ROBERT LOW

A DISH OF SPURS

CANELO

First published in the United Kingdom in 2020 by Canelo

Canelo Digital Publishing Limited
Third Floor, 20 Mortimer Street
London W1T 3JW
United Kingdom

A CIP catalogue record for this book is available from the British Library.

Print ISBN 978 1 80032 014 7
Ebook ISBN 978 1 78863 954 5

Grateful acknowledgement is made to Derek Stewart and Julia Stewart for supplying reenactment images used on the cover artwork.

Look for more great books at www.canelo.co

Printed and bound in Great Britain by Clays Ltd, Elcograf S.p.A.

In The Year 1542...

King James V of Scotland, capricious, prideful, paranoid and cruel, sent an army against Henry VIII. It won a victory at Haddon Rigg and then, a few weeks later at Solway Moss, fled before a much smaller English force ordered, paid for and commanded by Sir Thomas Wharton, Deputy Warden of the English Middle March. Wharton's army was composed almost entirely of Border reivers, the Scots and English along the frontier who cared more for their family Name than any sense of national patriotism and were happy to take English money to fight a Scottish king.

King James, hearing of this rout, suffered a nervous collapse and died, aged thirty. His only offspring was a six-day-old daughter, promptly hailed as Mary, Queen of Scots and served by the Earl of Arran as Regent. Arran refused to be cowed by English demands for the baby Queen to be married to King Henry's son, Prince Edward. So Fat Henry, old, gouty and pained by a bad leg and a bad wife – Catherine Howard had just been executed – looked for a way to force the issue.

He decided on a bold plan, using the skills of the Border reivers.

The Border lands, particularly that portion claimed by neither country and called the Debatable Land as a result, were already lawless, ruled only by fire and sword. That was scarcely to change for another sixty years... but change it did, with the death of a queen and the rise of a king with two crowns.

For some, all that came too late.

Chapter One

Never a place of joy, even in the green, bird-sweetened summer, winter made Hermitage a bleak grey slab that shouted 'bugger off' in stone. Set in a bleak landscape, the death of King James had it draped in mourning black, so that Mintie Henderson fancied she could feel the tomb-chill of the place just by riding up on it. She thought, then, that the stories concerning the laird who built it being boiled in molten lead for his wickedness could well be true.

It was also, she discovered, a great mistake to have arrived at this time. She had been sure the Keeper would have been here for Advent and more amenable because of it – but Lord Hepburn, Earl of Bothwell and Keeper of Liddesdale, was gone. As the sentry told her, the Keeper had 'sklimmed up to Embra, for a king's kisting and a bairn Queen's ascent into the arms of God.'

Mintie, though she sympathised with the reasons for it, could not help but be irritated and offended by the pomp and circumstance in Edinburgh which deprived her of a hearing. The wee Princess Mary, she pointed out, was hardly likely to sit up and give orders or favours after having been duly blessed and crowned. They could have waited until she was a full fortnight old at least. Or, better still, until she did not wet on the royal robes.

The sentry pointed out that the child's father, King James, had died, which news had sent the Keeper off on a fast horse, knowing what would follow and that the realm needed an arse on the throne, even one swaddled and damp – and anyway, what did a slip of a girl know about such matters?

Mintie crossed herself, a defiant gesture in these Reformer days in an undecided Scotland, and the sentry was not slow to note it.

'My own father is dead and our holding spoiled this past fortnight,' she told him stiffly. 'He was fell murdered by one Sweetmilk Hutchie Elliott – with two "T"s – who has also run off with two valuable horses, a deal of money and a brace of good weapons. I came to have a Bill and justice done.'

The sentry was sorry to hear of it, though there was little that could be done, seeing as how the Keeper of Liddesdale was gone to Edinburgh.

'Is there no man in charge of Liddesdale?' Mintie demanded primly. 'Or even of L'Armitage?'

The sentry was a Graham, a Border family never given to suffering fools lightly, so the proper name of Hermitage never even made him raise an eyebrow. He probably does not know it means 'guardhouse', Mintie thought scornfully.

Henry Graham knew well enough that Hermitage was the guardhouse of the bloodiest valley known to man or God, which was enough. He knew also that it was cold and that this young snip – Christ's blood, she could be no more than fifteen – was keeping him from the warm, with her steely eye and perjink way of speaking. She had a neat way of dressing and holding herself, iron eyes in a face too wary to be pretty, with lips thinned into a bloodless line – but that might have been the strain of riding here after dealing with a dead father.

Well, Hen thought, her da's wee rickle of acres was held from the Henderson chief, who in turn was bound to the Hepburns like a dog to a sausage, so she had done right to come here, though it would be no help to her. It was not more than a week since a Scots army had been routed to ruin on the Solway Moss – no more than a strong spit from here – and there were so many armed men everywhere that sensible men kept to their strongholds.

Still, he walked her over to Land Sergeant Will Elliot, since she had mentioned that name and he thought the sergeant might be kin to the reiver, a not uncommon occurrence. And because Will Elliot was the nearest thing to command that Hermitage currently owned. And because he was defiantly Catholic, when he was anything at all in these strange Reformer times, and Hen had seen this Henderson lass cross herself.

And, finally, because Hen Graham did not care much for Will Elliot, since he seemed to win more at dice than was reasonable for an honest player, while having the very job Hen himself coveted; let him deal with a purse-lipped wee snippy.

Will Elliot limped like a sailor on a rolling deck, courtesy of lost toes on his right foot, and was built in a series of squares, from the one that seemed to be his head, perched on the rectangle of his body, to the oblong dykes of his legs. He had a dark beard like stuffing spilled from a bad mattress and matching hair that straggled round his ears from under a bonnet that might have been blue once, but barely retained the memory of it.

He was cubbyholed in a room seemingly carved out of Hermitage's stones, a dark place on a dull day and lit only by an evil-smelling crusie; this at least allowed him to get to a bench and eat a poray with a spoon without missing the bowl more than once in four.

When Mintie came in he had just hirpled to a seat and paused in raising his spoon for only his second sup, so that Mintie saw drips pearl along the length of his moustache; he wiped them away with the back of one hand as Hen Graham explained who Mintie was and what she wanted.

It was clear to Mintie that the Land Sergeant did not care for it much, and he made that plain when he snarled Hen back to his post, then turned a jaundiced eye on Mintie and forced a smile.

'Hutchie Elliott,' he said.

'Known as Sweetmilk,' Mintie confirmed, 'though he is neither sweet nor milk. He killed my father and stole two horses, weapons and money. I have come for justice.'

'Hutchie Elliott,' repeated the Land Sergeant and Mintie was irritated, wondered if the man was slack-witted.

'He is. I understand your name is also Elliot – is he kin?'

The Land Sergeant's blockhouse face creased into a scowl.

'He is not,' he growled and then offered her a shadowed smile. 'Double "L" and single "T" are fine. Double "T" and single "L" are fine. As good Names as Graham or Armstrong.'

And then he sing-songed out the last: 'But double "L" and double "T" – no man knows who they folk be.'

'Yet you know him,' Mintie persisted and knew by the shift of him that she was right. He confirmed it with a nod.

'Hutcheon Elliott is from the English side. A brawler and a ramstampit hoormonger – begging yer young ears. Permitted to ride and commit all sorts with the Eliotts of Minto for all the extra "L" in his Name. Then they threw him out for his burning of a Ker house at Bloodyhaggs with the pregnant wife inside – that was a foulness too far, even for the furtherance of an auld feud.'

'You know him well,' Mintie said, trying not to show her shock.

'Until recently he was in Berwick, displaying a caged rat the size of a fair hunting hound,' Will went on. 'He claimed it came from the Paris sewers, whose rich foulness made it only typical of the breed there and no monster. It died and he was left with no living from it.'

The jest thudded, flattened by Mintie's cold regard.

'I know nothing of that,' she declared, but was not surprised at the revelation of Sweetmilk Hutchie Elliott's previous employment.

She had not liked Hutchie Elliott from the moment he had appeared, begging work on a quarter day last year. Hutcheon was not a name so much as a description, given to the black sheep or the albino crow, offspring that were odd and almost certainly unlooked for. If a father had handed out that name – and a mother agreed to it – then there was an understanding of an offspring unwanted and a contrite wife once less than loyal.

Mintie had said as much, and her father had frowned and pointed out that every decent man had gone for the army, which was headed to fight the English. And besides, he had added in his big, quiet, gentle way, such an unloved whelp needed more of a leg-up in life than others.

There was no arguing with that, and help was needed with the horses they bought and sold at Powrieburn, so Mintie had bridled her tongue on matters. But she continued not to care much for Hutchie Elliott.

It wasn't that he was ill-favoured – just the opposite, which was where, Mintie supposed, the hutcheon in him had lain for his father. It was plain to see in Hutchie's reasonable features, wavy hair, and good white teeth, which he cared for with a frayed hazel twig.

Finer by far, Mintie thought, than should have been bred onto poor flax labourers by themselves. And there is why the mother agreed to everything her man decided, out of shame and fear of abandonment for her clear adultery.

Hutchie also thought himself fine as the sun on shiny water and it came as no surprise to Mintie when, not long after he had put his feet under the Powrieburn table, he came to her all heat and heavy breathing in the dark of the barrelled undercroft. He had a hand pinning her arms to her waist and another fumbling at her quim before she could yelp.

'I am too young,' she gasped desperately. 'It is my menses—'

He grinned his white grin, pressing his hardness against her hip.

'Auld enough to bleed, auld enough to breed,' he pointed out.

She thought quickly, seemed to acquiesce, and when she had her arms free, hauled out the little knife she used to clean the Fyrebrande's feet and poked him hard with it.

'If it is blood you want...'

He yelped and sprang back, rubbing the forearm.

'By God, you have as well. You have drawn blood, you wee besom—'

'I will draw your insides out of your belly if you try again,' she declared, and he went off, muttering.

Later, when the tremble of it tipped her into sitting, she found it running over and over in her mind. She was sure he would try again, and having thought about it all the way to her bed, had made up her mind to tell her father the very next day – only to find that he had gone off early to deliver a brace of stolid horses to a farmer several miles off in Blackdubs. Because there were all sorts milling about in the wake of the great failed affray at Solway Moss, he took Sweetmilk Hutchie with him, for the protection.

All day Mintie knew there was wrong in it, but the bad cess only fell on them all with the sound of screaming and hooves the very next night.

She rushed out into the yard in her nightshirt and with a spark-trailing torch threatening her unbound hair, but was too late to prevent Hutchie riding off on Effie, the nag her father had lent him – and leading the Fyrebrande out of the undercroft.

Jinet, who had been dazzled by Hutchie, lay sprawled and weeping on the cobbles, having let him in quietly and suspecting nothing.

Her mother, screaming the whiles, was rendered all the more useless by the other pair of equally wailing serving women of Powrieburn. That trio of witches were no help at all and sure that everyone was about to be foul murdered in their beds and no man here to help.

Mintie, soothing and determined, ignored the wails and pleas and Jinet's sobbing apologies, saddled Jaunty the mare as soon as it was light and rode out with only her paring knife, fearing the worst. She found it not far off, a ragged bundle lying close to her father's own mount, which cropped grass all unconcerned.

He had been shot in the back, which must have been with his own caliver, given to Sweetmilk, ironically, to guard his back; the hole in was small and the one out of her da's belly was enough to make Mintie swallow once or twice, then turn away and be sick.

His own pistol, a good wheel-lock dagg, was gone, as was his purse, his leather jack and boots; the last caused Mintie more distress than any of the rest, simply because it left her father looking so vulnerable, even in death.

Blinded by tears and snot, she cut willow poles and fixed them as a sledge, then wrestled her father across it and dragged him home at the back of his own horse, despite the beast's protests. What followed was a great lake of tears and head-shaking from the women, fainting and despair from Mintie's ma. It was heartbreaking and brought Mintie to her own hot spill of tears more than once – but none of it was any help once he had been swaddled and put in the ground.

Not in any priory, either – though Mintie would pay Bygate for a Mass for his soul – but among the old Faerie stones that ringed their land, for the Hendersons had a pact with powries and the price, it was believed, was that the Faerie welcomed the dead.

The other Border Names, if they cared, simply made warding signs older than the cross, and the priests were all eye-lowered and huddled in these times, saying nothing at all and hoping they would not be noticed. Many of them remembered the burning of the Reformer preacher Patrick Hamilton by the Archbishop of Glasgow the year after Mintie was born – six hours it had taken because the faggots were wet, yet the Archbishop had sat stolidly through the whole of it, listening to Hamilton scream and praying, for the love of God.

There was little of God left in the Borders and even the Archbishop had known that – even before smouldering Patrick

Hamilton to ruin, Archbishop Gavin Dunbar of Glasgow had produced the Curse, an admonition so foul that every Borderer was breathless with admiration. The reiving men of the Borders were cursed awake and asleep, from the crown of their head to the soil on their feet, from behind and before, above and below – it went on and on, and not one of the reiving Names cared a black damn, even as they applauded the skill in it.

After all, these were God-fearing folk who made sure the right fist, which would be called upon to commit the ungodliest of sins, was left unbaptised. Or, if you were a Ker, the left, for all that Name were contrary-handed.

As Mintie stood by the stone-lined hole with the swaddled body of her father and the smell of the new-turned earth fierce in her nose, she remembered his big, gentle voice and the stories he told. Like the one about the Christians.

The Borders were lawless and proud, holding their Names higher than God Himself, and the story her father had told her was of a traveller arriving at a lonely bastel house on a dirty night up the Liddes and getting no charity from it, only suspicion and shut yetts. In the end, wet and freezing, he declared he was a good Christian and desperately called out to ask if there were any Christians within at all.

No Christians, came the wary reply. Croziers and Nixons, but no Christians. Try up the dale.

After the kisting-up, Mintie was dried of grief, replaced by an ember of anger which smouldered away on justice. She resolved that she must be the one to do it, since her mother was not capable; at the best of times her mother could tally using a notched stick, but neither read nor wrote more than 'God', and was not the one to ride off to the Keeper of Liddesdale and make a Bill against Hutchie Elliott.

Mintie had been taught reading and writing by her father, who wanted a clerk he could trust, and that role had been filled by his daughter since the age of twelve, so that she wrote a fine book hand and a fast charter script.

Will Elliot listened to all this, nodding and breaking bits off some bread, which he chewed. He barely read or wrote himself, so he was all admiration; and finally remembering his manners, he invited Mintie to sit and offered her some of the poray, but it looked particularly unattractive, so she refused. He offered her small beer, which she took and sipped.

'Well,' he said slowly, 'I can make a Bill for you, but nothing will be done until the Keeper returns. You should know also that we are men short since the English under Wharton are stravaiging everywhere in the wake of the defeat at Solway Moss. There are few even to guard Hermitage.'

'Is there no one will go after Hutchie Elliott?' Mintie demanded.

He thought of lying, then sighed and shook his head.

'No. He has gone into the Debatable for sure, where he either has friends or will be dead for the cost of his stolen purse and horses. I fancy the latter myself.'

'That is no justice nor consolation to me,' Mintie snapped back, and then, to her horror, felt the tears well and had to stop, biting her lips.

'It opens the lungs, washes the cheeks, brightens the eye and softens the temper, so weep away,' Will declared, so gently that Mintie was astonished. He offered her the contents of a black leather bottle, sloshing it meaningfully and uncorking it so that the pungent smell bit her nose.

'Drinking water neither makes a man sick, nor in debt, nor his wife a widow,' she flung back at him, and he shrugged, unperturbed by her poor gratitude.

'I am unmarried, never sick up good drink and spend not a half-groat on it – all confiscations.'

He winked knowingly, took a pull and stoppered it, making that strange grimace which seemed at odds, Mintie always thought, with the pleasure men took in strong drink.

'If you are unhappy with the Keeper of Liddesdale, try the Warden of the March at Roxburgh,' he went on, then split his bearded cliff of a face with a smile. 'Though I suspect Lord Maxwell is too busy with all the elbowing for favours at court. Or go to Carlisle,' he added with a larger grin. 'Hutchie Elliott is English, mind. It might be that the English Deputy Warden has men to spare, since he won at Solway Moss.'

The last was another attempt at jest, but Mintie thought about it on the ride back home, a long, cold, wet journey down past the Bygate Priory, all spoiled with burning and pocked with shots from the raids following Solway Moss. The reivers who had done it might well have been Scots paid by the English and hot for Fat Henry Tudor's Reforms, but it was more likely they were locals who knew the best shine was to be had in a Catholic priory.

They had also burned out the Armstrong wool mill at Mangerton, for all that the Armstrongs were in English pay, like a wheen of others Mintie could name – including the Keeper, she was sure, though she had that to thank for Powrieburn being untouched.

But war and greed knew no loyalties when blood got in the eye and fire the hand; cruck houses all the way down the valley were charred husks and she came down the frown of it, heeled by the black dog of despair, tempered by the thought of how her own home had escaped; the Faerie paid their debts, she thought. Her mother and the Powrieburn women did little to lift the mood and Tinnis Hill itself seemed to loom over them, drowning them in shadow.

Still, it was the Twelve Days and everyone tried to be merry for Christ's sake. Bet's Annie, youngest of the trio of serving women in Powrieburn, enlisted her brother's cousin, Wattie, as an ostler and because he was 'a man aboot the place'. She had to sniff at the questions Mintie put to her regarding his talents when he arrived a few days later, but in the end Wattie was accepted. He was fair with the beasts, though the job of man seemed beyond him, for he was a sliver with protruding teeth and scarce older than Mintie.

The point was made all the same – Mintie, for all her years, was the true Mistress of Powrieburn, even if she had to work through her distraught ma yet. Everyone knew it, accepted it, and life went on as normal as any household could which was perched on a lawless corner of Liddesdale, with the outlaws of the Debatable Land on one side and the ravaging thieves of England just across the Kershope Water. Not to mention the Scots reivers up the Liddesdale itself.

–

The day after Christ's Mass, Mintie rode off, despite protests and hand-wringing, to take her lament to Carlisle.

'You will be seized and robbed, so you will,' Bet's Annie declared across her folded arms as Mintie saddled up Jaunty. 'There is war abroad and neither side is welcomed by the other. Your ma is fair laid up with worry.'

'Then unlay her,' Mintie replied tartly, 'by making sure Wattie does his work as he should. I will be back in a day or two. Besides – the Hendersons of Powrieburn pay out blackmeal to every Name for Scotch miles in every direction. Who would want to kill that milch cow, war or not?'

In fact, she was back in two days, and never got further than Askerton, on the English side. The snow came down and hissed across the Bewcastle Waste until she could not see farther than Jaunty's head and stumbled into Askerton Castle with her feet and hands frozen and her face so numb she could hardly speak.

Tod Graham was the Land Sergeant there, and once his clucking wife had rubbed sense and feeling back into Mintie's limbs and plied her with possets, he sat down opposite and listened to her tale.

At the end of it, he shook his head.

'The crime was done across the Border, so it is no matter for Carlisle,' he declared firmly. 'The Scots Middle March Warden or the Liddesdale Keeper would have to apply to the English Warden here to have it resolved. That is the way matters work

– though I doubt they work at all in these days. I would not waste your time going all the way to Carlisle.'

'I would offer a fair reward,' Mintie attempted. 'I can manage five pounds, English.'

It was sum enough to arch Tod's eyebrows – as much as a skilled servant earned in a year in England – but still he frowned and shook his head. The English Deputy Warden, Wharton, had won a great battle against the Scots at Solway Moss. Hardly anyone had died in it, for the Scots had so clearly not wanted to fight that they had fled or given in, and it was said King James had died of the shame.

The result, Tod explained gently, was that the two countries were at each other's throats, and Wharton had forbidden contacts across the Border, knowing full well that Name blood was stronger by far than national pride. God forbid anyone is married on to someone on the other side of the Border now, he added, for Wharton has declared the death penalty for that. There would be no Truce Days, where Wardens on either side could sort out claims of criminality in a sensible manner – now March law pertained. Which is to say, no law at all.

'You should not be here,' he ended, 'and it is only out of Christian charity that I welcome you in.'

That and I am a Henderson and so no kin of yours that this Wharton can accuse you of consorting with, Mintie thought bitterly. Henderson was a Name feared by no one, a Name who paid blackmeal to all, just for the right to live quiet.

In her barely unfrozen heart, Mintie had known all this from the start and accepted a night's lodging in the warm of Askerton before setting off back home the next morning.

Tod Graham watched her go into the great white of the day and wondered if she would be fine; it was not a long ride back to Powrieburn, but the weather was false and there were all sorts out and about and up to no good in it.

'Is there nothing can be done for the wee soul?' his wife demanded, and Tod didn't know why it happened, but the words were barely in his ears before a face swam up into his mind. It was not a good face, even for kin, and he almost thrust it away.

Yet the more he thought on it, the more the idea formed. He was, if he admitted it to himself, ashamed that his Deputy Warden, Sir Thomas Wharton, was paying Armstrongs and Croziers and others, on both sides of the divide, to ride into Scotland for burning and slaughter. Tod was a Graham, of course, who had a long-running feud with the Armstrongs and any of the Names who stood with them, but even so, what Wharton was doing was black-hearted.

Besides, the kin Tod Graham had in mind for Mistress Araminta Henderson's task would benefit – and not just from the money. The man had, Tod thought, been languishing long enough in bitterness and the stews of Berwick and would be washed into the deepest stank of them entirely if left much longer.

He frowned about it a bit more, then got ink, quill and paper and painstakingly, tongue between his teeth, sharpened the implement and then scratched out a letter. There was not much in it – the man he wrote to would need to get someone else to read it to him – but the sweat had popped out on his brow like apple pips by the time he had finished.

Then he summoned Leckie Bell, who was young and stupid enough to consider the task an honour in this weather.

'Ride to Berwick,' he told the boy. 'Seek out the Old Brig Tavern and the thumper employed there. Give him this and tell him that his kin, the Land Sergeant at Askerton, would be pleased if he would consider it.'

He glanced at the boy, newest recruit to the trained band of Askerton, and hoped he would be safe, not only on the journey, but afterward.

'The man you want is called Batty Coalhouse. You will not miss him.'

Chapter Two

The dog stirred Mintie from overseeing the table, and she was concerned for she had heard no rooks, whose disturbance from roosting was usually the first warning of anyone approaching. She heard Wattie whining his annoyance at the hound, but even he was clever enough to realise why a good herd and guard dog had his voice raised.

Everyone else stopped as if turned to stone, with platters and spoons and horn cups clutched tight, looking at one another fearfully in the butter tallow glow. Then they all started clucking at once and her mother sank onto a bench, where Megs flapped her kertch in her face to keep her from a faint. Mintie dispatched Jinet to soothe her before turning to the trapdoor in the floor.

It opened to show the tousled head of Wattie, bright-eyed and blinking in the light, wafting in the strong, acrid stink of the beasts below; disturbed, they were shifting and grunting.

'A rider is at the yett,' Wattie declared solemnly. 'He is asking for Mistress Mintie Henderson of Powrieburn.'

A man. Come at night. Mounted. Where there was one, there could be two or more... Asking for her and not her mother, mind you, Mintie thought. Which means he knows how matters are at a Powrieburn so recently bereaved.

She scrambled down the ladder into the warm, vaulted undercroft of the bastel house; there was a brace of milch kine in it but only eight horses, all brought in from the fields. It was late for Riding – it was usually done in autumn, because folk had to bring their beasts in from their scatter of grazing and pen them, which made for easy lifting. Still, it was possible some of the more desperate would Ride, and Mintie did not want any livestock reived.

Any more livestock reived, she corrected. Particularly horses, which seemed suddenly few in number around the Border, so that the handful Powrieburn had were pure gold.

She had a lantern held high and almost dropped it as the straw rustled and a head popped up, half defiant, half apologetic. Bet's Annie smoothed her rumpled clothes and bobbed an arrogance of curtsey, but could not look Mintie in the eye.

Mintie knew the ways of it and marvelled – Wattie Crozier the ostler boy might be a skinny runt, and Bet's Annie might be a sonsie sometime aunt to him, but he was the nearest thing to a rooster this henhouse had. She had wondered where Bet's Annie had got to when work was involved, but was already too wise to be diverted from what was outside in order to scathe what was in. She ignored the pair of them and moved to the yett, shivering as the cold hit her and wishing she had brought a cloak.

The thick outer doors, a pace or two beyond the metal grille, were dark, silent and barred – but the voice from beyond made them all jump.

'Are you there, Mintie Henderson? I have a letter here from Askerton and I am informed you can read it fine.'

'It's a ruse,' Wattie declared firmly. 'As soon as we open the way, they will be in with fire and sword—'

'Shut up, Wattie,' Mintie said and heard his teeth click, though she took no delight in slapping him down; he was Borders-bred and what he said was marrowed into the bone by long and bitter experience.

For all that, she moved to the yett, lantern held high, then unbarred the metal grille with a squealing clank of bolt. She strode through with more bravado in her walk than sense, calling for Wattie to close and lock it behind her; there were only two steps to the outer doors, but her skin was puckered when she reached them, her breath coming in short gasps and none of it was because of the cold.

Now she wished she had taken the time to look out one of the small shuttered windows set high in the wall before she had come down, just to see what was in the yard. She tried the looking slat set in one of the wooden doors, but saw only a vague shadow.

She laid the lantern to one side, took the great wooden batten in both hands and lifted it off the trunnions, thinking, as she always did, that a solid sliding bolt, set into the thick wall of the bastel, was much safer and altogether more modern.

Well greased, the thick double doors slid open with a soft groan even before she had set the bar to one side and picked up the light.

Beyond was a figure on a horse, limned silver by moonlight. Moonlight, Mintie thought wildly – perfect Riding weather…

But the man was alone, it seemed, sitting on his hipshot Galloway nag and leaning forward with his right elbow resting easily on the pommel, the hand outstretched and holding a fold of paper. The other hand, Mintie saw, was hidden – possibly with a blade in it – and the moonlight danced along the peak and comb of a burgonet fastened casually to the man's belt.

That helmet was all too familiar, the workaday headgear of every Riding grayne on the Border, and even in the lantern light it shone golden brown from years of weatherproofing with lanolin-rich sheep grease.

She tore her eyes from it and raised the lantern a little, annoyed at a loose panel betraying her tremble.

'I am Mintie Henderson. What want you here?'

'Christian charity would be good,' the man growled back, his breath silver smoke in the moonlight. For a moment Mintie almost giggled wildly at the thought of replying with her da's old story – no Christians here. Hendersons only; try up the dale...

Then the rider thrust his face and the hand with the letter into better light.

It was not a comfort, that face. It was a long, lean affair with a tow-coloured raggle of hair and beard topped by a soft cap; under a glowering lintel of straw brows two eyes lurked in a surround like a parched desert, cracked and scored.

'A horn cup of something warming would be good,' the man added. His jaw waggled as he spoke, the curve of beard on it coming up to meet the swoop of a hawk nose, thin as a blade.

Undershot, Mintie thought, trying to herd her mad thoughts together. If he was a retrieving dog I'd have put him down for a jaw like that, for it will grip and never let go until you kill it...

She took the letter and then did not know what to do with it. He waited a moment, then nodded at her.

'Sooner you read that,' he pointed out, 'sooner you can offer that Christian charity. The wind is cold up here.'

She looked back up at him, while the moonlight blued his face with ugly shadows. Then, in a swift gesture, she thrust the lantern at him to hold and cracked the wax seal on the folded paper.

It was brief and painfully scrawled, she saw, by a man who had taken care to get it right and had probably sweated over every careful loop and dot. From Tod Graham at Askerton.

'Are you Batram Coalhouse?' she asked, raising her face from it, though she knew the answer. The man nodded, widening his beard in what Mintie saw was a smile.

'Batty Coalhouse. If Askerton Tod Graham says true, then I am bound for the recovery of your stolen horses and Hutchie Elliott, for the price of five pounds. English. No Fat Henry testoons in it neither. Good honest shillings. Even a bag of bawbees will suit.'

He had a strange accent, even for an English, and Coalhouse was not a name Mintie had heard, so she supposed he came from further south. She looked at the fierce face of the man. '*Do not be fogged by his appearance. He has been in the wars and is thus hardened in skill and resolve*' said the letter, and Mintie had no doubt of it. So she nodded and watched as Batty Coalhouse levered himself out of the saddle and onto the cobbles with a heavy thump.

It was then that she saw he was not concealing anything in his left hand at all and never would.

He had no hand, nor most of the arm it should have been attached to.

She tried not to think on that as she led Batty Coalhouse and his horse into the undercroft, ignoring the frowning white faces of Bet's Annie and Wattie.

'The boy here will care for your horse,' she said firmly, battening the door and the yett. 'You will eat with us upstairs.'

He only nodded and followed Mintie, who was aware of the dagger stares of Wattie at being referred to as 'the boy'; she heard him and Bet's Annie hiss at each other like snakes and was sure there was nothing good said about her in the whispers.

Upstairs, Megs and Jinet had recovered enough to bob curt-seys, while her mother was upright in a chair at least, though she coughed politely behind her hand now and then, a dry racking affair. Batty gave them a polite smile and a decent enough bow for a man with a belly on him, then sat where he was indicated, unloading himself of an ironworks of weaponry which made the women blanch.

'Do you need some assistance?' Mintie demanded as he struggled out of his bandoliers and unhooked the front of his lattice-sewn padded jack.

There was a moment of puffing and grunt, then he emerged from the fustian cocoon of it with a waft of staleness and a triumphant, red-faced grin.

'I do not, thank you. I have been dressing myself since I was a youngster.'

When Mintie tried to lift it, her arm buckled under the weight of the steel plates sewn inside it. Flustered, she fought to recover her poise and waved insouciantly at his missing arm.

'I thought only that that might have been a hindrance.'

'It was so until a barber trimmed it, all proper and perjink as a new preen – but that was when I was twenty and something and I am used to it missing.'

There was nothing much left to say, so they sat and the women busied themselves with platters and bowls and spoons. Wattie came up, with Bet's Annie trailing behind like a grey smoke.

'Your nag has been fed and brushed,' he announced tersely, just as a bowl of fragrant stew was plunked under Batty's beard, with a cup of small beer and a hunk of oat bread to go with it. He sniffed and then tasted it with a surprisingly delicate gesture.

'Well, well,' he beamed, 'there is mutton in this. It seems myself and the Saul have fallen into paradise.'

She realised he spoke of his horse – Saul meant 'soul' or 'spirit', and it seemed a long way from the mild beast she had seen, all winter tangle and mud-clagged hairy fetlocks. Nor was the beast's master much better; for all his initial grace he ate slovenly, Mintie noted, pausing now and then to run the drips off his beard with his hand, which he wiped clean on his stained shirt. Men will wallow, she thought sourly, if left to their own.

She was astounded at how pleased the women were by him all the same, all beams and quiet chaffer – and when he exclaimed with delight at their wobbling junket, flavoured with rosewater and honey, they laughed. Even her mother, Mintie saw with amazement.

'Now,' Batty said, pushing his plate away, with the last of the junket clinging to the ends of his moustaches, 'if there was a lick of *eau de vie* to wet my beak, I would be a content man.'

'Your body is a church to God – keep the Spirit in and the spirits on the outside,' Mintie said swiftly. Bet's Annie laughed bitterly.

'There is no strong drink in this house, Master Coalhouse,' she said and shot Mintie a hard stare – which she had back in measure enough to make her drop her gaze.

'Aye, aye, so I see,' Batty said thoughtfully, then shrugged. 'Well, I'm often ashamed of the way I drink. Then I look in my cup and think of the wee monks slaving away with their hopes and dreams of pleasing the Lord with their work in producing a good *aqua vitae*, and I think to myself – Batty Coalhouse, how can you be so selfish as to deny these folk their way to God?'

The silence was stunning and, beaming, Batty added 'Amen' to it, so that everyone repeated it by rote.

Mintie let a moment pass, then cleared her throat.

'You claim to be able to bring Hutchie Elliott to task and justice,' she said flatly. 'I know you can eat and I hear you can drink, but even allowing for the faith your kin in Askerton places in you, I see little evidence of your ability to do more. In fact, you seem poorly diminished for such a task as Hutchie Elliott.'

There was an embarrassing silence and Batty shook his head with wonder.

'God be praised,' he breathed at Mintie's mother, 'would you listen to the mouth on it? Goodwife Henderson, I can see why you leave the pursuit of justice for your man's demise on this sprig of the house, but you need manners with such spirit. Your daughter needs a lick of reminding now and then, certes.'

'She is a good girl,' her mother bleated.

'You are not in the first flush of youth,' Mintie snapped, 'with only one wing betimes. Hutchie Elliott, as I remember him, is young, strong and now well armed.'

'Ach – two-armed besides,' Batty said and Mintie flushed. She might have added 'belly like a cask' to Batty's list of faults, but would have had to admit that he had moved surprising fast and light, enough for her to have noted it as he climbed the ladder to the hall.

'Did you hear the rooks?' he said, closing one sly eye; it was so suddenly announced that Mintie had to open and shut her mouth a few times, unable to answer. Batty nodded with a satisfied triumph of a smile.

'You did not, for I saw that neat trap – ride close to it and roosting rooks will rise, as my da used to tell me. As good watchmen as any.'

'I heard the dog,' Mintie fired back, flustered, and Batty waved his one hand.

'I did not come to spoil the house, so I let the hound hear me,' he pointed out, and Mintie heard the murmurs of agreement behind her – and felt the flame of her face at the truth revealed. He was clever, right enough.

'I have enjoyed your Christian hospitality,' Batty went on and bowed like a courtier to the simpering women, 'and have seen the mutton in your dish. You have no sheep, though. A pair of milch kine and a handful of horses besides mine in the undercroft, but no sheep.'

'We do not keep sheep,' Mintie answered, only realising afterwards how much he had noticed in his brief trip through the dark-shadowed undercroft. 'Our fields are given to winter fodder for horses mainly – and grazing for same. Sheep crop the grass too tight for horses to follow. We get some ewes or lambs in barter now and then and slaughter them for the pot.'

He nodded, one eye shut and thinking.

'That is what we do,' Mintie added scathingly, wondering if he was lack-witted. 'We deal in horses.'

'You do,' he agreed. 'And keep no sheep. Yet you eat mutton, which means you are getting it in exchange for what you sell. No coin. And you have precious few nags – there are more empty stalls than full in your undercroft. The stall you have put the Saul in was made for a finer-bred beast than he – though I will not say so to his face.'

'The Fyrebrande,' Mintie answered blankly, the dull, leaden feeling of the stallion's loss settling on her like sea haar, as it did each time she thought of him.

'Just so. Stolen by Hutchie Elliott – a racing beast was he, this Fyrebrande? Winner of prize silver bells at Truce Day meets?'

'He could do that,' Mintie admitted, 'but he was not. He was a fine tourney-bred horse, fit enough to carry a plate-slathered king to battle, and would not be out of place in the royal stables at Falkland Palace. We were crossing him with decent mares, to breed good horses for riding or fighting by gentlemen.'

'A harsh loss then,' Batty answered. 'Which is why you will want him back.'

'He is eaten, according to everyone I have spoken to, including your kin at Askerton,' Mintie answered harshly, and her mother burst into tears, which almost made her turn with the guilt. But she kept her face like a dyke and set the stone of it on Batty's own.

'I do not think so and neither do you, Mintie Henderson,' Batty replied, which surprised her. 'Hutchie murdered your father – my pardon for intruding into your grief with this memory – and had a brace of horses, money, weapons and a good new pair of boots. Is that the way of it?'

Mintie nodded dumbly, remembering.

'He left a horse,' Batty pointed out. 'The one your father rode. And came back to Powrieburn to take the Fyrebrande. He left your father's mount because he could not control a pair and ride hard on a third. He left your father's – fine beast though it might be – and came back for the Fyrebrande, which he wanted in particular.'

The truth of it took Mintie's breath hard up into her chest so that it hurt. A lot of that had to do with her own stupidity in not having seen it as clearly until now.

Batty nodded, seeing the revelation scrawl across Mintie's face.

'Just so. He took the Fyrebrande and I do not think he wanted a decent meal out of the beast. Knowing Hutchie as I do, I also do not think he stole it to order, or with any regard as to what to do with it after. No fine-bred tourney horse is a use to Riding men in this country – Galloway nags is more their strength, beasts that can travel a brace of days through the wet on a handful of oats and the scum water from a tarn. So Hutchie must know someone he can sell it to, someone with the coin and the sense to know the value of such a beast. Find such a man and there will be your stallion. And a clue to where Hutchie has since fled.'

'You know Hutchie Elliott?' demanded Mintie suspiciously.

Batty waved a hand dismissively.

'Everyone in Berwick knows Hutchie Elliott, brawling swaggerer that he is. Him and his giant rat – though the truth is that it was no rat at all, but some creature he had off a sailor who had brought it back from the far Spanish Americas. I am surprised the ugly creature lasted as long as it did.'

Mintie was silent and Batty cocked his head to look at her.

'I am not surprised that the ugly creature that is Hutchie has lasted as long as he has,' he added. 'He is as dangerous as nightshade, with Bills filed on him in every March and no family name to shelter him – his own were no more than labourers at the flax, though his true father is nowhere to be found. I jalouse that such a da would keep well clear, for shame, from acknowledging the likes of Hutchie as any get of his.

'He is as bad a backstabber as any I have hunted,' he went on grimly. 'I mention all of this – and your lack of sheep and horse and coin – only because, as you doubt my ability, I doubt you have five pounds English to make it worth my while bringing him to task and your fine beast back to his stall.'

'I have it,' Mintie declared, equally steely eyed, 'though I will not be showing you any time soon, lest the shine ruin what sense you have. But if you bring Hutchie Elliott to task, there it will be, waiting for your hand.'

'A poor bargain,' he fired back, one eye closed in a villainous look. 'I have to trust you, when you have no trust in me at all.'

'That is the nature of master and hired,' Mintie answered, then cocked her head to one side. 'How many have you brought to task?'

Her mother cleared her throat pointedly then broke into a fit of coughing, which jerked Mintie back to the others, all ignored in this intense exchange. She felt herself flush under her mother's cool censure.

Batty blinked and fumbled inside his shirt for a moment or two, then produced a strange tangle of wool and fat sticks. He tucked one stick under the obscene waggle of what was left of his missing arm and took another in his good hand, letting the rest dangle.

'Alive?' he asked, and Mintie, mesmerised and only now realising that Batty Coalhouse was knitting, was forced back to her question.

Batty grinned at her face.

'That was a trick,' he said, winking to Mintie's mother, 'for all the ones I bring back are alive. The Wardens only pay for live ones. Two pounds Scots, usually, in order to see them decently hanged and view for themselves that the fouled Bill has been duly served.'

He paused, clicking dextrously, then leered at Mintie.

'The dead I leave where they fall, for they are no use to me.'

'What age are you, Master Coalhouse, if I may make so bold?'

The question came from her mother and was innocent as a white kertch. Batty smiled at her politely.

'I was born with the century, Goodwife Henderson.'

Then he was forty-two, Mintie thought, aware – with some pride – that she had calculated that more swiftly than any of the others, who were still frowning over it.

'Do you play cards, sir?' her mother asked brightly, and Mintie, aware somehow that the rug had been pulled from under her and that matters had been settled, sat back and gnawed a nail.

'I do, Goodwife,' Batty replied cheerfully. 'Primero, Cleke, Loadum, New Cut, Putt, All Fours, Post, Pair, Ruff and Trumps. Noddy for preference.'

'My,' her mother replied admiringly, 'you are a man of many parts. Then we shall play Primero, for the others are all much the same and Noddy is a game for hard gamblers, I understand. Mintie – fetch the cards, dear.'

Mintie did as she was bid and they played Primero, which Batty did with a reckless, stone-faced bravado and won as much as he lost. That was Primero all over, a game of bluff when all was said and done.

And all the while Mintie watched, with growing fascination, the way Batty's fingers flicked and purled the wool round the needle, a skill which she had trouble enough with using two hands. And this as well as playing the cards, so that he tucked the needle into his collar while he picked them up, studied them, then did not need to look at them again to know what he had, tallying their worth in his head.

When the tallow started to gutter, Mintie led Batty, festooned with weapons and jack back down the ladder to the undercroft, where he would sleep well enough in a bed made up in a stall next to his horse, the Saul.

'We have had worser billets than this, eh, old lad?' he said, speaking soft and quiet to the horse, which whickered and rubbed him with its nose.

Mintie had noted the scored and scuffed saddle with its big worn buckets of horse holsters and the great wheel-lock daggs snugged in them. He had two more such daggs for his belt, as well as a basket-hilted cutter and a bollock dagger, all expensive items; the helmet, she saw, wore the last glimmer of gilding like a proud memory of greatness. No longbow, no parry dagger, nor small shield, the familiar accoutrements of any man on the Border – then Mintie realised how useless they would be to a man with no left hand to wield them.

There were stories in everything that surrounded the man, and Mintie wanted to ask about them all, but did not dare.

She bid him a good night and left the lantern so he could find his way to the night pot. All the way back up the ladder to her own bed and long after she was in it, she thought on the strangeness that was Batty Coalhouse.

The rooks woke her, hooking her from sleep; Mykkel followed soon after, with his low growls and then brief warning bark, as if he was hoiking up his dinner. It was dark outside and Mintie realised she had slept no more than an hour or two.

There was a flurry of flustered women, moving in the dancing shadows made from the single reeking crusie kept burning so folk could find their night pots. More light was sparked and the sconces flared, even as Mintie peered through the shutters of the small, high-set window.

The yard held shadows and shouts.

'Goodwife Henderson – open up. It is Will Armstrong from Whithaugh come to visit.'

There were two others with him, and Mintie thought hard about it. Will was the lout son of Mattie Armstrong of Whithaugh Tower, a lick and spit away from Powrieburn. She paid Mattie blackmeal to let her alone and he had done so, for Powrieburn was held by the Hendersons from the Keeper of Liddesdale, a Hepburn who was not lightly crossed. But even he permitted Mattie to blackmeal Powrieburn just a little, because the Armstrong Name was powerful in Liddesdale. Just a little and no more, all the same.

Yet here was Fingerless Will Armstrong, past midnight and with two of his kin; she did not think they wanted to sit and play Primero.

'What want you here at this time of night?' she yelled back, and there was a pause.

'Is that you, Mintie? Well, it concerns you, but your ma is the one we have to speak with, so open the doors and let us through like a good lass.'

Wattie stumbled up the ladder from below, white-faced and shaking. Mintie heard Bet's Annie cursing – and then a low, harsh voice telling her to weesht. She almost laughed with delight, sure she had heard the click of Bet's Annie's teeth in her haste to obey Batty's growl.

She went to the wall and took down the caliver, then shoved it almost scornfully at Wattie, who took the weapon as if it was hot poison.

'Light the slow-match on that at least,' Mintie declared as she started down the ladder. 'If you can load it, do so. Check the priming powder – and try not to blow your own head off.'

Below, Bet's Annie was hunkered in a corner, more in fear of Batty Coalhouse than any outside.

'You know them, then?'

The soft voice heralded the face, then the bellied body shoving out of the shadows. Batty had his jack on and his baldric was crossed with a bandolier of apostles, the dozen dangling wooden powder charges softly clicking as he moved. Three pistols were stuffed in his belt and a fourth held in his only hand.

'Will Armstrong of Whithaugh. I suspect the others will be Clem and Sorley, his kin – cousins, I think.'

'Ach, yes,' Batty said thoughtfully. 'Fingerless Will of Whithaugh, son of the headman there, old Mattie. He and Clem and Sorley are a godless triumvirate of no good, for sure.'

'You know them?' Mintie asked and felt rather than saw the nod.

'We have had dealings, Will and I. In Berwick, where he lost a brace of fingers from the end of his left hand.'

'Open the door,' demanded Will Armstrong, his voice raising. 'It is chilled here.'

'Why have you come?' Mintie shouted back, and there was a great false sigh.

'Ach, Mintie, you have spoiled the surprise of it. I have come to wed you.'

'Aye, and bed you besides – so open the yett and your legs, lass…'

Clem Armstrong was roaring drunk and no amount of hissed commands to shut his lip had any effect, save that all three went off into argument.

'Well,' said Batty mildly. 'Have you a mind to wed him?'

'I would rather be wed on to a wet-sick dog.'

'Then tell him so.'

She did, while Batty hummed and sang, tuneless and soft, one wheel-lock dagg stuck under his lost arm's pit while he primed it with rasping turns of the key.

'Ach now, Mintie, is that a way to start a wooing? You'll lose that edge when you are proper married, my lass… for married you will be.'

Will's voice was light and laughing; Mintie's was a scorch.

'You moudiewarp. You want this only because your da has put you up to it. No man at Powrieburn, he thinks, and a way to get his greasy fingers on it. My mother is too greying for you, Will, but I am sure she was considered first.'

There was pause enough to let Mintie know she had hit the mark, enough for her to hear the low, soft lilt of Batty.

'*Her skirt was o' the grass-green silk, her mantle o' the velvet fine,*' he murmured. '*And ilka tett o' her horse's mane, hung fifty siller bells and nine…*'

A thunderous battering at the outer door made Mintie jump; Mykkel went off into furious barking; and Bet's Annie squealed once with the shock of it, then grew hard-eyed at Fingerless Will's bellowing, for she was Borders bred and had iron in her.

'Open up, damn your eyes. Or I will scumfish you out. Open, I say – Sorley, spark up that torch, man.'

Mintie was unfazed by threats of scumfishing – smoking them out – for Powrieburn was stone with a slate roof and anyone who wanted to scumfish them would need to start by getting up on the icy roof in pitch darkness. She did not think that would be happening in any great hurry from folk as drunk as these sounded.

She started to reply, and felt a heavy hand gentling on the nape of her neck; she turned upwards into the face of Batty Coalhouse, all shadows and pits. He was not looking at her, but through the yett and the big wooden doors to those beyond.

'You have had your answer, Will. The only way you will lay a finger on lass or lands is if you dig up the pair that were cut off and throw them at both.'

Batty's voice was not raised, but the slash of it brought silence for a long time. Then a suspicious, uneasy Will asked the obvious.

'The man who cut them off in Berwick town, Will Armstrong,' Batty answered back lightly. 'The night you thought a one-armed man was easy meat for a showing up with a blade. You were in drink then too, as I recall – I thought you might have learned.'

'Batty Coalhouse – is that you there?'

'It was me when I woke this morning, sure enough, so I believe it still is.'

'Why are you here? Have you an interest in my bride, Batty?'

Will Armstrong's voice was light but there was still a strain in it that Mintie delighted in; he is scared enough to wet himself at the idea of Batty Coalhouse, she thought. For the first time, she began to consider that the fat, old, one-armed man was something more than he looked.

'I have no interest in Mistress Araminta Henderson save in a business matter. And that she has asked my help in refusing your suit. You should go quiet back to Whithaugh.'

There was silence at that for a time. Then Clem spoke up and it was clear they had all remembered what Batty did for a living.

'Have you a made Bill on any of us?'

Batty's chuckle was low and feral.

'There speaks a man with guilt for something,' he replied. 'I will find one if I look, I wager – but I have no Bill on any, save the bill I will send to Will's father for the trouble his son persists in putting to me.'

'You speak mighty for a one-armed man behind a stout door,' shouted Will Armstrong, clearly stung.

'Get you gone before I open it, or rue the day.'

'Come ahead, you single-winged auld cunny. You can have but one pistol in your one hand with one shot – and we have three good matchlock guns here.'

'True,' admitted Batty and deliberately clattered the bolt on the yett to let them know he was coming. 'But what you want to worry at is who gets the one shot. At the range we are, it will tear some luckless soul a second dunghole.'

Mintie watched, amazed and afraid in equal measure, as Batty strode through the yett to the outer door and put his foot to hold the opening swing. He stuffed his pistol into the bandolier belt round his chest and carefully, slow and quiet, raised the bar and set it down; it was heavy that bar, and Mintie knew the strength it took to remove it silently. He might only have the one arm, she thought, but it is a strong one.

The doors, hooked by his foot alone, stayed shut, and Batty filled his lone hand with pistol, took a deep breath as if about to plunge underwater and shook himself like a dog in the rain.

'I can hear you breathing hard there,' he said loudly, and the nearness of his voice must have made them afraid, for Mintie heard a horse squeal as the reins were jerked hard by a startled man.

'I will count, Will. To three, so as you can all follow it even with your poor tallying skills. At the end of it, I am coming through this door with my single fist full, and if any are there to see it, then you can count shots instead. You can all manage to count to one, can you not? Them left alive, that is.'

'Will...' said Clem uncertainly.

'Weesht you – come ahead, Batty, you lack-witted by-blow of a Graham hoor. I owe you for my fingers and will take the five you have left in the world.'

There was a pause, then Batty shook his head. Mintie was surprised to see that the sorrow seemed genuine.

'One,' said Batty and took his foot from the door, so that it swung open. There were two loud bangs, the flashes bright as lightning, and Mintie jumped with the noise. For a moment, she thought Batty was down, but he had flattened against the wall and simply let the door open on panicked, eager men; the shots splintered wood. Wattie was hunkered on the ground with his arms over his head and Mintie heard Jinet start to wail.

'Two,' Batty said and stepped into the doorway, where Will and Clem sat their mounts, smoking matchlock pistols as empty as a Monday morning church. Sorley was frantically fumbling with his own weapon, which had misfired.

'Three,' said Batty. There was a whirl of sparks, like embers off a blown fire. Then a huge bang buzzed Mintie's ears, and for an instant Batty was lit up, all bloody red, his bearded jaw jutting and his hand full of wheel-lock dagg, smoke fountaining from it like egret plumes.

The sudden plunge back into darkness came with a mad, ghostly wraith of acrid stink which made Mintie choke. Half blinded, she heard a clatter and only later realised it was Batty dropping the emptied pistol and hauling out a second.

Another great flare of light blasted away the night, then a blackness more choked and darker than ever. There were squeals from horses and women, but the thunder of Batty's pistols had all but blown away Mintie's hearing as she staggered to the doorway, expecting to see Batty bleeding on the cobbles.

Instead, she saw him drop the second pistol and haul out a third, while Sorley raved and cursed, flung from his maddened horse and with his caliver spilled uselessly away. Batty pointed the pistol at him and it whirred and sparked – and nothing happened.

He gave a roar of frustration and hurled it to one side, hauling out his last dagg just as Sorley rolled over, grabbed the caliver and swung it like a club, catching the end of the long-barrelled pistol and hooking it from Batty's grasp.

'Ha!' Sorley yelled in triumph and swung it again, this time at Batty's head – but Batty was quick on his feet for an old, bellied man, moving inside the swing to drive his forehead into Sorley's face.

Sorley fell backwards, roaring with pain, the caliver spinning away to clatter on the rimed cobbles. He rolled over and got up swiftly, only to find Batty closing with him. Slipping and straining, the pair of them locked for a moment, and Mintie saw Sorley grin through the red mask of his face and thought – he has Batty now. Two arms against one is hardly fair.

Sorley was sure of it, exerted all his young strength and shoved Batty away, so that he could step back and start punching.

'One arm,' he roared triumphantly and cocked both his fists meaningfully.

'Two legs,' Batty answered and booted him in the cods. Then he clamped his one hand on the back of the whimpering, pain-lashed Sorley's neck like a mastiff's grip on a hare.

Sorley struggled and roared through sprung tears of pain, but Batty walked him to the dungheap and plunged his head in it, holding it there while the man thrashed. Then he drew it out until Sorley could splutter and gasp.

'Are you done?'

'You stinking bastard-bred—'

The powerful arm thrust and back he went, face first into the dung. Mintie took the hand from her stunned mouth and moved as if in an underwater dream, gliding to where Batty's last loaded dagg lay.

Sorley was thrashing less, so that when Batty pulled him out, it was all the man could do to breathe; he had no curses left. Batty let him drop to the cobbles and started to wipe his hand down his tunic, when the great blast of the dagg blew fire and smoke everywhere and brought him whirling round.

Clem, already bleeding from the leg, had his arms over his head and a great scar on the cobbles marked where the shot had hit and screamed off into the dark. An inch from where his hand had been reaching for Sorley's caliver.

Batty looked at Mintie, now sitting on the cobbles, feeling the damp and cold seep through her nightdress and the ache in her wrists, all done by the recoil of the weapon. He grinned, stamped the slow match on the caliver to blackness with one foot and booted the groaning Clem senseless with a single swift kick in the face.

'Well done, Mistress Araminta,' he said.

Mintie could only hear a strange low mutter, though she saw his lips moving and realised he was speaking. Panicked, she started to shake her head, thinking she had been driven deaf. Then, slowly, hearing ebbed back until the buzzed mutterings became audible.

'You dare meddle with me, eh?' Batty was saying mildly, and Mintie, blinking and rubbing the tears from her eyes, moved through the drifting smoke to where Sorley coughed and sputtered, climbing painfully to his hands and knees and retching. Eventually he looked up at Batty and found he had to do it down the length of a long blade.

'Get up and fetch Clem onto his horse,' Batty ordered and Sorley scrambled to obey. Clem, whey-faced and laid out, had blood all down one leg, and Mintie, seeing the great scab her own shot had made on the stone cobbles, swallowed hard, for she knew he would never walk again without a limp – if he walked at all. It was a mercy for him that he was senseless, for the pain from Batty's pistol ball would be bad.

Batty turned and saw her look.

'Get inside, Mintie. This is no sight for you.'

Mintie took a deep breath or two.

'I carted my dead father back, all bloody from what Hutchie Elliott did to him,' she replied stiffly. 'I just fired off yon dagg of yours and near killed a man myself.'

He nodded admittance of her iron and turned back to the groaning figure on the ground, just as Mintie started to realise what she had done and what had happened here; the shivering took her savagely.

Will Armstrong was struggling weakly to rise and not realising he would never do so. Mintie remembered the great ugly exit hole in her father's body and saw the bloody seep on Will's belly.

'Ah, Christ, you have belly-shot me, Batty. Help me up, in the name of mercy...'

Batty levered himself down to kneel beside Will and looked at him with a flat, blank stare and laid his sword down. He picked up a stalk of straw, wiped it as clean as it would go on his jack, then balanced it on his knee and made the sign of the cross three times on it.

Will saw it and his eyes went wild and round while he tried to sit up. Mintie knew Batty was following the custom in urgent cases, asking God of His grace to consecrate this stalk, a fragment of His creation so that it could serve as Host and himself as priest. It was so swiftly done, worn by long usage, that Mintie became aware of how often Batty would have had to perform this in a life of war and siege.

He offered it and Will spat at him, about all that was left to him besides curse. Batty shook his head.

'I can do nothing for you, Will Armstrong, save leave Sorley unharmed to cart the pair of you home. Clem may live, but you will not. I have blown your backbone through and you will not survive.'

Will closed his eyes to hide the panicked fear in them, but he was a Borders man and rode the bad cess and fear of it like a plunging stallion, rode it hard and all the way until his eyes flashed open to reveal the last venom he could muster. Blood lined his teeth and spilled from him with every word he spat.

'My kin will hunt you, Batty. My da will pay you full measure for this...'

'Blood feuds are meat and drink to me,' Batty answered. 'I might just have shot your horse out from under you, save that you had called my mother a hoor.'

'So she was,' Will raved. 'A dirty-quimmed drab of a Graham, and I hope the German bastard who sired you on her rots in Hell, where you will be soon enough...'

Mintie stood, stunned and unable to move, while Will's poison voice spewed on, then tailed slowly off into harsh breathing and, finally, nothing at all. Batty crushed the consecrated stalk and let it blow away into the yard.

Sorley, having loaded Clem on his horse, stood miserable and hunched as Batty ordered him to load Will across his own mount. Then Mintie saw Clem start to weep and was a turmoil of emotions, reliving the great bang and leap of the pistol in her hands, what it had done to the stone, what it might have done to Clem – and what had been done to Will Armstrong. The dam in her broke suddenly, so that she finally whirled and screamed at the grating wails from Jinet floating through the upstairs window.

She felt a hand on her shoulder and leaped before she realised it was Batty, his great ugly face full of concern. He did not speak, but the touch and presence of him made Mintie suck in a few deep breaths and recover herself. Batty nodded as if he knew, then turned back to the weeping Sorley.

'Take them back to Mattie of Whitahugh and make sure you let him know Batty Coalhouse took nothing from them, for all the trouble the three of you put me to. If he wishes, he can feud with me – but remind him that he is not the first to try. Then tell him Powrieburn has no need of any husbands he may send. The women here can take care of themselves, and what they cannot manage, the Keeper of Liddesdale surely can.'

Batty waited until the horses were all moving out and into the dark before he fetched his thrown-down pistols and, when he straightened, he found Mintie staring at the blood left in the yard. Behind came the ostler boy, his mouth a black O in the white of his face.

'You shot two men,' Mintie declared, feeling slightly sick and stunned – and admiring, all at the same time.

'I did too,' Batty declared. 'And killed one, which was careless of me, for there is no reward for the dead, as I have said.'

He frowned and gently wiped dirt from the barrel of one of the pistols he had thrown down.

'But he angered me. And now I will have to spend a deal of the night cleaning and reloading all of these, which is a business.'

'I will help,' Mintie declared suddenly and then flushed as he looked astonished at her.

'I can load a pistol as well as shoot it. My da taught me, and I would have his save that Hutchie Elliott stole it.'

'Indeed,' Batty said with a quiet grin. 'Then we must make sure we get it back.'

He moved into the dark of the undercroft, then stopped, the trembling lantern held by Wattie making shadows leap and dance on his face.

'Unless you think I am too decrepit for the business?'

'I do not,' Mintie replied vehemently, though she trembled and shook still. 'We can leave as soon as you care.'

He had taken two steps before the import of the words hit him and he jerked up as if roped, then spun on her.

'We? There is no "we" in this. I am unlikely to take a lass into the Debatable – why, I may as well tether a lamb in a wolf den.'

He broke off and shook his head until Mintie thought it might fall off.

'No, no, and again no. You will bide here and look after your mother.'

'I will not. I am determined to make sure justice is done and for five pound, English, I will be going with you.'

Mintie flung one hand at the dark beyond the light-pooled door.

'Besides – take a long run and a jump from here and there you are in the Debatable. The boundary stone of it is only a good walk away and I have lived here all my life.'

'Little good it has done you,' Batty replied grimly. 'Besides – what if Mattie of Whithaugh decides to come back? None of these here have any bottom to them save you – well, apart from yon Bet's Annie.'

'I agree that is a worry,' Mintie answered bitterly, 'though you might have more carefully considered that before you shot his boy.'

He muttered, unable to answer it, and then Mintie closed the argument like the jaws of a wolf trap.

'You said yourself that Hutchie stole the Fyrebrande knowing full well what he did. Now I know what he will do with it.'

'Do you now? And what is that?'

'He will find someone in the Debatable with the money and contacts to buy it cheap from him and sell it on at premium,' Mintie replied triumphantly. 'Do you know all the horse dealers for miles around, in or out of the Debatable Land?'

Batty's beard twitched as he chewed out his frustration on one lip.

'I do,' Mintie said and went up to pack her things.

Chapter Three

She was up before any of the others, dressed in the chill and never felt it, exulting in the feel of boy's hose and breeches. She went as silently as she could down the ladder to the undercroft, hoping Wattie had paid heed to her instructions.

'Two hours before first light, feed Jaunty a handful of oats and a little hay. Make certain she has enough water. At one hour from first light, saddle her up, but leave the bridle off. Nod to show you understand.'

'I am aulder than yourself and not witless,' Wattie had replied scornfully.

'Half right is all good,' Mintie had said and went off up to bed.

Now she crept past Wattie and Bet's Annie, tangled and snoring together – just for the shared warmth, they would argue, for sure – but Jaunty was saddled, and she put her travelling gear on, shoving the long-barrelled caliver and its coil of saltpetred slow match through the loops, so that it stuck out on either side of Jaunty's haunches.

There was no sign of Batty, nor of the Saul, and for a terrible moment Mintie thought Batty had gone off without her – then she heard voices from the yard and realised the yett and outer doors were open.

When she went to the entrance, she saw Batty, fully dressed in battered buff jack and tattered boots, standing by the head of the Saul. Next to him was a resplendent figure in black Spanish formality, slashed and puff-lined with red, though the marks on Will Elliot's finest doublet revealed where a back and breast had frequently been worn. Mintie had no doubt the metal armour was in the large bag hung on the saddle of Will's horse, beside the metal helmet.

Will turned as Mintie came out and nodded politely, smiling an uneasy smile at the scowl he was getting from her.

'That's a face to turn milk,' he joked and had no half ashamed apology in return.

'What want you here?'

Will shifted on his game foot a little, taken aback by her vehemence. I should have remembered her from last time, he chided himself silently, but determined to be polite a while yet.

'I am in conversation with Master Coalhouse here,' he said lightly. And then added, as pointedly as he could manage and stay smiling, 'A privy conversation it was too.'

'Concerning?'

'Concerning no matter you need involve yourself with,' Will said, barely holding his temper in check and thrusting his chin out so that his beard bristled like a badger's behind. 'Away, lassie – butter needs churning somewhere.'

'We have butter enough,' Mintie snapped back, 'and you are keeping Master Coalhouse and myself from important matters of our own. Feel free to enjoy bread and the butter you are so concerned with before you leave. You may tell my ma I said so.'

Will's face flushed and he quivered, looking from Mintie to the mild, amused eyes of Batty.

'By God, child, you are in sore need of a scold bridle.'

'Try such a thing and I will prick the bladder of you with something sharp.'

'You are not so auld that I cannot put you on my knee and slap manners into you, lassie—'

'You may dream of it.'

Will, unaccountably to Mintie, flushed even deeper and could not speak at all. Batty, his voice rich with laughing, laid his hand on Mintie's shoulder, so that she became aware of her own tremble.

'Enough, the pair of you, good entertainment though it is on a chilled morning.'

He hitched the wooden apostles round his padded jack and spoke seriously to Mintie.

'The Land Sergeant from Hermitage came to tell you a Bill has been duly made for Hutchie Elliott and he himself ordered to track the man and bring him to justice, returning your goods betimes. We were discussing the matter of it when you arrived.'

Mintie looked from one to the other, frowning. Will Elliot's face was suffused but triumphant, and he recovered himself enough to speak.

'My coming was timely,' he grated and nodded to the darkened cobbles, which a night's rime had failed to cover. 'Blood spilled and men slain is no light business.'

The memory of the night flooded over Mintie, so that she hugged herself tight and could not speak.

'Ach, now,' Batty soothed, 'it was properly done, as all here will subscribe – they came to do mischief and fired first. You can see the marks in the door there.'

Will glanced at the fresh scars and wondered at Batty Coalhouse having taken on three weaponed men with only the one arm. Killed one too, and there would be conniptions over that. He suspected foul play but there was no way of proving it, and he knew the man only by reputation, struggling to recall more which might be of help.

Batty Coalhouse had arrived at Berwick two years since and there was some scandal attached to his mother, who had been a Graham. His father had been some German mercenary who came with Perkin Warbeck when he was pretending to be Richard IV of England and persuading King James to launch a huge army from Scotland against the English. It had all been smoke and Scotch mist, soon uncovered. Warbeck was packed off to Cork in shame and eventually got himself hanged at Tyburn.

Some of the Germans had hung on in Scotland, washing round the Borders like slurry all through the last year of the old century. One had eventually washed over a Graham lass and had Batty on her. The pair of them, Will surmised, must have fled, for the Grahams would not have suffered either to live long.

That had been years back, but memories were long and grudges longer still. Since he had come back to his mother's homeland, Batty Coalhouse had been as shunned by Grahams as if no time had passed. Will knew most of this because Batty had been taking on the worst of fouled Bills for the Wardens of the Marches on both sides, hunting down hard men for the money in it and spending the rest of his time as a thumper, keeping peace in a tavern in Berwick.

He had his name from the German and Coalhouse was the nearest most folk could make of it. A morose, ugly name, Will thought, fit to match a man it was better not to cross, for all he had a bit of belly and only one arm. Will was polite, though determined to mark a little of his authority, which did no harm.

'Aye, it is surely as you say,' he said slowly, stroking his neat-bearded chin, 'but the Keeper will want it writ up, witnesses attested and all that.'

'It will be,' Batty said cheerfully. 'All done as if there was law on the Border right enough – but once we have brought Hutchie back out of the Debatable.'

'So you agree to my proposal then?' Will said, brightening.

'Which proposal is this?' Mintie demanded and had another scowl from Will, who sucked his teeth with frustration as Batty explained.

'Young Will here has been sent by the Keeper, as he says. He proposes we join forces to bring Hutchie to task and that he will claim only the two pound Scots for recovery, leaving your fee entirely to myself. Since he is well set up with a brace of decent latchbows and a good sword, I think that is a fine arrangement.'

Mintie, frowning, thought about it and was puzzled as to why the Land Sergeant at Hermitage, who could not be both-ered before now, was suddenly so hot to go after Hutchie that he would not even argue for a share of five pound English. She said as much and saw the flicker in Will's eyes that showed the next thing he said was a lie.

'I am the Land Sergeant out of Hermitage,' he declared stiffly, 'and Lord Hepburn – your feudal, I might add, and Keeper of Liddesdale betimes – has so ordered. I am the law.'

Mintie felt the heavy hand of Batty on her shoulder, almost at the back of her neck, as you would do to gentle horse or dog; she turned up into his mild, benign, ugly smile.

'By God, he is a man of parts right enough. The law, he says. Well, we are better served with him than without.'

'We?'

Will's face was wide with incredulity.

'We?' he repeated, then looked a sneer at Batty.

'You are not taking this girl with you? I wondered why she was dressed as a laddie, but thought that was just her way. There is no way under God's Heaven that I am riding into the Debatable with a girl in train – lad's breeks or not.'

'Then we wish you a good day and a safe journey,' Batty said before Mintie boiled over. 'Though the Debatable is less likely to regard a poor one-armed man and a wee ostler boy than yourself. I doubt a Land Sergeant from Hermitage will pass unchallenged.'

The fact had not escaped Will Elliot when Hepburn had put the scheme to him, and he had asked for a dozen riders besides himself. The lord had waved it away.

'I don't have a dozen. Nor half that,' he had told Will. 'The Hamilton Earl of Arran has turned Catholic overnight since he became Regent to the new wee Queen. He is thumbing his neb at English plans to marry their wee Prince to his charge, but might birl himself into a new condition in another eyeblink. The Stuart Earl of Lennox, who has a fair claim to the throne himself, is looking to be wed to the wee Queen's mother and Mary of Guise is giving him a poor welcome, so he scowls and plots in France – but he is hourly expected. Fat

Harry of England, bad leg or not, will not be backwards in coming forwards and we are at war, for all nothing seems to be happening. Yet. But every man will be needed for what follows, mark me.'

Which was no comfort, as Will explained.

Hepburn, his slab face bright, had clapped him on the shoulder. 'One man, sly and secret, can get in and find Hutchie where a hot trod of riders would only attract unwarranted attention. Go to it.'

Will Elliot would have loved to have broken his knuckles on the Keeper's smug smile, but he had paid fifteen pounds Scots for the position of Land Sergeant and had recouped half of the outlay in a year of tithes on returning stolen beasts; he was not about to slay that milch cow.

He thought about it now, blinking into Batty's bland stare. He would have refused save that the task he'd been handed was important, as the Keeper had been at pains to point out, the threats concerning failure only slightly veiled. There had also been a strange note, as if the Keeper already knew the outcome.

'You have been cozened by a slip of a girl,' he said bitterly to Batty and climbed on his horse. Batty, grinning from one cheek to the other, levered himself up on the Saul and looked at Mintie.

'Well, don't stand there like a millstone. Fetch your gear and horse.'

They rode a little way, long enough for snow to start in large, wet flakes. Will gathered his fashionable, short black cloak round him, and Batty drew out a long, hooded riding cloak, green on one side and madder on the other, though both colours had faded with time and stain.

They had stopped at the great slab of Faerie rock that was the boundary stone marking the north-east extent of the Debatable Land, as if Batty was giving Mintie a last chance to change her mind as he expertly looped the cloak around himself with the one hand.

43

'Have you a cloak, young Mintie?' he asked, and she admitted she had, a good Border shepherd one of cream wool and blue check, but it was wrapped up in her tied bundle and strapped to the back of the saddle. They waited while she climbed off to get it, and Mintie was annoyed at herself for having packed so badly.

'By God,' said Batty admiringly as she pulled the caliver free, 'that is a fearsome lump of iron – there must be a three-quarter-ounce of ball shot in that. Can you fire it?'

Mintie knew how but never had, though she tilted a defiant chin and lied. Will was unimpressed.

'Ha. It would tumble you backwards on your hurdies, girl. That is too much gun for the likes of you.'

'A man who cannot afford one should not give advice on what he has not,' she spat back, and Batty laughed out loud into the flush of Will Elliot's face.

'She has you there – is it cost that puts you off a decent pistol or two?'

'It is not,' Will said indignantly. 'I prefer a good latchbow – I can get half a dozen bolts off in between your reloads. Nor will the rain douse it, as it will that slow-match caliver. A longbow shoots faster still, but badly from the back of a nag. So a latchbow is best.'

'Fair points,' Batty said and nodded to Mintie. 'Coil the match length of that up under your hat to keep it dry. And tie a wee bit cloth ower the barrel-end to keep damp from the charge – I take it you have loaded it, but not primed?'

Mintie had done neither, and Will shook his head at the revelation.

'See? This is not some gallivant, girl. What would happen if folk came on us sudden-like, all drawn weapons and bad intent?'

She was searching for a stinger to fire back at him when he suddenly whipped out his broadsword and whacked Jaunty on the rump with the flat. Outraged, Jaunty squealed, bucked and ran, scattering Mintie's pack as she did so.

'Something akin to that, lassie,' Will roared triumphantly. 'Now, by the time you have gathered in your mount, we will be long gone beyond the horizon and you would be best advised to go home. Where you should have bided in the first place.'

Mintie was stunned for a moment, then the anger surged up in her. She put two fingers to her lips and blew a piercing whistle which brought Jaunty to a quivering halt. Another started the beast, almost shamefaced, back towards her.

Will was open-mouthed, then scowling, and Batty slapped his knee and roared with laughter. Will was too busy trying to get all the bitter flow out of his mouth at once that he never noticed Mintie at his knee until the knife flashed.

He yelped, thinking she was stabbing him in the cods – but then felt the grip on his big knee boot and realised, as he fell sideways at her tug, that she had sliced through the stirrup and hauled him off his horse.

He landed heavily and scrambled up, aware of the mud slathering his elbows and knees. Batty was hanging onto his pommel, helpless with laughter, and Will whirled to face the crouching Mintie, her knife held low and point up.

'Come near me and I will draw blood,' she hissed, and though her own blood sang in her ears and her chest was tight so that she could hardly breathe, she felt a great surge of exultation at what she had done. That will show you, Land Sergeant of Hermitage.

Will Elliot frowned. That stirrup leather had been old and tough and two fingers wide, yet the knife had sheared it easily enough, so he had respect for the edge. But no slip of a girl was about to outface the Land Sergeant of Hermitage – it was bad enough that she had tumbled him off his horse.

'Now, now, Mintie...' Batty managed to get out between haw-hawing.

Will darted, feinted, got in under her strike and twisted. Mintie did not know how she had missed, but felt the hand on her wrist, the sudden sharp pain that made her squeal, and knew she had lost the knife.

Then suddenly she was headlocked under one arm, and he had plonked himself on a fat tussock and dragged her over his knee. She did not believe it – could not believe it – but he slapped her, hard.

'This is what I promised you, missie,' he said, breathing hard. 'And so what you will get. Your hurdies will keep you warm all the way back – but you will have to walk for I am determined to make it too hard for you to ride.'

He hit her again, and she roared with indignation and outrage, struggling futilely in his iron grip.

'Aye, aye,' Batty said, wiping the tears from his eyes. 'Enough is enough, Will Elliot. Let the lass go now.'

There was a pause and Mintie felt the tension coiling.

'I will finish what I started,' Will Elliot declared, and another whack descended, though it seemed less hearted than before.

'Best if you stopped now. We have a long ride and we will be slowed enough by your lack of stirrup without having to wait for a walking Mintie.'

'I can ride fast enough without stirrups,' Will answered, and she felt the shift of him raising his hand, 'and she will not be walking our way when she leaves here.'

'She will be riding which way she chooses. And I said to let her loose.'

She heard the change in his voice, the laughter gone from it and the tone shifted to something low and soft, like the slither of a snake's belly on wet grass. Will heard it too, but Mintie felt only anger tremble in him.

'And who are you to order me, you Graham half-blood? I will finish what I started.'

They both heard the low, dreadful scrape of metal on leather as the dagg came out of the saddle holster.

'That will be your last mistake, you lack-toed fud of a father-less whelp.'

The air creaked with the coiled tension of the moment, and Mintie felt his grip slacken, tore free and rolled over to face them.

Batty sat his horse casually, leaning his elbow on the pommel, the hand filled with long-barrelled pistol; from where she sat, the damp seeping up through her breeks and hose, Mintie could see the big black hexagon cave of it and realised it must seem like the mouth of Hell to Will, who quivered on the point of launching himself, like wine in an overfull cup.

And all the time he was thinking: he knows of me as I know of him – lack-toes he calls me, so he knows that much. Fatherless, he calls me, which is true enough, though not as much sting to me as calling his ma a hoor is to him.

Which, even as he said it to himself, he knew as mostly lie. He let himself subside and breathed out slowly.

Batty nodded and carefully stowed the weapon.

'Mintie – collect your gear and repack it. We will wait. Master Elliot – can you ride without stirrups for a while? There is a sometime farrier a mile from here at Andrascroft who might be able to find a spare stirrup leather, or something like it. Beyond that, you may do as you please.'

Will said nothing, simply got up, fetched his hat and beat it pointlessly on his knee boots until he was assured it was clean enough to stick back on his head. Then he vaulted, lithe and easy, into the saddle. Batty nodded admiringly at that, as if he recalled a time when he could have done the same.

A thought struck Mintie and she aired it.

'I know the farrier Andra. Perhaps he has a pistol the same as yours. I will willingly trade this caliver for such a dagg, Master Coalhouse, which is one I can handle and load and which can still kill the likes of Hutchie Elliott.'

Batty shook his head like a weary dog.

'Mintie,' he said. 'Shut your bliddy bread hole, fasten your pack and climb up on yon clever horse.'

–

They rode on and heard the tink-tink-tink of hammer on metal before they came on Andrascroft, a straggle of cruck houses huddled like sheep; though they were all wattle, daub and thatch, they'd been there long enough to get moss and as long as Mintie could remember. She knew Andrew Crozier and his family well enough, but Will Elliot regarded it all with a scathing eye.

'No fixed raisings,' he muttered and Batty laughed. The law, agreed between both countries, was that the land none of them wanted was not to be settled by either side. No permanent structures were to be built – but since neither country upheld their laws in the Debatable, it was an instruction the residents thumbed their noses at, to the extent that an entire village – Canobie – existed within it.

'A substantial slab of Scotch mist,' Batty agreed wryly, 'as is the one being built in stone and belonging to the man who lets Andrew smith here.'

Mintie knew, as did Will, that he spoke of Johnnie Armstrong, once known as the Laird's Jock to distinguish himself from his father of the same name. The Armstrongs were the power in the land no government wanted and the Laird's Jock was now the power at Hollows, a great tower which had been the arrogant stamp of his father. He was also close kin to the chief of the Armstrongs, whose castle was at Mangerton.

A thought struck Mintie, though it was clear when she spoke it that it had fallen on both Batty and Will long before.

'Will the Laird of Hollows know you killed an Armstrong of the Whithaugh?'

'If I were Mattie of the Whithaugh,' Batty said flatly, 'I would have sent riders to tell him before first light. He may not know yet. Or he may.'

'Then it would be wise to put distance atween us,' Will muttered, hunching into his cloak and eyeing the wood-spattered hills as if a band of vengeful Armstrongs would ride over it at any moment.

Which they might do, Mintie thought, since Hollows is a spit beyond the horizon. It was also one of the places she thought likely for Hutchie to go with the Fyrebrande and said so. Will Elliot groaned. Batty paused in dismounting, then levered himself off the Saul with a grunt.

'Let us speak with this Andra first. He may have news more welcome than sticking our hands in a Hollows viper nest.'

'Aye, very good,' Will said morosely.

Mintie did not know the young man working the hammer and anvil at all, which puzzled her, but he nodded politely enough, set the hammer down and wiped a hand down the stained front of his leather apron.

'I am Geordie's Eck,' he declared with a smile. 'Wed on to Andra's girl, Agnes, this year. He bids me to make you welcome.'

Mintie was stunned. She had known Agnes all her life, though did not see her often and only when Andrew Crozier brought her to Powrieburn along with his farrier's tools, for her father would not take horses into the Debatable to be shod unless he had to. Such horses, needing shoes at all, were a station above the usual Marches mounts and so even more valuable.

Married? She is younger than me, Mintie thought.

'Where is Andrew?' asked Batty, while Will was thinking that Andrew was well informed as to who was coming up on him and from where. Which was no surprising revelation about a man living where he did.

'In back,' Geordie's Eck said, jerking his head for emphasis and then grinning at the sudden mad ratchet of cackle and honk that erupted. 'Shoeing geese.'

'Have you a stirrup strap?' demanded Will Elliot. 'Or leather to make same?'

He glanced bitterly at Mintie and added, 'Mine broke.'

While they fell to discussing it, Mintie followed Batty through the cruck lean-to covering the forge fire, out into the yard formed by a protective huddle of mean houses. It was a riot of geese, though there were only eight of them, being driven – with difficulty and protest – down a stick run, through hot pitch, then sand and grit and, finally, cold water to soothe and fix the mess on their feet.

They did not like it, and it took the combined efforts of Andra, his wife Bella, and a brood of four boys, all noisy, tumbling, laughing pups who got in the way more than helped.

The Goodwife straightened when she saw them, tugged her soiled apron and shoved a stray grey tendril back under her cap.

'Mintie Henderson – good to see you. How is your mother? Why are you dressed as a laddie?'

'She is with me,' Batty declared, as if that was all that was needed.

Bella looked uneasily from him and back to Mintie, while the geese flurried and stretched their necks with a honking series of cackles which all but drowned the conversation. The last of them flapped indignantly through the run and the boys cheered.

'We are out with the Land Sergeant at Hermitage,' Mintie added, 'looking for news of my stolen horses and the man who killed my father.'

Her voice, to her horror, caught at the end of this, and Bella, having heard of her tragedy and then forgotten, flung a hand to her mouth and was at once crease-faced with concern, gathering Mintie into the stale sweat smell of her, patting her like a dog. They went off towards the nearest of the cruck houses, leaving Batty with Andra, who made a last show of scattering his boys with good-natured curses for their cheek and noise.

'Did you see the man?' Batty persisted, and Andra blew out his cheeks and made a play of thinking, as if a man riding hard and trailing a superb specimen of horseflesh arrived at his door every other day.

'Aye, I might have seen the man – the horse anyways. I wondered why the Fyrebrande was in the Debatable with someone I did not know well. But who are you? Will Elliot is known here, but you are a stranger to me.'

'Batty Coalhouse,' he replied, and Will Elliot came sauntering through, dangling leather like a dead snake and in time to hear the last – and see the blanch on Andra's worn face which showed he was no stranger to the name.

'Andra,' Will said and nodded.

'Land Sergeant Elliot,' Andra gave back awkwardly.

The long moment persisted, filled with the mutter of outraged geese and the shrill of quarrelling boys.

'Did you wonder enough about the Fyrebrande and this chiel,' Will persisted, 'to inquire where he went with another man's horses?'

Andra had the grace to lower his eyes, then he shrugged.

'No business o' mine,' he answered determinedly and Will was hardly surprised. Saw nothing. Heard nothing. Do not know the man. It was the litany of the Border.

'Did you see which way he went at least?'

Andra waved a loose hand in the direction of north. Will thanked him politely enough, then went to fix the leather on his stirrup. Batty watched Mintie come back out of the cruck house and thought she had a strained look – but a smoke-reeked hole like that would make anyone blanch.

The inside of the howf never bothered Mintie, though she marvelled at how people could live in such a dark, stinking place and never want to at least change the rushes. The smoke from the pit fire was allowed into the thatch, to kill the vermin, rather than be sucked out of a sensible roof hole, so the place was an eye-stinging, lung-burning blue mist – yet light enough for her to see Agnes on a bed of stained blankets.

She was well enough but near her time, and Mintie only managed to stammer a few trite phrases, mesmerised by the greatness of her belly. When she stumbled clear of it, the vision of that swell stayed with her.

A child. Agnes was pregnant and a year younger than herself; Mintie found her hands on her own flat stomach and could not speak for the thoughts tumbling in her, all at once revulsion and wonder.

Will Elliot fixed his stirrup and then hauled his back and breast out of its sack, making a great play of it, while Batty sat his horse and smiled. When Will had fitted it on, with Mintie's help, he clapped his iron helmet on his head and climbed aboard his nag, scowling truculently into Batty's grin.

'Well,' he said. 'If I am to stick my head in a crowd of armed Armstrongs at Hollows, I had better look the part.'

'Just so,' Batty agreed mildly. 'Mars himself, no doubt of it. By God, someone will be tempted to try a shot at yon lobster shells you are wearing, just to see if they are proofed.'

'The bugger with Mars,' Will grunted, adjusting his new stirrup leather and trying not to look at Mintie to see her reaction to his oath. 'I wish only to look like the Land Sergeant of Hermitage and give them some thought on who they are shooting and the consequence of it.'

They rode in a mourn of windsong on the white-patched rolling hills, skirting the rimed woodland, heading for Canobie and on to Hollows, lair of the Armstrongs and site of the strongest fortalice in Eskdale.

All the way, Mintie thought of Agnes and how, not so long ago, they had spent a day making straw dolls and cradling them. Now both of us have changed, she thought – she has gained husband and bairn, I have lost a father. Is this what it means to grow up?

She was so lost in it that she did not realise Jaunty had stopped for a good minute, and when she looked up they were at Canobie's brig and looking across the patched snow and the half frozen tumble of the Esk to something new.

A mill had been built where nothing had been before and they all stared at it for a long time. Mintie turned to Batty, feeling something strange and tense in the man, seeing his glazed stare. He was looking at the slow-turning waterwheel, but Mintie was sure he was seeing something else.

'A mill,' Will said and then glanced sideways up to where the great nail of Hollows Tower struck arrogantly into the sky, perched above a loop of the Esk and with the new harling on the stone-built part of it as bright as the snow itself.

'In stone,' he added and shook his head. 'No fixed raisings, by God. The king had his snook cocked by these Armstrongs right enough.'

Mintie knew that the present laird's father had started the tower in timber – though it had been burned out under him by the English. He had thought his own king would be more considered and helpful over it, and so, arrogantly, he had started rebuilding it and broke off only to attend a meeting with the young King James, thinking that the deed being done, the royal boy would simply stamp his seal on the matter.

Johnnie Armstrong had arrived flaunting a finery of clothes and entourage which outdazzled royalty – and outraged a seventeen-year-old boy-king with bad skin and deep-rooted fears, only recently freed from the prison grip of other flaunting lords, the Douglases. So the young King James had ordered Johnnie seized.

Mintie had heard that Johnnie had pleaded the conditions of the truce, then offered half the blackmeal rents he took – a sum so vast it had only made the spotty youth of a king more wrathful, so that he swore Johnnie Armstrong would hang. Arrogant to the end, Mintie had heard that Johnnie's last bitter laugh into the petulant glare of King James had been on how foolish it was to expect 'grace from a graceless face'.

Now Johnnie's son, it appeared, had no less arrogance or riches. The Laird's Jock, now Laird of Hollows himself, had denied King James the Armstrong horse for war – which meant a deal of others who all owed the Armstrongs stayed away as well. The king's army had been defeated and the king himself was dead of shame, so that thirteen years after Johnnie Armstrong had been hanged, the Name had its revenge. That was a cold and relentless vengeance any man would have to consider when dealing with the Armstrongs.

With only a child on the throne – and a female one at that – Hollows was being finished in stone quarried from the nearby rock, with enough left over to build a mill. It was clear what the Laird of Hollows thought of matters in Edinburgh.

'Corn or wool?' Will mused. 'I hear grinding, but not tilt hammers walking cloth, so I am thinking corn.'

Mintie heard Batty shift, with a shudder like hare shaking itself free of a weasel stare.

'Neither,' he answered. 'It corns right enough, but not grain.' He pointed.

'See that? Three stone walls on the lower floor and one of wood. That's the weak wall.'

Will stared for a moment longer, while Mintie was simply bemused. Then the import hit the Land Sergeant and he jerked as if stung.

'Powder. It is a powder mill, by God's hook.'

'It is.'

Mintie looked from one to the other and finally asked, at which Batty shifted and turned to her, his face grim as a headsman's axe.

'It corns black powder, mills it into grains fit for calivers, pistols and larger. If it were not winter and the wind blowing from us, you would taste the stink of it, like the Earl of Hell's hall. That will be the sulphur. That big pile, all nice and clean white, is actually dung with snow on it, which is how you get the saltpetre. That store yonder probably houses the charcoal. One to three to nine gets you powder, all perjink and according to the *Liber Ignium*.'

Mintie did not know much Latin, save that which came up in legal documents, but she could make a lunge at it and, hesitantly, came up with 'flaming book'.

'Book of Fires,' Batty corrected. 'It has the recipe for powder in it and was writ by Auld Nick himself, some say, in order to visit Hell on God's good earth.'

'You know a lot,' Will pointed out suspiciously and Batty nodded.

'I do, for it was my task, *ingenieur* like my da afore me. I know every gun from a Cannon Royal to a Rabinet – which is the Spanish sizing. There are twelve of them, less for the French and sixteen for the English. I know bombards, petards, and how to cut a slow match to the second.'

'Is that what cost your arm?'

Mintie had blurted it out before she knew it and clamped her lips afterwards until they went bloodless white.

Batty turned and showed his teeth at her in what might just as well have been snarl as smile, then waggled the stump of his missing arm.

'In a way. If you survive them, such mistakes are instructive.'

Then he widened the grin until his beard end almost touched his nose.

'But it was not black powder that did this. It was Maramaldo.'

Mintie did not know who or what a Maramaldo was and did not pursue it; neither, she noticed, did a thoughtful Will.

Will said nothing but thought long on it. He had known the German who sired Batty had been a mercenary, but not exactly what – an *Ingenieur* was a skilled prize for any army, a man who knew powder and how to site the big guns for sieging, and how to blow up walls, or undermine them if he could not. His estimation of what Batty had seen and done went up a few notches.

'Why are they dressed so curious?' Mintie asked, seeing the workers pausing and staring back at them suspicious and wary. They had kertches on their heads and shuffled in wooden pattens in the snow, their hose and shirts loose; they looked to freeze, she thought, and said so.

'No iron on them, on belts or shoes. Sooner freeze than spark,' Batty answered and Mintie realised the significance. In a few more minutes she had learned that the powder store was called a magazine and was probably the little shed to the left. It was only little because the bulk of it was underground for safety and would be packed with milled cakes of black powder.

That kept the stoor down, for sometimes Auld Nick leered and caused even the dust to blow up, for no reason at all other

55

than devilment. Those milled cakes would be gently teased – corned – back into grains and dried, the result being a fine powder that would not separate back into the parts it was made from.

'It will bang and not fizz,' Batty ended, and then, musing softly and almost to himself, added: 'It is a rare thing, a powder mill. I do not think there is another in all Scotland.'

'Is that right?' Will said with ironic admiration. 'By God, you can walk some muscle onto your wits listening to you, Batty Coalhouse. Now tell us what we do about them.'

He pointed to the riders no one had noticed, ambling soft through the snow and coming from the direction of Hollows. A good ten, with upright Jeddart staffs winking sharp leers to the weak winter sun and scowls clapped low on their brows.

'Steady and quiet,' Batty said, seeing Will edge a hand to his hilt. 'Mintie, get behind us a wee bittie if you please. Keep your face lowered under your hat.'

She saw him, casual as smiling, rest his sole hand on the cantled pommel, an inch from the curving butt of the horse-holstered dagg; a slide of cold went down her, from neck to the crack of her buttocks.

The riders were soft-hatted, but padded with jacks and leather; Will Elliot eyed the Jeddarts they carried with a sour look, for one similar to them had taken off two toes of his left foot and four years had not dulled the memory of the pain.

Eight-foot iron-bound shafts, they had a spear point and a thin sliver of blade on one side, with a hook on the other. In capable hands, they could be deadly on foot or on fast horse – and the reivers of the Borders were, if nothing else, some of the finest light horsemen in the country, which was why rival kings sought them.

The man riding at their front wore only a bonnet, cocked at an angle on the forehead of his brosy face. He was bluff and round, with russet hair and beard, a doublet of striped red and darker crimson, plain hose, and his big knee boots folded down to the ankle. A black cloak swathed him, the white fox collar of it coddling his big chin.

The Laird in person, Mintie thought, for she had seen him once or twice in her life when he had ridden out to Powrieburn for horses. Her da had treated him politely enough, but Mintie had seen that he did not like the Laird of Hollows much; she was suddenly glad she was swathed to the eyes in cloak, with a hat pulled down to her brow. She was afraid of being looked at by him, as if the act of him singling out a body was the kiss of death.

Which it may well be, she thought with a sudden chill.

The light grace and unarmoured style of the Laird of Hollows made Batty a little easier, though he never took his eyes from the man, nor his hand further than an inch from the saddle holster. Yet he nodded polite greeting and had it coldly returned.

'Land Sergeant Elliot,' the Laird declared expansively, turning to Will. 'You are some way out from Hermitage and lightly entouraged for a hot trod, I think.'

'No trod,' Will replied, feeling the prickle of sudden sweat break out along his spine at what he had originally intended to bring – a hot trod meant a manhunt and every rider at the Laird's back was a Debatable outlaw who had experienced being so hunted at one time or another. I was probably in the pack chasing them, Will thought, feeling their eyes like claws. He was glad now that he had never brought men with him.

'We have a Bill, nevertheless,' he went on, pushing it like an uphill boulder. 'On one Hutcheon Elliott – two "T"'s – who has murdered the Master of Powrieburn and stolen a horse called the Fyrebrande.'

'I had heard,' the Laird said, stroking his beard with a fine-gauntleted hand. As if he was some considering judge, Will thought bitterly to himself, instead of an outlaw baron. Yet an outlaw baron with all the powers of judge, jury and hangman in the Debatable, he corrected a moment later, which it was always best to keep in the forefront of your mind.

'I am sorry for Powrieburn's loss. I hear that the daughter, Araminta, is much favoured these days as a result.'

Mintie held her breath and the Laird's eyes swung to Batty, resting like brief lamps on her as they passed.

'I hear also that one suitor has been rebuffed,' the Laird continued mildly. 'To death. You must be Batty Coalhouse.'

'Unless you are familiar with another one-armed man,' Batty replied flatly, 'then it is me myself.'

'I have Sorley Armstrong up at my hall, drinking and weeping into his mug about the loss of his cousin, Fingerless Will of Whithaugh. A father in Whithaugh also weeps, and sisters and mothers too. Clem Armstrong may never walk or ride again.'

He stopped and was clearly waiting for Batty to put some sort of case, but when nothing came back at him, his eyebrows rose a little, which was volumes from him.

'Sorley tells of ambuscade and how he fought like a tiger,' the Laird went on, 'despite being attacked by others from the house and even though he and his kin had arrived in friendly fashion and meaning no harm. He has come to me seeking redress.'

Batty shifted slightly, but Mintie saw that was only so he could rest his hand lightly on the side of his saddle holster; his little finger, spatulate and hairy, was snugged up to the butt of the pistol, and Mintie watched the Laird's eyes flick to that, then back to Batty's face. He did not seem annoyed or angry, simply amused, and that tightened the flesh on Mintie's arms.

'A brave tale, I am sure,' Batty answered. 'Has he scraped the horse shite from his hair and beard yet? I half drowned him in dung, for all his youth and both arms. Which taught him not to come in the night, expecting to abduct a wee lassie from a rickle o' women and an ostler boy.'

He stared levelly at the Laird.

'They found me instead and thought a one-armed man was an annoyance only.'

The Laird nodded thoughtfully, then rested his full gaze on Mintie, so that she almost cried out as if it stung.

'This will be the ostler boy,' he said and Will nodded.

'Brought to help with the horse when we recover it from Hutchie,' he declared loudly. 'If you have news of either, I am sure your grace as the Laird's Jock will allow it to be shared.'

The head turned slowly, like some horn-heavy ox, and his gaze was searing, so that Will had to brace himself, as if in a blast.

'I am Laird's Jock no longer. I am Laird of Hollows and my grace is none of your affair,' he declared thickly. 'I have horse and Hutchie both. The beast I will bring to you now, for the memory of a good man at Powrieburn. Hutchie I will bring to the next Truce Day. Will that suffice?'

'There were two horses stolen. And a dagg.'

Mintie had blurted it out before she realised and shrank under the eyes that turned on her.

'Sir,' she added, her voice trailing off even as she tried to deepen it a little. 'So I was told to say by the Mistress.'

The Laird looked at her a long time, then nodded.

'The Fyrebrande and the horse Hutchie rode in on, then. Plus his dagg. Take it and be gone. Land Sergeant, if you poke your neb in Hollows again, it will be bloodied.'

Will Elliot, for all he did not like the feeling, had relief wash him and knew he had let it show by the Laird's twist of sneering smile. Then the gaze was swung back to Batty.

'Master Coalhouse, you are free to leave, but not free of obligation. Will and Clem are kin and Whithaugh will not forget. Neither will I. It would be best if you left the Borders entire for healthier climes. I hope you are as legendary stubborn as I have heard, and do not, for I have a mind to see you dead.'

Then he smiled, an arrangement of face muscles his eyes knew nothing of.

'While you live, all the same, it satisfies me enough that you are a shame to the Grahams.'

Mintie held her breath. It was well known that the Armstrongs and Grahams feuded with each other, as harsh with hate as the Maxwells and Johnstones, and that viciousness had lasted decades already. She waited for an explosion, but Batty said nothing and his face showed only a mild, thoughtful surprise, which Mintie thought very fine after having seen Will Elliot almost fall off his horse with relief.

They sat in silence after the riders had gone, while the wind danced flakes of snow around them. Finally, Batty straightened and stretched, taking his hand away from the holstered pistol for the first time.

'That went well enough, eh?' he declared and had back a sour look from Will.

'You may say so, having got your five pounds English.'

Mintie thought that he was more annoyed by how much he had revealed of his fears and how well Batty had not, to the extent that Mintie was not even sure if Batty had felt any at all. For herself the moment had gone, and only later did she realise that it was the arrogance of youth, that certainty of immortality, that had chased away how she had felt when the Laird set his eyes on her.

At the time, though, she dwelt more on the boots Hutchie had stolen and that she had failed to mention. They would now never get them back — yet there was enough grown woman in her to then feel a wash of shame for considering it after what they had just escaped.

Batty was right — they had achieved a great deal in a day, and though the justice for Hutchie Elliott was a promise only, she had it in mind that the Laird of Hollows would honour it. He thinks himself as graced as a king, that one, Mintie said to herself, and his pride and honour no less. His father had been the same and look where that had got him.

The horses arrived, brought by a brace of sullen men anxious to be done with the matter and back in the warm. Mintie took the cloth-wrapped bundle and unwrapped it; the sight of her father's dagg and the inlaid vine-leaves that had delighted her as a child made her bow her head and choke a sob.

She felt that now familiar hand on her neck – the same hand which had gripped Clem Armstrong and buried him face-deep in dung, she remembered – and shivered. His rough voice was a soothe on the moment, all the same.

'A fine pistol,' he declared, peering. 'German. Ivory inlay. Good ebenist work on that, for sure.'

But the Fyrebrande was nearly all of the moment and she spent a long time looking him over, ears to fetlocks, while Batty sat patiently and Will fretted to be away 'afore the Laird alters his mind'.

In the end, Mintie had to admit that the stallion was glossed and gleaming, while her father's original mount was no less cared for. She climbed on Jaunty and took up the lead ropes as Will reined his horse round savagely and started back the way they had come.

'If we lift the pace,' he growled over his shoulder, 'we can be back in Powrieburn as dark falls. I trust I can beg the grace of a night's food and lodging.'

'You can,' Mintie retorted, 'even if your own grace in asking is sour as old gruel. What is bending you out of shape, Land Sergeant from Hermitage?'

Will did not reply, but had produced a leather flask from his saddlebags and unstoppered it with his teeth, before fumbling the cork into one hand and taking a deep swallow. Then he coughed, cleared his vision and realised Batty's hand was outstretched meaningfully; reluctantly, he passed it over.

Batty drank, his apple bobbing in his throat for so long that Will's mood was not improved by how much of his *eau de vie* was vanishing.

'Is there to be a glut of drink tomorrow?' he demanded, snatching the flask back. 'Is it that makes you swallow it as if so easily got?'

'A wee stirrup cup to success,' Batty expounded and reined in at the brig to allow four big carts to trundle past them, stuffed with covered horse fodder; the fresh smell of it brought the undercroft of Powrieburn back to Mintie with an intensity that was almost painful.

'Success, is it?' Will demanded with a growl, and Batty stopped looking thoughtfully at the carts and laughed.

'Not for you, mark you, who have to go back and tell the Keeper how you were foiled from getting the Fyrebrande.'

Mintie's head came up at that, and Will blinked, stopped in the act of raising the flask to his mouth.

'I don't know what you are saying, Coalhouse,' he blustered.

'The Keeper sent you to fetch the horse. The thief if you could manage it, but horse for sure. For himself, mayhap? As fitting a tithe as ever was claimed, eh, Land Sergeant?'

Batty Coalhouse was both right and wrong at the same time, but he might well have stood outside the door as the Keeper told it to Will, so that Will was flustered by it and had no ready answer. Mintie, bridling, was starting in to curse him when the cackle of geese arrested her.

Batty knuckled his hat brim to Andra's wife, Bella, herding the shod geese up the flinted track towards Hollows, with a stick and one of her boys to help. She bobbed a polite curtsy to the men, then looked at Mintie, taking the sting out of her with her smile.

'You got your beasts back – there is nice,' Bella declared, beaming. 'The laird is a good, fair man, like his poor faither afore him.'

'Keeps a fine table,' Batty added and the woman nodded agreement.

'These will not last long, if the last delivered are anything to judge by.'

She turned back to Mintie.

'Agnes was right pleased to see you, Mintie. She would have invited you and your mother to the handfasting and wedding, save that matters grew crowded at the smith.'

'Busy are you?' Batty asked mildly and the woman threw up her hands.

'Blessed be, aye, we are. Horses coming from all airts and pairts and not just Galloway nags – proper beasts, slipshod and needing my man's skills.'

'Honest-earned money is no toil,' Batty intoned. 'Fair journey to you, Goodwife.'

Bella, still beaming, added that Agnes would bring her bairn to Powrieburn for inspection, on the way to it being welcomed to Christ at Bygate, if the priory still stood. God be praised it were a boy.

Mintie watched Andra's wife hurry off after her waddling charges, and soured to silence now, hunched into her cloak and glared daggers at Will, who had the sense to stay quiet and suffer the sear of her look on his back.

But Mintie, when she eventually surfaced from her anger and sullen embers enough to look, saw that Batty was strange and still and thoughtful and wondered what was going through his mind.

Chapter Four

Towards dark on the way home, a mist came up and the day was over, though it was scarcely late afternoon. As the mist cleared, the moon unveiled and had some wind on it, so that scudding cloud left just enough light to glint the burn they followed; the cold came out, sharp as fox teeth.

At Powrieburn, the women clucked and clapped at their success and return. Bet's Annie declared she had thought never to see them again, and Wattie, who had never seen the Fyrebrande, was awed by the beast, as like the horses he had cared for so far as a dragon is to a lizard.

In the warm of the hall, fed and watered and listening to the quiet movement of her mother and the other women clinking pots and cutlery, Mintie hugged her knees while the fire danced shadows.

It had been a great adventure, if just for a day, and it hardly seemed only the previous night that Batty Coalhouse had killed a man and disabled two others. Or that her neighbour had thought to marry her by force and steal Powrieburn; it brought a strange feeling to Mintie, both of her power and lack of it.

Batty and Will sat, passing the flask back and forth in silence, and Mintie found herself embering up again at the thought of the Land Sergeant – and the Keeper – trying to cozen her out of the Fyrebrande. But she fumed inwardly, while Will had Jinet pull off his big boots and socks. Then he fell to massaging his three-toed foot, which clearly bothered him.

Mintie watched, fascinated and repelled at the sight of the puckered stumps. Batty grinned, drank and smacked his lips as he passed the leather flask back.

'Between us, we can nearly make a whole man,' he said and Will smiled wanly.

'How did you come to lose them?' Mintie demanded. 'Stealing someone else's sword maybe?'

'Ach, now, Mintie,' Batty admonished, but Will waved his attempt at mediation away into the flicker of shadows.

'No, no, she has a right to know, about the Fyrebrande if not the toes,' he answered and managed a grin. 'Though I will reveal both.'

'The toes I lost on a hot trod after one Dog Pyntle Eck Bourne,' he began and then saw Mintie's mother listening and made a hasty nod of apology. 'Begging your pardon, Goodwife, but that is his name.'

'I have heard worse,' Mintie's mother said and vanished to fetch sewing and a better light.

'He and some Nixons, with a peck of Croziers, raided across the Waste, slipping up the east bank of Hermitage no less. This was a few years back, when we were less vigilant.'

'In the time o' the Flood then,' Batty growled, 'for a band of tootling mummers could drive reived kine past Hermitage in the broad light of a fine day all the time I have known the place.'

'A foul calumny,' Will replied, his amiability at such a slur surprising Mintie. 'Unless it has been agreed aforehand.'

'A fine distinction,' Batty answered. 'Which garners black-meal for the Keeper and no good for the folk he is charged to protect.'

'One of whom is myself,' Mintie interrupted, 'who would like to hear the rest of the tale.'

It was familiar enough even to Mintie, who had heard similar in her few years of life. A raid had been organised from the north side of the Kershope, the water dividing Scotland from its neighbour. Hermitage had known of it, but had let it happen because catching raiders going out is empty of profit, while catching them laden on the way back in gathers decent results in claimed tithes when the beasts are returned to barely grateful owners.

Dog Pyntle and his collection of grim, veteran men had been reluctant to give up their spoil, and a sharp fight resulted in broken heads and fleeing reivers. In the hot trod – the official pursuit – which followed, plain Will Elliot of the Hermitage garrison had caught up with Dog Pyntle, whose horse foundered in a bog.

The fight had been vicious and learning for the Hermitage man – Dog Pyntle's Jeddart staff had sliced Will out of the saddle, his horse had been lifted, and Dog Pyntle had galloped off on it into the Debatable, where he had been laughing ever since. Will had all but bled to death before he had found help.

'A toe were gone entire,' he ended. 'One turned black and stank later, so a barber was fetched and he snicked it off like you would a wee pup's tail.'

Mintie made a face and Jinet, overhearing the last, made sucking noises, as you would to a child, then offered to soothe his wounded foot. Will seemed wary, but smiled nonetheless, so that Mintie thought the undercroft would be busy that night; she thought of Agnes and her swollen belly and hugged her knees tighter still.

'Now tell her about the Fyrebrande,' Batty grunted and Will sighed.

'It is much as you revealed,' he answered, with a quick, bitter glare at Batty for doing so. 'The Keeper was less interested in getting Hutchie as the horse—'

'Thief,' Mintie interrupted, sour with indignant accusation. Will waved an irritated hand, making the candles flap.

'Away – you may not believe it, Mintie Henderson, but I was to bring it back to you, all brushed and pin-neat, together with the news that Hutchie would be up for judgement at the next Truce Day Meet.'

Mintie's disbelief was clear in Will's exasperated sigh.

'I swear on any Bible you like that this is the truth of it. I would not be party to such a theft, even from the Keeper of Liddesdale.'

'Just so,' answered Batty mildly. 'I am sure of it. As sure of it as I am that when you tell him I and an ostler boy were there, he will hush you on the matter and wink and offer you a glass of wine and a clap on the shoulder for a job well done. Though he will not care to find my name in it. Best if you do not mention Mintie at all.'

'What are you saying?' demanded Will truculently.

Batty leaned forward so that his face was devilled by firelight and shadow.

'Think on this, Will,' he said. 'You were sent on your own to the heart of darkness itself, Hollows Tower, to recover a prize horse from a grasping man like the Laird. Does the Keeper hate you? Have you swived his wife or daughters or both? Stolen his purse?'

Will frowned. The Keeper, he had always thought, ranked him well enough, and the fact of that mission had puzzled and irritated him all the way there and back.

Batty swallowed from the flask, made a sad face and handed it back to Will, who found it empty and scowled.

'That should tell you enough,' Batty said, 'but in case you are struggling with it still, let me point up the ease with which the Laird handed back said horse – and more, beside – and promised redress on the thief.'

'As if he knew,' Mintie declared suddenly, seeing it clear. Batty nodded and indicated her with a triumphant flap of his hand, as if to say to Will, 'There, you see? A bliddy wee lassie can work it out in less time than yourself.'

Now that it was said, the fact of it stared Will back in his face. The Laird had known someone would be coming for the horse, possibly even that it would be himself, since Hermitage was man-short and he was the most likely to be chosen for the task. Which meant that the Keeper of Liddesdale and the outlaw of Hollows had arranged it between them. Which meant...

This last arrowed Will's brow, though he struggled manfully with it – and failed.

'What does it all mean?' he asked and Mintie wondered it as well. Batty closed one thoughtful eye and stroked his raggle of beard.

'Well – the Fyrebrande is no ordinary beast and neither is Mintie Henderson of Powrieburn,' he declared, so that Mintie felt herself flush with delight at his grin.

'She comes seeking justice for murder and spoiling, and when none is forthcoming, rides to Askerton – possibly on to Carlisle, for the Keeper has no way of knowing – to get it from the English.'

He paused and shook his head with mock outrage.

'A wee chit o' a lassie, stirring matters up, causing upset and ripples which the Lord Hepburn, Keeper of Liddesdale, would prefer to stop spreading, lest other folk start sticking their nebs into what is happening around Hollows.'

'The mill?' declared Will and shook his head uncertainly. 'It is new to us, sure, but not something you can keep hidden for much longer. An event, as you say – there is no other like it, and if the Keeper and the Master of Hollows have contrived mutual profit from such a venture, then it will surely come out sooner or later.'

Most likely later, he thought, since we have no firm hand in the land, only a bairn still drooling milk and a regent too occupied with greater matters to care, even about such a strange thing as a powder mill in Scotland. And in the Debatable, where no permanent structures are supposed to be raised and no writ of Law runs, save that of the Laird of Hollows.

'It is not all about the mill,' Batty declared. 'You will have noted how the Laird of Hollows was not facered in the least you reporting it to the Keeper, as you would do. He is, I suspect, put out by me and a wee ostler boy having set eyes on it, all the same. But the mill is part of it, mark me.'

'Part of what?'

Batty sucked his lip and then suddenly grinned.

'Ride to Hermitage the morn, Will,' he said. 'Tell the Keeper the Fyrebrande is returned and Hutchie promised for the next Truce Day meet, and see what he says and how pale he turns when he finds you were not alone, as planned. He will ask you if there is any Bill on me and whether one should be made, with a wink and a nod and a look that makes my future uncertain. He may even ask you to serve it.'

God forbid, thought Will, without a troop of men. Two. And possibly a wheeled gun.

After they had broken fast and Will Elliot had ridden off, Mintie left off from her work, the feeding and cleaning and tasks that kept Powrieburn turning quiet and smooth as a greased wheel. She fetched the agreed price from the bound and locked iron coffer, afraid at how little it left.

Still, she plunked it down in front of him, allowing some of the coins to spill forth to let him know what they were – a brace of them were bonnets, worth forty shillings each, the rest were shillings of the late king, with saltire, thistle and crown stamped proud on them. Batty's eyebrows went up.

'Five pounds, English, as agreed. No testoons.'

'So I see,' Batty said mildly and stirred the coins with one of his knitting needles. 'I had no doubt of it – now put it back and deduct what you think is fair for my keep for another day. Perhaps two. Unless you are weary of my company.'

Mintie was not – was, in fact, relieved if a little puzzled, for she didn't think he was staying for love of the Powrieburn company, even her own. But she took the money back to the coffer, hearing the click of his needles as he knitted his endless sock, with the dog's head on his knee, it cocking an eye and an ear, as if listening to Batty as he crooned like a sick crow.

'*Sing and play, Thomas, sing and play along wi' me. And if ye dare to kiss my lips, sure of your body I will be...*'

–

That night they spent as they had the others – playing Primero by the light of a tallow candle and the built-up fire, flushed with the heat at their front and chilled with the bite of increased cold at their backs.

Mintie, wrapped warmly in a blanket, half drowsing, watched Batty knit with his one hand and his waggle of needles, while he hummed about True Thomas and now and then winked at her mischievously to show that he had no cards to speak of, but was talking them up to bluff her mother.

She liked it, was aware that Batty soothed the loss of her father for her mother and everyone else in Powrieburn – herself included. She sat and listened to the mice scutter in the corners and the wind mourn in the eaves, sounds as soothing as Batty's tuneless humming, and all of it a lullaby of Liddesdale. Once, snapped back to wakefulness by Batty's sudden laughter, she was confused and thought her father was there again, wanted to run to him, to tell him about Agnes and her babe.

But it was Batty, making her mother laugh with old tales of a German trickster. Mintie wondered, with a sudden sharp pang of coiling emotions she could not untangle, if Batty was wooing her ma.

The next morning Will Elliot appeared, looking patched as hung mutton in the cold and wearing perplexity on the brows under his hat. He did not even dismount, but simply nodded to Batty as the pair of them talked in the yard.

'It was as you said. If I were a canting priest I would accuse you of deviltry and have you burned for it, so close to the mark were you.'

'Ach,' said Batty, stroking his beard thoughtfully. 'So you say. Well – is a Bill to be made on me?'

'Not by me, nor the Keeper,' Will declared vehemently. 'I would not serve it and he knows that. Nor does he have enough men to spare to take you down, Batty.'

He shifted, as if the saddle spiked him uncomfortably, for he did not like to speak ill of his employer and master, the Lord Hepburn.

'I have it in mind that he will come at you sleekit, all the same,' he went on, rushing the words from him as if they staled his mouth. 'I would get you gone, Batty, and soon.'

'Why would he do such a thing?' Mintie demanded, appalled by what she had heard, and more so because she was aware that somehow she had brought it down on all their heads.

'He would prefer me closeted,' Batty said and glanced warningly at Will, who was about to argue that the Keeper would find Batty's death easier and more final.

It came to Will then that the ostler boy, poor innocent Wattie, was as mired in all this because Mintie had pretended to be him. Perhaps no one at Powrieburn was safe... there was a secret to be kept and Will, sick at heart, was not even sure he himself had not been marked by the Keeper. For the moment, he thought, I am the Keeper's man; if there comes a point when he thinks that has changed...

He was sure all of that was known to Batty, and they shared the brief, wordless exchange of it in a mutual nod before Will turned and rode off. Mintie saw Batty suck in his breath and then let it out in a long sigh.

'Well,' he said, falsely bright, 'all is done and done. If you fetch me the remainder of that five pound, English, I will be gone and gone.'

Powrieburn's women wrung their hands and dabbed their eyes, and though Mintie was sad to see the back of Batty Coalhouse, she found their reaction surprising and put it down to the fact that his presence had been a comfort against retribution from the Whithaugh Armstrongs.

Wattie, of course, did not understand why he was being sent away, even after being told, while Bet's Annie, scowling furiously, all but accused Mintie of being jealous.

Over all of it, though, was the question Mintie needed answering, the nail-nag irritation that would not let go, so that she stood at the stirrup of the Saul and looked up at Batty even as he awkwardly said his farewells.

'What is worth all this?' she asked. 'And why?'

Batty checked in his reining round, frowning down at her.

'For what we have seen. Think on this, Mintie – shod geese and slipshod horses. Best if you say nothing of what you work out, all the same. Best if you never work it out at all. But the Keeper and the Laird of Hollows cannot depend on folk being witless.'

Then he turned the Saul's head and rode out of the yard, his laugh trailing behind him like a banner.

–

He rode north and east a little way, following a faint sheep track round the hunch of Tinnis Hill, deliberately avoiding the main routes but headed back to Berwick, five pounds in coin snugged up on the Saul's haunch, with the nagging annoyance that he had perhaps not earned it entirely.

Yet the doings of the likes of Hepburn and the Laird of Hollows were no concern of his, he argued. There were strangenesses at Hollows, for sure – the geese driven there were for no everyday dishes and had replaced ones already sent. Hollows was feeding more folk than it was used to and finer bred than any in the Borders.

Andra's forge was busy too, fixing horses whose shoes had been sucked off by the ground and bad weather of this part of the world, which is why no Borderer horse – the Saul included – had shoes at all.

That confirmed the fine folk at Hollows, and the fodder wagons revealed that horses were there in large numbers – had not Mintie been puzzled over a lack of horses for sale in Liddes-dale?

They were all at Hollows, it appeared, with their fine-bred riders — English garrison men from Carlisle or even further south, Batty was certain, as well as gathered Armstrongs from both sides of the Divide, plus their supporters. It appeared to Batty that the Laird was mustering with a pack of southern English and a great deal of the sort of horses you would need to mount a raid. The Armstrongs could put two thousand men in the saddle, armed *cap-a-pied*, in a day and a bit, and it would be no great surprise if they turned out in the service of the English. Half of them would be English anyway.

For why was what nagged Batty. There was war and the English were fresh from ruining a Scots army at Solway Moss, so the coming spring would brew the whole matter up anew. The English Deputy Warden, Wharton, was stirring up the Borders for Fat Henry in order to keep all those fine light horses out of the reach of the Scots and setting old feuds alight — Armstrongs against Scotts, Grahams against Armstrongs...

Yet this was particular, a large planned Ride in a season when Riding was done with — the depth of winter was no raiding time. Batty shook his head. He knew there was no good in it, but rode with his chin down and his shoulders up, trying to convince himself that it was no business of his.

He was so turning it this way and that that he did not notice the riders until a flash of weak winter sun flared off a lance point into the corner of his eye, bringing his head up and the Saul to a halt; Batty squinted at them.

Two men, riding easy and steady. Armed, one with a long lance slung to the back of his arm, and almost certainly both armoured with padding and leather. They would have latch-bows too, Batty thought, though not guns; most Borderers mistrusted guns. Yet they were hardly going about some ordinary business.

Batty turned the Saul more north, riding into the eastern lee of the stark, bleak mound of Tinnis, where the snow was patched more thickly; it took him only a moment or two of twisting backwards, grunting with the effort, to see that he was followed.

He was not so worried all the same, for he had a good head start and the Saul, though yellow-toothed, was not entirely past the business of running. He fretted on the certainty that they had been watching Powrieburn and seen him leave and was afraid for the ostler boy; he hoped these men were more intent on hunting him than Wattie, who would be like a mouse to questing owls.

Mind you, he added fiercely, the boy bliddy deserves a slap for what he has done to my stirrup; he shifted in the saddle, irritated by the leather having been notched one hole lower on his left side than his right. It unbalanced him, but he could not stop, nor reach down easily to change it.

They rode on, the men behind neither speeding up nor slowing down, though Batty was sure they were after him. He could not quite understand it – until the other pair appeared ahead and slightly to his right, making him check and curse. Driven, by God, like a plodding milcher into a field.

He looked around – the clear way out was a dart directly east, between the pairs before they closed, but that would be the intent and they would shut their jaws on him before he could get clean away. Though he hated to admit it, they would outrun him if they got that close, because the Saul was too old for seriously mad gallops over uneven ground, twisted with snow-covered bracken and studded with fetlock-turning tussocks.

So he turned the other way and started up Tinnis Hill at a slant, to take the sting out of the climb. He headed through the deeper snow in its shadow and up into the brush and willow scrub that led to the great round crown of it, seeming as bare as a bald man's nap, but deep with tangled winter moorland and drifted with snow that came up to the belly of the Saul.

He glanced back once and grunted with the satisfaction of seeing the riders meet and stop, seeming to argue. Not happy about heading up to the Faerie hill, he thought, where steel-clawed wee horrors would tear them from the saddle into pats of meat and soak their Faerie hats in the blood that gave them their name – redcaps.

Batty had been up the Tinnis before, chasing Ill-Made Wattie Bell who had robbed a Crozier farm in company with four others. Bell had been the last of them gathered up by Batty and thought himself safe up on the Faerie hill, believing only he had the iron in him to do it.

He had been right surprised, Batty remembered, coming back from some outing to find Batty sitting in his cunning wee hidey-hole cave near one of the Faerie wells, whistling about the Queen of Elfland and pointing a dagg at him. All the iron had leached out of him then and he had come quietly enough – had scarce even made a grunt when he was hanged weeks later.

For all that, even Batty could not prevent himself glancing round, fearful as some beldame for a second, before catching himself and shaking his head.

'Faerie, by God,' he muttered to himself and the Saul. Then he checked the wheeled flint and the priming on his daggs, one by one, as he turned the blowing horse in slow, plodding arcs up the hill; he planned to go on over it, and rode on until the Saul started in to wheeze with the effort of ploughing uphill through the snow.

He was considering halting entirely when the Saul did it himself – suddenly enough to make Batty sway. Alarmed, he saw that they had ridden to the edge of a drop which looked solid thanks to the snow but was a steep gill, as if someone had taken a Jeddart staff to Tinnis and slashed a cut in it.

He peered and marvelled. Two hundred feet down, he thought, and a slope with more steep than slant, choked with stunted gnarl and brush. He heard water at the bottom of it, a beck laughing its way through the ice that was trying to choke it.

'Sharp,' he told the Saul admiringly and patted the beast's neck. The long rough coat was winter-friendly, but made for overheating, and Batty knew the Saul was all but done up and wondered if he could rest a while; he was not entirely free of sweat and pant himself.

But not here, he thought, turning the horse south. Mayhap we can fool them, you and I, by skirting this beck and gill and doubling back the way we came, hidden by the bulk of Tinnis and a long, thin scar of stunted brush which was so thick even the bare branches were a fence to vision. He halted the Saul and lifted his left leg to take the weight off the stirrup, reaching round awkwardly with his only hand to get to the leather and raise it a notch.

At least we can lose the annoyance of this, he thought—

The Saul went sideways, at the same time as Batty heard a thunderous roar and a deep bell clang. He had time to realise that the ambuscade had been well ordered and the last part of it had been a man hidden up on Tinnis. A man with iron in him to sit alone on Tinnis and iron on him in the shape of a long gun.

Then he and the Saul spilled on the ground, the horse with a harsh grunt, and Batty's shout was drowned by the crash of undergrowth and the air hoiking out of him as he hit.

In a whirl of images he saw the horse rolling on his back with all four feet in the air, saw the dissipating spurt of egret-feather smoke from the bracken and scrub, heard the echoes of the crack.

Shot, by God, he thought – then he felt himself sliding and knew, with a horrible, sick certainty that he was going over the edge of the gill.

The men were moving in packs like dogs, wary and ruffed, looking this way and that while the smoke swirled. Black that smoke, and greased with the stink of old lives, all the carts and pots and benches people had coveted.

They did not covet them now, only their lives, shivering as they stood with shit on their legs, watching the Armstrongs and Bournes pillage everything.

The Laird sat his horse and watched a shivering man and his trembling wife, though he did not see them and only turned to the screaming to make sure no one was being killed. As few deaths as possible, he had ordered, and did not care for any disobedience.

Embers flew firefly trails in the dark. A shape, mounted, rode up and knuckled his steel cap; the Laird recognised Dandy Bourne of Clartyrigs, trailing riders as grim and armed as himself – and a woman.

The Laird stirred; this was what he had waited for.

'Megs, yer honour,' Dandy said. 'With a babe, as you said we'd find.'

He signalled and Megs held out the basket for the Laird to take, which he did, peering in. He pinched out a spark landing dangerously close to the fuzz of red hair and saw the rosebud mouth squall. It wailed. He nodded to Megs and she scurried off; he looked meaningfully at Dandy, who blinked back like an owl.

'Away, lads – Dandy, set your men free. Shake loose the border and plunder as ye will. Remember my tithes, mind... And if you take any of Buccleuch's sheep, check them for scab. That goes through a herd like wildfire and I dinna care for Scott scabies spoiling my ain.'

He looked down at the shivering man and his trembling wife, both torn from their house in nightshirts.

'Jock's Dandy Scott,' he said, and the man turned misery up at him; his beasts were already vanishing and the inside of the house was being thrown out into the yard for people to plunder – chests, chairs, pewter plates, all of it.

'Wicked Wat wilnae be pleased,' he went on amiably, 'at someone so careless with doors as yourself. Nae matter – you are in good company, for a score of your kin for miles aroon are so treated.'

He leaned down. 'Tell Buccleuch he kens where to find me – if he has the stomach for it.'

He turned away, listening to the sweet sound of the baby Queen of Scots wailing while scores of Armstrongs and Bournes and others went off to steal cattle and sheep and everything else they could from his arch-enemy, Wat Scott of Buccleuch.

He had done it. He had carried out Fat Henry's lunatic plan and stolen a Queen. Now all that was needed was to keep that secret until the babe had been spirited south to England.

The Laird rode into the moonless night, his men a hedge of Jeddart staffs around him, and wondered why he shivered at the memory of Batty Coalhouse's stare. Then he shook it from him; Coalhouse and everyone else who might have seen what was in and around Hollows would not be a problem soon enough.

–

There was a sour feeling round Powrieburn, sauced by the vanishing back of Batty Coalhouse followed shortly after by the pinch-faced Wattie, his feet slung into unaccustomed brogues laced up round his ankles for the walk, and swaddled in a cloak gifted to him by Mintie's mother. He was on his way to his Crozier relatives in Bellsyetts, which everyone hoped was a safe enough distance.

Mintie doubted it, but said nothing, just as she swallowed any comment on the cloak gift, particularly as she remembered it on her father and the lump that brought to her throat stopped her speaking entirely. So she watched in silence as Bet's Annie fussed and her mother promised Wattie he could return 'as soon as this unpleasantness is by us'.

Her voice was soft and steady, but Mintie saw the tremble in her hand and the waver of her smile and knew her mother was not nearly as strong with this as she was making out.

No one was. The thought of what Mattie of Whithaugh and all the Armstrong kin they could call on might do brought a sullen horror on them all, not to mention that they had seemingly angered the Hepburn Earl of Bothwell, Keeper of Liddesdale and their liege lord for Powrieburn, no less.

No one knows why save me, Mintie thought – particularly ma, though she does not need to know what is happening to know what might – and I can say nothing.

She remembered some nights, as a child, seeing the red glare and hearing the shouts and thought how much firmer those memories were for her mother. Without da, she thought, she will be fearful.

Mintie resolved to be stronger than all, so that when Bet's Annie and Jinet and Megs fell to telling terror tales, alternately lacing their fantasies and stuffing kertches in their mouths and squealing, she grew annoyed.

She recalled some of the tales herself. Winter harvests, they called them with grim jest, a reaping of black smoke and cinders and a threshing of luckless captives tossed on Jeddart staffs while the wind blew away the chaff of their frantic screaming.

She chivvied the women with work and scowls. With Wattie gone there was more to do, so that the day went swiftly, and eventually Mintie found time to climb up to her private place, the floored space above all and just beneath the roof, where there was only her and the scuttle of mice in the kist which held her mother's treasures.

She sat and thought about shod geese and slipshod horses and was so nearly on the edge of understanding that it fretted her, so she opened the kist, just to remind herself of better times. Must and mice piss rose up from the folds of what had been her ma's wedding dress and her own Christening gown. The Nottingham lace, aged down to the colour of old bone, was gone for handsome ruffs and bonnets and fine bedding for the long-tailed family of field mice who had tunnelled through the leather and made it a home, safe from harvest.

Harvest. Winter harvest, where the frozen riggs blossomed only blood. She shivered and felt her own breasts then, felt the hardness of the nipples, the sensation of it turning her armflesh goosed, and she stripped suddenly and stood, running her hands over her body, pretending they did not belong to her. Will

Armstrong, she thought of, with his beard combed out – but she recoiled from it, for she suddenly saw him as if in a vision, lying there all blue and not talking to worms.

Then, with a sudden flush as if she had been dipped in fire, she felt where Will Elliot's knee had dug in her, the pit of the stomach, felt his hand. She touched the buttock cheeks of herself, felt the heat as they had been when he slapped them…

The Virgin bothered her, perched high and looking at her even though Her eyes were raised to Heaven; Mintie turned it to the wall, but the moment was gone, leaving her strange and desolate, mired in the memory of Agnes. She cupped her hands on her own flat stomach and felt like weeping and laughing at the same time.

The clatter of cooking and the smell of new bread brought her back to the moment and the cold under the roof space, so that she realised with a shock that she had fallen asleep and did not know for how long. Not long, naked, for she might have frozen to death, slipping into the coverlet of coldness as easy as sliding into the burn water on a hot summer's day, feeling it lave you like a lover…

The frantic shouting and the barking of Mykkel snapped her into her clothes and spilled her down the ladder to the hall below, and then to the undercroft and out to the yard. Bet's Annie stood in a circle of women, all silent as crows in a pecked field. One hand was at her breastbone, as if it hurt, the other was clutching the bridle of a horse.

A limping sick horse, wheezing and sore, and with blood on the saddle and both holsters emptied.

The Saul, scraped and bloody and minus Batty Coalhouse.

Chapter Five

His shouts had been wild and ugly, he knew that. Driven out of him when a shoulder smashed into a twisted tree, bouncing him off in a star-whirl of arm and legs until he struck again and crashed through thick bushes and hard stone.

He skidded and slithered for a moment, then dropped again, struck again, bounced again, falling feet first through a ripping tangle of whin and stunted willow that clawed him almost to a standstill. The final drop, into the reeds and choke along the burn, was almost a kiss in comparison.

For a long time Batty heard nothing, felt nothing. Then the cold woke him, shivering and shaking him into its bite and the world of pain that was his body.

And the voices, which froze him more than the air.

'Christ's wounds – why does himself fret so on this man? He is just a fat auld Graham bastard with the one arm.'

It was a voice at once irritated, tired – and afraid. Batty would have grinned if the pain had not already twisted his mouth into a rictus of gritted teeth so he would not cry out. Afraid o' the powrie, he thought, with night coming on the hill of Tinnis...

'It's not for you nor me to put the Laird to the question, Dog. Find him, kill him, bring proof that it is done. That's what he said and that's what we do.'

This voice was firm and hard, so that Batty knew who led and who followed. The other's reply was a whine.

'Are you moonstruck? The old fool was shot off his nag by Francie, who has won prizes for his caliver skill. He fell a score of feet at least into the burn.'

'Fifty at least,' the other corrected, his voice like a splintering of midwinter ice, 'which is neither here nor there, Dog. Certes, his body isn't here, nor is the body of the horse Francie swore was downed. So we keep looking.'

Batty lay on the wet cold, trying not to shake the willows and alder to a betraying clatter, while the sound of plootering and slashing through the choke faded and died.

The Saul was alive then, Batty thought, so Francie is not as good a shot as everyone thinks. Still, he checked himself as best he could, feeling himself over for the mush of a hole or the sticky of blood.

There was enough of the latter to almost fool him, but it came from his scraped face, clawed by branches and scree as he fell. His shoulder – the one with no arm to speak of on it – was a mass of agony, and he wondered if they had missed the entire left side of his body when he was baptised, for it seemed to be such an affront to God that He was determined to crush it. Then again, mayhap just the opposite – had he not already lost the arm, it would be gone now, ripped to ruin.

His leg thundered with pain, but the armless shoulder pulsed with a red, beating heart, and he had to stuff his scarted knuckles in his mouth to keep from any noise as the voices drifted back with the crash and slash through the underbrush.

'Ah, Christ, Dand – enough is enough. It is clear to me he is in Hell, for no man I know will survive a shot of lead from a caliver and such a tumble into a cut like this. It is cold and miserable wet as a witch's cunny here and... besides.'

The last was a mutter of fear that let Batty know the man was mortally afraid of the Faerie now, for it was darkening and starting in to rain, a cold slanted sleet.

'Aye, well, you can tell it like that to the Laird, Dog,' the other one said with a bitter sigh, 'for I will not search here alone, nor be blamed for giving it up.'

There was a pause and then an uneasy laugh.

'Mayhap the Faerie have him, horse and all, which is why we cannot find him.'

The other grunted, grabbed the idea eagerly.

'That will be it, Dand. Lifted into Elfland entire, to be seen in a hundred years.'

Then they were gone, although Batty lay a long time still and quiet, with the rain soaking him from above and the damp seeping him from below. His thoughts were all fuzzed because of the pain in his shoulder and made no sense, save that he realised that the cold-voiced man had not been insulting the other when he called him 'dog'. Dog was the man's name and Batty recalled Will Elliot speaking of a Dog Pyntle who had fled to Hollows, so it might have been him. Dand and Francie he did not know – but he would. If he lived...

His leg hurt and would scarcely move, but his shoulder was a great red blossom of agony. His helmet was long gone and his head felt swollen inside and out, his stiff sausage fingers brought away viscous streaks of blood. Yet he was not shot...

He took the thought into darkness for a time, then woke suddenly, as if broaching from a stream. Cold. Wet. He had to move...

He did so, slow and pained. He had his sword, though the baldric was tangled up and it was somewhere at his back and so as far removed as the moon – but he still had a bollock dagger sheathed in his belt and another hidden down a boot. His pistols were all gone and the bandolier with charges. He mourned the expensive loss of them and then wondered about the Saul and five pounds English, snugged up in his pack.

No use here, even if I had it, he thought. Cannot eat it, or make a heat with it. I must find shelter...

He crawled along the bracken and reeds to the burn's edge, stuck his face in and sucked until the cold ached his teeth and his thirst was slaked. Then he rustled and cracked a slow way away from the water, each movement a lance of hurt from that shoulder. He found a curve of rock, dry and sheltered with brush, crawled into it like an animal, dragged in his numbed leg and curled as best he could, wondering if this was his time, the moment Batty Coalhouse left the world.

It would be a relief from the pain at least, he thought. Like being broken on the wheel... He threw that from him. He had seen it and knew that what he experienced, ravaging as it was, did not compare to being broken on the wheel.

He remembered the millwheel turning, how it had mesmerised him, shot him back to that day when, just a blank face in a crowd of gawpers, he had watched his kin displayed on the spokes of a breaking wheel.

His half-brother had been strapped to it, the executioner had slammed an iron hammer on the limbs between the spokes, then braided the broken remains into the wheel and left him to perish, turning slowly in the vagrant wind. It had taken Hans Kohlhase five days to die, while the Elector of Saxony had declared himself well pleased with the judicial removal of such an outlaw. All his breed and those who rode with him, he promised by public decree, would suffer the same – particularly the one called Balthazar Kohlhase.

It had all been because of horses, Batty recalled, and a wee noble who thought to rob a horsedealer and use his position to get away with it. Mayhap that's why Mintie Henderson's request had fired him to an answer – though it had only come to this in the end, just as the last time had resulted in his kin breaking on the wheel.

He woke later, in darkness, with hunger an egg he had hatched in his throat. Which was a good sign, he thought, trying to move the leg and no longer able to feel it, for a man who has lost his appetite is not long for this world.

He had kept his appetite, even if it seemed he had lost his leg. God whittles me like an auld stick, he thought bitterly, and yet grinned, cracking the stiffened blood mask of his face, dreaming of food. Kail obsessed him, the wonderful Border stew which folk spoke of in the plural. 'They is good the second day, best the third' ran the saying. Yet when the mutton in it was fished out into a bowl, it became singular again. No matter the grammar, it was good eating.

He thought of the wedding feast of Von Zachswitz, the noble who had cozened Hans out of his horses and bought the law in his favour. He had then discovered that a hard, stubborn man like Hans Kohlhase, ruined horse dealer, made his own law and his kin acted as jury and executioners.

They had stormed the noble's wedding feast, which had been the talk of Saxony. They had tied Von Zachswitz and his new bride up, then eaten the salmon steaks stuffed with cress on a bed of white lilies, the snipe pastried with bilberry jelly and speared with their own beaks.

Then Hans had asked Batty for his expertise and entertainment, so he had stuffed the groom's mouth with poor powder and hung sausage charges round the forehead of the bride, so that they could both watch the slow matches burn down on each other.

They were cut to exactly the same length, but no slow match burns precise as its neighbour, which was the entertainment in it; they took wagers on which would be first, mouths full and laughing, long shoved past morality by all that had been done to them in turn.

The bride's match was slightly slower, so she just had time to see the fire fizz out of her new husband's eyes and mouth before her bridal chaplet blew her head to bits. Everyone cheered...

He shifted slightly, starting in to shiver again, seeing the moon rise up like a silver coin to dance with the burn water. A vixen musked on the bank paused to fix her mask with a delicate paw like any proud lady, sniffed the presence of him and slid away. An owl, shroud-silent, scraped the slightest powder of snow off a branch as it whisked in, then sat and swivelled its blink.

Batty huddled, smelling damp loam and what lay beneath it, the faint green spikes of bracken, whin and willow. The deep churn of rotted oak leaf and wormcast, warm beneath the frost. He lay there and thought about Dog and Von Zachswitz. About food. About revenge, which is a dish best served cold...

He found himself sliding into the dark, like a worm burrowing into the loam, and he tried to shake himself, though he was shivering hard enough as it was. Keep awake, he thought. Keep awake. Sing...

'*True Thomas lay o'er a grassy bank, and he beheld a lady gay, a lady that was brisk and bold, come ridin' o'er the fernie brae.*'

–

The Saul had a broken rib for sure and had been banged about so much that Mintie was certain a lung had popped. He had swelled up with the air trapped in the skin, so that Mintie not only had to cut the girth from him to get the saddle off, but to carefully lance him.

He grunted, too done up to protest much, but seemed easier after the spurt of watery blood and the hiss of escaping air. Mintie knew there was nothing you could do for his ribs or lung save let him rest in the warm and light a candle to Saint Elegius, but she bathed the smaller cuts and found a nastier one on a hind leg which was deep enough to need stitching. When he was stronger than tonight, she thought.

She shunted him into the Fyrebrande's big stall, putting the fine horse in a smaller one, which he did not like and showed with snorting displeasure.

It was when she finally got to moving the saddle that she found the money in Batty's pack, still snugged up in a shirt to stop its betraying jingle. There was a peck of oats in a similar bag, and then Mintie found the griddle plate, which no sensible Borderer goes without. With that on a fire, a little water mixed with a handful of oats, you could have a hot bannock or two and enough of a meal to keep you until shelter was reached.

Batty's griddle, like all of them, was tucked under the flap of the saddle and the hole in the flap led Mintie to it, to the great dinged dent in it and the surety of how the Saul had come by his injuries. Someone had shot him and it was only by the grace of the Virgin's hand that the animal was not dead.

But Batty might be, for that's just where his knee would be, and if the shot had gone through it to do damage to the griddle, he was injured and out in the cold. Yet there was no blood here, and suddenly Mintie was sure that Batty was not dead, though she wondered at her strange certainty.

The women were flustered as chickens sensing a fox, and her mother had collapsed on her bed so that Bet's Annie and Jinet were fussing round her. So it was Megs who brought news that Will Elliot was at the gate, wringing her hands as she did so.

He was a shadow in the gathering dusk, sitting politely and waiting to be asked to dismount, which Mintie did. She was wary of him all the same, arriving into the middle of clear sign that Batty had been hunted and perhaps killed; he was, after all, the Land Sergeant from Hermitage and thus the Keeper's man.

She could not stop the blurting from Megs about the return of Batty's horse, and was forced to watch Will examine it, then nod.

'Good work, wee Mintie. You know your horseflesh.'

'As you might expect,' Mintie replied tartly. 'I am my father's child.'

He looked at her, judging her demeanour and getting the glimmer of why she was so stiff. He sighed and passed a hand through the tangle of his beard.

'Mintie – I am not the enemy. I came here because two men arrived at Hermitage not long since, asking for the Keeper.'

Mintie said nothing, just waited, so Will went on, encouraged.

'One of them was Dand the Lamb Ker, whom I know slightly. The other, bold as you please, was Dog Pyntle.'

Now Mintie's interest perked like hare ears.

'Him who removed your toes yon time?'

'The same. As if there never had been a Bill made on him, nor did it matter if there was. Asking for the Keeper.'

'What did you do?'

'Slapped the pair of them in the jail, o' course. My, they howled, though. Demanding the Keeper, roaring that they had news, had been on his work – though they would not say what it was.'

'And what did Keeper Hepburn have to say on it?'

Will shrugged.

'The Keeper left for Edinburgh earlier, with only Hen Graham for company, the pair of them sleekit as wet seals.'

Mintie sucked her bottom lip at that news, and Will nodded, moving back and forth now, talking as much to himself as her.

'It is clear who the Keeper trusts,' he added bitterly. 'Hen Graham is a greased wee fox who hunts my job. The pair I have in the jail made me wonder, Mintie, by God's wounds they did. I just knew they were up to no good – and the Keeper and Hen Graham are as bad, it seems. Whatever Batty thought was about to happen is happening – and I came here to find him.'

'He is out there,' Mintie declared, bright and wide-eyed. 'That pair had a deal to do with shooting the Saul and might well have shot him as well.'

Will tore off his blue bonnet and scrubbed his head in a fury of fluster.

'Och, what a God-damned bliddy slorach. Batty shot and a Ride out on the Moss. Nor any wee Ride neither, if Batty has the right of it.'

His swearing in front of her was proof enough of his concern, but Mintie ignored it and told him what she had worked out about shod geese and slipshod horses. Will nodded, for he had worked it out himself. The whole weight of the matter sank him to his hunkers, where he chewed his cap and shook his head, muttering barely audible swearing that would have stripped the gilt off a saint's statue.

'Well,' said Mintie smartly, bustling with the cloth and saddle for Jaunty. 'Dead or alive, we can't leave Batty Coalhouse lying in the wet cold.'

'You have no notion of where he is,' Will declared, appalled at the prospect. 'He could be anywhere. Unless the Saul can speak, we might search forever – and it is dark.'

'The Saul can barely breathe,' Mintie pointed out scornfully. 'So might Batty also be – and he is not anywhere out there, he is close by and to the east, for he rode for Berwick and did not get far – the Saul could never have got back to us if he had.'

'Aye, aye,' Will said, climbing to his feet and beginning to see it. 'And if I were he and found myself hunted, I would have turned for a good place to hide or fight.'

He looked at Mintie.

'Tinnis Hill,' he said, and she had a hand to her breastbone and had said 'bugger' before she knew it. Then the look of Will, all raised eyebrows and shock at her language, made them both laugh and shred the fear of Faerie.

'He might have been shot from cover and never knew,' she pointed out, but Will gave a short bark of laughter, harsh as rook song.

'Not him. I learned more about Batty Coalhouse and why the Keeper fears him. Hen Graham knows Batty Coalhouse.'

He told it in fits and starts as they rode into the cold and the night, where it started to rain, a misery of persistent sleet fine as flour.

'His name is German – Kohlhase. His da's kin are from the Brandenburg, Hen says. Batty, it appears, is cunning. Knows everything and the price of it – how much a fool married on to a cuckold will pay for a kertch found in a wee gorse love nest when the fool was in Berwick. Which lass with a redhead man will pay what for news of a wee ginger newborn two steadings away. Who will run where with a fouled Bill on them – and how much they are worth to the Wardens.'

He broke off, his wet face pearling with what might have been pale sweat or rain as he turned into Mintie's wide-eyed listening stare.

'They say he did terrible things with the rest o' his kin in the Germanies. Since he came back he has been called many things. Corbie is one, from the way you can run from him, far and fast, then turn to find him sitting there, looking at you like a crow in a tree. Slow match is another, from the way he seems to smoulder, relentless and steady, down to the powder of the matter, then – bang.'

Will clapped his hands in a spray of water and Mintie jumped, then shook herself.

'He is an old man with a single arm, drookit and shot,' she smarted back at him.

'His ma was a Graham lass,' Will went on, ignoring her. 'Bella, from Netherby.'

Mintie looked up at that, wiping rain from her face, and Will nodded grimly to her.

'Aye – a lick and spit from here. Batty came right back to his Graham home like a calf to the teat, to the shame of all that grayne, according to Hen. It might even be them as has done for him this night.'

'He is not done,' Mintie answered determinedly. I would know, she thought.

They rode on into the fox-screaming night, and the rain slackened off, allowing the cloud to clear and a moon to let them see the glint of water in beck and burn, which was a relief from the crush of dark. Mintie felt better when she could see – for a long time, it seemed, she had been letting Jaunty pick her own way, but now the great black hunch of Tinnis loomed over them.

'How did he lose his arm, then?' Mintie asked, more for the sound of her voice and his than for an answer.

'I don't know,' Will answered, 'but his da died in a siege fighting for the Frenchies. I think Batty lost his arm at the same time and was a young man when it happened.'

'Twenty and something,' Mintie said, remembering Batty tell it. Will glanced at her, wan in the darkness.

'His ma took fever and died not long after, so he's had sore loss,' he went on.

They stopped when it became clear they were at the edge of a spated run of water, white as new snow where it racked over the rocks.

'He went to the Germanies after that,' Will said, as they picked a way along it, heading northwards he thought, but always pressing as close as they could get to the glower of Tinnis. A great weariness came rolling over the pair of them, though neither admitted it to the other; it was composed mainly of despair that this was a fool's journey and that Batty would not be found.

'The Germanies,' Mintie echoed, trying to keep Will talking, to hear the sound of his voice and using it like fire to drive back the dark.

'The Germanies,' Will confirmed, and the tone of him was a chill that stopped Mintie dead.

'That was when Bartholomew Graham became Balthazar Kohlhase,' Will went on, flat and hard as napped flint. 'And had himself a newer name still, from the way he and his kin took their revenge on those who had wronged his half-brother, Hans.'

His face was pale in the moonlight, a lily-coloured match for Mintie's own.

'*Brandfackel* they called him, for the way he set the land to flame.'

He looked at her and wiped wet from his bearded face.

'You know the name in a decent tongue,' he added wryly, 'and there is the Devil in it – it means "firebrand".'

The silence that followed was ripped by scream of a hunting hoolet owl and brought them back to the sighing wind and the soft rush of the burn.

And the singing, cracked and faint as a weary bell.

'*And see ye not that bonnie road, which winds about the fernie brae…*'

Mintie's head snapped round and she yelped.

'Batty…'

'*That is the road to fair Elfland, where you and I this night maun gae...*'

The crunch and clatter of stalks made Batty start a little. The voice, when it came out of the dark, was eldritch and tinkling like bells.

'Batty. Batty Coalhouse.'

The Queen of Elfland, he thought, and laughed aloud. As ye are summoned, so must ye come...

'Batty. Batty.'

The voice was closer, the whin broke apart and a Faerie face shoved through and stared down at him as he stared back at her. Well, almost Faerie – he wondered at the Queen of Elfland having a great drip on her nose.

'Batty,' Mintie said, her voice bright with relief and concern at the same time. 'What have they done to you?'

–

They struggled him up on Jaunty, and Mintie crept up behind to hold him on. She even found his helmet nearby and clapped it on her own head, so that it might fool any night riders to thinking she was a warrior.

Jaunty, dogged wee besom that she was, blew out her displeasure but plootered home without a twitch, while Mintie clung desperately to Batty as he wavered right and left and in and out of consciousness.

Back at Powrieburn, drenched as voles, they manhandled Batty into the undercroft, where the women stripped and salved him expertly and without fuss. He had cuts and bruises and his leg was 'swole bad', according to Bet's Annie, but the worst of it was that she was sure his shoulder was out of joint.

'We can put it back in then, while he is out of his wits and feels nothing,' Will declared, but Bet's Annie pointed out the flaw in that – it was his left shoulder and how you put it back was with a sharp and particular tug on the arm. Which Batty did not have.

Mintie thought about it for a moment, then fetched the birthing rope, the one they used to haul reluctant foals and calves into the world. Will got the idea at once and they tied it to Batty's withered stump. Will snapped it expertly, and grinning as if they had built a palace between them, they swaddled Batty back up like a bairn.

There was little chance of getting him up the ladder, so they bedded him alongside the Saul; the undercroft was dry and they smoked up a steaming because the fetid heat of beasts was driving the drench out of them.

When Batty finally slept, Mintie passed a weary hand over her face and shivered, then felt the touch of Will's concerned hand on her arm.

'You are soaked, lass,' he said softly. 'Away up and change. I will watch him.'

She saw that he was as wet and said so, but he only laughed.

'A wee bit weather is neither here nor there to a man used to hot trods on worse nights,' he declared, so she went, gratefully. It occurred to her in the middle of changing into her only other dress that he had perhaps arranged it, that he had been sent to make sure Batty Coalhouse was dead.

She was ashamed of herself when she half fell down the ladder in a panic, only to find Batty snoring and Will in his undershift and smallclothes, smoking with steam as if he was on fire and working up a sweat by mucking out the Fyrebrande. He had already looked to his own horse and Jaunty, both forgotten in the moment of caring for Batty.

His clothes were neatly hung over a stall rope, and for all he was half naked, he looked up at her and smiled, such a calming, warming thing that Mintie stopped dead, feeling as if she had been struck by some unseen lightning, fizzing from crown to the itching soles of her feet.

They never spoke more than an instruction or a question and answer while they worked together with the kine and horses. When that was done, Will climbed back into his damp things, the better for them to dry on him during the night, put a horse blanket round his shoulders, and they settled down beside Batty.

'You should get away to your bed, lass,' he said eventually, as the crusie guttered in the last gasp of oil. She shook her head and smiled at him.

'I am happy here,' she answered, and it was all the truth.

Chapter Six

She was there, sitting in the dark listening to the wind batter a fury at the unyielding bastel, feeling the odd swoop of it, thick with rain-damp, where it had fingered under the outside doors and through the grilled yett to the back of her neck.

The Fyrebrande, blowing out unexpectedly encountered cobwebs as he hung over a stall side, made her turn her head to check him. When she turned back, Batty was awake and looking steadily at her.

Neither of them spoke for a heartbeat or two.

'I dreamed I was in Elfland,' he said in a rheumed growl that was heavy with relief and disappointment both.

'What was it like?'

He thought a little, then a smile split his beard – which she had combed out, taking the opportunity of him not being able to resist or protest.

'Like a Lammas Fair,' he answered, which made her frown, for she had expected something better and more magical. All the Lammas Fairs she had attended in her time had been places of noise and drink, with all the strangeness invested in a lass with a beard, or a calf with an extra leg.

'I thought you were the Queen of Elfland,' he added and she laughed at that.

'God forbid.'

'As beautiful a sight, for all that,' he said, and she felt herself flush to the roots of her hair and busied herself with his blankets to cover the confusion.

'The Saul?' he asked and she nodded reassuringly.

'Behind you, bruised and scraped but fine as spun silk. Your five pounds still intact as well.'

He nodded.

'The Saul would have been good enough. I have lost my pistols, mind, which is hurtful. Them daggs are expensive engines.'

She fetched his griddle and showed him where the shot had struck, so that he whistled through his teeth.

'They were set on my death right enough. Give Wattie my thanks, then, for setting my stirrup badly and making me lift that leg to fix it. If not, they would have blown it clean away and I would be of a different standing entirely.'

The humour clanked like poor tin. There was silence while Mintie thought of Wattie and wondered if he was safe. Then she told Batty of how she and Will Elliot had searched the night for him, but he drifted away before the end of it. She was comforted, however, by his easy snore; sleep is best, she thought.

She sat there a little longer, breathing in the pungent reek where one of the mares had staled, listening to the rain and wind and the sound of his steady, regular breathing, comforting as the sighing Solway sea.

He was still asleep when the crusie guttered down to little more than shadows flickering on a wall, and she rose stiffly to refill it, moving past the soft stir of the beasts, their warm fug as familiar and comforting as memory.

She felt ruffled and strange, the shadows around her meeting, flowing, smoking into nothing and forming again; she felt as insubstantial as the fingering wind. Tomorrow, she thought, the horses will remember my hands on their mane's bristle, the yard's morning ice will crackle under my clumsy feet. Tomorrow I will fork hay and fetch water – but tonight...

96

Tonight I am as Faerie as the Queen of Elfland.

When the awakened light bloomed she went back to where Batty snored, sitting with her knees hunched and her arms clasped round them, listening to the wind and the soft, regular chewing of Jaunty at the straw.

She felt like clouds over a hill, but it wasn't the night and wind which had unleashed her, though she did not know what had. Mykkel did as dogs do, coming to stare at her with melancholy eyes until she scratched him behind the ear, feeling his pleasure in the delighted muzzle pressing harder against her knee.

What did Batty dream? A person was as much what he thought and dreamed as a dog was locked to a mistress or master, and Mintie looked at the sleeping Batty, remembering all that she had learned about him.

What did he dream? Nothing good, she thought and pitied him.

The light was pale as bad milk when the sound of hooves in the yard woke her and brought Bet's Annie spilling down the ladder into the undercroft.

'My cousin Tam, from Bellsyetts,' she hissed, as if he was a wolf at the door.

'How is my mother?' Mintie demanded, tugging her clothes straight and raking straw from her hair.

'Sleeping soft,' Bet's Annie said, and then took a deep breath, as if about to plunge into cold water; Mintie felt her own constrict in her throat.

Tam Crozier was little more than a boy, chap-cheeked and chilled; he slid awkwardly off the swaybacked old mare he was riding, his breath smoking and his face pinched. Mintie did not like the look of him and saw that Bet's Annie had seen it too. She stopped, her hands folded into her apron against the cold, almost hugging herself.

'Bring her in,' Mintie declared, signalling him to lead the mare into the undercroft, but Tam shook his head.

'I will not bide long, Mistress.'

He nodded to Bet's Annie and his eyes were raw now, so that Mintie saw Bet's Annie bring one hand up to her throat.

'What news, then, Tam Crozier?' she demanded, almost defiantly.

The boy stood and shuffled, pulled off his cap and wound it round and round in his big, red-knuckled hands.

'Wattie is dead,' he finally blurted, and Mintie saw Bet's Annie rock under the wind of it, like a boat caught broadside.

'Two men came for him, dragged him out. They beat old Ferg and one held a latchbow on us while the other carted Wattie to a tree. They hung him with his own belt.'

The words spilled out now, rotted and sodden with grief.

'They set a burning brand to the roof tree. Then they poked poor Wattie's feet with a torch and dragged him off to be hanged like a side of slaughtered beef. They were grinning like hay rakes as they rode off. I have been sent to yourself and then to the Keeper to make a Bill. We don't know the men at all, but those are faces none at Bellsyetts will forget.'

He stopped, dumbed with the horror of it, and Mintie, who had wanted to stop the slew of words pouring from him – words so careless of what they did to those who listened – now found she could not speak at all. For a long moment there was no sound save for the hiss of the cold wind and the distant, harsh laugh of a rook.

Mintie felt frozen. She had done it. Pretending to be an ostler and the only one at Powrieburn, so that they had hunted poor, innocent Wattie Crozier down, who knew nothing, had seen nothing and died, choking and bewildered and swaying...

The touch on her shoulder snapped her back to where Tam was swinging stiffly up onto the mare, turning away to ride to Hermitage. Bet's Annie's hand was light, her voice stronger than that.

'Hush now, Mintie. The fault in this belongs to the pair who hoisted Wattie Crozier. He will be revenged and not by the Keeper.'

'Not by Hendersons neither,' Mintie declared, fighting the bitterness of tears. 'We pay blackmeal to everyone.'

'There are some who will ride if called,' Bet's Annie answered firmly. 'And Croziers of my own with them.'

Mintie was struck by the iron in the woman, which she had not known was there; it was a stark contrast to the wails of Jinet and Megs announcing the news to Mintie's mother.

'I will go to her,' Bet's Annie declared, then nodded to the undercroft door and the stable beyond it. 'You care for Master Coalhouse.'

She paused and looked hard into Mintie's face, as if to drive the words through her eyes.

'They will come for him next when they know he is here.'

The truth of it sank into Mintie's belly like a cold stone into a burn, so that she stood for a while looking down at the snoring Batty.

For all Bet's Annie's iron, the truth was staring, if not stark; no one feared the Hendersons, and even if some would ride, it would not be enough. Black rent had been their only recourse, and with a sick certainty, Mintie knew that still remained the way.

When Bet's Annie came down into the undercroft, trailing gulping sobs from the other pair behind her, she found Mintie dressed in her best and leading out a saddled Jaunty and the Fyrebrande on a tether rope.

'What is this?' she demanded, folding her arms determinedly, but the stone misery of Mintie's face robbed her of resolve and hard words.

'Blackmeal.'

It was all Mintie said and all she needed to say, so that Bet's Annie closed the undercroft doors, then the grilled yett, and went upstairs to the thin slit of window, where she watched the small, slim figure and the two horses vanish softly into the fading mist of the winter's day.

Later, she brought a posset down to the waking Batty and told him what had happened to Wattie and what Mintie had done.

'By God, I am sad to hear of the boy,' Batty said, then shook his head and flung off the blankets.

'Gone to Hollows with her fine horse,' he added in a voice as dull as poor pewter. He shook his head again and added a pungent curse even Bet's Annie had not heard, then apologised for it.

'No offence taken,' she answered, 'for I am thinking the same.'

'She will do no good,' Batty answered, and started to drink the milk posset in order to free up his hand to help him rise. He made a face at the taste.

'Is there nothing to add life to this?' he demanded, and Bet's Annie brought out a small leather bottle from under her apron, though her smile was strained.

'Put some life in it with this,' she said and winked. 'Don't tell the others – especially wee Mistress Mintie.'

Batty saluted her as she tipped a considerable amount of it in the posset, then he drank and sighed.

'Saints bless ye,' he said, making a nest in the straw to sit his cup in so that he could stroke his beard, which felt strange. He realised it was because it had been combed of raggles and nits.

Then he stuck out his hand, and after a pause, Bet's Annie took him by the wrist and leaned back, hauling him up. He grunted and Bet's Annie was sure that there was more pain in him than he let on, particularly from that wrenched stump.

For a moment he swayed, testing the limits of his battered leg, while Bet's Annie tried not to look at the fat naked thighs and sinewy legs sticking from under his bulging shirt.

'Fetch me breeks and hose,' he ordered in the end. 'And hand me that cup up, for the place is swimming round me.'

'*Eau de vie* does that,' she answered, obeying him, and he laughed.

'Not now. My head is widdershins and this fine posset will spin it back the right way – did Mintie take her da's pistol?'

She had not taken any weapon at all, and Batty, struggling into his clothes, sent Bet's Annie to fetch the pistol and load the caliver. He knew the Keeper would release Dand and Dog Pyntle as soon as he arrived back in Hermitage, finding good excuse to do so into the outrage of his Land Sergeant.

'Men will come,' he said when she returned with the pistol. 'Two, possibly three.'

Bet's Annie nodded, then recalled what she had heard Will reveal earlier and told Batty about Dog Pyntle and Dand the Lamb Ker. Batty nodded.

'I heard a third name,' he added. 'Francie. I don't know him, but he was the one who shot and I have it that he was considered to have killed me because he seldom misses.'

Bet's Annie frowned over it a while.

'Francie Bourne it will be,' he said firmly. 'He wins the Truce Day shooting more often than not – when he is sober. Never been known as a man for following Hollows, mind – but he's a cousin to Dog Pyntle.'

'A man will follow money, drink or quim if offered in sufficient quantity,' Batty declared, smacking his lips and raising the pewter cup to Bet's Annie. 'But he will exert himself for the Name for free. A fine posset. I taste honey and… is it gingifered a bit?'

'It is,' replied Bet's Annie, beaming. 'Four eggs, boiled milk—'

'By God, Powrieburn keeps a rich spice chest,' Batty said admiringly and smiled. 'Load the caliver with peppershot, so you don't miss.'

Bet's Annie was swallowing hard but nodded firm enough and stood for a moment watching Batty, sitting with his back against the stall, loading and keying up the wheel-lock with his knees and one hand. When he picked up his basket-hilted sword and tested the edge with his tongue, she went up the ladder and fetched the caliver off the wall.

The other women watched her load it and tried not to whimper.

Mintie came up on the hunch of buildings through the bad cess of a wintering day, Jaunty plodding through the swirling sleet, head down and moving like a dog. Mintie rode astraddle, her dress howked up and tucked in, leaving her with breeches and her best blue wool stockings exposed; her legs were chill. Behind, dragged like an unwilling bairn to church, the Fyrebrande fretted and followed.

The forge fire was a welcome ember, the sound of the hammer and anvil like a tocsin – but the place was filled with men, which Mintie had not expected. They had buff doublets and puffed breeches, slashed to show the reds and greens, wore ribbons round one thigh and an upper arm – a livery which showed they were professional soldiery, a trained band. She had not seen the like since her one visit down to Carlisle, the year before last – but these men were not Carlisle men.

They were harder men, with flint eyes and iron stares, hands on hips or stroking thoughtful beards as she rode into the yard. Mintie did not know whether it was her or the Fyrebrande they fancied more.

Andra and Geordie's Eck hammered iron and sizzled shoes in their forge lean-to, surrounded by horseflesh and the buzz of talk, strange and foreign to Mintie; with a thrill she realised that these were men from the south, further than Carlisle or even York. Brazen and unafraid in a land they were at war with, which told Mintie a lot.

Andrew Crozier looked up briefly, sparks smouldering in his beard and his face a runestone of blank misery. When Mintie caught sight of the pinched face of Geordie's Eck, red-eyed from weeping or lack of sleep, she knew something had happened.

Bella confirmed it, bustling up through the men and dragging Jaunty by the bridle away from the lean-to forge and the stamp of horses and men; Mintie felt their eyes raking her, griming over the fine lines of the Fyrebrande.

'Mintie, Mintie, you should go home, lassie.'

Bella wrung her hands in her apron and her face was clearly marked with hours of tears, so that Mintie felt a cold stone settling in her.

'What has happened?'

There were still tears left, but the tale spilled out, hot and sorrowed, as they fell.

Agnes had birthed a stillborn, a wee soul of a boy now swaddled up and buried. It would be a Christian mercy on him and Agnes if Mintie would ask the priory to say a prayer and light a wee candle for him. They could not do it in the nearest church, which was across in the Reformed England.

'What of Agnes?' Mintie demanded, cutting harshly into Bella's weeping. The Goodwife wiped her eyes, hiccupped once or twice and ignored the clamouring for 'ma' from unseen bairns behind them.

'That, at least, is good news,' she managed. 'Agnes has gone to Hollows. As a wet nurse. Which is a gift from God that will save her from grief and milk fever.'

She saw men swaggering over, the better to look at the Fyrebrande – or Mintie – and slapped Jaunty's rump.

'Away, lass – this is no place for fine born, neither horse nor lass.'

Mintie went, dragging the Fyrebrande and only dimly aware of a few cozening calls for her to stay. Her mind reeled, not only with news of poor Agnes' loss but of a new babe at Hollows.

Mintie did not know any woman at Hollows other than the wife of the Laird and she was too old to be birthing new weans. There would be other women there, of course, to fetch and carry – and no doubt other matters with such men around – but none of them warranted the expense of a wet nurse for any birthing they may have had.

The snow fell like drifting oat flakes, melting on her lashes. By the time Hollows loomed, her toes and fingers were pinched and cold and she rode over the sluggish crow-black slide of the Esk by the bridge, looking at the nestle of the powder mill. It seemed as dark and cold as the water, with no one moving near it.

There were watchers who saw her come up, appearing from nowhere it seemed. They held her by the bridle, grinning up at her, but any mischief they planned was halted by the slash of a voice. It chilled Mintie, but not because of what it promised the men if they did not leave off, nor because of the way they slunk sideways like whipped dogs.

It settled ice on her spine and brought her hand to her throat because she recognised it only too well. One step more brought the owner of it out of the swirling veil of snow to stand and grin his fine teeth at her out of his handsome face with its wave of thick hair.

'Aye, aye – well met, Mistress Mintie,' said Hutchie Elliott. 'I know that excellent horse as if it were my own. Did you also bring me back that fine dagg?'

She found her throat constricted and fought for control of it, was suddenly aware of her indecently exposed ankles.

'The things you see,' she managed weakly, 'when you have no weapon.'

He laughed easily.

'With that tongue, Mintie, you are never unarmed.'

His riposte stung her, both by the insult and the fact that it had bettered her own, so that she found her voice at last.

'I am bound for the Laird,' she snapped. 'Either stand aside or take me.'

His eyes narrowed like button slits.

'Mintie,' he said, and added a sudden twist of nasty grin to her name. 'I will take you, Mintie. Never fear.'

Will Elliot came with the dusk, a clatter in the yard which brought everyone alert and snapped Batty out of sleep in mid-snore, cursing as he fumbled for the dagg. By the time he had it, Bet's Annie was leading in Will's horse, blowing on the slow match of the caliver to keep it glowing in the sleet.

'Aye, aye,' Will grunted, beating wet off him with his hat and looking like a slab of metal in his gleaming back and breast. 'You are up and about then – how fares it with you?'

Batty, more relieved than he cared to admit, eased the hurt in his leg a little and stuffed the dagg back into his waistband.

'Well enough,' he grinned. 'I have a touch of gravel in the back, lime in the right foot, and hourly expect my rotted liver to fail. Apart from that, one arm and a gammy leg, I am fine as the sun at morning.'

'I have news that might bring on a new malady,' Will said grimly, unburdening himself of a brace of latchbows and a basket-hilted sword. 'Spleen, for sure. The Keeper is back and has freed the men I jailed. He was not best pleased to find them locked up and less pleased with me for doing so. I am suspect now.'

This last was added bitterly, and Batty had some sympathy with the man, who had put his living – and even his life – at such risk. He thought he knew why, all the same, and dreaded having to answer the inevitable next question Will Elliot would ask, his bluff face miming unconcern and hiding eagerness.

'Where is Mintie?'

Batty told him and saw the grim cliff of the Land Sergeant crumble like old bread. He sank down on his hunkers, heedless of the cold iron back and breast biting his hips, and stayed there a long time, shaking his head and unable to speak.

In the end, it was Bet's Annie, bringing food and drink to him, who chivvied him from despair.

'Get this down you,' she declared, 'and never fear. Between us, we will see Mintie safe and justice done.'

Will looked up at the pair of them, dog-eyed with hope. Batty grinned his jut-jawed grin.

'The posset is good. Better with a wee finger of *eau de vie* in it, mind.'

Bet's Annie went back upstairs with the caliver while Will finished his posset in a gulp and tended to his horse. Batty went to the Saul for a while, murmuring and soothing, then levered himself down to the straw and shared bread with the dog when it came to lay a head on his wounded knee. Will came and joined them after a bit, watching Batty click-click his needles on the endless swathe, but the waiting and what lay at the end of it was a rasp. After a time, the grate of the silence on Will's nerves grew too much for him and he nodded at the knitting admiringly.

'You are skilled with just the one wing,' he said. 'How came you to lose it?'

Such a simple six words, yet it washed Batty with sudden, sharp memories – so sharp that he had to glance down to make sure the stump was there, for the blinding agony of the moment of his arm's loss almost sprang tears to his eyes.

It had been after Pavia, where the Black Band died under the Imperial cannon fire he and his da helped with. All those proud, beautiful Landsknechte with their gaudy finery and plumes and ribbons, shredded to blood and splintered bone.

He remembered the sweating hell of it, his mouth dry and salted from the powder, gagging at the sulphurous reek like the Earl of Hell's own arse. Swabbing until his shoulders ached, ramming, pricking, laying, with his da grinning at him out of a stained black face like some mad, white-haired imp.

At the end of it, Maramaldo had ridden up, all smiles and rewards as befitted the Grand Captain of a mercenary band which had six good rabinets served by such fine gunners as the Kohlhases. He had tossed them a purse and ridden off to hang all the looters who had not turned in their plunder to him; he was a byword for cruelty even then, was Maramaldo.

After that, the French had been on the run and Maramaldo, bright with triumph and seeing himself as a *condottiere* of the first rank, had been made Captain General of the siege of Asti.

It wasn't much, a little walled place on the plain of the Tanaro River, but Maramaldo set up the guns and invited its surrender. It refused. He pounded it for a day or two and asked again. It refused. He hung captives. The city still refused and paraded its patron saint, Secondus, along the battered walls, chanting prayers for the martyrs. Maramaldo lobbed dead people over the walls like the Romans did in ancient times. It still refused.

And all this time Batty and his da sweated at the guns, while his ma brought them water and food as if they ploughed fields on some peaceful farm.

Then Batty saw Maramaldo speaking head-to-head with his da and his da frowning and unhappy. A little later, he came to Batty and explained what they had to do, his bluff, black-powdered face sheened with sweat.

'He wishes us to set charges under the walls at the Torre Rosso.'

Asti's claim to fame was that it was a 'city of one hundred towers', and two of them formed the main gate. One of these was the Red Tower, the Torre Rosso, and a more defended part of the walled city you could not hope to find. It was here that the defenders had perched the image of their saint, for protection and defiance.

That night, Batty and his father crept out, with five men carrying charges close behind them, picking a slow, nervous way through the singing night and the old dead, slithering through stinking fluids and farting rot that had once been men.

At the walls they had stacked the charges, and in the dark Batty's da had prepared the slow-match fuses. The problem, as they had always foreseen, was that someone would have to remain to make sure the fuse was lit. And that would be at dawn, when light betrayed him to the watchers fifty feet above as he sprinted away from the explosion. If he cut the match for safety, the defenders would have time to put it out; and if he cut it shorter he would risk blowing himself up.

His father sent Batty back, of course, and he was unmoved by protests. Batty was moved to obey by entreaties about his ma and had spent the rest of the night with his mother, watching and waiting by the guns, ramrod in hand and worry in his gut.

At dawn Maramaldo assembled his army, then gave the signal for the breaching charges to be lit. But it was clear that the defenders had spotted Batty's da; sally ports opened, men spilled out, and Batty's da got ready to run for it.

Maramaldo, who had expected this, simply pointed his sword at Batty and his ma, a gesture Batty's father could not miss, even across the swathe of scarred, corpse-littered ground. If you run too early and fail, that sword said, then everything you love dies.

Batty reared up then, roaring with anger, and made a grab for Maramaldo's wrist, missed and sliced his palm along the sword blade before men dragged him off.

Batty's da waved to them. Then he blew the charges on a short fuse. Blew himself and the wall to flying flesh and stones to save his son and his woman, and had known he would have to do it, for the charges he had laid were four times more than needed, with more than half angled to blow out from the wall.

Stones and earth scoured across the littered ground, the blast tearing up bodies, helmets, discarded weapons and shields, slamming them into the waiting ranks like cannon fire.

The statue of Saint Secondus launched itself like an avenging angel, arcing into the sky, bouncing a gouge out of the earth, whirling across the ground, ripping through the scattering men until it whipped all four legs out from under Maramaldo's horse.

Batty was a screaming angel of vengeance himself, so that Maramaldo found himself, dazed and sprawled, looking up at Batty Kohlhase's unbloodied good left hand, full of ramrod and righteous anger.

Batty almost beat Maramaldo to death with it. Almost. He had to be dragged off while the milling, half confused and leaderless army launched itself at the breach. But their heart was not in it and they fled, while the defenders shouted about the 'miracle of Saint Secondus'.

Next day, with face bruised and his head bloody-bandaged, Maramaldo had paraded the remnants of his army before lifting the siege and marching away.

There, in front of the mercenaries, a limping, wincing Maramaldo had taken a farrier's axe to Batty's left arm, strapped at the wrist with leather thongs and pulled across a rabinet trace by leering men who had never liked him, for his wit and his wage as a skilled man.

'You dare to strike me?' Maramaldo had shrieked, his mouth wet and working, spittle flying. 'Me?'

He had been too injured by the ramrod and botched it, leaving the barber to cut the last few shreds, cauterise the stump with hot pitch, and tell Batty how lucky he was that Maramaldo had left him an arm at all – and that he would be worse off now if he had beaten the chief with his right hand.

Batty had almost died of the fevers that followed, and his ma, worn out with grief and harshness, had died some weeks later, simply turning her face to the wall. After that, Batty had stumbled on to fresh wars, seeking revenge.

Captain General Fabrizio Maramaldo went on to fight for the Duke of Orange and the restoration of the Medici against the Florentines. At Gavinana in 1530, he took prisoner his old enemy, Feruccio – already badly wounded – and stabbed the bound and unarmed man in the neck in a fit of furious temper, then assaulted the corpse. That had earned him no favours, so that even his own mercenaries deserted him, shaking their heads about how he would 'kill a dead man'.

Will sat stunned and silent while Batty stared blearily through the littered ground at his past.

'I never caught up with him again. I heard he is at the siege of Boulogne this year, but the Pope bans him from any army he finds him in, because of his black heart,' Batty ended bleakly. 'He is not a man to cross is Captain General Maramaldo. But we knew that when we joined him, for there was talk even then of his having murdered his wife in Naples, and my ma argued against us taking up with him at all. But he paid well.'

Will had nothing to say and wondered all the rest of that night at what it must have felt like to have your arm cut off with a farrier's axe. And what kind of man survived such a thing.

He would have been surprised to find that Batty could not tell him, that only a little of the pain and horror of it leaked through now and then; the rest was buried so deep even Batty could not find it if he chose.

He recalled some moments of sweating dim, hearing his ma chant in her lilting Border voice — but since she knew only charms against wens and birthing and water-elf disease, he was never sure if she helped heal him.

If she had not. If he had died...

Batty thought about that now and then — especially now that Will had asked.

What would he miss, being dead? Good drink? Soup? There was not much to Batty Coalhouse, he thought, if you put him in the balance.

A list of tavern owners who knew him by name. A longer list of snarling growlers who knew him by reputation. An even longer list of folk he owed money to.

Wife, none. Children, none. Future prospects... None.

He would not miss any of that. Nor his arm, which itched him now and then. A whore had once asked him, looking at the scars and puckered remains of his body, what had kept him alive when everyone seemed out to kill him by slow degrees.

Batty told her. The secret of staying alive, he had said, is not wanting to.

He showed no sign of all this with his calm knitting, let the storm of old memories sink back into the slorach of his soul, while the wind guttered and wheeped, full of conversation about snow.

Chapter Seven

The men slithered in with the dark, which Batty had expected. There were more than three, which he had also expected, though Bet's Annie, upstairs at one of the small windows, sent Jinet down to tell them she was sure there were forty or more. Batty scorned that, while hoping it would not be the case, just as he had hoped for one more day for the swelling in his leg to go down a little, for the aches and bruises to ease some.

But you play the cards you are dealt, in life as in Primero, he thought, soothing the dog from squeezing out barks; it subsided, stiff-bristled from neck to tail and trembling. He checked the pistol and wished for three more like it, stuck the basket-hilted blade in the packed earth of the undercroft where he could easily snatch it, and waited for the ritual dance of it all.

'Ho the house! We seek shelter.'

The lie would usually be answered with demands to know who was at the door, a snappy riposte of refusal, an exchange, a threat, and then matters would move to battering on the door and fistfuls of fire.

Bet's Annie, though, was clearly too fretted to jig in the ritual dance. There was a fizz and bang from upstairs, followed by a scream and a series of shouts and curses from beyond the walls.

'Away wi' ye, ye foutie, hunker-slidin' hempie infames, or there will be more of the same.'

Will and Batty listened to Bet's Annie's shrilling and laughed grimly to each other.

'By God, she has iron in her,' Batty declared, and Will, with a sickening shiver, thought that was more than physically likely by the time matters were done here. The dog started in to barking again and Batty gentled it to silence; it looked up at him and whined. Outside was chaos and shouting, with a threnody whimper and a final, plaintive moan.

'My eyes – I am blind—'

Peppershot will do that, Batty noted exultantly.

'One less is all good,' Will growled.

Jinet clattered down the ladder again, half falling into the undercroft and breathing hard.

'Bet's Annie thinks she has hit one,' she reported breathlessly, and Batty nodded and smiled.

'So I hear. Help her to reload – keep her match lit while she does,' he told her, and she scampered back to the ladder, happy to have something to do, and so thrilled with fear that she had already wet herself and blessed the skirts that hid it and the brogued shoes that let it run out.

Batty took a breath or two, then waited, singing softly to himself as the moaner outside was soothed to soft bleats.

'*She turned about her milk-white steed and took True Thomas up ahind. And aye whene'er her bridle rang, the steed flew swifter than the wind.*'

'Is that you in there, Batty Coalhouse?'

The voice cut through the tuneless hum, trailing dead sound in its wake.

'It was when I woke this morning,' Batty eventually answered, and there was a pungent curse from outside, a moment of hissed exchanges culminating in a command. Batty grinned; so it was Dog Pyntle who had got the peppershot.

'Is that Francie Bourne arguing on how it can't be me since he never misses?'

There was a pause from beyond that let Batty know he had struck true and hammered a sliver of fear into them. Faerie-spelled, they would be thinking now – especially Francie, who would sooner have the Queen of Elfland's hand in the way than admit he had missed.

'You know some things,' said a voice, grim with purpose and clearly unimpressed by Faerie.

'You will be Dand the Lamb Ker,' he said, smiling at the effect he knew this would have. 'Is Dog Pyntle bad shot in the face?'

He could almost see them look around to see if he hovered in some ethereal form, watching them with the powrie lurking at his heels to do them harm.

'Christ, Dand – get me to my horse...'

'Shush, Dog. We are not done here yet. Francie – fetch our bags.'

So they'd come prepared. Oil, probably, for the scumfishing – but you needed into the undercroft at least for that. Or up on the roof to put smoulder down the chimney; the women would be ready to hook it down and smother it in a covered bucket before it started to reek.

Will Elliot's head had come up at the sound of the last voice and Batty looked inquiringly at him.

'That's Hen Graham,' Will whispered savagely. Batty nodded; so the hand of the Keeper was in it more surely than before. And Will, sensibly, was keeping his presence here secret, for such a surprise might make the difference later.

'Has the Keeper men to spare?' he asked, and Will nodded, sheened with bitterness.

'He can find them for this,' he hissed. 'Armstrongs, no doubt.'

'With a Graham at their head? That will not sit easily,' Batty noted, and then hummed quietly, looking at Will and placing a finger along his considerable nose.

'*But, Thomas, ye maun hold your tongue, whatever ye may hear or see.*'

'You know we have come for you, Batty Coalhouse,' the voice shouted. 'It will be faster and easier if you do not make us work.'

'I am warm and sheltered, Hen Graham' Batty replied. 'If you have to work up a sweat in the freeze there, I am happy to watch.'

He heard the fall of silence, almost saw the frantic head jerkings from men convinced that they were truly being watched, impossibly, through Powrieburn's thick walls. More power to the Queen of Faerie, Batty thought, who makes Powrieburn so feared.

'Dand... Francie... Help me.'

Dog's plaintive whine ended in a yelp and then silence.

'Listen to that,' Batty said with as much laugh as he could put in his voice. 'Kick the Dog when you can kick nothing else.'

He was looking at the brindle Powrieburn hound when he spoke and added another laugh at the seeming brown-eyed reproach he had from its look. There was silence, then a thunder at the door that made Batty jump and set the dog to crouching and growling; Dand and Francie had clearly fetched a balk and were using it as a ram against the outer doors of the undercroft.

Bet's Annie came slithering down the ladder, the caliver in one hand and the match smoking in the other.

'I can't get to them from the window,' she announced savagely, 'but there is a looking slat in the door—'

'I had seen it,' Batty said matter-of-factly. 'I was coming to get the yett keys but I see you have brought them.'

He watched her open the grilled yett and then turned to Will, who had said nothing and sharpened his blade.

'Lock the yett in case Dame Fortune smiles on them and the door collapses.'

Bet's Annie snorted.

'That door will not be broken open in a month of hammering.'

Batty nodded and lumbered into the small space between grille and main door.

'For if you speak a word in Elfyn land, ye'll ne'er get back to your ain countrie.'

The great rhythmic shudders on the door hid his soft singing and the sound of him drawing back the looking slat. He saw vague shapes, heard ragged breathing – more than just two, he thought, and stuck the pistol out.

The wheel whirred and the smoke flashed in the pan. Someone gave a curse, then the pistol went off with a deafening bang and Batty drew it back and slammed the portal shut. He did not think he had hit anyone, but it did not matter.

He limped back to the yett gate, laughing at the shouts and curses beyond. Will opened it and Batty went through, tucking the pistol under his armless oxter and starting in to reload it, while the dog capered and spun and leaped, sharing the joy of the moment with a reef of slavered teeth and a lolling wet tongue.

'Here – give it here and take the caliver, just in case,' Bet's Annie declared.

Batty obeyed and leaned the gun against his belly, his only hand swinging the slow match in mesmeric, glowing circles, while Bet's Annie reloaded the dagg, tongue between her teeth; the horses and kine shifted and made little noises of disapproval, restless with the stink of powder and match and the ratchet grind of the dagg wheel being wound.

He stood for a long moment or two until the sudden boom on the door resumed, then he looked at Bet's Annie.

'But I have a loaf and a sup o' wine, and ye shall go and dine wi' me,' he sang, gentle as breathing and with as much lightness as he could muster.

'Lay yer head down in my lap and I will tell ye farlies three,' Bet's Annie finished – in proper tune too, he noted ruefully and took the loaded dagg back.

'I will fetch a loaf and a sup,' she declared, taking the caliver and match. 'It will be a long night.'

She turned briefly to the dog and weesht it to silence, which command it ignored. Batty watched her hunch herself into the bell-boom of the ram on the door and the mad barking, watched her all the way up the ladder.

Will laughed softly, jerking Batty's eyes from the sway of hurdies.

He wagged a mocking finger at Batty, then smiled.

'*O no, O no, True Thomas. That fruit maun not be touched by thee. For a' the plagues that are in Hell, light on the fruit of this countrie.*'

Hollows Tower
At the same time

The Laird looked Mintie up and down with a liquid eye. Then he switched his gaze to Hutchie Elliott and, finally, to the coiled snake of a man in the seat next to him.

There were others in a crowded hall, Mintie saw, but none that mattered more than us three – save perhaps the richly dressed man who looked like a snake.

'Black rent,' the Laird muttered and shifted his weight on the seat; his face was a bag of sweating blood and his hand kept moving to the blue glass goblet of wine sitting in front of him. Twice he did this, Mintie noted, then he sighed, took it, drank deep and replaced it as he began to cough; there was white at the corners of his mouth, and Mintie had the idea that he had been drinking for a long time.

He scarcely seemed to be listening as Mintie made her plea – the Fyrebrande in return for the safety of all at Powrieburn, Batty Coalhouse included.

'We are all loyal vassals of the Keeper and the King,' she declared, then remembered and corrected herself, flustered. 'The wee Queen, I meant, my lord—'

'Loyal vassals,' the Laird repeated. 'Oh aye, so you say. Yet you have befriended Batty Coalhouse, who has murdered your neighbour's boy, Will. He was an Armstrong and a loyal vassal of mine own.'

He coughed again, pressing his hand flat on the table to take the strain of it. The hand twitched towards the goblet.

Mintie explained the whole sorry story of Will Armstrong and there were a few mutters and growls at it. Someone began to shout out from the draught-flickering shadows and was quickly muffled. That will be Sorley, Mintie thought, trying not to look for him.

The Laird belched, drank more and sat heavily back in his seat.

'Still,' he said, 'I am minded to forgive, which is Divine—'

'Forgive all you like,' the snake-man declared flatly. 'But after I am gone with what I came for.'

Mintie looked at this one, took in the slashed doublet and puffed breeches, the *ronde-bosse* enamel of the *etui* for some holy relic hanging round his neck, the jewel-hilted dagger.

He was thin, fine-featured, with long fingers which were never still, either brushing back the flop of auburn hair falling over his brow, touching the *etui*, his dagger hilt, his close-cropped beard. A beast too well bred, Mintie thought. If it was horse or dog, you would put it down – little stamina and too nervous – but here was one of the men eating Andra's shod geese and used to such fare and better too.

'Never fear, Tom,' the Laird began in a patronising soothe, his smile slack.

'I do fear,' the man interrupted, sitting forward with irritation. 'I fear that I will never be able to leave this God-forsaken Scotch hole with the King's prize. I fear you will throw out at the final hazard. And I am Sir Thomas Wharton, not "Tom", nor "coz", nor "English".'

The Laird had eyes like a boar, a red-rimmed stare that shrank all who saw it.

'You are what I decide,' he said, slow and harsh as a blade on a grindstone. 'Son of the Deputy Warden of the English March or not. And you are stuck here with your prize until I have my purse. Speak less on it afore your tongue runs you down a blocked road.'

He leaned forward himself.

'Do you know where your men are? Where my purse is?'

Wharton waved a dismissive hand and then stuck it in his mouth and started gnawing. A knuckle, Mintie noted with distaste, because all his fingernails are bitten away.

'I thank you for the gift, Mistress Araminta,' the laird went on, as if nothing had transpired. 'The beast has lost a deal of topline, but the weather is to blame for that — and for keeping you with us. It is too inclement for me to allow you to leave the hospitality of Hollows.'

Mintie knew better than to argue, so she curtsied.

'I hear Agnes from Andrascroft is here,' she said. 'I hope she is well and that I can see her.'

Hutchie laughed and the laird glared at him, then studied Mintie for a time before sighing.

'Hutchie will take you to her,' he said. 'The Lady of Hollows is there and will see to your needs.'

'What of the horse?' demanded Hutchie.

The Laird turned his red-eyed glare on him, and Mintie had the joy of seeing Hutchie shrink under the heat of it.

'Quite right, Hutchie, to remind me of your station,' the Laird said. 'You will take Mistress Araminta's mount to the stables and see to it. I will see to the Fyrebrande's needs, for it is a finer beast and needs a proper hand on it.'

Hutchie was scowling now and slouched from the hall with an arrogance that was breathtaking. He will not enjoy Hollows for long with that attitude, Mintie thought with savage satisfaction.

Up a level were the women, sitting in a brazier-warmed room and playing cards or sewing. They looked up when Hutchie ushered Mintie in with bad grace and made the sketchiest of dues to the oldest of the clutch.

'Lady,' he said sullenly. 'Your man bids you see to the needs of this lass. She is a guest, if ye take my meaning.'

118

'Everyone takes your meaning, Master Elliott,' the woman answered, purse-mouthed, then waved him away. 'You have the subtlety of a falling tree.'

The wife of the Laird was called Margaret, had a careworn air, a threadbare style worn away by too long pretence at being finer than she was. She introduced the others, four or five younger gauds the Lady of Hollows was pretending were tire-women, or ladies-in-waiting, as if she was the Court at Falkland Palace. They were hipshot and arrogant and whatever serving they were doing was not upright, Mintie suspected, for there were a lot of languid well-bred southrons draped all over the Armstrong tower with little to do but gamble and wink.

Mintie heard the names of these women but did not mark them, other than as fornicatrices. She had eyes only for the one she knew, the shining-eyed Agnes and the bairn she cradled.

'I heard of your loss,' she began, but Agnes smiled only a little sadly, then with a sudden blissful radiance held out the bundle for Mintie to see.

'Look what God blessed me with, Mintie,' she declared. 'A wee lass to replace the Eck I have losted.'

Mintie glanced at the prune-faced wrinkle, the hair bright as red gold against the yellow satin wrap, fit to coddle a royal. Her heart went cold then, for she knew now what the secret of Hollows was, and that neither she nor Agnes were likely to be going anywhere in a hurry.

The little Mary, Queen of Scots, opened her bright eyes and yawned her rosebud mouth sleepily up into Mintie's stricken face.

Powrieburn

Later that night

Towards dawn the door splintered, a great sliver flying off the inside of it, leaving the wood bright as moonlight in the crusie-lit dim. The men outside heard it and gave a hoarse cheer, quickly hushed by a snap of voice.

'We need this ended, Hen,' growled another. 'We are already late for Netherby and it is snowing now, by God.'

'Silence on that, you blatherer...'

There was a pause, then the voice both Batty and Will knew belonged to Hen Graham raised itself a little.

'Surrender now and hand over Batty Coalhouse, who is Billed for the murder of Will Armstrong of Whithaugh. The women of Powrieburn will not be harmed. Are you listening, Mistress Mintie? If you do not, it will be March law, which is to say the Law of Deuteronomy.'

There was the bang of a shutter from upstairs and the scrabble of leather on slick, sliding cobbles as men scattered from the expected blast of the caliver. Instead, they got Mintie's mother and the peppershot of her scathing was almost as harsh, seemed to swirl the flakes of snow.

'Mintie is safe gone, ye hempie-deedit kithans,' she shrilled, a sound to ruche up armflesh like a nail on a slate. 'Ye custrin yaldson... ye will hemp yer necks for this, so ye will, and the Land Sergeant of Hermitage will stand witness to it.'

'Ah, well,' sighed Batty, 'there ends our wee surprise.'

'Shame,' agreed Will with a tight grin splitting his beard, 'but, my, she can curse, can she not?'

There was a pause after Mintie's ma's blast – spoiled a little by the sound of her bursting into hysterical tears at the end of it – then Hen Graham cleared his throat.

'Are you in there, Will Elliot?'

'I am, you two-faced hunchbacked wee rat,' Will answered mildly. 'And by the time I am done, you will swing. There is no Bill on Batty Coalhouse that is perjink, since I never made it and I am the only one who can.'

'The Keeper did,' blustered Hen, as men muttered uneasily. 'And since you stand with a black murderer, then you are as guilty. Set to, you men!'

'Who are you to give orders to Armstrong men?'

The voice was deep and thick with truculence, but Hen Graham did not need to struggle long for a reply; someone else cut through his bluster.

'He is the Keeper's wee dog and of no account at all,' it declared, and both Will and Batty knew it at once as Dand Ker.

'But I am of account,' Dand went on, soft as plague breath, 'and if you want to argue the bit, speak again, Hen Graham. I warn you, though, I will have so many teeth from your head for it that beldames will have to suck your meat soft from now until the day you no longer eat.'

There was a silence, then Hen recovered his saw-whine.

'Nothing meant by it,' he muttered, and you could hear the uncertainty in his attempts at firmness, the fake depth and shredded dignity; Will grinned at Batty in the shadow-dancing dim.

Then Dand told them to set to and the ram splintered the door again.

Hollows Tower

That same night

Mintie tried, but it was clear the joy of bairn was all over Agnes, smearing her grief and unlikely to be wiped away by the truth.

'They have stolen the babe,' she whispered, a repetition that was making no difference. 'A Queen, Agnes. The mite will have to go back to its own in the end. You must know that.'

This last speared Agnes, so that she looked up from her bliss, frowning.

'I am caring for her. The Lady of Hollows said so.'

Mintie glanced to one side, where the Lady of Hollows, too normal and too bright, sat talking with her 'ladies' in a brittle banality which fooled none, least of all herself.

'The entire land will be out hunting this bairn on behalf of her ma,' Mintie declared. 'Who is the Dowager Queen Mary of

Guise, if you need reminding. The Lady of Hollows is neither here nor there next to her, and when wee Queen Mary goes back, the Lady will swing for it. Her and her Laird.'

'It appears to me that you are upsetting this wet nurse.'

The voice made Mintie jerk and stare up into the agate eyes of the Lady Margaret of Hollows. Red-rimmed they were, the cheeks beneath them planched and on the wither; she might seem dry as an old stick, Mintie thought, but she moves swift and does not creak at all.

'It seems to me,' the Lady went on coldly, 'that you need to be elsewhere, or you will curdle the bairn's dinner.'

Someone sniggered at the back of her, and Mintie, recovering as best she could, rose up and smoothed her hair, a gesture that gave her a measure of confidence. This 'lady', she thought to herself, is more fearful than I am, more lost than this bairn. Her proud, golden Laird is not the man he was, if ever he was that at all, and she is living beyond the means of her heart, trying to keep up appearances of an era beyond repair.

'They will come for you and the stones of Hollows will not save you,' she said levelly. 'What were you thinking to steal a Queen? If the babe is harmed—'

'The bairn will not be harmed,' the Lady retorted harshly, then flapped one ringed hand. 'She is only to be wed, that's all. To a prince, no less. Bringing peace to the land before war ruins us all. It is for the greater good.'

Mintie did not understand the greater good, only saw folk jigging about for advantage and profit for themselves. She said as much, and from the sag in her, knew that the Lady of Hollows had seen it too.

For all that, the Lady drew herself up and had one of the fornicatrices fetch Hutchie Elliott. When he slouched in, the Lady indicated Mintie with a haughty, dismissive wave.

'Take this girl to the undercroft and place her there for safekeeping.'

Hutchie smiled his dazzling smile, winked at the gauds and then took Mintie by the elbow out of the room and down the wind of stairs, down and round and down into the dark.

She knew what he would do in the dark of the deep under-croft, knew it as she knew the saw-rasp cry of geese as they fork the sky, knew it as she recognised an individual horse by the way it whinnied. She wanted to scream. She tried to scream. But her throat closed around the sound, so that the 'no' came out strangled and faint.

'Shush, wee Mintie,' he said, as soft as if he soothed a trembling lamb. She felt metal on her neck and saw the wink of his knife.

'Please,' she said and was appalled at the fear in her own voice. 'Don't hurt me.'

'Just in case,' he said and grinned his white grin, startling in the undercroft dark.

'In case you decide to draw blood on me, like last time,' he whispered, as if calming a child.

He pushed Mintie against the rough stone of the wall, tomb cold and so thick it swallowed noise, so that the hand on her mouth was not needed and he took it away again. Then he showed Mintie the knife, a small eating one with an antler handle.

'You drew blood on me once,' he said. 'I could kill you for it, but I won't if you do what I say.'

His free hand took her round the shoulders and the knife hand vanished; Mintie felt the looseness and knew he had cut the lacings of her kirtle. He drew the knife back and caressed her cheek with it, ran it up to remove the kertch, pins and all, so that her hair fell free to her shoulders. Mintie trembled then, felt more naked than a moment later, when the top of the kirtle slid from her shoulders and exposed her breasts. Cold and terror nubbed the ends like an invite and she tried to cross her arms on her body's betrayal, but he would not let her.

She was shaking hard, but too terrified to weep, though a moan broke from her when he forced the kirtle down, then sent the petticoat to puddle at her feet. She wore no smallclothes, so the lie of menses would not work.

'Wait,' she said and started to flail, weak with panic.

'Hush,' he said, harshly now, and there was a sensation that her mind ran hard to catch up with. When it did, she put her hand to her neck, where the knife had touched. It felt sticky. She looked at the bright red smear on her hand. Her blood.

Her blood. She looked down and saw more of it on her crumpled kirtle, and her mind wavered as if it was no more substantial than a haze of heat. Never get the stain oot o' that, she thought, not proper. Ruined it is.

In that instant everything came into sharp focus, as if God had brightened the lens of the world. Ruined like me, she thought. I am fifteen years old, and this is the day of my death.

She felt his hands on her naked breasts, but it did not seem quite real. She saw the blade wavering, winking its edged leer out of the corner of her eye, felt the scrape of the wall on her bare back.

But that was only her body. The rest of Mintie had slipped away, up the curl of stone stairs, up and round and up into the rafters of Hollows and beyond, away out of this place, out of time.

There she watched, suspended and detached, feeling neither fear nor panic, seeing it as she had once seen the two-headed calf at the Lammas Fair, or the mummers in the play. She felt only a slight pity for the girl she saw, backed to the cold stones while Hutchie Elliott fumbled at the lacings of his breeks.

When he struggled his hose to his knees, he pushed Mintie against the wall with his body, tried to get it in her, standing there. When that didn't work, he turned her around, face to the wall, but that worked no better, and he growled then, pushing her to hands and knees.

That worked. The pain was only a faint thing, as if it did not belong to her at all. After a while of it, he turned her over and put it in her again. He moved fast, his face staring at a point beyond her head, at the rough stones of the wall. He seemed detached, almost disinterested, and she saw the little pewter medallion on a chain round his neck, swinging in rhythm, back and forth, back and forth into her face.

He suddenly kissed her, but would not look in her eyes.

'D'you like this, wee Mintie?' he demanded, and from her eyrie she was amazed. What was this? He is treating me as if we were courting, she thought, like he thinks we would be together after this.

With a shock, she realised that this for him was courting.

He froze once, at some noise real or imagined, and put his hand over her mouth and brought the knife back into it.

'Hush, now – keep quiet.'

Eventually he took his hand away and pushed her to the floor again.

She lost her sense of time after that and did not even know when it slipped away, leaving her in the undercroft like a sealed tomb, like something out of a tale told round a warm fire to frighten bairns.

She knew when it stopped and he left her, panting and pulling his breeks up. Mintie got her own clothes, though the kirtle was ruined with blood and could not be re-laced, so she held it round her with the wrap of her arms. They did not feel like her arms. Nothing felt like it belonged to her, save the slow, insidious realisation of the pulse of pain.

Hutchie smoothed his hair and grinned his white grin.

'Told you I would take you,' he said, then put the eating knife to her arm and pushed the point in just enough so she could feel it.

'Not so proud now, wee Mintie,' he said. 'Know who is master now.'

He stepped back from her, exposing the stairs, and she almost fell, almost lost the use of her legs at the idea of bright. Sun. Air.

'Say nothing,' he ordered, looking her in the face for the first time. He licked his thumb and rubbed at the blood on her neck. He smoothed her hair.

'I am away soon,' he said. 'Away with the English when they take the bairn south to Fat King Henry to be wed to his son. Say nothing of this to anyone when I am gone.'

She felt sick at the sound of herself, at the whining-dog eagerness to please.

'I won't. I promise.'

'Och, I will miss you when I am away, wee Mintie,' he said, almost cooing. Then he kissed her on the lips and swaggered away.

Powrieburn

Around the same time

The undercroft stank of dung and fear. The truth is, Will thought, that it reeks only of animal because my arse muscle is strong. It would not have mattered much to the stink if he had shamed himself, for it was so pungent that he stood at the rearmost of the beasts crowded into the walkway between wall and stall and breathed through his mouth.

The rearmost beast was one of the brace of milchers and he had heard Bet's Annie cooing to it, calling it 'beautiful Maggie'. Maggie, with her smeared hindquarters and desperate, lowing panic, was anything but beautiful, Will thought.

Batty watched the horse next to it, which was standing in the open yett gate and trembling at every booming smash on the splintering outer door. The noise was almost under its nose, and for all it had been the late master of Powrieburn's placid riding horse, the gelding was snorting and trying to back off, only to bump into the beast behind. It did not help that the dog danced at its hooves, birling and barking alternately.

Only the Saul, wheezing and too weak for all this, was in his stall, and Batty turned to soothe him with quiet murmurs, while checking the winding on his dagg. He never soothed the other beasts, though; for this desperation to succeed needed all the beasts the opposite of quiet.

The bar broke in two with a rending crash and the great double doors of Powrieburn swung wide. Beyond, dark shapes, panting and feral, hung on the ram, while others crowded past them, expecting to have to break the inner iron-grilled door.

Batty fired the dagg, a great fizzing boom of white smoke and noise. He dropped it and barely had his hand on his sword hilt when the bellows and roars from Will Elliot, the smoke and the flame and the mad barking finally reached the point, like a slow match on a charge.

The beasts, snorting and squealing, sprang forward for escape through the already opened grille of the yett, through the broken door and into the snow-slush yard – and over anything in their path. The maddened dog rushed through with them, biting and snarling.

Will Elliot saw Batty lurch out of the Saul's stall just as the shitty end of the last bawling cow trundled past; he balked Will's own rush and the pair of them crowded through the yett door almost shoulder to shoulder.

Batty was first, hopping nimbly over a limp bag of rags on his way out into the courtyard, swinging his stiff leg, his sole fist filled with the basket hilt of a notched sword.

Will did not see the bag of rags, stumbled over it and almost went on one knee, and was cursing and rising when he saw the face, twisted unnaturally to one side and the one eye left to it showing a cracked bewilderment.

The beasts had not been kind to Francie Bourne, Will Elliot saw, swallowing the bile at what hooves had done to him. He would win no more Truce Day shoots.

Out in the yard the wind was snell and swirled the snow. Figures danced and shouted; torches flickered. Something went off with a bang and a flare in the dark, and Will's heart lurched at the thought of Batty down and himself being left with all these shadows.

Someone staggered towards him cursing, and he slashed, feeling his blade catch, seeing the man reel away screaming and holding his neck where something blacker than the night spread like a stain.

Will heard Batty then, roaring in the dark, and where the voice was, sparks flew from ringing steel.

'You bastards – meddle with me, is it? Who dares meddle with me?'

Will started towards the sound and a shadow came out of the night, forcing him to turn and shoot the latchbow in his left fist. The bolt took the man square on his metalled jack and the range was close enough to knock him off his feet and all the wind from him. Will heard the frantic, high, wheezed whimper and felt a savage joy – that has cracked a rib bone.

Someone else came at him, and he hurled the bow, so that the man flung up one arm and had it smack the bone of it; cursing, he reeled away, only to let yet another move in.

This one was big, in battered pot helm and leather jack padded with straw and badly used, so that wisps of it stuck out and made him look like a mad scarecrow. He had greasy black hair spilling out from under the helmet, dripping with the sleeting snow, and his beard was a tangle, pearled like a lady's hair with a net of melting-ice gems.

The sweat-reek rose from him like steam, he had a scar down one cheek and another across his nose, which was bent sideways like a badly-made gate. The wound was so recent it wasn't yet healed from the scab. When it did, it would become one more in a patina of nicks and little pocks.

Will danced with him, seeing the yellow bared teeth and the two missing on the left side, the incongruous little dangle of pearl earring, as if it compensated for everything else and made him a fine-faced courtier.

Nothing would do that. His was the face of a man who had lived fight and raid all his life, with the hands that held the buckler and broadsword scarred and scored from countless other battles. If I cut one off, Will thought, it will fight on with just the memories of its own wrist.

They clashed and circled and lurched like a fool's parody of lovers in a wedding reel, and the man snarled from out of his ugly, hair-shrouded face. Their blades sparked; Will feinted, twirled, struck the buckler and wrenched the man's arm sideways with the blow, but the counterstrike spoiled his plan and he had to hirple backwards.

They traded blow on sword blow for a bit, until Will thought the man used to the rhythm – then he birled on his good foot, shoved a shoulder in the buckler and stabbed downwards with the sword.

It should have taken the man in the instep, the shoulder shoving him off-balance at the same time. Instead, Will found air – then the world sprang out of the side of his eye and slammed stars and moons into him.

He found himself on his arse in the wet, looking up at the ugly face while his own burst with pain and he tasted blood on his teeth; if there was a new dent in the buckler that had fisted him to the yard's cobbles, it would not be noticed.

'There was fancy,' the man snarled, and Will, blinking in the snow-whirl, realised he was done for, though at the same time he thought it was strange how many there were in the yard, and some mounted...

The man grinned, yellow and gapped, then gave a lurch and a choking sob; a great gout of black vomit steamed out down his beard and he dropped buckler and sword to grip the bloody sliver of metal sticking out of his chest.

Bewildered as the man who suffered it, Will watched the sliver suddenly vanish, sliding through the blood-slick fingers the man tried vainly to grip it with; released like a straw mommet, he fell in a heap, and then Will saw the horse, a snorting Galloway nag on top of which perched a boy with a bloodied lance and a feral smile.

'Ho, ho – enough I say. Enough...'

The booming voice brought everyone struggling in the yard to the sense of too many men they could not account for. There was a stepping back, a wary lowering of weapons; the sudden moment of silence was broken by a clatter of hooves and a shrill scream.

'Davey Graham – leave off stabbing folk. Leave off, I say.'

The horsebacked boy reined round, a sullen pout spoiling his old grin while greasy blood coiled slowly down the shaft of his raised lance.

'That's better – mind you, you have accounted yourself well. Has he not, lads?'

Voices barked and growled assent, and Will finally saw the speaker, tall and thin, with a halo of tow-coloured hair on his unhelmeted head and a curve of yellow beard like a Turk's golden scimitar. He looked like Batty, Will thought bemusedly.

Bewildered, Will struggled up, staggering a little. Now there was only the wheeping snow wind and the moans of the hurt and the distant lowing of an unhappy milch cow.

'Which of you is Batty Graham?'

There was a stir then and Batty hirpled out of a throng which parted before him, revealing several men on the cobbles. He was breathing hard and had blood on his cheek.

'I am Batty Coalhouse, if that's who you mean?'

The old man leaned on the crupper of his horse and nodded.

'You are Batty Graham, son of Bella Graham of Netherby. She was kin to me and I am kin to you. I am Dickon Graham of Netherby, son of Lang Will. That there is Arthur of Canobie and Fergus of the Mote, a brace of my many brothers. The other is Tam Graham of Kirkandrews, also kin.'

'What brings you here?' demanded a new voice, and Dand Ker stepped up, his beard and hair swirling in the wind. 'This is no matter of yours.'

'Who are you?'

Dand told him and Dickon stroked his beard a moment, while subtle shifts showed everyone not on a horse that the mounted men had them neatly penned and needed only to lower their lances. The wee boy called Davey looked at Dand as if choosing a target.

'You are a Ker and so of no account. If you are clever, you will be silent.'

It was an iron dismissal and Dand bridled at it. That is a mistake, Will thought.

'This is a hot trod,' Dand persisted, 'seeking Batty Coalhouse, a murderer, and the Land Sergeant of Hermitage, his accomplice.'

He flung one hand behind him.

'Here is Hen Graham, another of your kin, to tell you how he comes from the Keeper of Liddesdale—'

The fizz of powder in the pan gave Dand an eyeblink warning that his mouth had run him down a closed road. The bang of the matchlock pistol was loud, the flare bright and the foot-long barrel of it kicked into the air like a salute. But the range was too close to miss and Dand went backwards three yards and skittered over the cobbles in a half-circle. Those nearest backed away, wiping bits of his blood and brains and bone off them.

'You are Armstrongs,' Dickon Graham declared, waving the reek from his pistol shot and speaking as if the name was a bad taste. 'Hunting a Graham. Now you have found more than you cared to and will hang for it.'

'No, no,' squeaked Hen desperately. 'I am no Armstrong. I am Hen Graham from Hermitage, here on the Keeper's orders—'

'Liar,' Will growled, finding his voice at last, and Batty stepped into the echo of it, looking quizzically up at Dickon.

'It is gratifying to find I have kin after all this time,' he said wryly. 'And timely, no doubt of it, so that I am Batty Graham if that is what it takes. Does this mean your five other brothers are waiting to welcome me with open arms?'

Dickon grunted and scowled down at him.

'You are a by-blow of a German bastard,' he said flatly, 'but you are our by-blow of a German bastard, and as long as there is a lick of Graham blood in you, that Name will never let a bloody Armstrong spill it unchallenged.'

Batty looked at Will and neither could fathom what the other thought other than relief. Suddenly Will found he could no longer care, or hold his sword up, or even rise, so that when Batty half fell onto the cobbles beside him, he knew why.

They sat there, with the wind bleating like a lost sheep and spraying snow in everyone's eyes, while Dickon had the Armstrong men disarmed and sent out riders to bring back the scattered beasts.

'I thought they had shot you dead,' Will said eventually, and Batty stirred as if from sleep, looked wearily at him and then waved his hand at the nearest rag-bag corpse.

'Not me, but a sad loss all the same.'

It was then that Will saw the four legs on that particular corpse; he felt suddenly – and strangely, considering all the blood spilled and lives lost – struck dumb with sadness at the sight of the brindle dog sprawled dead.

In the end it was Bet's Annie, shawled and with her arms folded, who stood looking down at them and shaking her head so that snow spilled off it.

'Get your arses up off the wet,' she ordered as if talking to bairns, and meekly they obeyed, struggling to do it. Bet's Annie scornfully held out a hand and Batty, unashamed, took it and was hauled up and into a fierce embrace.

'Silly auld fools,' she said, gripping Will equally hard. Then she turned as Dickon walked up, leading his horse. Behind him came the boy, like a small parody.

'Well, what shall we do with the ones taken, Davey-boy?'

He did not even look round and the boy, well used to this, simply replied without looking up.

'Hemp them.'

Dickon smiled and nodded admiringly.

'This is my son,' he said to Batty and Will, as if they could not already have guessed as much. He turned to the boy.

'Aye, tree and rope as your grandfaither tells us all,' he went on, stroking his beard and grinning. 'Lang Will is a byword for harsh, even in such a land as this.'

He glanced slyly at Batty.

'What say you?'

'I offer my thanks for your timely rescue,' Batty said, flat and hard as a whacked blade on a stone, the smoke of his breath seeming more scorched than any other. 'Even though I have been back a few years and never had so much as a cheery wave from any of you before.'

'Aye, well,' Dickon answered uncomfortably. 'Your kin at Askerton watched out over you, so we knew when you were in real danger.'

'Knew when I was of use to pull the beard of the Armstrongs of Hollows, more like,' Batty answered, and Will grew alarmed, for this was not only staring the gift horse in the mouth, it was pulling out the teeth to inspect them. Dickon had lost his grin now.

'I add my thanks to your boy,' Will flung out hastily, and tried at one and the same time to be generous and still hint that he had had the matter under control the entire time.

The boy nodded matter-of-factly, but there was enough lad left in him to beam with pleasure. He will be pleased of the dark, Will thought, which hides his blushes. There are few boy-blushes allowed to pass in Netherby, I suspect.

Dickon laughed and clapped his hand on the boy's considerable shoulder.

'Big enough to manage horse and lance, big enough to Ride,' Dickon declared. 'You can never be bloodied early enough.'

'Aye,' the boy replied, 'it was a fair stroke. But not my blooding. That was last year when I was ten, da, as you well know.'

'Ten,' Will echoed weakly.

'Aye,' Dickon said proudly, then closed one eye and looked slyly at Batty. 'That's Graham for you. I see by the wee spoil you made of your own here that there's a fair amount of grayne blood in you. We welcome you.'

'Late,' Batty replied flatly, 'but welcome this night. Why this night, mind you? How did you know that we were hard-pressed here in Powrieburn?'

Batty saw Dickon struggle with the lie that nothing that went on was missed by the Grahams of Netherby, but then he shrugged and truthed it out.

'Your kin at Askerton, the Land Sergeant there,' he replied, then frowned. 'Also a great many of foreign folk tramping up and down between Hollows and God knows where back across the Border. None of them are decent Names, but southrons all. The latest came yestreen – a score, well armed and well paid by the look, escorting a fancy carriage full of plush and decent springs and nothing else – empty as a Monday morning church.'

He shook his head at the very idea of such a contraption.

'They had a sick man they left at the Auld Tavern, saying they would pick him up on the way back and that it would only be a few days. Their captain was grumbling about the weather, which was sticking his fancy cart in every patch of soft between Netherby and York. And because those who were supposed to meet him were sieging a Batty Coalhouse in some place called Powrieburn.'

Will and Batty exchanged looks; they remembered the comments they'd overheard about finishing the business and getting to Netherby. And how Hen Graham had hushed them on the subject.

Batty said as much and Dickon nodded.

'They left in the night, saying they could wait no longer,' he went on. 'They went on to Hollows and we followed for a bit, then came here.'

He broke off as other riders came up, coiled ropes over their shoulders.

'I hope you have not hanged Hen Graham,' Will added, alarmed.

'Not at all,' said the new rider, his face blood-dyed by torches. 'Cannot hang kin. I came to find out what you wanted done, brother.'

Dickon grinned and clapped Davey-boy on the shoulder.

'Davey-boy says we should hang them all but Hen, and our da would agree — how many are there, Fergus?'

'A good dozen, Hen Graham included. Some of them are cut about a bit and one's blind,' Fergus of the Mote replied, and nodded admiringly to Will and Batty. 'There are five gone to Hell besides. You gave good account, for sure.'

'A dozen,' Dickon echoed and cocked a sly glance at Batty. 'My question remains, Master Batty — what would you have us do?'

'You can't hang them,' Will interrupted sternly. 'Turn them to me and—'

He broke off, because taking them back to Hermitage for justice was hardly an option when the Keeper of Liddesdale was up to his lace collar in the business. Frustrated and feeling foolish, he flapped a weak hand.

'He is right,' Batty declared, to Will's astonishment. 'You dare not hang them, and even your da, Lang Will of Arthuret, is not daft enough to do so, for the Laird of Hollows would never forgive nor forget. Pulling a few hairs from his beard is one thing, but blood feud is another. Bad enough that I am up to my armpits in feud with the Armstrongs — but I am a disgrace to the Graham and so can be ignored when it comes to the bit.'

He winked and smiled, but the chill in it made Dickon look away.

That was the bare truth of it, and Will wondered how the Grahams would take it. They had neither men nor weapons for a bloody feud with the Armstrongs; and once begun, such affairs could stretch generations unless one side was markedly stronger than the other. Inevitably, they became a struggle not of pride but of survival, and the Grahams were not as well set up for such an affair as the Armstrongs – but Will knew the mountain of stiff pride in the Names that would never wish to admit it.

Will should have known better. A bigger mountain owned by Border Riders was the size of their practical and when that tipped the pan, pride could wait. He saw Dickon recover some of his calm and turn to his son.

'Mind this lesson. Here is a master Graham at work, for that is just what I had decided myself. We will keep them for a while and then ransom them back—'

'Hand them back, more like,' Batty replied, and Will saw that Dickon did not like that – he had expected better of his clear Graham embrace of Batty than to have it shrugged carelessly off as if of little account.

'Netherby,' he said, before things started in to boiling. 'Hen Graham.'

Batty turned to him, remembered.

'Dog Pyntle,' he countered.

Hen Graham was sullen and fearful, yet buoyed by the surety that he would not be harmed in any meaningful way by those he shared a kinship with. This gave him enough courage to shake his head when asked about the carriage at Netherby.

Dog Pyntle, on the other hand, was a moaning, shivering wreck, his face clotted with half dried blood which no one had bothered to clean from him, and the eyes shot from his head, which he turned this way and that as people spoke, lost in the dark forever.

'Dog,' Will said sternly. 'You know me.'

'Is that Will Elliot? Oh God, has enough not been done to me? I am blinded, Will. For the love of Christ's mercy, leave me be.'

'What is the carriage for, Dog?' Will demanded. 'Tell me and I will see to your wounds. It may be just the blood in your eyes.'

Which was a flat-out lie, since everyone was staring into the raw holes where they had been.

'Carriage?' Dog repeated, then moaned.

'Shush, you,' Hen Graham shouted, and a sharp crack spilled him to the cobbles with a cry. Fergus of the Mote sucked his knuckles and scowled down at him.

'Another word from you and I will choke them all from you with hemp,' he growled. 'Kin or no.'

'Oh, God take my pain,' Dog moaned. 'Help me, in the name of Christ...'

'The carriage,' Will persisted.

'For the babe,' Dog groaned. 'For the wee bairn...'

Hen made a noise and then lost the power of speech completely when Fergus kicked him up in the cods. He rolled, gasping and retching, while Dog, bewildered and afraid, turned his head this way and that at the sounds.

'Bairn.'

Batty's voice was a slap in Dog's bloody face and he knew who it was at once. There were mangy curs who could learn cringe from Dog Pyntle, Will thought.

'The bairn they stole,' Dog moaned. 'The wee Queen. On Fat Henry's instruction. They are taking her to London to be wed to the wee prince. Don't hurt me more, Batty, for the love of Christ.'

There was a moment when no one could believe what they had heard and looked from one to the other.

'The wee Queen Mary?' Dickon demanded and gave Dog a kick as emphasis. His head lolled and he shrieked and nodded.

'Christ in Heaven,' Will said weakly. 'What have we stepped in?'

Chapter Eight

Near Hollows Tower
The next morning

Morning was a sketch of landscape unfolding under a broken sun, snowed to flawlessness with no people in it bar the cavalcade winding through it and no other seeming life besides puffed birds.

If there had been green left in the trees, the night's driving sleet and cold had twisted it all off, leaving them damp, black claws that sucked up the dark of their own shadows.

The men were not happy with the cold, nor the great sprung coach which had been wrestled with curses and sweat all the way up to Hollows. It was no more than box suspended on chains for smoothness, but it was monstrously heavy and had already got stuck twice in the time it took to travel the short way back to the rutted mud street of Canobie.

They were also fretted by the place and the strangeness. The mewling of gulls was only part of it, for it seemed to Wharton and the men from further south and inland that they sounded like crying children. There should not be gulls, they thought, with no sight of the sea.

Mintie knew, all the same. The Solway was not far off and the gulls were sweeping inland, driven in by bad weather and the promise of more of the same. She felt like a gull herself, hatched on a cliff's edge and raised by rocks.

The bairn mourned as if in answer to the gulls and she turned to where Agnes nursed it, all soothing sighs and coos. They exchanged glances and Agnes tried a smile which fell between them.

She had come into the undercroft later, to where Mintie hugged and rocked, knowing what happened and lying to herself that she had not come earlier because the bairn could not be left.

The truth was that she had come down right when Hutchie was grunting on her like a tup on a ewe; he had heard her, and for a moment her heart had almost stopped. She had been too afraid of Hutchie, knew that she might well have been where Mintie was, save that she was 'too milky' for his taste. When the babe slept and Hutchie was drinking and shouting with others, Agnes came with a bowl of hot water, which she knew Mintie would need.

It was not hot enough, nor was there scrub enough, but Mintie did it until Agnes caught her wrist and stopped her scraping herself to a raw wound.

The carriage had arrived in the night, a great grinding of wheels of the coach; there had been shouting and banging, and Mintie, as if through a slow-lifting fog, realised that the Laird now had his promised money and that Wharton would be moving the wee Queen south. Then he and the elder Wharton would proudly present the babe to Fat Henry, for the reward and advantage that would result.

Agnes argued for the inclusion of Mintie, thinking she was saving her from worse, not knowing that Hutchie Elliott would be coming with them; when Mintie saw him, smiling as if they were handfasted, the fire in her should have melted the ice-white teeth of him to blackened stubs.

Now she lurched in the rocking box with Agnes and the babe, hearing men curse as they levered the fat iron-rimmed wheels out of the slushed snow and mercilessly lashed the sweating Mecklenburg horses.

'This is too slow,' she heard someone complain.

'Then go faster,' Wharton snapped back.

He was past worried and galloping into frantic, Mintie thought. With the last kernel of her that cared, she had heard the mutterings from the men about reports of armed Scots coming down on Hermitage.

It would be the Regent, the Earl of Arran, equally frantic and sending what men he had to find out what had happened to the royal bairn and how she had come to be stolen so easily, and who had taken part in the ruse of a Ride that had assisted the abduction. The Armstrongs would be suspect at once, and sooner or later the Keeper's part in it would be unveiled. And slowly, slowly in the deep midwinter, an army would be gathered to wave at Fat Henry and demand redress and return.

So Wharton and his English wanted to be gone. There was not an Armstrong in the riders flanking the carriage, Mintie saw; they were all English retainers of the lords persuaded by Wharton to lend themselves to this enterprise for the reward in it, with no Name that mattered along the Border. She saw it through a dull veil and could not bring herself to care much.

Wharton, hag-ridden by the idea that matters might fail at the last, that the Scots forces, though hardly an army, could overtake them before they reached the safety of Carlisle and beyond, was gnawing his knuckles to the elbow joint.

He remembered his father on the day he had gone demanding – not asking – for money to pay for mercenaries to assist in the enterprise of stealing a queen. Scathe was one of the elder Wharton's many skills and he was free with it, even on his son.

'You are not stealing a Queen,' he had growled back. 'That will be done by others. You are merely sent to fetch her, boy. Any decent carter could achieve the same and at less expense.'

He had made it clear, too, the fate that failure would birth even for his son, and Wharton shivered at the memory of it, hoping folk took it for cold. The best thing his father had ever done for him, Wharton thought, was send him to Court in London, and despite a mountain of debt and a surety that he was poxed, Wharton never wanted anything more than to be back there now.

The appearance of the rider, stark against the mantled snow, made him blink and squint to see if it was real – he had a moment of panic at the idea of Faerie, for he had heard all the tales while lolling indolently at Hollows.

It was real. A man on a hipshot Galloway nag, sitting all unconcerned and doing… something.

Knitting, Wharton saw with astonishment. With only one arm.

A figure appeared at Wharton's elbow, and he turned to see the frowning face of Sir John Otley, his vein-threaded cheeks raw with cold and swaddled almost to the eyebrows.

'Who is that there?'

'I believe,' said Wharton as languidly as he could manage while his heart thumped, 'it is the one-armed man sought by the Lord of Hollows.'

'This?' Otley's scorn dripped like the ice melting off his furred collar. 'This is what the Hollows Man could not find or deal with?'

Behind him, William Patten looked uneasily left and right and saw only virgin snow. He was a sometime scholar and secretary to the Earl of Arundel and had been leant to Wharton to put some legal on the affairs at Hollows. The Hollows Man was a good name for the Armstrong chief, he thought, a big black spider who sat in his stone finger and wove webs, sucking dry anything he caught as if it would fill the void in him.

It would not fill such a void, of course, any more than whores and drink and gambling would fill the one inside the younger Wharton. Patten glanced at the man, seeing his fretting tension, and wanted to warn the youngster that things may not be as they seem; he had been around politics and armies enough to know that. He knew also that pointing it out was futile; these sneering well-born had already made clear what they thought of an 'ink-fingered clerk' and his opinion.

Patten was no soldier, but even he could see that the one-armed man was too calm, too at ease in the face of a score and more armed men. There had to be something more to it.

Batty was feeling good with the world, even though the bruising ache of his stumped arm, a memory of the dislocation, made knitting awkward and painful, and his leg thumped with pain after only a short ride. He had come out of Powrieburn with only a scratch on his cheek and had found two of his lost daggs on the bodies of Francie Bourne and Dand Ker, so half right was all good by his tallying.

Besides, he had all these English by the throat, even if they did not know it yet.

'What want you here?' demanded Otley, and Batty tucked his rickle of sticks and wool down the neck of his jack and smiled out of the raw scars on his face.

'To rise with the sun,' he said mildly. 'To enter the night.'

'You may have done the first,' Wharton retorted, 'but I doubt you will enjoy the second.'

Otley haw-hawed at that, and Wharton felt pleased with himself, but Batty's smile only broadened, thrusting up the knife of his beard.

'It is all up with this enterprise,' he said flatly. 'The Keeper is surely taken, the Earl of Arran is at Hermitage with an army, and if you do not hand the royal babe to me and go your way, you will hang for it. All of you.'

There was more lie and hope than truth in what he said, but Wharton did not know that, nor the men behind him, who started in to muttering; this one-armed man should not have known anything of the enterprise, never mind the whole of it. Wharton did not like the panic he felt. Yet it was a fat old man with one arm... what could he hope to achieve? He asked it aloud, and Batty nodded, as if it was a reasonable question requiring a sober answer.

'Well, I cannot fiddle a tune as I would like, nor clinch a woman proper in a jig, nor even lace a pair of brogues,' he admitted.

His voice dropped an octave, grew chilled as the air.

'But when I fill my only fist with pistol, my lord, I can shoot the cods from under a midge at two hundred paces.'

Wharton was blanched with respect, but Otley narrowed his eyes and sneered.

'Can you shoot a score and more with the one pistol?' he countered.

In the rear, Hutchie looked right and left, eyes narrowed, for he was the only one here who knew the Border way. The men who surrounded him looked formidable, with their metal breastplates and helms, long lances tipped to the weak sun. Two of them had matchlock guns, long affairs needing a forked iron rest to take the weight of the barrel. The rest had the English longbow, equally lethal and faster-firing too.

But Hutchie doubted that the muskets were primed and the slow matches were wrapped against the wet. The longbows were unstrung and coddled with wraps against the damp, while neither was any use from the back of a horse.

He shifted, using his legs alone to back the Galloway as far as he could, then began, gently and slowly, to rein it round. Those next to him scowled and one said something which Hutchie could not understand, the accent being thick and English.

In front, Batty seemed to consider Otley's question seriously, then patted the two loaded holsters in front of him.

'I have three,' he pointed out, and Otley laughed, though it was uneasy now.

'Besides,' Batty declared with a lofty wave of his hand, 'I have these also.'

There was a sharp crack, like a branch breaking under too much weight of snow. Next to Hutchie, a man's horse staggered, gave a squealing grunt as if it had been kicked in the belly by its neighbour – then fell sideways, clattering into two others.

More cracks, almost at once; men and horses spilled, the column shattered into mad plunging, rearing and shouting. Hutchie dragged his mount's head full round and raked it with his heels, while something vengeful whoomed past him and hit on the breastplate of a bewildered rider with a dull whang of sound, knocking him clean out of the saddle.

Batty filled his fist with pistol, while Wharton and Otley and the others at the head of the column looked frantically right and left, in time to see the pristine snow erupt. On signal, as the hidden caliver-men in the trees opened fire, the shrouded Grahams burst from their snowholes, roaring heat into them and cold stiffness out.

They stumbled and leaped down on the chaos of Englishmen, slashing and shrieking. Wharton saw one spring entirely off the ground, smack into a rider and knock them all over, horse included, in a whirl of legs and arms.

Otley dragged out his sword, waving and shouting, but Patten levered himself off his mount and stumbled to the lee of the carriage, knowing what these men had come for and that the carriage was the safest place to be – there would be no shooting or fighting near the royal babe.

Batty saw Hutchie, a fleeting glimpse through the throng.

What he had said to Wharton had not been entirely true – he could not play the fiddle at all, and when he took a woman by the waist, one-handed or not, he was fairly sure of the dance by that point. Nor was he as good a shot with a pistol as he had made out. If he wanted to hit a midgie's cods, it had to be only one hundred paces away – but he could hit the broad running back of Hutchie Elliott with his eyes closed.

He fired, the wheel whirred reassuring sparks, the pan flared into smoking life – and the man called Otley surged into the line of it, waving his ridiculously feeble court rapier and yelling, until the fat lead ball blew his head to shards of bone, blood and brain.

Cursing, Batty stuffed the smoker in his belt, feeling the barrel burn as he hauled out another from the saddle holsters. The horse he rode was not the Saul, all the same, who would not turn a chin hair at the sight and sound of blasting powder;

it stamped and snorted and shifted so that the second shot went into the pack, and if it hit anyone at all, Batty did not know of it.

It did not hit Hutchie, that was certain, for Batty saw him, leaning low on the horse's neck and flogging it unmercifully through the gripping snow, heading back to Hollows.

Wharton, dazed and afraid, finally thought of hauling out his own sword, only to end up gazing down the barrel of Batty's third pistol.

'Eighty-four,' Batty said with an evil smile. 'Knock or draw.'

There was a little white needle and something grey-slimed lodged on Wharton's sleeve – he saw with a sickening lurch that it was Otley's bone and brains. With that part of his mind not still gibbering, Wharton realised the one-armed man was quoting Primero – eighty-four was a massive overstated boast of what points he might hold in his hand, and he was inviting Wharton to challenge or throw in his hand.

Wharton threw in and then threw up.

Will Elliot was on foot and shivering stiff from hiding in the snow – Christ, how did these half dressed Grahams manage that so easily? He let them leap and shriek and do their work, wanting no part of it and trying not to look or listen to the bloody screams. They would hold their killing hand from Armstrongs, but these were English and all English could be slain, in the worst ways possible; Will could hear that the Grahams knew some of the worst ways.

He made for the carriage just as the driver was dragged off, bleating. The mad grinning Graham who did it worked his arm like a forgeman at the bellows and the blood flew up in gobbets; the whole area around was clotted with red, stark against the snow.

Someone wept from inside the sprung-boxed affair, and Will shouldered aside the man who was making for the sound, scowling at him until Davey-boy, all fired eyes and blood lust, blinked some sane recognition and grinned like a fox in a coop, before darting off to collect a horse. The looting had begun.

Will wrenched open the carriage door and the whimpering grew to a shriek. He saw the man who made it, hunched on the floor and covering his head with his hands. Agnes, holding a bundle close to her, looked defiant, and with a lurch of relief Will saw Mintie sitting beside her.

'They are here,' he bawled. 'Safe and sound... Shut up, you.'

The last reduced the whimpering man to sobs.

Batty rode up, leaning down from the saddle to peer in, his lean creased face taking in what he saw. Will dragged the sobbing man out and the sight of the bloody slush finally choked all sound from him, so that he lay in it and shivered.

'Mintie,' he said, nodding. 'Agnes.'

He tapped his iron hat with the barrel of the dagg, knuckling his forehead politely as if they had well met on a pleasant winter ride.

'That's mine,' Mintie said suddenly, seeing Davey-boy leading a horse, and Batty saw that Dickon's son had Jaunty, probably tethered at the rear of the carriage.

'Off,' he said companionably, and for a moment it looked as if the boy would defy him — but then he scowled sullenly, slid off the back of it and tossed the reins contemptuously up at Batty.

'There,' Batty said easily, smiling at Mintie. 'All is rescued.'

It was then he saw her eyes, sunk deep in her face and the light in them no more than wary creatures peering from caves. He saw the blood on her dress and cut laces and the way she held herself, and knew, with a lightning stab from crown to heel, what had happened to her and who had done it.

Mintie saw that he knew. He can tell just by looking, she thought, how ruined I am.

And the tears came at last.

They left the English, stripped to the marbled flesh and lip-gaping wounds, for the Armstrongs to find once Hutchie had stumbled back and gasped it all out. Not one of the soldiers was alive.

They left the fancy foundered coach and the whimpering man called Patten, his piss freezing his breeches to him as he curled up in it, but they took the big Mecklenburg horses, for Davey-boy had taken a fancy to them. Patten would, once unfurled from his fear, tell what had happened after Hutchie had run off.

Wharton, whey-faced, shivering and with slime all down his front, was eventually led away from staring at what had been Sir John Otley and joined Hen Graham and the Armstrong prisoners taken at Powrieburn; they would be huckled back to Netherby. Dickon would usher Wharton politely on to his da, which would be as much punishment as beating him unmercifully for a week.

So they came down on Andrascroft, much to the alarm of a band of travelling folk, Egyptianis as they called themselves. There were six wagons and a cart, six men, four women, innumerable weans and even more dogs. Their leader called himself Seb Bailzow and styled himself, with an elaborate scarlet and green bow, Count of Cipre.

No one cared for the Egyptianis much and the feeling was mutual – in some parts of Scotland you could be hung just for being one. Yet the late king had favoured one of them, a certain Johnnie Faa, with a Writ of Protection – and they were in the Debatable, which had no law, so their safety depended on how useful they were.

Dickon was minded to be generous while Andra and Eck fixed the cracked shaft of one of their wagons. Davey-boy had barebacked one of his new prizes and had tired of the Mecklenburgs even on the short ride to Andrascroft; his da, Will Elliot saw, was pleased about that.

'By God,' Dickon exclaimed when Davey-boy announced he had traded with the Egyptianis, 'I am glad of that, for you looked like a pea on a four-legged marrow. There is nothing so useless as a big-arsed horse with shod feet in this country.'

Then he eyed the boy gravely and asked what he had traded it for. Davey-boy presented the caliver with a flourish, and even Will had to admit that it was a fine-looking gun, all silver and ivory inlay from muzzle to stock.

'Christ's bones,' Dickon had exclaimed with wonder, 'yon is a fearsome engine. A lord's gun, no doubt of it.'

Snaffled from the ruin of Solway Moss, Will Elliot thought to himself, by clever folk with an eye to such a business and timing their arrival to perfection, so that they could plunder the litter of discarded arms without fear of becoming prey themselves.

It was certainly a lord's gun, possibly Turk to begin with, and if the lord ever set eyes on it again it would no doubt go badly for the new owner, if only because the lord had thrown it away and so it glared proof of his cowardice. But Davey-boy was beaming, and even though his da distrusted guns, in common with other Border folk, he was pleased that the boy had bartered with Egyptianis and come out of it well.

Batty never saw much of the Count of Cipre and his brood, being too busy leading a stumbling Mintie to a warm place near the forge where she could rest. Then he drew Agnes aside and asked what she knew he would ask. She told him, rocking the bairn as much to comfort herself as it, and watched his face grow into something that made her shrink.

Then he nodded and unsaddled Jaunty and the horse he had borrowed, groomed them, fed them, and told Will and Dickon that Mintie would rest here the night and go on to Powrieburn in the morning. He did not say why, but everyone saw the face on him and thought he had blood in his eye and kept quiet.

Dickon wanted to be away back to Netherby, for this was too close to Hollows, who might take vengeance when they woke up to matters – but one of the Egyptianis was a rare exponent of the fiddle and so he decided to stay and listen a while; they could ride well enough in the dark, and some would stay to escort Will, Agnes and the bairn to Hermitage.

Batty sat and brooded while men jigged, and all the time Agnes watched, joggling the bairn in her arms while matters were sorted out all around her.

Like a slow match, she thought, as she watched Batty. Burning down…

Bella knew what had happened and folded Mintie and her daughter into her as if into a down coverlet, stripping Mintie of the stained clothing and burning all of it, for she knew Mintie would never wear it again. She left a dress of her own, which though faded and patched was at least clean; Agnes knew it was one of the only two she owned and the other was already on her back.

In the end, soothed and balmed and wrapped, Mintie slept despite the wild music and the wheeching, while Agnes looked at the bruise of shadows under her eyes and wondered if what had happened would break her friend, or whether she had true iron in her.

Will Elliot knew too, in the end – or at least suspected it from the way everyone behaved. He did not ask, merely spoke fact to Batty, softly where none but the pair of them could hear – he would ride with some of the Grahams to Hermitage in the morning and hand the babe back to the men he hoped were gathered there. If they were not there, they would ride on to Edinburgh, for he would not hand the babe to the Keeper for any reward.

Nor would the Keeper interfere, Will knew, for Hen Graham was held and he was the witness to his treachery. The Grahams would not want Hen strung up, for he was kin, and that bond would not be broken just because he was a sly wee conniver. Besides, they had the Keeper of Hermitage by the cods and would squeeze coin and favour from him as long as Hen lived.

The Keeper would know his plans were all scattered. He would welcome the Grahams, his Land Sergeant and the returned wee Queen as if he had planned it all, playing out the mummery for all his life's worth.

Which it was, Batty was sure. Some kin or bribed lady's maid in Falkland Palace had almost certainly spirited the babe away when it was being hastily moved for safety against the great band of raiders who had appeared so close to the capital. The Laird and his well-horsed Armstrongs, of course, making noise and flame to order.

Later, the Grahams, not having had nearly enough drink to make them reel, climbed back on their nags and prepared to head off into the dark. Those remaining chaffered loudly about how they were not having to leave this good music and warmth to plooter about in the wet dark.

'You will have to return her,' Will said softly to Agnes, as the music skirled, and Agnes sighed, for she had known it all along. The babe had done enough, all the same, to balm the loss of her Eck. There would be other babes... She thought of Mintie then, and the sweetness that had been soured from her by Hutchie.

Men are swine, she thought, feeling her own man's comforting weight slide into the bed. He was too tired from having struggled with the wagon wheel to do more than grunt a welcome back, and Agnes, exhausted by events, slid off to sleep listening to the babe stir and mutter beside her.

When she woke into the dim and clatter of a new day, she blinked and looked and blinked again. Her heart stopped.

The bairn had gone.

Chapter Nine

The Debatable Land
The next morning

Christ in Heaven, Will thought frantically, they could have gone anywhere. He was aware of the men at his back, waiting patiently for his orders, could feel the sick heat of the burning peat on the lance tip, signifying that this was a perjink, organised hot trod in pursuit of felons.

It was a jest, of course, to have a hot trod riding out of the lawless Debatable into an England they were at war with, and led by the Land Sergeant of Hermitage, but it gave some semblance of legality to what was a frantic bloodhound of a chase.

Pursuing phantoms, it seemed, for the Count of Cipre had vanished.

'It must be him as took her,' Will had argued, when Agnes had come shrieking out of her smoky hole of a cruck house, ashen-faced husband in her wake. Batty could only agree, though it crossed his mind that Dickon and the Grahams might have taken the babe, for the chance at profit.

But they had left men to escort the wee Queen and Will back to Hermitage, which seemed a strange thing to do if you had lifted the said Queen in the night. Besides, Batty thought, they are not so daft as to cross the Regent and the Dowager Queen Mary of Guise.

'They have Wharton with them,' Will pointed out, keeping his voice low and away from Graham ears. 'They might do a deal with him yet, hand over the babe and take more of Fat Henry's siller.'

That was all very possible, Batty had to agree – save for the presence of Davey-boy in the escort party, proudly showing off his new gun he had already shot twice that morning, scaring horses and geese.

'Dickon would never put his golden boy in such danger,' Batty pointed out, and Will was forced to agree, tearing off his hat and rubbing his shaggy head with frustration.

'Curse it,' he said vehemently. 'It must be the Egyptianis, then. Stealing bairns is what they do.'

Trading is what they do, Batty thought. Stealing is what they enjoy, and bairns is the least of it. Yet you would not steal one unless you had a market for it.

'There is hardly a bairn-fair, same as for horses,' Will scathed. 'Christ, if they find out it is the wee Queen of Scots...'

'Mayhap it would have been better if they had known that from the start,' Batty growled. 'They might have been circumspect about lifting it.'

Will, whose idea it had been to make no mention of the bairn in their presence, recognised the truth of that and scrubbed his head again, adding another gilt-stripping oath. Then he straightened.

'Well, there is nothing for it but a trod. We will fetch some burning peat from the fire and bind it to a lance and be off.'

'Good luck with that, then,' Batty said mildly. 'I would head for Carlisle – I surmise that is the most likely route for horse-copers like them. They will be headed down to Stow's fair. It's a long way and they have to reach it before May.'

Alarmed, Will looked at him. 'You are coming?'

Batty shook his head, his beard quivering.

'I will take the lass back to Powrieburn. Then I will go on to Hermitage and lie to the Regent on how the babe is safe enough, if not quite in our hands.'

'Christ,' moaned Will, remembering that part of matters with a lurch that sank his stomach to his knees. 'The Regent...'

He had seen the wisdom of that, even as he had dreaded a hot trod with strange Grahams at his back and no Batty to at least provide some measure of kinship. Some time later, his back felt more exposed than ever, for he had no idea, among all the cart ruts of the crossroads, which belonged to whom.

'They have split up,' one of the Grahams noted, though Will had already seen that and thought it little help.

'They have signs,' another declared. 'The Egyptianis have signs that tell others of their like where they are headed. A mark on a tree,' he added helpfully, 'or a stem broken in a particular way.'

'Can you read such signs?' demanded Will sourly and knew the answer before the huffed silence revealed it.

'On,' he declared, as firmly as if he had spotted something they had not, which was a lie. He hunched up his shoulders against the stares at his back and led them down the wet mourn of road towards Carlisle, already sick with the certainty that they had lost the Queen of Scots.

Carlisle

Conversion of St Paul (25 January)

Sebastiane, Count of Cipre, vanished somewhere along the road to Carlisle, climbing into the back of the lurching cart as a scarlet and green mountebank with red hair and coming back out as a sober perjink and slightly damp drover with black hair and a plain jerkin.

His wife, the magnificently named Amberline – Lena for short – lost her hooped earrings and garish clothes to become plain Jean Gordon, which was her real name anyway. Her hennaed hair vanished under a proper kertch and the pair of them, with a brace of other carts, women, weans and anxious men, came down to Carlisle's Scotch Gate with all hope for a deal of money.

The babe, as Seb said often enough on the trip, was all luck. Last year, he and others had got drunk with a mason, a German who had come with Master Stefan von Haschenperg to rebuild the Citadel of Carlisle for Fat Henry, adding a new half-moon battery. The work was almost done and the German, Stahlmann, would be going home to Cologne with his wife sometime soon.

She had come with her husband so as not to waste a moment in trying for a child of their own. Trying and failing.

'I need a child,' Stahlmann had confessed, 'for I fear my wife is barren and will never have one on her own. Since we are leaving it will excite no curiosity if we suddenly appear back home in Cologne with a child. With no disease and who will not be missed. A girl child for preference...'

Seb had his own ideas on which of the pair was barren – Stahlmann the mason was a thin, dry stick of a man who drank too much – but the German was well stipended for his skills and could afford to pay what was asked; the deal had been done then and there.

Seb and Jean had thought it would take at least nine months and had assiduously sold the charms of their own daughter, Kezia, to anyone who would buy. Seb had even sacrificed a few nights on her, though Jean had thoughts of her own on that.

'It will not sell if it comes out drooling daft or has three eyes,' she growled and he took the hint and stopped.

Kezia, thirteen and wayward, had stayed stubbornly unconcerned by weans all the same, so the arrival of a perfect wee girl child right under Seb's eager nose had been sent by God, clearly; it had been the easiest of matters to lift the bairn and be off, scattering carts left and right to fool pursuit. They would all meet up down at Stow-in-the-Wold for St Edward's Horse Fair and everyone would get their share.

Once inside Carlisle, Seb sent Jean with the good news and she came back, frowning.

'He seems less sure than he did,' she reported and Seb dismissed that with a wave of one hand.

'I will tell you how this will happen,' he declared. 'The wee mason and his wife will have the goods examined – only right and proper, after all, as you would a decent horse. But they will have milk or a wet nurse and wee geegaws for it to play with, for all their seeming change of heart. It will take ten minutes, mark me – they will not want us once the deed is done.'

The next day they took the child through the thronged streets to the home of the mason. At the door, before knocking, Seb asked if the bairn was clean.

'Aye,' Jean replied and frowned again. 'She is an uncommon beautiful wean to belong to a plain-faced wee besom like the lass at yon forge – and nurse-fed, so that she won't take to anything but a breast. And these cloths in the cradle are yellow silk and fine wool.'

'Then the mason and his wife will be doubly happy that we have taken so much trouble and expense,' Seb answered and chucked the babe's fat wee chin.

'She's our golden bairn,' he cooed and had back a gurgle and what might have been a smile.

The mason and his wife lived in a rented house, very fine but with nothing of a home in it. He welcomed Seb and Jean with the air of an old friend, effusive and polite though none of it hid the sweat on his forehead. The wife, a buxom Dutch piece, Seb thought, looked even worse, all waxed pallor and hand-wringing.

They had brought a physicker, a sober-suited auld yin called Ridley who tried to be superior and had that knocked out of him by Seb's growl; if the ancient reprobate was involved in this, then he was scarcely an upright citizen.

The Dutch wife chewed her fingernails and apologised for the state of the place, which looked to Seb as such places always looked – unnaturally neat and clean coffins.

'You should have allowed us more notice,' she said and Jean simply presented the basket; for all her alleged surprise, the

Dutch Goodwife was all ready with blankets and shawls, just as Seb had predicted. Right down to a rattle.

'It would be better if you did not raise your hopes so high,' the physicker declared pompously, sniffing down his nose at Seb and Jean. 'The chances of this being undamaged or without trace of sickness are slight.'

'Ach, away,' Seb growled. 'See for yourself.'

The physicker fell to poking and probing and peering through spectacles on a stick, while Seb spun a magnificent, dazzling web of lies about how the babe came from a fine family, hinting at a great lady and a doomed love affair with one of the handsome Egyptianis, with this babe as the result. It had been the plot of a play he had seen once at Appleby Fair, but he found he was talking to himself in the end, for all attention was on the physicker and the bairn.

She was right as new rain when the old man listened to her breathing, but fretted when he stuck things in her ears and tried to measure the spacing of eyes, mouth and nose. The physicker looked in the babe's mouth, felt the belly, examined the bud of a cunny and then exclaimed when a small fountain of piss came up. He dabbed a finger in it and tasted.

'As clear and fine as I am sure my own was once,' he exclaimed joyfully. 'Alas, I fear that has been much tainted since.'

He turned to the mason and declared the infant not only well but near perfect and much cared for.

'Did we not say?' Seb declared, then beamed at the mason. 'Well done – you're a father.'

The physicker was on the point of asking about the yellow silk and expensive wool blanket, but the babe started in to wailing with lusty vengeance, while the mason splashed wine in goblets and passed them round, gulping and grinning at the same time. His wife, unsmiling, sipped and stared at the babe.

Seb and Jean stayed for a quick swallow or two, took their money and left. The physicker took his fee shortly after and also left. The mason and his wife looked at the bairn.

'It's a good sign,' the mason declared, more in hope than sound judgement. 'A noisy babe is a healthy babe.'

'Suddenly an expert you are,' his wife declared and put her hands over her ears.

'It will need fed,' he suggested and she shook her head.

'I am too afraid to pick it up.'

The mason did, awkward and afraid, tried to feed the bairn from a clay bottle with a sheep-gut nipple, as you did with calves, he had been told. The baby spluttered milk everywhere.

'It will not drink,' his wife said, alarmed and the babe wailed.

'It will have been breast-fed,' the mason offered. 'It needs to become used to this way – you should have hired that wet nurse, as we agreed.'

His wife bridled.

'She was asking too much – besides, we are leaving in two days and she would not travel, as you know. And would have talked, besides, about where this babe came from. So it was pointless.'

The babe wailed, hungry and in need of changing. The mason tried, but the wife would not. Exasperated, he turned to her.

'This child cost a fortune. If you are going to care for it, as you so often wished, you will have to at least make an effort, *schatzi.*'

'I never wanted it,' she declared sullenly and winced at the noise. 'Make it stop.'

'Never wanted...'

The mason could not go on, struck near senseless for a moment. Then he recovered himself.

'You have spoken of little else for months. I wish I had a child. I wish I had a little girl of my own...'

'Of my own,' she said and began to cry. 'Mine. Ours. Not someone else's.'

The sick realisation of it hit the mason then and he went pale and sat heavily, listening to the bairn roar and his wife weep, thinking of the monstrous expense and wondering what in the name of God they did now.

Hollows Tower
At the same time

The Laird looked at them with a watery and wandering eye, his face sheened with sweat despite the chill, in a hall grey-dim with smoke and bad light, where the stone dust drifted like distant diamonds.

'You are sure, wife?' he demanded, and the Lady tapped an impatient foot, while Leckie the steward folded fat fingers over his paunch and smiled blandly.

'Bella came to Leckie last night, wondering if we needed more fowl now that the English were gone,' his wife said urgently. 'She told of it — her visit was no more than a ploy to find out if her Agnes was in trouble with Hollows, since she was holding the babe when the Grahams struck.'

Gone, the Laird thought. There is understatement. The English were gone right enough — all the way to Hell. The road from Hollows was littered with stripped corpses, bluing and rotting in the iced rain until the men he sent buried them as decent as possible.

A score were dead at least. More yet from the failed endeavour at Powrieburn. The young Wharton taken. An English lord slain. The babe taken and Fat Henry's wee clerk of an envoy shivering in his piss-stained hose. The truth of the enterprise now out and dangling like a swinging corpse on a gibbet for all to see.

It was all a huge festering cesspit of no good, and he knew who was to blame for it.

'Not the Grahams,' he growled, feeling the sick wine-roil of his belly. 'Batty Coalhouse.'

His wife dismissed that with an angry flap of a hand.

'Leave Coalhouse. The babe was taken from them, d'you hear. They do not have her. We do not have her. Egyptianis have been mentioned and Carlisle spoken of as a likely place.'

The Laird nodded owlishly and seemed lost for a moment. English Armstrongs had gone off, south and west, with the plunder they had taken, and though it had eased the cost and discomfort round Hollows, it left the place light in men if revenge came. He had counted on there being little revenge from the Scott of Buccleuch, whose lands had been worst affected, and if it came at all, it would not be in the depths of bad weather. Now he was not so sure.

The Lady watched him and wondered; she was scouring the whores out of Hollows, but at least two had been 'retained' in some capacity and by order of her husband. She did not care for the implications of that, nor for his increasing use of the goblet; she sighed with relief as he slapped a hand on the table, belched and then squinted at Leckie.

'Men,' he said. 'For Carlisle. Find the babe and bring it back here.'

Leckie nodded, having already arranged it beforehand on the orders of the Lady; the Laird knew that and was not as foxed as either his wife or his steward imagined. Nor did he like the alliance between them, seemingly against himself.

He paused a moment as a thought struck him, then cackled out a rook's laugh.

'Hutchie Elliott can go – Leckie, you will lead. Tell Hutchie if he values living he will exert his utmost to succeed in it.'

'He will most probably run,' Leckie advised carefully, alarmed at the prospect of riding anywhere in this weather, never mind armed to the teeth and with similar growlers at his back. The Laird shook his head and tapped the side of his nose.

'No, not him. He fears Batty Coalhouse if he leaves the protection of Armstrong men. And he fears me if he stays. Who do you think he fears most, eh, Leckie?'

He cackled again and looked pointedly at his wife, then at Leckie.

'Who do you fear most, Leckie?'

His wife looked sourly at him.

'We will find out,' she said.

The physicker was in a scramble when the door was pounded. He was also in Ganny, and so near that point of whimpering release that he had started to babble about love and white marble, as he always did; the thunderous noise jerked him out of his trance and out of Ganny.

'Christ, Christ – we are undone.'

'You are undone,' the boy declared viciously, and hauled up his hose. 'Do yourself up – I will answer it.'

'No, no,' the physicker wailed, clawing his hose up and trying to find his fat breeches. 'Wait, wait – oh God—'

His head was full of fire and hot irons, for the physicker was not a man of the medical – though he knew some aspects of it – but a priest from a dissolved priory far to the south. Father Ridley of St Mary Merton in Surrey had been looked on askance at the best of times, for his 'unhealthy' interest in cutting up perfectly good small animals before they reached the pot, 'just to see how they worked', and brewing up potions, ostensibly for use in treating the sick.

That would have been bad enough when the hordes fell on St Mary Merton with hard words, torches and sticks. But Father Ridley had another weakness, and Ganny was spirited away before the full wrath of the Suppression Act consigned them both to a pyre.

Now, at last, he was sure they had been found out, was trembling and trying to be brave when Ganny came back, his arms full of basket and his beautiful face full of frown.

'Don't,' Father Ridley said automatically. He loved the beauty of Ganny, his Ganymede, and had run off with him when the boy was eight. Ganny could not remember another name now and three years had not yet ripened the delicate beauty into the harsh beard and sinew of youth that Father Ridley knew, sadly, would turn him to pastures new.

'A babe,' Ganny said in his pipe of accent, his voice full of wonder. 'A man pushed it at me and babbled something about not wanting it, then hared off down the Shambles like a cat with a burning tail.'

Ridley blinked once or twice, stared at the basket, then back at Ganny as if the boy had performed some marvellous trick.

He looked so ludicrous, standing with the failing remains of his erection poking beneath the shirt, his hose puddled round his ankles, that Ganny laughed.

Snapped, Ridley darted to the basket, and the familiar babe gurgled at him, then started to wail.

'Christ in Heaven, no, no,' Ridley said and snatched the basket, darting for the door, half falling over his hose and realising what he was about to do. Appalled, he dropped the basket and the babe screamed. Ganny collected it, scowling blackly at Ridley.

'Oh Christ, fuckpishshit,' Ridley said, hauling up his hose and hopping. He would run back to the German and give him babe and a piece of his mind – by God, the man and his wife were leaving this day, mayhap they had already gone…

In a fever, he was struggling into his breeches, the babe wailing and screaming, when the thought struck him that the last thing he wanted to be seen doing was rushing through the streets with a babe in a basket. Especially one that was wailing – though that, mercifully, had ceased enough to let him think…

The wailing had ceased.

Ridley whirled to where Ganny, bouncing the creature gently in his arms, was feeding it from a contraption of bottle and gut nipple. He stared, open-mouthed, at this apparition.

'She was only hungered,' Ganny declared, then looked at the babe fondly. 'Weren't you, little 'un. Just hungered. Well, by God, you will think your ma has the biggest dugs in Christendom by the time you have sucked all this milk up.'

Ridley stared.

'Where did you learn this?' he demanded and Ganny scowled.

'Don't,' Ridley pleaded. 'It will leave a mark.'

'I had four sisters and two brothers, all younger than me. Two were babes no older than this.'

And your ma was less of a Goodwife and more of a whore, Ridley recalled, while your da was a drunk – so the task would fall to you, even at that tender age.

He sat down suddenly, realising that it was all too late to go after the German and that somehow he and Ganny had been stuck with a baby. He looked at Ganny, cooing away, and knew the boy had been struck by the child; jealousy rose in him, even when he knew how foolish it was.

They would flee north where priests were less hunted. He wondered if he could get rid of the creature on the way without upsetting Ganny...

Chapter Ten

The courtyard was the same, without the bodies nor the blood, and the rain lisped down from a pewter sky as cold as a witch's tit. The earth was a manged dog, leprous and mottled with mud and patched snow, the trees clumped and bare as poor hair; along the gills and burns the reeds whispered, and the willows clacked bare branches like wry applause.

The bastel door had been patched, Batty saw, though it would need replacing in full and by more expert hands if it was to resist another battering. The rooks were the same as before, rising and smoking through the damp air, rasping away.

No dog, he saw and felt sadness for the loss. It was not the only one and Batty wondered if a month would have balmed her much.

Bet's Annie came out, all shawl and folded-arm grim. Her nod was welcoming but lacked smile; men are not liked in Powrieburn now, Batty thought, and his heart sank. Not balmed at all, then...

'She is fetching fodder,' she said, nodding towards the store and then hesitated as Batty levered himself off the horse; she took the reins with a sudden gesture, as if ashamed of her previous lack of smile.

'Be easy with her,' she said, leading Batty's horse into the comfort of the undercroft; later Batty would go in and murmur to the Saul, but for now...

For now there was Mintie and her summons. Batty did not think she wanted the borrowed horse back so badly, or to insist the Saul be removed from eating Powrieburn's winter feed.

The store was solid drystone capped with a thatched roof weighted with rope and flat, heavy rings of stone. Inside, it smelled of summer, and Batty stilled in the dim of it, to allow his eyes to catch up and just to breathe it in.

Meadow hay, he thought, with wildflowers and clover in it, cut from a field that had never seen a plough. It was a marvel to him, thrawn cynic that he was, that it was still here at all, that the grizzled, dark-souled reivers could smoke folk from a house like shelling crabs, slaughter them, steal all the livestock they possessed, and all the goods they could lay hands on – and yet not burn winter feed.

For the loss of winter feed was sure death to beasts, and beasts was what everyone depended on. What everyone stole from each other.

Mintie, in the dark recesses of the place, heard him and felt a rise of panic which she quelled savagely. It had been recent, her return to the world, and she knew the day and hour when she had woken to the urgency to tend to Powrieburn, unveiled as if from some dream. Yet her new resolve wavered in the face of Batty, that seamed, bearded face; smiling or not, it was a man.

'Mintie,' he said with a nod, and she speared the fork into the hay and then stopped to push a stray wisp of hair back under her kertch, wondering what to say, where to begin…

'Master Coalhouse,' she said. 'You went without your five pounds English.'

'Hardly earned,' he replied levelly. 'Since the Fyrebrande is still in the Laird's stable and…'

He stopped, not wanting to mention Hutchie Elliott, but the omission was loud as a shout.

Mintie felt the blood thunder up in her ears, a rush of sound like pouring water. Suddenly she was back in Hollows, feeling him, feeling the pain of him, seeing the pewter medallion swinging back and forth, back and forth…

The pain. She had not felt it then, so why now? Was it a memory she had buried? A memory of a memory? A fable – had there been pain at all? Had it been, God forbid, a pleasure for her? That was the only way you could get a child, she had been told. If you fetched off. She knew the feeling, had experienced it the first time riding bareback on Jaunty in the blaze of a summer sun pouring on her skin like honey. She had felt it since, using her sinful fingers. She knew the difference – had she felt that at Hollows and buried it?

Batty's hand touched her shoulder, that old reassuring gesture – but she twisted away from it and stepped back, so that it fell limply between them. The sadness in his face then made her ashamed, want to explain.

'I didn't…' she began and then stopped. Didn't what – fight hard enough? She had not fought at all, she had grovelled and begged.

'I am not offended,' he lied, and she blinked back into his concerned face.

'Lose it,' he said suddenly, urgently. 'Lose it or he will have his way with you every day for the rest of your life, Mintie. Put it behind you and get back into your life—'

'I am with child.'

The words clattered out like china falling on cobbles. There was silence, broken only by their breathing, the smoke of it mingling and vanishing.

'Is that why you called me?'

She was surprised; he had not asked – as everyone else had asked – if she was sure. She was sure, as sure as when she felt any other black humour descend on her, from winter snotters to summer chills. Something dark was in her and she was sick with it.

He saw it in her face, waited for her answer.

'The road is dangerous alone, I am told, so you must take me to the Solway Coast,' she said, tilting a defiant chin, an echo of the old Mintie returned enough to make his heart glad even as the request settled coldly in him like sea haar.

'To where?' he asked, though he knew most of it already.

'There is a woman there, near Graitna...'

Her voice fell away, and he looked at her until she dropped her eyes. He remembered other times, when women in the camps had come to his ma with similar requests. He remembered what they had looked like after, all drawn and sunken-eyed and sick; one, he knew, had gone mad and hanged herself, the loss being too much to bear. More than one had died of fevers afterwards.

He said as much, harsh as a metal file, and watched her flinch, then right herself and come back on the same gait.

'Will you go with me?'

Her voice was defiant, filled with the implication that she would go anyway, but she had called him all the way here from Berwick, him in particular, and not just because of the protection he would offer on such a journey.

Will Elliot would have done it, he knew. He had met Will only a week ago, found him sitting in Berwick's Old Brig Tavern one day when he had lurched in to fill his one fist with more drink, as he had done since the day he had quit Powrieburn and the whole festering boil of Liddesdale.

The aftermath of everything had seemed unreal, a calm as sudden as the storms that had swept everyone. Will had arrived back empty-handed, the trail of babe and Egyptianis gone cold. The Regent had not been happy, but had decided on silence, decided to wait for the inevitable haughty announcement from Fat Henry that wee Queen Mary was in his hands and about to be wed to his Prince Edward and they could like it or lump it.

Nothing had come; and even allowing for delays and deliberations, the time was stretching to where the Regent was beginning to wonder – and the fretting mother, Dowager Queen Mary of Guise, was growing less inclined to be politically patient and more inclined to start howling to her French relations about kidnap, murder and the ineptitude of Scotland's nobility.

Will had suffered a lot of that, passed down from on high. He had been glad to escape from under it, if only into the scowl of Batty Coalhouse.

'What news, then?' Batty had asked heavily, after a suitable ritual of buying and tasting in a quiet corner. The Old Brig Tavern was a favourite with the drovers, an evil-smelling bunch of hard drinkers reeking of woodsmoke and wildness – yet carved above the fireplace were the words 'Wisdom and science which are pure by kind, Should not be writ in books but in mind', and that hint of fineness in a place like the Old Brig gave Batty pleasure.

'The Fair Earl is fled,' Will reported laconically. 'Only to Bothwell, mind, where he is trying to avoid being looked at too closely by the Regent and the Auld Queen.'

Batty merely nodded as if he had known that. Hepburn, Keeper of Liddesdale and Earl of Bothwell, had always been a byword for treachery. 'Fair Earl' had been given to him for his looks, all golden and handsome, though they had faded ever since he had been imprisoned for two years back in 1529 for 'harbouring robbers'. He was hot for Fat Henry – or his money, at least – which did not prevent him being the scourge of Reformist preachers, for he was a fierce Catholic.

He was also a cunning political and knew when to lower his gaze and his head.

'Which leaves Hermitage and Liddesdale in your charge,' Batty noted shrewdly, and Will shook his head moodily.

'Scarcely. Maxwell is in the Regent's bad books as another of Fat Henry's friends, so he isn't permitted in Hermitage lest he fortifies it for himself. Scott of Buccleuch may get it, but not yet. So it is left to me for now.'

'I would have thought you would relish this,' Batty said, squinting at him. 'A rise in station, no less.'

'Until they appoint another,' Will answered shortly. 'Wicked Wat Scott of Buccleuch, no doubt – the Scotts are growling for it, so that they can be all legal when they visit revenge on the Armstrongs for what the Hollows Laird did to them.'

Batty had heard that the Armstrong Ride to scare the court into moving the bairn – and allowing it to be more easily stolen – had fallen hardest on the Scotts. The Laird of Hollows, unable to pass up the chance to swipe at old enemies, had burned a deal of them out and stolen horses and cattle. Yet the reiving in that was an old tale, which the Scotts would revisit on Hollows and its dependants in turn when they could. So the world turned, ordered by God and the Devil in tandem.

'No matter who takes the seat, it will be all up with me – who wants a Land Sergeant prepared to turn on his Keeper?'

Batty had no answer to the truth of that and so said nothing and supped instead.

'Every time one looks at me they will see those bodies everywhere,' Will added, his eyes back on that snowy road with Wharton's men scattered like winnowed stooks, the Grahams dragging shirts and boots off them. Some had not been properly dead, but were not even given the grace of a knife. All had been left to freeze, including the English lord, Otley.

'Just so,' Batty agreed with a dismissive wave. 'Hard times and only a wee lick of what will come in the spring, when Fat Henry turns his army north. Which he will do, even in the teeth of the French threatening invasion in the south. He hates the Scots even more than before, which is a considerable feat we have achieved.'

Silence closed them off like a yett.

'How is the lass?' Batty asked eventually, and Will shook his head.

'Sore, in mind and body. Hutchie Elliott broke into her and broke something in her, that's sure. She will not speak to any man now, let alone one with that cursed surname, no matter the spelling.'

'You have tried,' Batty answered, and it was less a question and more a bleak, sad statement of fact. It spilled from Will then, like rot. How he had gone and fetched and carried, tended livestock and repaired the door, all in the hope of seeing her, of soothing her. But she would not speak nor stir to even look.

Hutchie was with the Laird of Hollows, the pair of them still untouched and now untouchable, since the Regent would need the Armstrongs for the coming war and was inclined to forget if not forgive. Unless presented with red-handed evidence that they'd a stolen Queen, of course.

'All is over and done with,' Will ended bitterly, 'and everyone served with their reward. The prize for Mintie and me is bitter.'

Mintie and me, he had said; Batty knew love when he saw it. Knew it too when it was doomed. He could not say that, nor that he cared for Mintie himself in a strange way, for her spirit and the loss of it.

He stared into his mug of ale and thought on bodies, stripped and scattered. And what would come in the spring, worse than anything Will could think on, even though he was no stranger to hot trod and night reiving.

This would be a vengeful old Fat Henry at war, and Batty knew that well enough, had seen his fellow monarchs, the French and the Holy Roman, wage the same and even been part of it. The memory of rubble and flames, shrieking and corpses made him blink and grip his emptied mug until the leather buckled.

Then Will had gone off and left Batty glowering and nursing drink in a corner of the Old Brig – until word had come from Mintie that he was wanted back at Powrieburn. Even then he had wondered why – and now the truth stood in front of him, pale as poor milk and with her chin tilted defiantly.

'Will you go with me?'

The question wrenched Batty. He looked into the whey, anxious face of her and knew she would go alone if he refused, knew that she had called for him because he was the least threat of a male she knew. So he agreed and saw the relief wash her and her attempts to hide it by forking up more hay.

'By God, you have a mountain to barrow into the undercroft,' he added lightly. 'Must be the Saul, eating his fat face off.'

Mintie managed a wan smile at that. The Saul was healing well enough, but it would take a long time and he would not be the mount he had once been. She said that, watching Batty intently and swearing she could see another line or two crease the grim sadness.

'Ach,' he said heavily. 'I know that well. Keep the five pounds English and the Saul safe and warm for the rest of his days. If I can visit him now and then, that would be fine, but I do not insist on it.'

She knew why he had offered that last and bit her bottom lip to stop her weeping. She did not want to feel the way she did about Batty, or Will, whom she knew now had come time and again out of concern; she suspected Will wanted to woo her, and the thought settled like a cold sinking sick into the black bile humour that lurked in her, that must be got out of her before...

Batty stayed the night, sleeping with the Saul after he had eaten upstairs, as he had done before. This time there was no Primero, for Mintie's ma had taken to her bed following the events and horror, and the other women were not much better. The unease of Mintie seeped into them all save Bet's Annie, who led Batty back to the undercroft with a horn-panel lantern and set it down slowly in the old place where Batty had bedded before, bruised from falling off Tinnis Hill.

'You are moving better,' she observed as he struggled out of his padded jack.

'I am that – possets had a deal to do with it,' he answered smiling, and she remembered them, then looked at the grilled yett and the battered double doors beyond, draught wheeping in through the holes. She shivered at the memories.

'Is she sure?'

The question turned her to face him, and for a moment she thought he spoke of her being with child – then realised he did not, and knew at once what he meant.

'She is set on it. I said it was too early to tell and that if she had missed a bleed it was as much because of how she had been mishandled as having his plant in her.'

Batty shook his head and the unspoken words 'bad business' seemed to coil out of him anyway. He squinted at her.

'Is she good, this woman from the Solway?'

Bet's Annie thought on it. Auld Nan had as good a reputation as any, better than most, and would send away all the young ones who came to her begging love potions, or spells to ruin rivals in their affections for some man. Those she scourged away with growls and strangeness – but folk like Mintie, with good reason and deep fears, were differently treated.

'Auld Nan,' she said, nodding. 'I went there once with my mother and a cousin in trouble. She took a long time, did Auld Nan, and most of it was to make sure the cousin knew what she was set on.'

'Did she?'

'She was relieved of her condition,' Bet's Annie said, and saw Batty shift. Then suddenly she realised why, and the shock of it almost brought her hand to her throat. He had been the unwanted bairn, got on Bella Raham of Netherby by a German. But for the merest chance, he might well have never been born at all, scourged to oblivion by the likes of Auld Nan.

'What does she use – pennyroyal? The tail hairs of black deer?'

She looked grimly back at him.

'You know a bit,' she answered, and he waved his one hand and then used it to balance himself against the stable stall while he heeled off his boots.

'My ma did some for the camp women.'

Bet's Annie did not doubt Batty had seen the results – another reason for him not liking the business much.

'Pennyroyal keeps fleas off a dog,' she answered flatly. 'That is because it is poison. Deer hair will make you sick, for sure, but you can't sick up what is inside Mintie.'

She handed him blankets against the cold, busied and fussed in getting him comfortable, as if he was a wee boy. Then she straightened.

'She used black hellebore and savin, which is the juniper, on my cousin. Boiled it all up in milk and ale. Then she potioned her with dittany, hyssop and hot water, which is balming to the aftermath.'

'Safe?'

She set the lantern carefully on a hook, so it would not fall and burn the place down.

'Nothing is safe. My cousin was as sick and near death as any woman I have seen. But she recovered. Went on to have a brace of healthy boys for the man she eventually got married on to.'

All night Bet's Annie felt him, awake and staring at memories, even through the corbelled stone floor of the undercroft.

Solway Coast
Three days later

Fiskie, he called the horse, and Mintie suspected Batty did so to provoke a response from her. Normally she would have been stung by this renaming of her da's old mount, especially since it was the term given to a horse prone to kicking, which was a great lie for her da's gelding.

But Mintie had no arguments in her, only a dull dread that kept her from saying anything other than the answers to direct questions about when to start, when to stop and which way to take.

They had avoided Andrew's forge and any encounter with Agnes, skirted Netherby and any contact with the Grahams, avoided Graitna and slept in the cold and the damp until Batty's bones creaked. All rather than meet folk she might have to speak with.

They came down on the River Sark in a dawn of milk and gold, with the wind hissing off the firth, fat with cold and running snell fingers through the hawthorn and gorse and willow. Red-legged little waders waddled and wheeled back and forth, and Batty looked up at a skein of geese making a black fork in the silver sky.

'Mayhap we will find their tree,' he laughed softly to Mintie, who nodded and almost managed a smile; it was well known that such geese were grown on a branch, hanging by their beaks until they matured and fell into the water. Though no one had yet found such a tree.

The shape of a man rose up, dark against the sky, and Mintie reined in while Batty rode up to him. It was moot who was more afraid, Mintie or the man out with his bow, poaching from some mean hovel in Graitna and as anxious to avoid being seen or spoken to as Mintie herself.

But he stammered out what Batty needed to know and then scuttled off. Batty kneed his horse back alongside Mintie and jerked his jut of beard at a rise of coast.

'That headland splits and between is a sandy cove. Auld Nan's cottage is there.'

And so it was, a wattle and daub affair built almost into the earth and invisible, swaddled by willow and yew. It faced onto the opening in the headland, along a wind drift of sand in as sheltered a cove harbour as you would find anywhere. Smugglers, Batty thought, with a professional eye. For sure.

There were seabirds on the boundary wall, hung out and dried to black crosses. A whole fox was nailed to a post, gone to a rickle of bones with ribs like a set mantrap. And as they rode up, the bitter firth rolled through the gap of the headland in long sighs, already withdrawing to leave the great stretch of sucking mud that was low tide. The wind mourned and danced spirals up from the sands.

A woman opened the door as they dismounted, so that they paused in what they were doing and looked at her. She was neither old nor young, her hair unbound and a colour that might have been, in the dawn light, silver or gold.

She said nothing, merely waited for them to duck under her lintel and enter, Batty with his nerves raw and his one hand on the hilt of his sword. The room was dim and grey with smoke, flowered with dancing flames from an open fire; mad shadows reeled on the walls.

A chittering, like rats, made him crouch and half draw, but then he recoiled a little and blinked his eyes to get used to the poor light until he saw the figure. It hirpled out, rolling like a sailor, naked save for a scrap of cloth across its hips, and Batty felt the hackles rise on him because he did not know what it was, let alone male or female.

The face was beautiful as a girl's, the head hairless, the haddock eyes wet and bright, seeming blind as a slow-worm, and the jaw slack. The hands were held in front, like a prayer, and looked like flippers; the feet, Batty saw, had all the toes fused.

'Christ in Heaven,' he said and would have crossed himself save that he did not want to take his hand off the hilt; Mintie stood and stared. The creature made a chittering sound and a grimace which Batty realised was meant to be a smile.

'My son,' said the woman coming up behind them. Close up she was older, the eyes set deep as caves in a face once beautiful and now ravaged by time... and worse, Batty thought.

'He bids you welcome and says you should eat.'

Batty looked at the son, seeing now that the eyes saw well enough, just kept rolling up into his head. His hands flapping, he hirpled past them out of the hut, and the woman smiled.

'He goes to swim,' she said and looked at Mintie. 'He swims well. But you would have guessed that.'

'Is he... selkie?' she asked wonderingly, and the woman laughed, bitter as the wind.

'His da was, so I think,' she answered. 'At least he vanished swift as one when he found I was with child.'

Mintie stared at her, at the surrounds and the fire which poured silver smoke up to the sucking roof hole, like a fall of water reversed.

'But you could have...' she began, bewildered, and the woman tilted her head, then looked at Batty.

'Eat the broth,' she said to him, ladling it into a bowl and fetching him a horn spoon. 'Then leave. This is no place for a man, be it father, husband or lover. Come back in two days.'

'I am none of these,' Batty answered levelly, though his heart thundered. The woman nodded and Mintie said nothing.

'And more than all, I think,' the woman answered. 'I know you, one-arm. You are Corbie. Slow match. I know your work, for I have had the spill from it here – wee husbands presented with evidence of cuckoldry from you and now convinced what lies in their unfaithful wife's belly is not any get of their own.'

She looked at him expectantly; Batty looked her right back.

'Fathers,' she added, 'told of their daughter's sins and determined to end the dishonour of it.'

'They could take it to term,' Batty answered in a growl, 'but would only have it left on the moss, so there is little choice for them, which is what happens when you sin. Besides – you could have refused them, woman. Them and their menfolk both.'

'And leave them in fear and with the loathing of those they have to live with after,' she replied tartly.

'Losing the fee betimes,' Batty countered, because he thought he had the measure of the woman now.

He nodded grimly to Mintie, but kept his eyes on the woman.

'She wants to know why you did not use your skills on your own self. Will you tell her?'

Auld Nan said nothing, merely worked the fire so that it flared and a small log rolled out into the ash on one side.

'You had none, of course,' Batty answered for her. 'That artifice all came later, as if in answer to your misbegotten, who might be selkie-born and might not.'

He leaned into the flames a little, blood-dyed by them.

'Every wee silly lass you root out,' he added, 'is yourself. But that horse has long bolted, Mistress – does your son know you never wanted him?'

'Firebrand,' she said bitterly, and whether she spoke of the log in the ash or of Batty's other byname, the one that set flame to everything it touched, was never certain. Then she turned to Mintie.

'We will speak on it more,' she said, 'but I say this for the Corbie's sake. I know why you are here. What you have in you was put there by a man and is now rooted. If it be your wish, then we will uproot it – but the part that is him will come also with the part that is you, and that will tear your soul.'

'Do not forget the rip of the body in it,' Batty added harshly, and Mintie finally stirred.

'Leave,' she said, and there was a deal of plead in her voice. Batty thought about it, while a cat with one eye wound itself round his legs. The broth was rich and good and welcome, so he ate it, wiped his beard and then nodded to the women and left. Mintie never looked at him.

Outside, he found himself breathing hard, as if to take clean air into him. It was the smoky hut, he told himself... But he looked for the selkie son, half expecting to see him rolling in the Solway's cold slide on his back, eating raw fish.

But there was nothing. He crossed himself, took the horses and rode away to Graitna.

Solway Coast

Two days later

He rode back, his tongue furred and his head thick and heavy from too much brooding drink at the Forge Tavern. The place was the same, with its black crosses of hung birds and rickle of fox bones, and the full light of day did little for it; even the cries of the gulls sounded like lost children.

Auld Nan was waiting for him, though there was no sign of the selkie son, and he asked after him, out of politeness.

'I send him away at times like this,' she said, 'for fathers, husbands and lovers sometimes do not take kindly to the work's aftermath.'

The work's aftermath lay in the smoking dim on a draggle of old furs covered with grey blankets she would never have let touch her in normal times. Her breathing, as far as Batty could tell, was slow and even, so she was asleep and not dead.

He turned into the woman's stare, and she nodded at him.

'Alive,' she agreed, then frowned and handed him a slip of paper. It was clear neither of them could read it, and Batty simply turned it over in the calloused fingers of his hand until she told him what was in it — as he knew she would.

'The lass says it is a writ, with a call on her for five pounds, English, and the name of the man she will not soil her mouth with. Justice, she says.'

Batty closed his eyes against the beating storm of it, hearing Mintie's voice even as the woman spoke. He felt the bleak, welling sadness rise in him.

'Ach, Mintie,' he said, slow and heavy and sad, then realised that Auld Nan was holding something, presenting it to him.

'Last time,' she said, 'you supped from my pot. This time the lass bid me serve a harsher meal, and then you must leave. She will make her own way home.'

Batty looked and saw the battered pewter dish and the spurs lying on it. Rusted, leather-rotted and useless for the purpose they had been made for, they were bright and sharp for the one they were being used for now. She must have brought them with her, Batty thought, all secret with purpose even then...

It was the pointed way a Border woman said it was time a man did his duty and went on the raid, to ensure the survival of the household.

A dish of spurs.

Chapter Eleven

He came out of night and the moon, that lover's lantern, chart of womb tides, accomplice of murderers. The dawn was a dance of loveliness by comparison, even though it dripped; the trees were grim and doves mourned.

Batty eased himself in the saddle a little, watching lapwings skim the yellow fields, squinting down at the black Esk and the lumped hunch of the powder mill, its wheel turning. The snow was patched now, he noted – but this was the north, so it was no indication that there would not be more.

Dark and cold it looked, Batty thought. Milling was done when there was enough daylight to spill in the windows and there would be no flame for heat or work. He saw folk moving there, shuffling in their rag-bound feet, breeches and hose loose without belts. No metal on them at all to cause a spark.

Beyond on the crag, the finger of Hollows stood half built in stone and caged by scaffolding mottled with damp. No one worked on it now, for mortar would crack in the cold and all the undone walls of it were stuffed with straw to keep the freeze from the ashlar and the fresh-cut stones.

Yet the barmkin was high enough, with a walkway on it where folk moved, sluggish as old snails. The outbuildings, hidden behind it, were up and about; Batty heard the whinny of horses and saw the thread of smoke from the kitchen fires.

He waited, knowing he had been seen, and did not have to suffer it long until four riders came out, the leader's bounce in his saddle showing he was no horseman.

Batty knew Leckie Armstrong, the sometime steward of Hollows because he could tally and read. Learning, Batty confirmed to himself, leaves little time for the important matters such as riding and fighting, which was survival in the Debatable. Yet Leckie was valued, used his mind like a sword and had to be considered because of it.

Flanked by surly scowlers who knew Batty, Leckie jounced up and reined the horse in gratefully, raising himself painfully in the stirrups. The long and fruitless ride to Carlisle in pursuit of the German had rasped him raw; there had been no child with the man and his wife, and he had babbled about handing the babe back to the physicker who had examined it. Of such a physicker, there was no sign.

They had killed the German and his Dutch wife anyway, though Leckie had not liked that. Hutchie did it, grinning and getting the others to make it look like a robbery while he did things to the woman, then killed her. They had rolled the bodies under a gorse bush out on the empty moss and then ridden back to Hollows with the bad news that sent the Laird into a spleen folk walked soft round.

The arrival of Batty would not help it, Leckie thought.

'You might not have a brace of arms,' he said by way of greeting, 'but your neck is of purest brass, Master Coalhouse.'

'Unlikely to be stretched, then, Master Leckie. Will your Laird speak with me?'

Leckie eyed Batty sideways for a moment or two, then shook his head with an awe that was only partly mock.

'By God, man, you have attacked his guests and left twenty of them cold and stripped in the road, a sprig of the English gentry among them. It took us a whole day to gather them in for decent burial.'

No doubt, Batty thought, though you never soiled your own palms with the business; mind you, you have been riding until your arse bleeds. I wonder where?

But he said nothing, simply waited, and Leckie did not disappoint.

'You have turned out Grahams against the Laird and, we hear, are spreading scurrilous telltale about him and the Keeper being involved in this awful business with the wee Queen.'

He shook his head and tutted at the outrage, all mock sorrow and innocence.

Batty shrugged and offered his undershot grin of admiration.

'Ach, Leckie, you are as fine as a mummer's show when you get started. "Scurrilous telltale" is it? Christ be praised it never comes to question and trial, where the wet nurse and the wee woodworker who made the cradle in Hollows are called to witness. And let us not speak of a wheen of Armstrongs and their friends thieving and burning all over Scott's land.'

Leckie's face was stiff now and Batty leaned forward, his voice harsher.

'The Laird got the English money, Wharton's wee lad got a lesson and is safe returned home, and the Regent of the realm is proved to be too weak yet to bother the Laird o' Hollows. So half right is all good, as they say.'

He leaned easily on the pommel, reining himself in from any more mention of the babe, since he did not know if Hollows had got her back, or even knew she was missing.

'Only a few English were slain,' he added.

'Armstrongs are held,' Leckie replied, recovering himself a little. 'Are you here to negotiate for them as a Graham?'

'I am not. And I am here to negotiate with the master, not his wee hound. Either turn me away or stand aside.'

Leckie did neither; he led Batty up to Hollows, the riders closing in and scowling blackly, though they flexed gauntlets on their lance shafts and looked right and left for hidden men, remembering the English corpses on the road.

It was not a long ride and not much was said between himself and Leckie, but by the end of it Batty had gleaned that the Laird of Hollows knew the babe was missing, but had no more idea where the wee Queen of Scots lay than anyone else.

Hollows smelled of stale rushes and stone dust, the clack of it under his boots seeming strange and empty. The hall was grey dim and the fire in the great hearth a mean affair of smoking sticks; there was no sign of the Lady, but the Laird sat slouched in a chair, his face thunderous.

'You are a rogue and a bastard-born son of a whore,' he growled as Batty came up, and watched Batty's eyes narrow.

'Aye – squint at me all you dare,' he added. 'You might well squint at your own arse by the time you have finished turning in the breeze, for I have a mind to hang you.'

'Every Armstrong held will fruit the trees at Netherby,' Batty replied shortly, 'which you well know, so enough of your bluster.'

The Laird found his own trap turned on him and could only scowl redly and hold his temper in check.

'Hutchie Elliott,' Batty said levelly. 'You need to turn him over to justice, for what he did to Mintie Henderson's da – and the lass herself. If you have not heard of what happened to her, then you will be the only one left still in ignorance.'

'No matter of mine, that,' the Laird replied, but Batty could hear the unease in his voice. Unwilling guest or not, Mintie had been under his roof and protection and it did his honour no good to be associated with such an assault.

'Then hand Hutchie to me and see justice done.'

'Justice will be done,' the Laird replied, recovering a little of himself and drawing up in the seat. 'I am justice here, not some Graham by-blow. When I decide Hutchie Elliott needs punishment he shall have it, and not before.'

Not before long either, the Laird thought to himself savagely, for bringing this down on us and for failing, him and Leckie both, to track down the babe.

'That is the second time you have mentioned my parenting,' Batty answered. 'It is not a wise thing to do with such a tone.'

'I speak as I please in my own hall.'

Batty nodded sagely.

'As you can do. But with so many of your men under a Graham noose, it seems a careless way to appease the hangman.'

The Laird knew those words would whisper their way round his hall and beyond; now his own eyes narrowed, for it was clear Batty Coalhouse had more skills than the ability to kill with just one arm.

'Are you here to offer for their release?'

'I am not. I am here for Hutchie – but all matters are chained under God's good Heaven.'

The Laird sat back, waited, then spread his hands.

'Is that all?'

Batty looked suddenly weary as he stood.

'I wonder if the Lady agrees,' he answered harshly and saw that dig strike hard enough to make the Laird shift and scowl. Batty made a slow show of pulling on his one gauntlet, using his teeth.

'I give you a final chance,' he said slowly. 'Hand over Hutchie or face the consequences.'

The Laird's face grew plum-coloured and he half rose, tipping the chair backwards with a crash.

'Consequences!' he bellowed. 'You threaten *me* with consequences. In my own hall? By God, Coalhouse, it is as well Mintie Henderson paid for your head with a good horse, else I would pike it up on the road outside for the world to see what I think of your consequences.'

Batty nodded soberly.

'Return the Fyrebrande to Mintie at Powrieburn,' he declared. 'That agreement is no more.'

'Return...'

The Laird spluttered, lost for words, then resorted to a bull roar until he found some and threw them at Batty, along with a shaking finger.

'I could kill you here and now.'

'You could,' Batty answered like mild steel. 'But then you would be an echo of the poor king who so ignored honour as to seize your da – and who would have the graceless face then, Laird of Hollows?'

The Laird was all tremble, like a bull on the end of a straining rope. His voice was hoarse with anger.

'Get you gone and be grateful for my honour that allows it under hospitality. I will keep the Fyrebrande, but if you want the agreement torn up, so be it. Keep clear of me and mine, Batty Coalhouse. The next time you are seen by an Armstrong, that man will kill you in the worst way he can find.'

He glared around the hall and bellowed echoes into it.

'You hear that? This man has an hour. Beyond that, any man here or a friend of this tower may kill him and gain my pleasure and reward.'

—

The Laird waited for a long time after Batty had slouched out, then called for Sweetmilk Hutchie Elliott; most in the hall thought he was making sure Batty had put distance away from the tower and would not hear him roar some curdle into Sweetmilk, but the truth was that he needed so long to bring his heart and temper under control.

Margaret appeared just before Hutchie did, slipping quietly up to stand at his elbow like a chill wind from the grave; the Laird did not want to look at his Lady, but her words pulled his head round.

'You would defend this foul wee wen?' she demanded, flat and heavy as a thrown iron, and he winced at her tone. Cold broth and lumpy porridge from now on, he thought, if I am so lucky; the thought made him waspish with her.

'It is not about him,' he replied. 'It is about Armstrong honour. My father would not have been half as merciful—'

'Does Armstrong honour permit the violation of women?' she snapped back. 'Would your father?'

He knew she was waspish because she had contrived to put Hutchie and Mintie together in the undercroft, but he had no mind for soothing. He rounded on her, savage as a bloody-muzzled dog.

'No, he would not have stood for it and Armstrong honour does not. Consider yourself fortunate in that, for it also does not permit its chief to be spoken to by anyone – *anyone* – as if he was a chiel of no account.'

'You were not always so arrogant,' she replied, soft and wistful – then put the pepper back in her voice. 'Like father like son. Mayhap if he had tempered his own hubris, a wee plooky boy-king might have spared him.'

They glared at each other for a long time, then the anger left him like an ebb tide. He waved one dismissive, apologetic hand.

'My doe,' he said. 'This is not worth a quarrel.'

The term made her blink, filled her with sadness for the way it had once rang truer than the false tin it now sounded, for the way it had once thrilled and delighted her as now it did not. She could not speak for the sorrow of it – and then Hutchie Elliott clacked into the centre of her search for words.

He was cautious, for he had heard who had come, so his bow was tolerable, neither too fawning nor too arrogant. His tone, too, was deferential; he was all sweetmilk now.

'You wished to see me, Lord?'

'You are a whore-slip who would fuck a haired floor,' the Laird said and watched the blood rush up into the man's face, daring him to do something about it. Instead, Hutchie choked it down as if it was another man's spit and said nothing. Disappointed, the Laird found his goblet and drank, then wiped his mouth with the back of his hand.

'You brought this on Hollows, this Batty Coalhouse,' he added, and Hutchie, recovered a little, raised his chin in a pinch of old arrogance and a hint of aloes.

'I thought that had been settled with the gift of a horse. Which I had stolen and you returned.'

The Laird waved that away with the flap of a hand.

'Not that. Mintie Henderson.'

Hutchie started to speak, but the Lady got to it first.

'Do not try to deny it, you filth,' she said loudly, and someone sniggered, reminding Hutchie that folk were listening; his flush went pale round his mouth and the corners of his eyes. Then he smiled his white smile and spread his hands. There was a plump heart on a ribbon round his doublet wrist, a last Valentine token from one of the women left in Hollows; the sight brought rage into the Lady, as if such a man had no right to love tokens.

He saw her look, mistook it and raised the plush heart to his lips, smiling sly as he kissed it.

'Mintie? Aye, well, it is hard to resist an old love when she insists on it. She was always hot that lass, even when I was at Powrieburn. By God, she was asking for it.'

The Lady struck him, so hard that his head rattled and the ring on her finger smashed a tooth from his mouth, so that he saw it bounce on the flags like a pearl.

'My tooth—'

The words came out muffled and with a spray of blood from his burst lip, but the thought of ruin to his smile was what brought Hutchie forward at her, his face like a boiled beet and his hand reaching for his dirk.

'Would you, by God?'

The Laird's soft, almost gentle voice snapped Hutchie from his next action and he recoiled from it as if scorched. The Lady curled a sneer at him.

'It is your tooth no longer,' she pointed out and toed it into the rushes with an elegant gesture of one leather-slippered foot. Then she leaned forward a little.

'You were asking for it,' she declared and strode off, while the Laird watched her go and felt a surge of admiration and remembrance as to why he had married the woman.

Hutchie touched his lip, looked at the blood on his fingers and then at the Laird, who scowled back at him.

'You brought this on Hollows,' he said. 'You repair it.'

'On my own?'

The Laird heard the desperate whine and glowered.

'Take what men will go with you for friendship or fear,' he growled and then looked round pointedly. 'If there are, as I suspect, too few of them, take those who seek reward and my good graces.'

He leaned forward and gimleted Hutchie's eyeballs with his stare.

'Find Batty Coalhouse. Kill him, for the honour of the Name.'

Near Canobie, Liddesdale
Two days later

On the crusted rock rimming the Esk, Batty knelt on his good knee under the branches of a twisted rowan, with the creeping moss crystalled with melting snow all around him.

He did not care for rowan, for it was Faerie, more so than any other of the trees – save, perhaps, for yew. But you could make a good bowstave from yew, and providing you didn't take the shade of a hot day under it, you were safe enough. Forget that rule and you were transported away to the land of Faerie, taken up on a horse and hag-ridden through mire and gorse and never able to get off.

The rowan was worse. It came from Elfland, Batty knew – well, everyone knew. The Faerie loved the berries and brought them from their own land, spilling them carelessly in this one so that rowan grew.

Batty had heard that eating one of the rowan's berries would make a person drunk, but he had never tried it, lest he lose all sense and eat two. Eating two would ensure that the person would live to be a hundred years old. Eating three would make the person thirty years old again, which seemed a fine thing – but they would stay that way for a hundred years.

Batty wondered if it regrew arms, for if it did he might chance the giant called Sharvan, whom the Queen of Elfland had asked to guard the rowan tree…

The sound of hooves on wet road jerked him back to the crusted rock and the rowan roots. Below, the riders swayed gently down the line of the river. Heading north, he saw. For the Mosspaul, most likely, all eight of them bound for drink and women in the best tavern for miles, and though a longish ride, well worth it; a cruel grin curled his lip at what he could have done to them. Even with only the one arm, he added to himself. Who needs bloody rowan?

He could not see who they were, for they had swaddled themselves in cloaks against the cold and damp, so he waited until they had passed and then levered himself up and moved back to where he had left Fiskie.

He rode away, stiff and sore, heading for the greater steep of bare Tinnis Hill and Ill-Made's old hidey-hole snugged up in the Faerie stones. It was a cave in a hollow, hidden from view, and Batty had already determined on it when he had ridden up to Powrieburn for the last time, just after leaving Hollows. No rowan round Ill-Made's hole, he remembered, and tried not to admit that the shiver he felt at having to stay there at all was more than a snell wind through the trees.

He had ridden from Hollows to Powrieburn earlier, and found Will Elliot's horse at the door, the man himself stroking his beard and looking grim.

'Is Mintie returned?' Batty had asked, and Will's scowl had been rank as musk.

'She is – how could you leave her to manage on her own?' Will burst out, shaking his head with disbelief. 'There are week-dead corpses looking livelier and better than Mintie.'

'By God, she will not be glad to hear it,' Batty had replied flatly. 'Nor will your case be advanced telling the lass that.'

Megs had appeared just then and bobbed warily to him, so he told her what was needed and she went off to let the others know. Powrieburn was running by committee, Batty thought, which makes an elephant out of the designs for a horse.

'Why are you gathering in such supplies?' Will had asked, breaking Batty's reverie. 'Where are you bound?'

To Hell, by the fastest road Mintie Henderson can devise, Batty thought. Well, he corrected, her and myself both.

'I am to bring Hutchie Elliott to justice,' Batty told him then. 'Mintie has hired me for it – five pounds English, which is fast becoming my set fee and the hardest coin I ever earned.'

Will's scowl deepened.

'That is my job,' he'd growled back. 'You will set the Border aflame if you try it.'

A sudden thought struck him and he squinted.

'Is that why you are pursuing it? Is it to further your own names – Firebrand? Slow match?'

'It is not,' Batty had replied coldly. 'It is because I was asked and because I did not finish the business before.'

Which was not all truth, though Will did not know it. Even not knowing, he had dismissed it with an impatient wave.

'It is done with now. Leave Hutchie Elliott to me and the law... besides, if you bring him to a trial it will simply drag Mintie through the mire of what he did, for all to see and hear.'

'Too late for that,' Batty had answered. 'Hollows rings with it and so it will spread like a canker from there. The Lady does not care for it – but the Laird of Hollows cares more for his Name than his wife or her honour.'

'Christ in Heaven,' Will had declared, crossing himself for the impiety. 'It will reach Henderson ears – Ower-The-Moss Hob is not so beaten down or hagged by black-rent payments that he will not rise at such an insult.'

Batty had nodded. The chief of the Hendersons in Liddesdale would have something to say about Powrieburn, certes.

'Jesu and all saints – you are already burning the Border.'

'Then forget Hutchie and extend your energies to putting it out.'

Megs had come out then with a bulging flour sack of provisions, which Batty heaved up on his saddle with a one-handed ease that Will had not missed.

'Why are you doing this?' he'd asked, catching Batty's bridle as the man reined round. 'Mintie will not thank you for it when she comes to her senses.'

Batty had not answered him, simply tugged himself free and rode off. But he had thought about it since and thought on it now, as he picked his way up Tinnis to Ill-Made's hidden lair.

He had thought it was because of the business with Hans. Mayhap it was in the blood – Hans Kohlhase could have gone his way and accepted that his horses had been snaffled out from under him, that the law he relied on to get them back had been bought by the same arrogant, powerful noble.

He had not. He had become his own law and thrown down a challenge to the whole of Saxony. Blood and fire had followed; robbery and death had followed. War had followed. In the end, it had fallen out as Batty had always known it would – the Kohlhases had been caught and broken on the wheel.

All but me. Mayhap I am still fighting the same war, Batty thought. Or it is in the blood – and though Dickon might argue it, the ruthless murder in me is Kohlhase as much as Border Graham.

Will thinks I burn his Border and that may be true – but it is already smouldering and will burst into flames in the spring, whether he knows it or not.

Mintie thinks she is barred from decent life and even Heaven – there is no soothing her with the truth. Which is that, in the end, no one will care whether one more quine in the Debatable lost her maidenhood unwillingly. No one but Batty Coalhouse, he added and smiled to himself, for that was closer to the meat of the matter than he liked to admit, even to himself. Never, of course, to Mintie or, God forbid, Will Elliot, whom Batty liked as much as any man.

I care for Mintie, he admitted. Not in the way Will does, not an old man chasing a young lass like some panting wee pup. But for the spirit in her, for the memory it brings of what I once was, before...

He felt the stump twitch.

Before this, he thought. Before the axe cut it and my old life away, plunging me into the knowledge, icy as winter water, that neither God nor the Devil cares.

This world is Hell and there is no other.

He ducked into the darkness of the hidey-hole, into the smell of old stone and must. Something had staled here a time ago – badgers or rats, he thought, but inside the eggshell of hidden dark, he fetched out the dried kindling stuffed inside his doublet and placed it at his feet, then grunted his way down to a knee. He whirred sparks from his tinderbox and blew life into a flame, then a fire, and by the light of it inspected the hole.

It was much as he remembered it – even the little stack of cut wood, bone dry and cobwebbed in a corner, and that gave him pleasure, for he could have a dry wood fire enough to cook and not smoke overly much. Filtered out through the brush of the entrance, it might not even show at all.

There was dressed stone here too, which made his skin crawl. Good stone galleted – big pieces, infilled with smaller bits and mortared with clay, now crumbling – and fine as any bastel. Yet old; Batty could feel the age of the place and held a brand from the fire higher, squinting at the part of his hole which was bared rock.

There were marks there, sometimes looking as if a hen had walked up the stones, sometimes no more than the scarts a man in jail will make, to keep track of his days. Yet Batty thought there was something regular about them; he thought they might be a message from the Faerie.

A warning, he thought, which was his usual experience of marks on gates or walls; and though he could neither read nor write, he knew these marks were as different from the ones men made as an egg is to a plum.

He tossed the brand back into the fire and turned his back on them, ignored them. It was what he had always done with such marks, whether on a Faerie wall or painted on a sign over the gate of a tower house. If folk wanted him gone, let them say so to his face.

So he tended the horse, fed the fire and made bannocks with one hand and his knee. He had oats and water enough for him and horse both for a long while, cheese and even some bran bread, which he chewed, spitting the quern grit to one side while the bannocks scorched up.

As he did so, he smelled the staleness more keenly and followed his nose, holding up a brand from the fire until he came to a ball of rough little twigs and straw. He touched it warily with a toe, felt it move and sat back on his heels, holding the torch high.

Adders, by God. No guests to be sharing a house with, even though they had prior claim with their wee hibernating nest.

They would be sluggish, but Batty knew they did not sleep constantly through the winter and he did not care for the idea of them, so fetched his emptied flour sack and struggled on his thick gauntlet with its maille backing. Then he scooped the lot up and tied the neck using his teeth and hand, watching the bag roil and bulge and hiss.

The bannocks were well fired by the time he got back to them and the cheese had to be gnawed, but Batty was well content, full bellied, warm and in the dry.

He sat and knitted until he started to nod, then pulled his cloak round him and lay down, watching the shadows dance and listening to the hoolets screech.

Then he slept and dreamed of Florence and the siege and Maramaldo.

Chapter Twelve

Mosspaul Tavern, between Langholm and Hawick
At the same time

It had been a long traipse in the cold and wet, but worth it. Hutchie was well content, for he had discovered that the tooth he had lost had been inside his jaw and not at the front – his smile was intact, though the jagged nag of what was lost kept rasping his tongue and his memory.

One day, he promised, that bitch who calls herself Lady of Hollows will find the price for such a blow...

The whore winced at his savagery, converted it to a whine of seeming pleasure and waited while Hutchie thundered to the end, with a strange little-boy whimper and a shudder, like a dog taking a shit.

At once she lost her charms for Hutchie, became a besmeared, sagged woman with missing teeth, wiping the sweaty grime and his own mess from her with a much-used cloth. He pulled his hose and fat slashed breeks together, threw coin at her and left, clattering down the stairs into the fugged reek of the tavern proper.

The others were bleared with drink, creishie with food and women and the knowledge that they would not be shifting from Mosspaul this night. Most thought it a good thing to have come out with Hutchie after all, though those not entirely lost in drink knew they would not be spending a lot more time here. Soon, matters would get cold and wet and possibly dangerous

– but, for now, there was drink, food and women, and someone else was paying.

Only one man was unhappy with his lot, did not raise a cheer at the sight of Hutchie stumbling downstairs, lacing his cods. But of them all, Hutchie was pleased to see this man the most and said so.

'Wattie Bourne,' he added genially, flinging himself into a bench seat and calling for drink. He waited until the dripping man had taken the leather mug in both hands and raised it to his lips, watched the apple of his throat bob and bob until, finally, Wattie let the mug down reluctantly, paused, then belched a gust of warm beery breath.

'By God, I needed that.'

'Now tell me where Batty Coalhouse is,' Hutchie demanded.

'Up Tinnis Hill,' Wattie answered, his answer muffled by the burying of his nose in the leather mug again.

Hutchie preened a little, aware that everyone was hanging on Wattie's words, aware that his clever ruse had worked. He had been sure Batty had been watching them, would move to watch them – and had set Wattie apart, instructing him to pick up Batty's trail and see where he went.

Tinnis Hill – well, Batty could hardly go back to Powrieburn, where he was too easily found, or any other roofed place along the edge of the Debatable. Hutchie had thought of Kirkandrew or some other Graham stronghold, which would have made matters awkward, but not impossible; sooner or later, Batty would have had to poke his neb out of doors and they'd have him then.

But Tinnis was clever. More awkward still, but not impossible.

'Where on Tinnis, then, Scarted Wat?' he demanded, and Wattie, dribbling ale from the strake along one jaw that had cut him to exposed teeth and tongue, blinked slowly and dabbed the ale off his beard, delicate as a cat.

'How would I know that?'

Hutchie went a little still and cold then; men saw it and went quiet, moved careful.

'Because you followed him, Wattie. To his lair.'

Wattie's headshake scattered ale droplets like a dog out of a stream.

'Up the Faerie hill? By God, I did no such thing...'

The blow scattered him and the ale cup, sent him tumbling backwards and struggling like an upended beetle. When he finally spluttered upright, red with anger and indignation, he found himself staring down the length of Hutchie's knife.

'Faerie, is it? I will give you Faerie, you white-livered wee drooler. Follow him, I said, and you should have done so if he had walked through the gates of Hell. Now we are only a little wiser as to where he is...'

He eased a bit and the knife was suddenly removed from Wattie's face; everyone's breath went out, then back to normal, as Hutchie sat brooding.

Of course Scarted Wat would not go up Faerie alone. Few would and Hutchie could hardly blame them – but Batty had, and where he went, Hutchie could go. And where I go, he thought savagely, these bastard-bred hounds will follow.

So he made his face pleasant, even if the smile on it was shaky.

'Well,' he said eventually, 'we will do it the harder way. We will plooter our way up it and down the far side and scare him out in the open.'

No one spoke. Even in the cold light of day, Tinnis was no place to be hunting, especially when it was a man like Batty Coalhouse.

'And you can lead the bloody way,' Hutchie finished, smiling nastily at Wattie, who found his mouth surprisingly dry for all the ale he had just swallowed.

He was big and dark. He had a beak of a nose pitted with clogged pores and the scars of old boils. With his speckled beard and his cropped black hair, matted with blood and dust, he looked like a Moor, or a mad prophet who had fallen off his pole.

There was a smear of blood across his forehead and a new scar down one cheek. His eyes were dark and desperate, his teeth were yellow and bared, and he had spatulate fingers with hairs like black spider-legs on them.

The called him Simoni when he appeared, covered in dust and shit like the rest of them, though he was one of Florence's best citizens. Once he had appeared in a silver back and breast, with a gilded helmet adorned with plumes; Batty and the rest of his Company of gunners laughed themselves sick until, eventually, he joined in. He had never dressed like that again down at the walls.

He came with plans for the fortifications of Florence and had been put in charge of rebuilding them, while the army of Emperor Charles and Pope Clement raged on the outside. In between, he sketched on the back of his plans, using rough charcoal and all his skill, so that people saw themselves come alive.

Now he struggled, him and Batty both, lumbering about like drunks fallen out of a tavern, lurching and tugging, clutching and gripping, while the grumbling noise sounded distant and faded, though it was a thundering din to folk who could hear properly. Someone had blown out the convent floor. Someone had dug into the sewers and blown it out... it was no comfort to Batty that he had predicted as much.

He and Simoni fought their way over the rubble, panting dogs in the smoke whirling round the convent of St Theresa, halfway up the street that led down to the Gate of the Cross and Gallows; Batty saw men stumble past them, shadows in the mirk; then the sound roared back in like water out of a broken dam.

Batty hauled Simoni over the broken beams and the cracked rubble, while men piled down the street and enveloped them like lovers. There were shouts and bellows and the crack of matchlocks.

Someone reeled past screaming, and Batty lost his concentration, stumbled, fell and dragged Simoni down with him, rolling over broken stones and broken bodies, wallowing in the last expelled filth and tarns of blood turning to gory slush.

Simoni climbed wearily to his feet and hauled Batty up, shook his head as if to clear it and put his mouth close to Batty's ear; his breath stank of onions.

'They blew in the convent. Someone showed them those sewers, as we suspected... a secret way.'

It would do them no good, Batty thought, for he and Master Simoni had thought of this – and now the defenders were forcing them back. He had a moment, a sudden spasm that brought him upright, banished weariness, that it might be Maramaldo in the convent; he would have had the cunning to work out about the sewers next to the wall. He spoke the name and Simoni dragged him away up the street from the fighting, shaking his heavy head.

'Even a Medici Pope would not allow the likes of Maramaldo in his army. Hurry – your match...'

The world roared like a muffled bear, tilted, turned to whirling dust and ruin, and everything blasted away, even sound. There was a long time of lying, half aware of nothing much. Then, as if from far away, he heard his name and felt a brush of sensation on his cheek.

It was repeated and the cheek stung a little, so that he tried to lift a hand. Then the voice came, louder this time, though as if from underwater.

'Kohlhase? Kohlhase.'

This time it was a slap on the cheek that sprang his eyes open and made him try and ward off another blow. Simoni's face swam in his vision, his grey tongue pressed into the gap where his front two teeth should be as he concentrated. The great face creased in a dust-caked grin.

'Good,' he said in his Tuscan grate. 'Back with us. Up. We cannot hold this and are falling back – your match burned down perfectly to our countermine.'

So Batty let himself be dragged off behind the comforting metal backs of Michelangelo's guards, back through the smoke and the screams, over *the rubble of the crushed Gate of the Cross and Gallows, and back across the shattered dead to safety.*

Batty woke from it, felt the sweat on him and lay blinking, confused and trying to hang onto the shredding tendrils of the dream. By God, he had not thought of that in years – the day the enemy almost took Florence. The day he and Michelangelo had thwarted them.

Michelangelo, the one they called simply Simoni, had been no more than one more annoyance in the life of Batty and his company, another Florentine gentleman given command with no knowledge and less skill.

Except that he had been both skilled and learned, shared his bread and onions and wine with them, was right in every point he made regarding enfilades and defilades, and could draw their faces on the backs of his plans so that the men laughed to see themselves.

He tried to show Batty the trick of it, but only because he was fascinated and repelled by Batty's missing arm. In the end, Batty had tossed the charcoal back at him and told him that he had never had the skill of it, even with both arms.

The fortifications expert Simoni nodded and gave a little shiver, touching the stump as if it might infect him with loss. He blessed God with fervent wonder and the hope it would never happen to him, since it would be the end of the world and he might as well die as not be able to sculpt.

'For painting, Master Kohlhase, is an inferior art. There is no *terribilità* in painting,' he added and passed the wineskin round again.

When the creator of the *Pietà* of St Peter's, *David* and, more recently, *The Last Judgement* on the wall of the Sistine pronounces on art, you listen. You listen too when such a man, with his ear to the Council, tells you to quit Florence before its hired commander betrays it.

He had left the city himself shortly afterwards, and Batty had taken the hint. A week after Batty and his men had slipped away into the autumn mists and trees, Malatesta Baglioni, the city's commander, abandoned Florence to Emperor Charles, the Pope and his Medici cousins.

And Fabrizio Maramaldo, whom even the Pope could not keep away from the plunder and the victory. Batty only learned that much later and cursed Michelangelo for it, for making him lose even that slim chance of revenge on the mercenary captain.

That was then and this is now, Batty thought. He lay in the hidey-hole on Tinnis for a while, listening to the birdsong outside, smelling the ash from the fire. Then he moved, careful not to wrench the stiffness into something worse. He raked the embers, blew life back and warmed himself at the flames; like the adders, sluggish in the bag, he thought, I need heat to move.

He remembered the sketch Michelangelo had given him, of himself done on the back of a detailed plan of the fortifications of the Porta al Prato in Florence. He had given it away for drink, but he could not remember when or where. He wished he had kept it, if only for the memory of how he had once looked, when he was young and had the same soul in him that Mintie has. That Mintie had, he corrected, and felt the bleakness of that loss as keenly as his own.

It also had an invite on it, that sketch, to be the guest of Michelangelo di Lodovico Buonarroti Simoni in Florence when it was at peace and free – for remembrance of when they were brothers in arms. The man he had sold it to had read it to him, before he asked Batty if he really wanted to part with it.

He had been surprised at that, at how a piece of fine paper with some scribblings by the likes of Michelangelo was worth anything at all – and how anyone could weigh it in the pan against a good bottle of *eau de vie* and find the balance tip in favour of the scribble. He had realised, somewhere in the sot of him, that Michelangelo had done well for himself if even his discarded scrawls were revered by some.

Later – sober – he had known what he had lost, but shrugged and consigned it to a matter of God, a matter of the Devil. How changed would his life have been if he had taken up the offer? Christ in Heaven, what would the likes of Batty Kohlhase do in Florence, in the company of Michelangelo and his like? It is not as if I could paint as much as a door even when I had a brace of arms, he thought and chuckled to himself and the bag of adders.

The artist had seemed old even then and is probably dead now, he thought, while his city is as free as it will ever be, for the Medici are now dukes in it but the Emperor Charles is pulling his troops out. With a sigh of relief, no doubt – a dozen years it had taken to calm the Florentine feathers and secure it for the Medici.

Maramaldo's trail had not been hard to pick up, a snail-slime of terror and blood, first for this ruler, then his rival. Batty had followed him to the Germanies and lost him, lost his Company to the obsession of it – who wants to be led by a mumbling madman, passing up good paid service to chase rumours? Finally, he had stumbled to his kin in Saxony, penniless, alone and sick to his soul.

After that... well, after that came the whole bad business, all of it broken from me by Hans and the wheel, yet here I am, brooding on Florence and Maramaldo and Michelangelo Buonarotti Simoni. What might have been instead of what is. Sitting in a cold Faerie cave in the Hell that is the world, and in the deepest pit of it, which they call Liddesdale. He laughed and shook it all from himself like rain from his eyes. By God, he thought wryly, I have done well for myself; Michelangelo would be proud...

He hirpled out and tended to Fiskie, who was hipshot and chewing browned, frosted grass, draped in a warm blanket and happy enough with his lot. He was as Borders as the rest of us, Batty thought, patting him on the neck – enduring a lick of cold, a deal of wet and the wrath of God and the Devil on a peck of oats and a sip of water.

The mist had come down on Tinnis during the dark of the morning, descending like a dank wet cloak and coming so far that it had dropped below where Batty stood, which was now bare of it, like a bald old man's crown surrounded by a fringe of white.

He shouldered his saddlebags and moved on down into the chill embrace of haar, for he had work to do before those lads came back from Mosspaul. He smiled to himself, for he knew that whoever commanded them had thought himself smart as new paint on a Michelangelo portrait, sending a tracker out, all sleekit and creishie.

For a time Batty had thought he might have to kill the man, but Tinnis's Faerie had stopped him cold and now his leader and companions would be back to hunt the hill, not knowing exactly where Batty lay on it.

The mist was handy and they would balk at stumbling around in it, but they would soon find a trail or two, fresh and clear as a torch-guide on a cobbled street, leading through the gorse and alder at its foot. Batty smiled, vicious as adders.

He did his work amid the dripping mirr, his panting and grunting muffled and falling as dead sounds to the mulched moorland. Teeth and leather thongs and his one hand worked, while his feet were careless with twigs and his knees with branches, bending the whip-thin trees. There were few enough of them, wee hardy affairs huddled together in clumps as if trembling at the loom of Tinnis above them; Batty's clear trail led from one to another, like a fox sliding back to its lair.

Then he hunkered and waited, chewing damp bread in the soaking mist. It would be down all day now, he knew, for it must be mid-morning and would have burned off or blown away if there had been a sun anywhere beyond it, or a puff of wind.

The lads were tardy, he thought and smiled. Sore heads and bad bellies, no doubt of it. Wishing they were laid in the warm and dry to shut their eyes and sleep off the thump and maze inside their skulls.

He heard them with the jingle of a bridle and was instantly alert. He did not move, but let them come to him, and they were slow about it, for this was Tinnis in a mist, which was worse than Tinnis in the dark.

'Here,' called a voice, which made even Batty start.

'Shush,' growled another. 'Why leave him sleeping safe in the mist when we can wake him up and have him run us all over the hill? Ye capernicious gowk.'

It was Hutchie. Batty would know the voice anywhere and sat back on his heels, stroking his raggled, wet beard and thinking on it. It was a surprise that Hutchie was here, and no doubt the Laird had ordered it. Had he done so with the intent of putting Hutchie within reach?

No doubt. The Laird of Hollows was cunning as a weasel hunting rabbit. If Hutchie succeeded, the matter was done. If I take this opportunity, Batty thought, then Hutchie dies and the matter is still done; both rescue Armstrong honour from it at little cost. And if Hutchie dies, the Laird will find a sleekit way to dispose of me later, with no honour in it at all.

He had not considered the possibility of Hutchie and so his plans altered then and there, from simple to red murder in an eyeblink. For now, he followed the original path of it and warbled through his cupped hands.

'Men of Hollows. Begone.'

'Christ in Heaven.'

They stopped, confused and afraid. Scarted Wat crossed himself and mumbled wardings; Hutchie was scathing.

'Off. Dismount, you fools, It is not Faerie, but Batty — here is his trail.'

'He can see us,' muttered Red Dand suspiciously and Hutchie rounded on him.

'Then he will have eyes like burning coals to see through this mirk,' Hutchie retorted scornfully, 'which was no part of the Batty I knew. He needs eyeglasses, I am told.'

Now that was a foul lie and Batty bridled at it. He would need them to read with, he admitted, but since he could not read at all, there was no need for eyeglasses.

He reached in the bag of adders with his gauntleted hand and plucked one out, watching it curl sluggishly and flick the air with its little Devil's tongue. This one was near black, with a faint lightning streak pattern, but it was as mazed as any drunk with the cold.

'Begone – or accept a gift from the powrie of Tinnis.'

He lobbed it at them, heard the slight body hiss in mid-air. There was a moment's pause, then a frantic rustling as people sped away from it, followed by cursing and the sound of fevered beating. Batty laughed and drew out another.

'Medusa's combing,' he fluted and lobbed that one too.

Red Dand was whirling this way and that, for he was not sure the first one had been properly killed and was heading back to his horse to get off the ground and trust to it to spot the wee beastie. The second one plopped on his shoulder, and for a moment he could scarcely believe it. Then he yelled, 'Serpens! Serpens!' Folk saw him do a wild jig, flailing his arms furiously. Buttery John laughed and then Red Dand felt the sting of the strike and could not believe it.

'I am bit. I am bit – oh God...'

Hutchie stamped on the fallen snake, but the ground was soft and he saw it slither out from under his foot. He chopped at it, saw it hit and writhe, curling round the wound. When he looked, only the tail was there.

'Now you have made two,' Scarted Wat said bitterly, and Hutchie, blinking and sweating despite the chill mist, rounded on him, bellowing so all of them could hear.

'Get on. Get after him. Find his lair and end this.'

Red Dand was sitting stunned and holding his neck. He looked up at Hutchie with the eyes of a frightened bairn.

'I am bit,' he said. Hutchie cursed him and moved on.

Batty listened to the crack and scramble of them through the tussocked moorland grass and the knots of trees, following the clear-made trail of snapped twigs, the white new bark of them bright as a blaze. There was a sudden swishing sound and a slap, followed by a sharp cry. Then there was silence for a moment, until a voice, thick with pain, broke the stillness.

'My neb. Christ, my neb is broke.'

Batty nodded with satisfaction; if the man had stayed mounted, the whipping spring-trap would have slapped the chest of his horse and made it rear and buck. But the nose of a man was better, and blind with snot and blood and tears, he would be less of a problem.

A few steps further in and a scream rent the air; Batty knew that one was the stake on a pole, at fetlock height for a horse, shin height for a man. That would hurt...

He lobbed more adders until he heard one man curse him, and then Hutchie, the Faerie, the mist and Tinnis all one after another, and knew he had broken them; he checked the powder and priming of his brace of pistols.

Now was the new part of his plan; he took a deep breath and started to move.

Hutchie, scowling and red-faced with fury, ranted and roared so that Batty could have found him in the dark, never mind the mist. But his men had had enough of him and mist and Batty and Tinnis all.

Two had contrived to toe out some of the moss in a dip and were getting Red Dand to leap the seep of puddle in it – it was well known that leaping over water in the presence of the adder that bit you was a cure.

'Sheepskin,' Scarted Wat was saying firmly. 'Fresh killed, wrap it round you and you will be cured of the strike.'

'An ointment of rosemary and betony,' said another and then frowned. 'Or a potion of goosegrass juice and wine.'

'That is for thorn pricks,' said Buttery John, levering himself painfully onto his mount; Hutchie saw the blood on his leg and the man saw Hutchie look.

'An inch or two more,' he said bitterly, 'and I would be picking my cods off them spikes.'

'An inch or two more sense and eyesight,' Hutchie spat back, 'and it would never have happened.'

He turned to them, about to wheedle and plead now, but most were concerned with the getting of their mounts, and Red Dand was beginning to have trouble breathing, his neck red save for the two purple spots where the snake had bit.

'A live pigeon,' Scarted Wat was saying, snapping his fingers as he remembered. 'Laid against the bite.'

'Does it work for nebs?' demanded Maggie's Tam Armstrong, the blood drying on his beard and his voice bitter with pain and the bad cess of his lot.

It got worse with the sudden fizz and bang, a great gout of smoke that milked into the mist. The ball intended for Hutchie missed because Hutchie had just turned away from them with exasperation, throwing his arms into the air – it went between the fingers of his right hand and struck the life from Maggie's Tam with a smacking gout of throat blood and torn flesh.

There were shouts now. A second shot cracked, the flame of it tearing the mist to shreds for a moment, so that everyone saw the dark, hazy shape of a one-armed man.

The ball went hissing towards Hutchie, but it was a hasty shot and struck Scarted Wat's horse, which barrelled over with a thin shriek and a whirl of leg and hooves.

Cursing, Batty thought of throwing down the second pistol and dragging his sword out, but there were too many of them still – so he stuck the hot barrel in his belt, swept up the dropped pistol and hirpled off into the mist, worried now about being pursued.

He need not have done. Hutchie was second in the saddle only because Buttery John was already mounted and reining round. The others scrambled for their horses and scurried out, leaving Scarted Wat trailing after them on foot, screaming at them to wait and take him up.

Panting, sweating and chilled, Batty stopped eventually, hand on his knee and his bead bowed, the drool falling on his beard and his lungs burning. After a while he pounded his knee until it hurt, venting his frustration until he calmed and breathed normally.

Too much to hope that he might have ended the business here. Instead, he had killed another Armstrong outright and maybe done for more, if venom and wound rot were allowed to run.

The Laird of Hollows would not like that, for it was not the outcome he had sought.

Hollows Tower
Later that day

The Laird of Hollows did not like it. Which, to all those who stayed wisely in the shadows and did not draw attention to themselves, was a bit like saying the plague would make you cough a bit.

He roared and scathed and saved the worst curl of his wrath for Hutchie, who had to stand there and take it, though it was flaying the skin from his face.

'You are a hotterel, skrinkie-faced bauchle. A dawlie dwaffle. One man deid, twa hurt and anither like to die of pizen frae an adder. By God, you left the deid man out on the Faerie hill.'

He paced, red-faced and sweating off his jowls like rain, his fine manners gone and his Borders accent thick as clotted blood in his throat.

'You couldnae even bring him safe back, to be mourned and kisted up.'

Hutchie stood, blinking under the blast, but holding his ground until the Laird rounded on him with a dismissive wave, recovering himself enough to speak clearly.

'You are a useless scrap of nothing at all. You could not find a crawling babe. You could not bring a one-armed fat old man off a hill. Leckie – take this dung fly to the undercroft, before I forget myself and hemp him up like the filthy wee bugger-back that he is.'

Hutchie went to prison and gladly, knowing he was needed alive and would no longer be trusted to face the likes of Batty;

the wind of that ball between his fingers puckered his nethers even as he stumbled down the wind of stair to a safe prison.

Those left in the hall saw the Laird turn and scowl for a while at the fire, until the whisper of slippers on flags brought him from the reverie; he turned into his Lady's stare.

'Another death,' she said pointedly. 'An Armstrong left in the Tinnis bracken – how does that balance the pan with Hutchie Elliott weighting the far side of it?'

'We will fetch poor Maggie's Tam back – no more on that,' he growled, waving her away, and then turned to Leckie, who was waiting, face like a floured bap and well used to the Laird and his ranting.

'Where is Clym these days?' he demanded, and folk looked one to the other, while Leckie coughed and thought. The Lady made a sound of disgust and a face that would curdle milk, seen by the Laird out of the corner of his eye, though he ignored her.

'Clym... in Jedburgh, I believe,' Leckie replied hesitantly.

'Fetch him,' the Laird declared savagely.

'Clym Hen-harrow,' the Lady said, icy as the draught curling round everyone's ankles. 'Is that your solution? Set a rogue to catch a rogue, is it? A Nameless man to bring honour to the Name? By God, husband, you are piling mistake on error here – you hand over Hutchie Elliott and the horse and be done with it all.'

The Laird cared little for censure and less for it being done publicly and not at all for it being done by his wife, who could get away with it. His face grew white and pinched, which was something even Leckie had not seen before and he did not care for it at all.

'Aye,' the Laird said, stiff as a starched collar. 'The horse. I had forgot that. Batty spoke of the horse.'

He strode to the wall and hauled down the Armstrong Sword from where it hung, a rasping ring of steel that set everyone's teeth on edge. It was an awful blade, as everyone said, a great affair whose hilt could take four fists, and the length of it was as tall as the Laird himself, who was not a small man.

He wielded it as Champion of the Name and it was said no one in Liddesdale, Eskdale, Cumberland or elsewhere was the match for him – and though it had been a time since he'd had to prove it, it was clear he had the strength to lift it still.

The strength for even more, as everyone saw and marvelled in horror at.

He strode to the stables with it, scattering people from his path, brawled his way into the place and watched the Fyrebrande lean over in hope of a titbit. Then he swung, without a single word.

He had the strength and there might have been old webs on the length of the blade, but it was sharp. Save for a last ribbon of flesh, the Fyrebrande's head came off with a meaty chunk of sound and the blood hissed like one of Batty's adders.

People screamed; a stable lad fainted, for he had taken a fancy to the fine beast, and even those who had not been so enamoured were scalded by such a treatment of good horseflesh.

But the Laird simply leaned on the dripping blade, watching the steaming tarn of blood leak from under the door and the head flop. Besides a kick or two from the headless corpse, that was the end of the Fyrebrande and everyone knew it.

'Take the head to Powrieburn and stick it up on a pole,' the Laird commanded and no one needed to ask why.

He handed the sword to two others to clean and restore to the wall, then worked a wrenched shoulder muscle, and paused only once on his way out, to stare into the flint of his wife's disapproving stare.

'Hutchie is mine. The horse is mine. Everything in Hollows is mine, to do with as I please, when I please and for my honour.'

Then he walked back into the reek-dimmed hall, bawling for someone to fix the fire.

Chapter Thirteen

Powrieburn
Lent (February)

Will rode over from Hermitage – which he did like a determined dog even when the rain lashed and even when there
seemed little hope in it. The day Mintie had consented to
welcome him in herself, stiff and polite and cold-voiced though
she'd been, was a heart-leap of joy which had made it all worth-
while.

The horse head was a slap to the face, and Bet's Annie,
shawled against the drizzle, had met Will at the bastel door,
her face grim as Tinnis in the dark.

'Aye – the Fyrebrande. Death of Powrieburn's hopes,' she
said, and a voice from the dim had corrected her at once, steeled
and sharp.

'The Fyrebrande was gone from us the day I took it to
Hollows.'

Mintie stepped out into the yard, heedless of the rain spot-
ting her kertch, heedless of the tendrils of hair escaping from it.
She looked up at Will with eyes like agate.

'It is important only because of the mark it sends,' she said,
'that black rent for the safety of Batty Coalhouse is rescinded
by the Laird. I am sorry for it and him.'

Will stirred himself then and pointed out that the horse had
been used to ransom everyone's safety, but Mintie was flint and
iron.

'Powrieburn will look to its own,' she said and then nodded politely to him. 'You would do me a service were you to convey the Laird's message to Master Coalhouse.'

Then she turned and went inside, Bet's Annie trailing after like a gull following a fishing smack.

Will sat for while, the rain dripping off the brim of his hat, his gloves sodden with it and his fine cloak seeped through. Part of him cursed her for her casual latching of him to the finding of Batty and the way she had worded it, the way she knew he would do it because of how he felt.

The other part sang at the thought of pleasing her with it.

So he turned and rode up to the wet bleak of Tinnis, riding open and taking his time about it, making sure he could be seen. It took a long time and he was just on the edge of being convinced that he had soaked himself to the bone in misery for no reason, when the voice had spoken to him out of a tangle of whin.

'Well met, No-Toes.'

He rose out of bracken and rowan, so surprisingly close that Will was flustered by it, until he realised that Batty had honed these skills long since; being a wolf-head in Saxony would have sharpened them, certes.

'You are looking fine,' Batty said with his old undershot grin making it wry. 'Being the law in Liddesdale agrees you well.'

To Will, Batty looked wood-smoked and rough, but no less kettle-bellied and no less determined, so he forswore all the pleasantries and laid out the meat of what he knew, and watched Batty's face set like moulded iron.

'Tell her I will come,' he said, and Will bridled finally.

'Tell her yourself,' he spat back. 'Am I a herald for the pair of you?'

Then he checked his furious reining round, the rain flying from the bit end.

'Mark me, Batty,' he said. 'I hear a man is dead at Hollows and others sore hurt. Did you know that Clem Armstrong died at Whithaugh, of the blood fever in his leg? It turned black and crept to his soul and ended him.'

Batty had not, but was not surprised. Will nodded, vehement and savage.

'Yet another to your tally. There can be no more, Batty, for I will be forced to move on it from Hermitage. I will not have more murder in Liddesdale.'

Batty wiped drips from the end of his nose and nodded sagely.

'Whether you want it or not is neither here nor there,' he replied flatly. 'Murder is in Liddesdale, as it was when you were Land Sergeant and was when you were all snotters and skinned knees. As it will be when you are cold in your grave. Murder in Liddesdale is a right.'

'March law,' Will scorned. 'I have heard that thrown about all my life, and by harder men than you. That is why we have Wardens on either side of the divide and a Keeper, special and singular for Liddesdale. So there can be true law, not whatever the red murderers make up as they go.'

'You would do better to exert yourself for the protection of Powrieburn,' Batty countered, 'for you'll have better success with it. Since you have taken over from Hepburn as Keeper, however much for the moment, you take over his duties to that house as well. They are as much in danger there as me.'

'You are their bloody danger,' Will spat back, his face angry and his arms waving veils of rain up. 'You, you red-handed cantrip. Enough is enough—'

'Until Hutchie is handed ower, there is not enough,' Batty said, and his voice was bleak as the Bewcastle Waste, a sound to make Will stop his angry reply.

'Is the babe found yet?' Batty asked as the rain lisped into their silence, and Will shook himself from his sodden scowl.

'No, nor is there word that the English have her.'

Batty sighed and cocked a squint at the sky.

'Pity the poor mite, then, if she is out on a day like this.'

There was a pause and then he wiped rain from his face with his one grimy hand.

'The lass of Powrieburn wants justice, Will,' he said, almost sadly. 'If not me bound to it, then you will be. And go willing, as willing as you came here in the wet and cold.'

Shakily, Will wiped his mouth and then forced a laugh.

'You make Mintie sound like a witch with a bad spell and a lock of your hair...'

'Worse than that,' Batty answered slowly, turning away to find his hidden horse. 'Worse than wee apples driven with summoning thorns. Worse than mandrake dipped in man-milk and blood.'

Will was silenced by the tone as much as the man's knowledge of a cunning woman's arts. Batty's voice was wistful as lost youth when he turned his back on Will and started to vanish into the trees.

'We will do it for the spell of love, Will.'

It trailed after him, faint as his tuneless singing.

'*For a' the blood that's shed on the earth, runs through the springs o' that country.*'

For a time after, up in the shadow of Tinnis, Batty had watched Will sitting there, dripping in the rain. He had not meant to be so hard on him with talk of love and wondered if Will understood that what he felt for Mintie was not the same thing at all. Will's was a hotter, saltier affair. Not that it mattered, since Mintie would not be comforted or loved in any way by any man now.

Still he came to her in Powrieburn as promised, singing as he rode into the courtyard, loud enough to let them know who he was and trying to keep to the tune under the glaucous dead eye of the Fyrebrande.

'*I doubt neither speak to prince nor peer, nor ask of grace from fair lady. "Now haud yer weesht, Thomas," she said. "For as I say, so must it be."*'

The rooks wheeled and screeched, making crosses in a sky blue enough to make every Virgin a robe, though the sun in it was a red-gold coin with no heat at all.

He rode up with a wind at his back, dragging itself through the claws of the trees and whipping the bundled cloak; he did it so everyone would see, and at first Bet's Annie, peering through the upstairs window, thought it was some peddler, come early and horsed for the trade.

Then she felt her stomach lurch and her heart rise in her throat.

'Batty,' she said.

He stopped in the yard and looked round as if it was strange to him, which it seemed. He remembered the first time he had come here – though it was not so long ago, it felt like another age; he missed the bark of the dog.

There was little difference to it, save for the horse head stuck on a pikeshaft in the dungheap. The beast's muzzle was bloody, withered back to show the yellow grin, one eye frosted, another pecked out, and the neck a vicious hem of torn flesh, for the rooks had been at it and would be again when folk stopped chasing them from dinner.

Bet's Annie unbarred the door and stepped out, wiping her hands on her apron and nodding politely.

'Have you eaten all you were given? There is more and as much as you need, Mistress Mintie says. Step down and sup – there is fish.'

'And a good day to you, Bet's Annie,' Batty said. 'How keeps this house?'

He made no move to get down, and Bet's Annie finished with her hands and folded them across her bosom.

'The mistress's mother is bedridden. All that has happened has taken the legs from under her.'

And the wee bit sense she had left, she would have added, and Batty saw that, suspected why she was silent and merely nodded.

'Megs? Jinet?'

'Fine well,' she answered to each.

'Mintie?'

'I am well enough.'

She came quietly out of the dim undercroft, as Batty had known she would, and he was facered by it, for he had not expected the whey cheeks and sunken eyes. As rough as a week-dead corpse, Will had said, and he had not been wrong. Mintie was either sore-sick or hag-ridden. Probably both, he decided.

'They have brought you an answer to black rent, I see,' he said, and she took a deep breath and nodded. Bet's Annie snorted.

'I wanted to bury it with the dirt flies in the dungheap they stuck it in, but Mistress Mintie insisted we leave it until you saw it. Have you seen it, Batty Coalhouse?'

'I have, Bet's Annie, so you can fetch a mattock and dispose of it. If there is a wee prayer for horses, say it.'

'Christ forbid,' Bet's Annie declared, crossing herself piously. 'A horse has no soul.'

'Tell that to mine, stabled behind you and with more soul than the likes of Clem Armstrong, who I hear has died – do you still want me to pursue your justice with the Laird of Hollows?'

The last was fired at Mintie and designed to catch her unaware. If it did and revealed the truth, or if she had been ready for it all along, Batty could not tell, for the answer was swift and firm either way.

'Aye. Pursue my justice.'

Batty knuckled his brow to her, turned Fiskie and rode off singing.

'"*Now haud yer weesht, Thomas,*" she said. "*For as I say, so must it be.*"'

Bet's Annie, bustling with the mattock, all disapproval and scowls, commenced to muttering and digging, but Mintie stood and watched Batty go, feeling nothing but a faint wistful loss, as if her kertch had been blown away in the wind.

Chapter Fourteen

Netherby, Cumbria
Later that day

'Give them to me,' Batty said harshly. 'All but Hen. Do what you will with him, since he is kin, though I would not expect ransom for him if I were you – the Regent is not interested in pursuing the Keeper of Liddesdale now.'

Dickon Graham glanced at Batty, seeing the dance of shadows and flame from the torches all along the curved beard and the hook nose of him, so that, for a moment, he resembled Auld Nick himself; he shivered, despite himself.

'What will you do with a puckle o' Armstrongs?' demanded Dickon suspiciously.

'Nothing that need involve the Grahams in any feud with Hollows, since Batty Coalhouse will be doing it.'

'You are known as kin to the Grahams now,' Dickon pointed out and Batty shook his head.

'I am Batty Coalhouse until the day I die and you know it. You used me and the kin in me to put a crimp in the Armstrong slow match, no more.'

Dickon did not care for the plain speaking, nor for the way Davey-boy was listening, head swivelling one to the other; he did not like to appear less to his son and so he made a show of careful consideration, then closed one eye.

'I planned to keep them a few days longer, then let them go. I have asked no ransom, nor do I want them hemped.'

'Hanging and black rent is not in this at all,' Batty replied. 'They will be released to the care of the Laird.'

He is trying to fawn on the Laird by bringing these ones back to him, Dickon thought. Saying how he had persuaded the fell-cruel Netherby Grahams to part with them. Still suspicious, he gave a grudging nod.

'Take them. They are eating me out of all larder.'

—

Dog Pyntle knew matters had changed for him again when he heard the gruff, off-tune singing and the rattle of keys in locks.

'*And see ye not yon broad, broad road, that lies across the lily leven? That is the Path of Wickedness, though some call it the Road to Heaven.*'

'Batty. Batty Coalhouse – is that you there?'

The answer was cheerful, with a hint of smile in it – like a sun in the dark of Dog's life now.

'It was when I woke this morning.'

Other voices joined in, gruff and suspicious, but Dog Pyntle turned this way and that, with only dark wherever he pointed his face.

'You are coming with me,' Dog heard Batty say. 'How many are here – eight is it?'

'Aye, eight. The other four were let go days since. Ransom paid by kin, no doubt.'

That voice was slathered with bitterness; Sandie Armstrong it would be, who came from Canobie with his brother, Sim. Their ma was a wee widow, too poor to ransom her boys, who had been left to the grace of their master, the Laird of Hollows. Who had paid ransom at last... Dog Pyntle almost sobbed with the relief of being included in it, even though he was only a Bourne, a Name long recognised as supporters of the Armstrongs, but even so...

'Has ransom been paid, then?' demanded Sandie.

'Step lively, lads,' Batty said, which was a jest as Dog found out, for his ankles were roped like a hobbled pony and none of them could do more than shuffle. Dog felt his hands being slapped angrily by whoever owned the tunic hem he was trying to hang onto, so as not to be left behind. He cried out in anguish at it.

'Soft, soft, Dog,' said Batty, his voice all soothe and reasonable. 'You come up behind me on this fine horse and we'll let the others shuffle, shall we?'

Dog could almost feel the hot hating stares on his back as he was lifted up on a hobby and sat sidewise, because his legs stayed roped; the cold bit him, but it had been as chill in the Graham undercroft and worse still.

He bounced on the back of the horse, realising that it was a wee pack pony and that Batty rode alongside it; the others, Dog suspected, were lashed behind and stumbling after, a sorry wake of misery.

They moved for a long time and Dog recognised only one part of it for sure – passing through Canobie, where the sharp stink of mould and damp and privies let him know it.

He remembered the village with a sudden sharp pang, how it had looked all the times he had gone through it, the street so narrow two horsemen could not ride side by side, the road no more than two deep ruts of brown water, the soil yellowed with years of dumped manure from ox and horse. The houses would still be wizened cruck affairs of wattle and weathered daub huddled round a square with a mercat cross.

Dog heard some chaffer from village folk to those Armstrongs they knew, but none hailed him, nor came within a loud shout of Batty. In the end, Dog did what he always did when the hunger bit and the cold gnawed; he fell half asleep, running towards oblivion, where it was warm and dry and he was fed and could see sunlight on meadows.

The halt and the voices woke him, so that it took a while before he sluggishly rolled back into the ache of the world, into the endless dark and the cold; his eyes blazed with pain and he could feel the leak of something on his cheek, from under the bandage that had been put round his head the day his eyes had gone.

Shot from his head by someone in Powrieburn. No one had cared and Dog thought the leak might be tears, though he knew the peppershot had blasted away eyes, tears and light, all in an instant. And no one had cared then, nor now... no, that was a lie. Someone cared now, for he heard her voice.

'Poor wee man – yon cloth on his head is a pure disgrace. Here – light him down to me and let me look at it.'

'You were ever for caring, Bella,' Dog heard Batty say, and then he was dragged from the horse and ushered stumbling over unfamiliar ground to where a hand on his head forced him to duck. He realised from the change in sound and the smoky reek that made him gasp that he was indoors; the heat of the fire drew him like a mad moth.

There was an exchange of greetings, Batty to someone else, and then he realised as the woman tutted and fiddled that it was Andrew the smith, and his wife was the one slowly unpeeling the cloth from round his eyes. It had crusted to him and something tore and made him whimper.

'Christ in Heaven, what a mess,' a new voice said, and Dog heard the goodwife shush him. Agnes's man, Dog thought, and did not want to know what was a mess. Not ever.

He felt the wonderful balm of warm water, the gentle sponge of cloth and would have wept save that he had no way of doing it. Instead, he made mewling noises that tore Bella's heart.

There was a soft murmuring exchange, conversation like a swirl of bees; he heard Batty cough and growl and give thanks to Andrew for what was clearly water and bread.

Then Dog felt horned fingers on his matted chin, tilting his face up.

'By God,' Batty said, 'she did a work on you, did Bet's Annie.'

'Bet's Annie?'

'Aye. Shot you from the window of Powrieburn. In bad light and hasty with anger, so this shows how poorly you stand with God, for that shot should never even have hit the cobbles, let alone your face.'

The fingers were removed and, stunned, Dog let his chin fall, feeling the utter bleak, black misery of his life settle on him like a moan. Shot by a woman. Shot against the sort of odds that could never be worked out with quill and pen and clever wee men in university gowns. He felt a hand on his heaving shoulder and then the goodwife's disapproving voice.

'Christ save us, Master Coalhouse – have you no mercy in you? Bad enough the man is blinded, without that you taunt him with it.'

'Then he should have stayed clear of me and Powrieburn,' replied Batty, indifference ripe in his voice. 'And not have me shot off Tinnis Hill.'

Dog felt something thrust into his palm, hard and curved; a handle.

'Here,' Batty said, 'carry this.'

It was a pot of cold pine pitch, almost solid to the touch and distinctive, acrid to the nose. Dog did not ask why they carried it, or what Batty wanted to caulk with it, but he had heard of the feud with Hollows and thought Batty had a secret lair that would need some proofing against the weather.

The hawthorn faggots strapped up behind him gave off another scent he knew – good wood, burns hot and slow, and more importantly, gives off almost no smoke; Dog was sure Batty was headed for his lair once he dropped them off.

Near Hollows, he thought. Batty will not risk going close to the place, but will fasten us up until he finds a way to negotiate with the Laird.

So when he heard Sandie, Sim and the others start in to mutter among themselves, then finally burst out with asking why they were headed towards Tinnis, Dog was not worried.

'Free us if the ransom is paid,' Sandie demanded truculently, and Dog could hear the struggle of him, testing the bonds on his wrists.

'It is not,' Batty answered. 'Not yet.'

'Then it is yourself has ransomed us?'

Dog heard Sim snort. 'He thinks to buy his way back into the favour of the Laird with us.'

Batty chuckled.

'If that is true,' Dog heard him say, 'you had better hope Johnnie Armstrong of Hollows favours you. Else you are no use to me at all.'

That closed mouths, and they went on with the wind hissing through them and the hunger gnawing. Dog's eyes felt raw, felt as if they were still there but full of grit, and he marvelled at that, almost wondered if they were growing back.

They stopped. Batty hauled Dog off the horse and he heard the others muttering about where they were. One – a youngster called Cock Davey – pointed out that they were at the dule trees and that gave everyone pause. The dule were fine oak, a grove of eight or ten of them and much used by the Laird of Hollows – dule were hanging trees.

'Are you hemping us?' Dog asked, trembling, and Batty's laugh was reassuring.

'No, Dog, your neck is safe and everyone's besides. Hemping is not in it at all.'

He instructed Dog with brief, harsh phrases – knot this, hold that – and Dog realised that he was lashing the wrists of the men so that they each embraced a tree, their arms stretched round the fat trunks, cheeks pressed close to the rasping bark.

It was as fair a way of fastening them as any, Dog thought. He will send me to Hollows to fetch the ransom and tell me where to deliver it; even without eyes I can follow the road to Hollows with a tapping stick. And after, he will seek me out when he is sure I am not followed.

So he sat, douce and in the dark, listening to Batty make a fire, which he thought was for mercy's sake, to keep the cold from them while they waited. Yet the cauldron went on it which was a puzzle, and the sharp, acrid tang of the resin coming to the boil was a surety that it was the pitch cauldron and not another with soup.

That and the tuneless singing of Batty was rasp enough on everyone's nerves – '*O see not yon narrow road, so thick beset wi' thorn and briars? That is the Path of Righteousness, though after it but few inquires*' – but the harp to his carp was the slow, steady rhythm of him whetting his blade against a stone held between his knees.

'Batty – what are ye about?'

Sandie's voice was grim and had more anger than fear in it, for he thought matters were still bound for freedom; Dog was now not so sure, especially when Batty grunted and levered himself up.

'Here,' he said and closed Dog's fist round a stick. 'Hold it carefully, for it is dripping hot and I would not have you burned.'

A slather of boiling pitch on a rag-ended stick; Dog held it though his hand shook, and he heard Sandie give a growl.

'Batty – for the love of God, what are ye about—?'

It ended in a sudden deep thunk and a shriek, so that Dog trembled so hard he almost lost the pitch-brand, but it was plucked from his fist, and he heard the sizzle and the sudden smell of roasted meat.

Now everyone was bellowing and screaming, though Dog could hear Batty returning to the pot, still singing, slow and tuneless.

'*O, they rode on and farther on, and waded rivers abune the knee. And they saw neither sun nor moon, but heard the roaring of the sea.*'

'Batty, for the love of Christ...'

'Hold this.'

And the stick was shoved into Dog's fist again. Another thunk, another shriek, and Dog, when the brand was plucked from him, fell to the ground, hearing the roaring of Batty's singing sea.

On and on it went, endless and dark as Dog's world.

Mintie had dreams in her wee place in the roof space, dreams where the wind blew and she heard a baby wail, though she could not find it when she waked, more often than not chilled and drenched with sweat. She did not sleep much at all, and when she did, it was all dreams.

Once she found herself lying in the middle of the floor, while one of the kist-mice cleaned its whiskers and looked at her with a bright black bead of an eye; somewhere the wails of a lost bairn faded.

She wished Agnes would come back, but knew she never would now. Mintie suspected Jinet or Megs had told her what had happened, when they'd been sent to trade winter feed for goose eggs and been resentful of struggling the cart through the mire, fearful of being fallen on by one or all of Powrieburn's many enemies.

They had not, of course, but excitedly spilled all their gossip about Mintie's visit to Auld Nan, and afterwards Agnes had come on her own, come no more than an hour since, to offer some soothe. Since her own loss was something shared, Mintie had welcomed it, been fervent for it, for she wanted questions answered and could not turn to her ma, nor any of the women in Powrieburn – even Bet's Annie, least chook-brained of them all.

She wanted to know why Agnes had named her bairn. Eck, she called it, even though it had died before it was even born and so was unbaptised. You never revealed a bairn's name save to the priest – Reformed or otherwise – who was wetting its head for the first time.

'So your Eck was unprotected from witchery,' Mintie said, staring fervently into the whey face of Agnes. 'Or the Queen of Elfland's Faerie folk. But since he was not even born when he died, does that place him still in the grace of Christ? Is a babe innocent and in the embrace of God until he tumbles from the womb?'

'I don't know,' Agnes had mumbled, not liking this, not liking the way it brought memories she'd thought balmed enough to suffer this, surfacing like turds in a blocked privy.

'I mean,' Mintie had said, hugging her knees in the old girlish way she had done when they had both been young; it lumped Agnes's heart into her throat, that remembrance of the way they had been and how far it was from what they had become now. She could not believe, sometimes, what they had gone through in so short a time.

'I mean,' Mintie repeated, 'if your babe was in the grace of Christ, then he would not have died unshriven, wandering lost forever.'

'What became of him?' she asked suddenly, catching Agnes by the hand. 'Was he buried at a crossroads?'

Agnes knew that was the haunt of suicides and the moon-mad, the unshriven who had died; she did not want to think of it, for her ma and da had actually buried wee Eck at the Debatable boundary stone, which served the same purpose and for the very reasons Mintie had dragged up. They rasped across Agnes, opening the old wound to new raw.

She knew why Mintie did it, thinking of her own bairn, the half formed, unborn wee soul sent spinning back where it had come from.

'Mintie,' she said. 'Don't, please, if you love me...'

'My ma told tales of such,' Mintie had gone on, oblivious to Agnes's distress. 'I heard her tell them with old Mary, who was servant here until she died four years since. About a woman whose bairn had died and she kept it hidden, for she was not married on to anyone and feared the wrath of her lover if he found out about it.'

She turned liquid eyes on Agnes, who did not want to hear more but could not move.

'But you can't keep such a thing hid in a house full of women, can you? They found out and tried, for mercy of the woman, to bury it on holy ground at night, in the graveyard of their wee chapel. The priest caught them and forced them to bury it at the crossroads beyond the village – and then told everyone, as wee priests will do.'

Mintie stared unseeing at the peeling whitewash of the walls.

'They heard it wail every night. Every one of them and others for a twenty-mile round. Some saw it too, bone-white and crawling, trying every shuttered window in the hope that someone would let it in, to the warm and a mother's embrace—'

Agnes broke then, ran wailing from the room, spilling past Bet's Annie, busy carding wool, down the ladder to the undercroft and out, away home. She would never come back.

Mintie remembered Bet's Annie's scathing curl of lip.

'By God, you were a wilful lass and have now become an uncaring woman. Yours is not the only bairn lost in Liddesdale, and if you had an ounce of love left in you, you would have been more merciful to poor Agnes.'

She had then huffed off, trailing her cardings of wool like an indignant veil, and Mintie had sat for a long time, watching the slow, whirling drop of a wisp, remembering when she had watched her own mother do that, hearing her laugh at Mintie's attempts to stagger up on little chubbed legs to chase them.

Her own mother. Mintie glanced at the bed and the rattle-breathing heap on it, who would never card another thing, nor laugh with Mintie again. Nor would any bairn of Mintie ever stagger on fat little legs, to be laughed at in turn and smile a rosebud smile back at her. She thought then of Will, of what might have been, of falling into him like a spell, of drinking the air from his lungs like the sweetest French wine.

Now she picked all that by the edge, holding it at arm's length until she could find a safe enough place to rest it upon the earth and walk away forever.

She wept then, the tears squeezed out like fat apple pips, slow rolling on her cheeks like the lost drift of carded wool – then gulped, stopped, and dried her eyes, sniffing. Tears would not serve. Work would serve. That and her justice.

Later, washed clean of tears, had come the long burn, like the time she had found her da with a hole in him the size of a dinner plate, the size of a wee unformed bairn in a belly. Justice, she thought. Or revenge.

It did not matter which, to her or to Batty Coalhouse.

Chapter Fifteen

Hollows Tower
The next day

The Laird was eating porridge and smoked fish in the reeking dim of his hall, brooding on the fact that his wife was up in her bower, embroidering with a furious intensity and allowing only the two women culled from the ones sent away from Hollows.

He ate alone and was conscious that those coming and going around him did not linger and moved as if they walked on plover eggs. All save Leckie, of course, who knew he had more leeway than anyone else and took advantage. He had known the Laird since he was wee Jock, son of the arrogant, infamous Johnnie Armstrong. He knew the burden that had heaped on a wee boy's shoulders and the crushing grief when the da was hanged by the king. No grace from a graceless face...

There had been other Armstrong deaths that day and since, at the hands of Grahams and Musgraves, who had been visited in turn by Armstrongs from Willieva and Langholm. All of it had forged a hot iron of hate in the boy who took on the mantle of Hollows – yet even Leckie had never seen the Laird's Jock so intense with brooding as he was now over this Batty Coalhouse.

So far, Leckie was pleased to see, it had not warped him enough that he did something foolish – like burning the Grahams out of Netherby and starting a war within a war, or routing the Hendersons out of Powrieburn and bringing the wrath of that name, as well as their supporters, the Hepburns of Bothwell. It had been a sweaty moment when Armstrongs had burned the Musgraves out of Bewcastle this very year for a ten-year-old slight, but the nations were at war so no one had blinked an eye.

The Laird had not been able to resist a dagger swipe at old enemies the Scotts when the Armstrong Ride had gone out to force the moving of the royal babe, and Leckie saw a fester in that which might grow poisonous in years to come – but there was God's hand yet in the Laird's forbearance over Coalhouse.

So far. It was a constant alarm to Leckie that he could not be sure of this remaining unchanged, that the slow match that was Batty Coalhouse might burn down to something designed to make the Laird burst with a madness of anger.

The arrival of the peddler and his hooded companion made for unease then, even though the peddler had been expected and Leckie set to watch for him, among others.

Leckie was heading for the yett and had to pass through the hall, pass the Laird spooning porridge and fish into a beard that needed trimming; a mark of the times, he thought uneasily, when a man who usually prides himself on his appearance starts to let his barbering slide.

'Who is it – Clym or the packman?'

Leckie hesitated.

'The packman, though there is another with him. Not Clym.'

The Laird pushed his bowl away, wiped his mouth with a napkin and rose up, the rasp of his chair bringing the servitors quickly, more for the scramble to get surreptitiously at what he'd left in his bowl than any assistance.

Leckie obediently allowed the Laird to precede him across to the yett and the doorward, already squinting at the pair below. The peddler waved a greeting with as much enthusiasm as he could muster; he was known the length and breadth of the Debatable and left alone for his usefulness – the women saw to that – but still, arriving in such places as this could be dangerous if you put a polite foot wrong.

The other man moved little, simply stood there hunched and shivering with cold, the soft shroud of rain-mist dripping off the frayed edge of the loop of cloth he had covered his head with. They took in his ragged, stained clothes and the sack on his back; alarmingly, Leckie noted, it leaked watery red down his leg onto the ground and away in tiny runnels of pink thread. He took him for a poacher of fish and rabbit.

'Needle Tam,' the Laird announced. 'Come up into the dry and warm. The women will bless your arrival, and once you have seen to me, you can see to them.'

Tam the Peddler nodded sagely, hefted his snail's-home pack and started up the steps to the tower door. He had silk thread, good needles, ribbons, buttons, geegaws and much else besides – but the true wealth in Needle Tam's pack was a crumpled, crinkling square of sealed envelope, carried secretly from the English Deputy Warden to the Laird of Hollows.

'Who is your companion?' the Laird asked curiously, peering at the man. Leckie gave a short, sucking gasp as the man swung his head to the sound of the voice, the soaked cloth band round his eyes revealing that he was blind. Despite it, despite the filth and the mad beard and the tangle of infested hair, Leckie knew the face. So did the Laird, whose voice went quiet and hard.

'Dog Pyntle,' he said, and the blind man jerked.

'The Laird,' he cried. 'Is that yourself?'

'Dog,' the Laird replied, and the man suddenly fell to his knees and started to moan.

'By God, Laird, he made me. He made me bring them and I could see nothing of it, but I heard, Laird, I heard. The screams and the chopping, Laird...'

Tam the Peddler was alarmed himself now and stepped back from the moaning Dog Pyntle, disowning him.

'I met him on the road,' he whined apologetically. 'I could hardly leave him, blind and stumbling as he was, for Christian charity. But the sack bothered me, Laird, then as now, but he widnae let me look...'

227

Men spilled down the stairs at the Laird's command and he came out himself to the top step, heedless of the rain dripping on him. The men took the sack from the grasp of Dog Pyntle and upended it.

The harvest of arms tumbled out like bloody kindling, so that Tam stepped back with a cry and Leckie had to shove a fist in his mouth at the sight. All left arms, he saw with horror, bloody stumps still leaking, cut off just above the elbow...

As a message it was as unsubtle as a blow to the head, Leckie thought. As unsubtle as a horse head on a pole. A message from a one-armed man, ramping up the vicious mean of this pointless feud – eight strong arms, culled from eight Armstrongs. Left arms, like the missing one on the man the Laird hated.

He waited, holding his breath at what the Laird might do now, and after a long pause broken only by the rasp of breathing, the Laird turned to Leckie.

'Find out from Dog Pyntle where the rest of these men are and if any live yet,' he said, and the harsh, quiet voice was as discomfiting as if it had been a raging shriek. 'Then have Clym come to me the minute he arrives – the very minute, Leckie. I want to see him dripping puddles in front of me.'

He turned away and Leckie could not be sure if it was rain making the runnels down his cheeks.

Hollows Tower

The next day

Clym watched the brace of two-wheeled carts lurch up to the dule trees, the luckless Armstrongs and Bournes trailing after them faced with the task of untying the men and loading them.

Two were dead, one would die, and the rest, as Unhappy Anthone noted, 'will ne'er play the fiddle again.'

No one laughed and not only because Anthone's savage wryness was so familiar to them that it was little more than noise these days. Clym looked at these, his Bairns; they were bog-brown with ingrained dirt and weather, careless of clothing, careful with weapons and any armour they had, since life depended on it.

None of them had Names. Red Will's Tam, Sore Jo, Corbie Mart — they had bynames, given for appearance or character, but not one had a Name, for they were all the worst of the worst, the broken men.

At some point, they had committed the one crime that the Borderers would not forget or forgive — they had sinned against their own and were now shunned by the grayne. Once they might have been Croziers or Bournes or Grahams, or Forsters and Hetheringtons from across the Divide, but now they were only Clym's Bairns and that was the sole family they knew. They skulked in the worst wastes of the Debatable, trying to scratch a life and avoiding everyone unless they had advantage in it.

Clym had been an Armstrong once, but no Armstrong would give him even the loan of the title; not after he had killed his own da and ma and sisters while deep in the drink and quarrelsome. Clym had woken to the horror of it, but it was too late then and he had been forced to flee before the world came down on him.

It had turned his hair white, and that, with his round face and beaked nose, gave him the look of the hen-harrow, that pale merciless hunter of the moss. Clym, in the years between then and now, had gathered other broken men to him, and they called themselves his Bairns in a bitter parody of the family they'd all once had.

It was strange, then, for them to be riding openly up to Hollows and they did so cautiously, though Clym was reasonably confident that he had carefully avoided annoying the Laird of Hollows in all the Rides they had done — wee affairs, for oats and the odd cow and a bit of shine to spend in Mosspaul.

Reasonably. But you could never fathom the Laird of Hollows, for he was his father's son after all.

So, with his men scowling filth into the enclosure of the barmkin, Clym trailed his moss-trooper reek of woodsmoke, leather and old death into the hall and stood, neither arrogant nor subservient, while the Laird slouched in his high seat and looked him over.

Christ, he was an ill-made scourge of a man, the Laird thought, taking in the monster dagg stuffed into his belt. Worn wood and old iron, it had a handle that ended in an axe blade, so that if you held it by the muzzle you had two weapons for the price.

And that face, he thought, looks as if it had been set on fire and then put out with a shovel.

'You know Batty Coalhouse,' he said without greeting or preamble and saw Clym's head come up, knew he had hooked the man as sure as a trout takes fly.

'Aye,' Clym answered, and the Laird tossed a leather bag across the table, so that it slid and chinked and then fell off the edge to the floor with a satisfying shunk of coin.

'Find him. He is on Tinnis Hill, hiding like a wee rat. Find him, half kill him and bring the live half to me here.'

Clym pursed his lips, squinted, ran grime through his beard with his fingers, and then finally bent, picked up the purse and weighed it.

'If I find these are coppernoses,' he said without a smile, 'I will be back to demand double.'

'Speak to me like that one more time,' the Laird said coldly, 'and I will break your limbs and hurl you in the Hole.'

Now it was Clym who narrowed his eyes; the Hole was a great scar out of the rock Hollows stood on – the name came from it, for once the Tower had been named Hole House – and was where the quarried stone had come from. It was as deep as the Tower was high, steep-sided and treacherous.

'Aye, so you say,' he managed, though his throat was dry. 'But you need me.'

The Laird said nothing, and Clym, with a last curl of lip around the silent, staring hall, turned and clacked out, aware of the disapproving scorn like a heat on his back.

Now Clym watched the Armstrong servitors struggle with the bodies and let his own sneer of triumphant scorn hold sway at them labouring while he watched. Hard labour too – dead weight and groaning wounded were lending little help. Clym had heard that a victim of an earlier affair was gasping and unlikely to ever recover from a viper bite at Hollows.

It was a fearsome tally on its own, never mind the others Clym had heard laid at Batty Coalhouse's feet. And all for a dead horse and a man called Hutchie Elliott.

Still, it didn't matter to Clym what the Laird's reasoning was, for his coin was sound – no poor testoons in it at all – and besides, Clym would have done it for much less because it was Batty Coalhouse and because of Ill-Made Wattie Bell. The day Batty had taken Ill-Made Wattie and had him hanged was the same day the man had been out delivering much needed succour – drink and oats – to the Bairns.

Clym had thought that unfair then and had not changed his opinion, especially since Batty had gone on to rout out other Bairns with his fouled Bills and his big spinning-wheel daggs.

He looked up at the drip of Tinnis, the glower of gathering pewter promising storm over it, and wondered if Batty knew who Ill-Made's friends were. And if he knew how many times Clym Hen Harrow had visited Ill-Made in his wee hidey-hole, spending the night with good drink, all snug, warm and dry up on Tinnis Hill and not bothered at all about the Faerie.

It was a good hole and if Batty did not know of it, Clym Hen Harrow would be surprised. And if he was not using it, Clym Hen Harrow would give up drink for a month. Well – a week, at least.

Black Penny Davey came up then, the brindle hound leashed tight in his hand, though the smell of the blood was making it whirl and whine. Black Penny looked expectantly up at Clym, who shook his head and looked fondly at the dog.

'Not yet, Penny,' he said. 'Keep a tight leash on Beauchien there and don't let him chew on any of the Armstrongs, else there will be words said.'

The others laughed; the Armstrongs loading their stiff or groaning kin onto the carts scowled, and Beauchien whipped the ragged stump of a tail and danced on the end of the leash.

Higher up, among the dripping trees, Batty hunkered in the rowan and whin, watching the men stack his work on the carts. He felt no remorse, felt no more than if they had been logs cut and left for carriage. The only thing he felt was curiosity and a sharp thrill of wariness at the sight of the white head.

Clym Hen Harrow. He knew the man and his Bairns well enough – so he has been set on me, he thought, him and his slewdug. He remembered the beast, with its sliced tail and torn lugs, straked lip and old, badly knitted scars. It was as ugly a beast as the man who held it, Black Penny Davey, so called for the pennyroyal he used to keep the fleas off the beast.

Beauchien. Batty recalled the name and smiled. It might be ugly as old sin, look as if it was sewn together from three or four other dogs entire, but it was worth five pounds English for the nose on it.

Mayhap I should offer to buy it with what Mintie owes me, he thought with a grim smile, for it is certes that they will put it to the smell of me and track me up Tinnis. Clym hates me because of Ill-Made, who was his friend.

He looked at the sky and nodded quietly to himself; the ache in his joints, the strange, oppressive calm and the lowering dark of the clouds all gave him satisfaction. A storm was coming and even Beauchien would not follow scent in the pissing rain.

He had time yet and would make good use of it.

For a long time more he watched them, sitting on their horses and seeming to laugh and take their ease while watching the Hollows men take the one-armed away; but Batty was sure Clym was sporting himself to be seen, giving Batty the message that his time on Tinnis was limited, for the Bairns were coming for him.

He watched them ride off, heading for Andrew's forge, and wondered if the folk there were in danger – then decided not. Clym would shelter, ask questions and be skilled in extracting what he could from the innocent answers. Batty tried to remember if he had said anything to Bella or Agnes that would lead Clym and his Bairns to the hidey-hole.

Agnes mayhap, he thought in the end. I have said nothing, but she has been to Powrieburn, and though none there know the place of it, I may have mentioned Ill-Made's hole in the hearing of Megs or Jinet. That pair had little in their heads but gossip, he thought and sighed. Besides – Clym might know of Ill-Made's Tinnis hideaway, them being such good friends...

He would have to leave the hidey-hole once the storm was done. Then a thought struck him, feral and vicious, and he hunkered back and stroked his matted beard with his one grimed hand and, eventually, smiled.

Powrieburn
At the same time

The women were easier these days, for it was now late February and everyone knew it was the lean time, so bad that Rides were forgotten.

Michaelmas to Martinmas was the Riding time – the end of September until the start of November, when the fells were dry and the cattle strong enough to drive and the moonless nights clear. The dead of winter meant foul weather, weakened cattle and, worse still, weakened horses. It was now weeks past Candlemas and the days were short and dark, oats dear, and no one wanted to be out and about.

Save Batty Coalhouse and me, Will thought, standing politely and aware he was dripping all over the Powrieburn floor. The women were welcoming enough, as they always had been, but this time Bet's Annie moved them away to the other end of the house, while Will sat opposite Mintie and studied her.

She seemed smoke to him. All cinders and grey ash. Her eyes were stone when they had colour at all, and he remembered them as blue, with a wee touch of amber in them. Yet they held his gaze, seemingly blank and set deep in the pit of her face, but with menace all the same, despite the wee lick of false colour in her cheeks and lips.

Bet's Annie would have done that for her, he knew, for Mintie no longer cared. Yet the effect was not what Bet's Annie would have wished; her face reminded Will of a knife in a nosegay.

'There is news,' he said, and she sat and waited for it, saying nothing.

'From Hollows,' he added and saw the flicker at that, sighed with the weary drag of all of it and ploughed on.

'Batty took the Armstrong men, the ones he and the Grahams had for ransom here. Batty cut off every left arm and sent them to Hollows on the back of blind Dog Pyntle.'

The eyebrows went up at that a little and she blinked. Well you might, Will thought angrily and his voice was bitter.

'If a peddler had not chanced on Dog Pyntle, blinded as he is, he might well have plootered his way into the Esk with them.'

Still nothing, and he shook his head at her, exasperated and afraid.

'Eight men are maimed, Mintie,' he said, cold and flat as bad charity. 'Two, I hear, are dead, and if the Laird of Hollows Tower exerts himself to complain, I will be charged with making a Bill on Batty.'

'*The shadow of that hideous strength.*'

Her voice was soft, gentle as doves and distant; Will blinked at what was said all the same, not knowing it and saying so.

'Lyndsay's description of the Tower of Babel,' Mintie said softly. '*The shadow of that hideous strength, six mile and more it is of length.*'

It was from Lyndsay of the Mount's *Dialog* and Will had begged a copy from the man when he had arrived at Hermitage, travelling as Lord Lyon of Scotland on a mission to England. Taking the Garter geegaws of the late King James back to Fat Henry – collar, statutes and garter itself, on the orders of the Regent – though what difference that would make to matters was something Will couldn't see.

Lyndsay, a pompous man in an ill-fitting hat, had been anxious to convey the Regent's regard, equally anxious in his sharp reminder that the Regent of Scotland was impatient at the lack of result in Will and Batty's attempts to locate the missing queen.

There was more and Will had listened to it and nodded, though he was really mulling over the revelation that matters were now leaking out in the open if the likes of Lyndsay knew of the bairn's disappearance. He would have been told because he would be trying to find out if the court at London held her in secret, with Fat Henry waiting and gloating for a perfect moment to produce her, wed on to his wee son.

Sir David Lyndsay did not inspire Will much with the notion that he would not be telling Fat Henry all he knew within an hour of arriving in London. A wee man puffed up with poetical and inclined more to his role as Scotland's Makar than that of premier herald. Proof of that was how easily he was diverted from scathing Will's shortcomings by a request for his *Dialog*.

At least Mintie had read Will's gift, and the memory of his fawning to get it was tempered a little. It also recalled more news…

'Scott of Buccleuch was at Hermitage to welcome wee Davey Lyndsay,' he told Mintie, then added as lightly as he could: 'He will become Keeper of Liddesdale and my time there is now measured.'

Even in the pewter reaches of her mind, Mintie's sharpness could not be dulled. The Keeper of Liddesdale was a Warden in all but title, she knew, his sole duty to clamp down on the

Debatable. Now Wicked Wat Scott had taken on the mantle of it and was clearly making a move to keep it for himself and strike back at the Armstrongs, whom he hated almost as much as he did the English. In return, the current Laird of Hollows hated only one man more than Batty Coalhouse and that was Wicked Wat Scott of Branxholme and Buccleuch.

It was a cake of black powder, with Batty, the aptly bynamed Slow match, burning down to it – and Mintie knew all that, gave it away when she raised her eyes to Will's face. He saw... something there. Sorrow? Regret?

'Aye,' he nodded to her, trying to fan the faint spark into some flame of true interest. 'Scott has now taken the duties of Keeper until a new one is appointed – or the old one sneaks back into favour. Either way, there will be a new Land Sergeant, I am certain, before midsummer. One who doesn't care for Powrieburn or Batty Coalhouse. One who will not be able to divert that hideous strength, Mintie.'

Now he leaned forward, reached out and grasped her wrist, heedless of what she might feel for that, or that it transgressed the unsaid boundaries they had set up.

'Call him off, Mintie,' he said hoarsely. 'Leash Batty Coalhouse before you bring ruin to him and Powrieburn both.'

She tore her wrist free, and for a moment there was fear and anger chasing each other across her carefully constructed face, so that the powder on it cracked and turned her into a parody of wrinkled age.

She drew back and got up from the table, conscious only of the burn on her wrist, as if fired. Once she had been soft and golden, her womb like rose water; now her mind was a well where she peered up at the world in each droplet's clear tremble.

The thunder banged like a clap of hands and everyone jumped; Megs shrieked and Mintie looked at him with eyes like black embers.

'Justice,' she said, and he recoiled at her fierceness. 'I will have justice.'

She walked away from him like a wraith, up the steps to the house.

'Put him out, Mintie,' she heard him call as she moved like a drift of lambswool, away up the last ladder to the roof space, hearing the hiss of the rain like a writhe of adders.

'Put out the Slow match, or he will fire the Border and burn us all to Hell.'

Near Tinnis Hill

Last day of February

The storm had betrayed him, come late to necks and heads of men and horses – and the nose of the spooring dog; Batty heard it, baying like a mourn for the dead, dragging Black Penny and the men with him onto his trail.

The stunted cripple of trees was thinning, leading to a meadow; in summer it would be a place of wildflower and clover where bees and butterflies flitted, but now it was a long, dark wasteland of withered grass which would have sucked the shoes off Fiskie if he'd had any.

Batty didn't like the open of it, headed Fiskie across at a spraying trot to where the trees thickened up again; he found a burn in his way, with a slight sheep path along it. The path followed the twisting bank, narrow and climbing up and down, which was nothing at all to Fiskie, and Batty marvelled, even as he felt a pang for the Saul, who could never have gaited this as smooth and breathlessly.

The dog split the night again with its howl and Batty paused, half turned to the sound, then urged Fiskie down the tussocked slope and into the burn; a waterhen beat out of the tangled broom, fleeing across in a ruffle of feather, spray and outraged cackle.

Fiskie did not like the water, not the cold of it nor the stoned bottom of the burn, where his unshod feet slipped and caught.

The water came up to his belly, up and over the spurs of Batty's big cavalry boots, and Fiskie tossed his head with annoyance.

Batty forced the nag to the task, no longer marvelling – the Saul would have picked a way along this, sure as sheep; a pity, he thought sadly, that when the sense is finest, the legs and wind have to go.

The baying snapped his head up. Save for that bloody old slewdug, he added bitterly, whose nose is full of ancient cunning enough to track me through mud and mire and whose legs and wind seem undimmed.

They moved slowly, for Fiskie was shy of the footing and the burn was spated and cold, so that the rush of it made him wary. The cry of the dog grew louder and they moved on, Batty pushing aside the overhanging branches of the trees. He knew that a dog as good as Beauchien would pick up the scent once it had been established where the prey had come out of the water, but was reasonably sure no one could track the telltale scrape of moss on rock in the moonless dark.

The thunder growled, distant and angry. Come on, you bugger, Batty thought. Rain.

The burn broadened, the bottom turned to sand and the spate of it eased, so that Fiskie relaxed into it more; then Batty spotted, as he had thought to when it started to widen, the other stream coming in from the left, so he turned Fiskie up it, back into the rounded stones that fretted the nag so much.

They grew larger, it grew shallower and more narrowed until, finally, Batty was forced to scramble Fiskie up and out of it. Here he stopped, reached into his slung bag and pulled out the body of a snared hare, scored deeply with his dagger to let the blood scent loose. It stank from being marinaded for hours in what else had been shoved in the bag, and he dropped the hare and moved on.

Twice more he led Fiskie into and out of the burn until it narrowed to a thread and too-steep banks; a steady roar made him think the thunder was rolling in on him. But it was a froth of falling water, white in the darkness, white as the lace round a fancy lord's throat, spilling down a cut of the Tinnis like rain spouting from the eaves of a chapel.

It might be the very burn I landed near, Batty thought with some amazement. He looked up at the wet slick of rock, black as a hog's back, and thought that it was certainly high, that cut. Same as the one I fell off, he thought, and the memory of it brought a twinge of pain to his leg.

The water tumbled and roared and Batty had to turn his whole head and cup his ear to listen for the dog. He thought he heard shouts, faint on the sudden rise of wind, but he could not be sure. A hoolet screeched, a feral sliver of sound.

If it had been a fine story of derring-do, of knights and ladies and questing beasts, there would have been a handy cave in behind that fall, Batty thought. But there was not and he would have to ride right or left. Left took him across the steep-sided burn and on into the cold dark of Tinnis, and he chose that, forcing the reluctant Fiskie into the water and up the other side.

Here he stopped, fumbled in his bag and then dropped another hare slashed with cuts to make it bloody. He hoped it would work, wished the rain would come and make it unnecessary. He hoped the slow match snugged under his hat stayed dry. He wished the flask he had was full of *eau de vie*.

Poor hope and Faerie wishes, he thought. Not a hook to hang your life on.

Batty urged the nag on, backtracking in a half-circle – or so he hoped, for there was no moon and fewer stars, only the shroud of unseen cloud in the dark. The thunder clapped, hard and sudden overhead, so that Fiskie snorted and danced sideways.

They went on, shouldering through alder; the thunder banged again and then a great fist of blue-white flare glared into the night, throwing everything into a stark parody of daylight. Fiskie squealed and Batty soothed him.

Not long after, feeling the slope of Tinnis start to make Fiskie grunt and bend to the work, the rain emptied on them, sizzling like fire through the clawed trees.

Not far away, Black Penny felt the first drops of it and nodded to himself, while the other three with him stumbled at his back, making more noise than a boulder rolling downhill through gorse. It did not matter much, for they'd had little chance of bringing Batty to heel – though Black Penny was pleased with the dog's efforts in the damp.

When he came on it, he found it whining uneasily and circling, sneezing now and then in a quiet way and shaking its head when it did it. Black Penny saw the hare and smelled the reek, knew it at once.

Clever wee Batty, he thought, sitting back on his hunkers and gathering the dog to him.

'Swef, swef – good Beauchien. Never you mind – you did well.'

'What's up?' demanded Sore Jo, and Penny glanced up at him, seeing the man's fingers stray to his scabs, as natural a gesture to him as breathing.

'Ransom,' he grunted. 'The beast is ruined.'

Beauchien snuffed out a wet agreement; the ransom – wild garlic – Batty had tumbled the hare in was all he could smell now and all he would for hours. Penny was admiring of Batty's trick, for it spoke of knowing how trail hounds worked, that Beauchien had the sense not to wolf down some left titbit of meat, but would be unable to pass it without at least a sniff to taste any taint.

At least it was not pepper, Penny thought, which would have caused distress and injury – might even have blinded the beast – and that made him contemplate Batty Coalhouse in a new light.

'Christ – is that us, then?' Sore Jo said with relief. 'Now we can get out of the wet and the dark.'

Penny leashed the dog and rose up as the rain started in earnest, nodding to himself. Clever Batty, he thought, having shrugged off the dug, would think himself safe and us lost in the rain. He would think it better to get back to the warm and dry of his wee cave.

Where Clym and the others were already waiting, having planned it all aforehand. Clever Batty – but not as clever as the Hen Harrow; Black Penny almost felt pity for the one-armed man.

The rain lashed down and Sore Jo cursed it, while Black Penny held his cupped hands until they were overflowing, then wiped them over the dog's nose; it wagged the ragged tail in an ecstasy of love.

The others, hunched and dripping, started to make more whine than the dog, so Penny straightened and nodded.

'Clym,' he said and set off.

Up high on Tinnis, Clym and six others huddled round the grey ash that had been Batty's fire, wishing they had one of their own but shackled to the dark by Clym's order to give nothing away.

Clym wound his axe-dagg in the velveteen black, the ratchet sound of the turning wheel a grate on everyone's nerves. His was the only gun they had; like most Borderers, they distrusted the unreliable weapons, preferring the longbow, or in tight spaces like this, the hand-spanned latchbow – though not powerful, at these ranges it would stick a man in his vitals well enough.

The place was tight, certes. And empty – or so they thought at first arrival – beyond a bracken bed and the ashed pit fire and some stacked dry wood and kindling. The dog had snuffled round the bracken bed and Black Penny had been satisfied that Batty had slept there long enough to reek it, though Penny was worried there would not be enough smell to salt the dog's nose.

Then Unhappy Anthone had found the wee rickle of knitted wool and held it up like a Truce Day football prize. One sniff of that and Beauchien had stretched his neck and bayed, shattering the dark and bouncing the echoes all round.

'Go and get him,' Clym had ordered, and then settled to wait. They had heard the dog baying since, heard the low sullen rumble of the thunder and sat in the dark hidey-hole, waiting.

The flash and flare of lightning made them all jump, but the entrance was around a wee elbow and so the worst of the light only made Faerie stone shadows dance on a wall of it. Corbie Mart was sure they could have had a fire anyway, since it could not be seen outside at all, and Clym hushed him angrily and then put him right on it.

'The smell of the smoke,' he growled. 'And us shown up between it and whoever is outside, easily seen and shot at.'

Not in the wet, Corbie thought moodily. Unless he has a bow, and nothing told of Batty had revealed an ability to bend a longbow with one hand, even if the tales were already crediting him with walking on water.

Even a latchbow would be a trouble for a one-armed man to span – so it would be a dagg or two, which is what Corbie had heard. In this weather, you might as well bare your arse and fart, for the result would be the same – a funny wee noise, some noxious fume and not much else.

Corbie Mart did not voice it all the same, and hunkered in the dark with the rest, waiting and thinking of Mosspaul and decent drink.

He warmed himself at the thought of Batty, one arm dripping, miserable wet as a drowned rat, half crouched to get in the low entrance and raising his head at the last to discover himself and Clym and all the others, with basket-hilt blades, parry daggers and Clym's fearsome axe-butted dagg.

The rain rushed down like a wind, blew damp in the entrance and the smell of mulch and grave earth. No one other than Clym liked this hole. The others had all seen the Faerie work in it when they had ducked in, their shadows capering madly in the torchlight, and marvelled at anyone having risked staying here at all. Corbie Mart, for all the storm banged and fizzed and lashed outside, would not spend one eyeblink longer than he needed to. Clym, who had spent nights here, was scathing with his glare.

'D'ye think they got him first?'

'Shut your hole.'

Corbie Mart subsided moodily, no longer warmed by the wait. He sat and listened to the rustling rush of the rain, the plip and spatter of it off the rim of the cave entrance. He saw a little red eye winking at him. He blinked, rubbed his eyes and looked again. It winked at him like a one-eyed rat; his belly dropped away and he felt colder than snow.

'Clym?' he said and, exasperated, Clym growled inchoately.

'There's an eye.'

'What?'

'A wee eye. Outside. Winking at me. Like a rat with one eye shut – but it is a bit big to be a rat if that is its eye. Mayhap... it might be a bogle.'

'Christ, Corbie – are you wittering witless?'

'A bogle,' repeated Red Will's Tam and laughed scornfully. Unhappy Anthone sniggered an echo.

The sudden arrival of the object made them all leap and curse. It bounced into the cave and rolled quietly around for a moment, while everyone brought their weapons up, and Clym only avoided shooting the thing by the sheerest willpower.

'See?' said Corbie triumphantly. 'A wee red eye...'

The thunder rolled, but as Clym saw the flash of lightning, blue-white and blinding, he knew it was Batty, even before the black shadow of the one-armed man lit the wall of the cave.

That was a blink before the wee red eye of the nubbed slow match burned down with scarcely a sound against the sizzle of the rain, burned down to the neck of Batty's *aqua vitae* flask, long emptied of the contents and refilled with all the powder and shot Batty had, stuffed full as an egg is of meat.

It blew up with a sound that shattered the world of everyone in Ill-Made's cave.

To Batty, it was no more than a dull thud and a dragon's breath of hot air from the entrance, blowing out dust and the stink of powder and blood.

He sat back and let the rain run off him, blinking it from his eyes; 'no match with a slow match' had been the proud boast of his company to all the others. Balthazar Kohlhase has no peer when it came to making and trimming fuse to the perjink second, none for the making of *granadas* with powder and iron scraps and shot.

He had spent a long time at it in the last moments of refuge in Ill-Made's hidey-hole, knowing he would have to leave it and could never come back. He had been vindicated with the very first bay of the dog, its exultant cry at having picked up his scent. There was only one way it could have been given a marker for that – and that had been deliberately left in the hidey-hole cave when Batty had quit it. He had been right – Clym Hen Harrow had known of Ill-Made's cave.

That bloody sock, he mourned to himself. You could never get the blood and brains cleaned from it. I will have to start knitting it ower again…

There was no sound from inside the cave and Batty did not expect one – the packed flask of shot and powder would have been a pepperpot spray in such a confined space; if the Faerie lurked in the shadows of it, they were out now, dipping their hats in the gore and whetting their wee steel nails.

Batty did not want to go in, but the plan called for it, so he went into the entrance enough to gain shelter from the drive of wind and rain, hunkered and sparked his wee tinderbox until it flared into life. Then he juggled it and the torch with his knees until he could raise the sputtering, windblown pitch high enough to see a little better; finally he ducked the rest of the way into Ill-Made's hidey-hole.

He kicked a body almost at once and held the torch high to see the lurid horror of what he had made. They were flung everywhere, shredded and bloody and not like they had ever been people at all.

Batty found Clym, a look of surprise on what was left of his face and a hole in his cheek the size of a pistol ball; the exit of it had taken the most of Clym's cunning brains out the back of his head. Batty stuck the torch in the firepit ash, took the axe-handled dagg, admired it briefly and shoved it in his belt; he drew out his whet-sharp bollock dagger, drew in a deep breath and, grim as old reef, began butchering.

Some time later, Black Penny came up on Ill-Made's hidey-hole, gripping the dog tight because it was whining and straining, which Penny did not like and said so. Behind him, breathing hard and sullen, Sore Jo was soaked and quarrelsome. He wanted shelter, wanted the business done with, and himself off Tinnis with its Faerie and its bang and flash. Everyone knew this because Sore Jo was repeating it like a litany.

'Christ, what now with that dug? Bloody useless whelp when needed and now you say it is facered by something?'

Sore Jo was facered himself, more by the strange taste on his tongue and the sizzle of blue flashes; he wore a steel cap under a blue bonnet and a home-made back and breast, and did not like wearing all that iron with lightning forking about. Besides – the rain was hammering on it and he would have to spend a goodly time with cloth and sheep grease to keep the rust at bay.

'I want off this place,' he began again; and behind him, the other two argued with one another, equally uneasy – but Rob's Davey and Rob's Tam would always do that, regardless of what it was. If one of the brothers was for something, the other was against, and they fell to fighting more often than not, though it meant nothing in the end.

Sore Jo was also a Borders man and hated walking; no Borders man would walk when he could ride, but their horses were tethered up on Tinnis, all them and their gear getting wet; Sore Jo wanted back to his nag.

They came up cautious all the same and hunched under the thunder, the rain and the flashes, which all seemed harder and closer up on the bare waste of Tinnis. They went down a dip and up the other side; the dog, which had led them unerringly, now stopped suddenly, the sodden coat of it bristled along the backbone like a hedgepig.

Now even Sore Jo was alarmed and drew his blades.

'It will be that Batty,' hissed Rob's Tam.

'Away – he is a score of miles from here,' Rob's Davey replied. 'Or else prisoned by Clym. Or dead.'

Then the lightning flashed, blue-white and fierce, and for an instant they all saw Clym, peering at them from low on the ground, as if he was hunkered and waiting for them.

Just for an instant, then he was gone and everyone was blinking, even Black Penny, who had shut his eyes to try and keep his dark sight. It never worked – the flash seared right through his closed eyes and it was all just a white spot to him now – but the dog was barking, squeezing it out as if sicking up bad meat.

'Clym?'

Penny's querulous shout was drowned by the roll of thunder; cursing he went forward and now he had to haul the dog with him, and that had Penny's own hackles up.

They crept up to where the blob of Clym's face started to loom. Penny called out again, squinting through the rain on his face. Then the lightning flashed again.

Clym's face was strange, lopsided, but it was him, the white hair on it plain. He was not hunkered – or if he was, then he had lost a deal of weight.

Blinking in the afterglare of the flash, Penny tried to make sense of it, the thunder crashing overhead now, so hard on the heels of the flash that he knew he was under it, felt the sheer power and weight of it like a giant hanging anvil.

'Clym – is that you?'

The next flash made Sore Jo scream, and they all saw, in the brief starkness of it, the head of Clym, ragged neck trailing tissue and stuck on the hilt of his own sword, which had been driven into the sodden turf of the moor.

And beyond it, eldritch as any Faerie the sharp silhouette of a man with one arm, stark and not inclined to hide at all.

'Christ,' yelled Rob's Tam.

'Christ, Christ,' echoed his brother. Sore Jo whimpered and backed away, flexing wet hands on the hilt of his own sword and parry dagger, and the dog jerked and danced in Penny's hand, barking and snarling.

'Let it loose,' Sore Jo roared out. 'Let it loose.'

'I would keep it leashed were I you.'

The voice was low pitched but came in a moment of sharp silence at the end of a rolling grumble of thunder and was just audible above the hiss of rain.

'I have loaded daggs here, Clym's among them. My powder is dry and I will shoot yon hound if it comes at me.'

There was a pause while they all considered matters, then the air puffed out of the moment and it wrinkled and sagged like an emptied wineskin.

'You have killed Clym,' Sore Jo yelled, and it was clear he was wondering how it had been done and where the others were. Batty confirmed it tersely.

'I have killed them all,' he corrected. 'Dead as stones in the cave.'

'You cut off his heid,' Penny roared out suddenly. 'After he was gone. God's blood – that was an ungodly act on a dead man.'

'He should have thought on that before he came after me, with his fists full of steel and pistol.'

Which brought the memory of Batty's words concerning his own pistols; Penny looked from one to the other and they all had the same thought. They had no pistols, not a longbow, nor even a wee latchbow, only good steel.

'We can get him,' Rob's Tam declared savagely. 'He is lying about his powder being dry. In this weather—'

'Away—' his brother replied, and they knew he had daggs under his cloak – knew that one or more of them would die killing Batty Coalhouse. They winked on the brim of it – and Batty spoke at the tipping point.

'In my time on the Devil's earth,' he said in a grindstone grim of voice, 'I have killed at least one of most everything that breathes air.'

The thunder bawled an agreement to it. The flash showed where he had been and then left them blinking blind.

'I know the insides of men and women and weans better than any barber-surgeon. I have opened bits of the Lord's creation up and let light wander where it had no right to be.'

The thunder growled sullenly and the men turned this way and that, no longer sure of where the voice was coming from.

'Do you think I would harp and carp about you four?'

The voice came from behind them and that broke them apart. They scampered, stumbling and falling over the tussocked grass, jarring themselves on sudden dips and spilling to roll over, then leap up like hares in March.

Batty watched them go, watched the dog drag Penny a little way, because the leash was wrapped so tight round one wrist that he could not let go; every time he lurched back to his feet, the dog would haul him off balance.

Behind, he felt the glassed stare of Clym's disapproval of his Bairns, of their rank white-livered running in the face of a cask-bellied auld man with one arm.

And only the one shot of Clym's own dagg left to him.

Chapter Sixteen

Hollows Tower

Feast of St David (1 March)

He was no more pious than any other man, but William Patten could hold his own in a theological debate and felt bound to defend the reforms of his king. The Laird of Hollows, on the other hand, expressed outrage that Bishop Barlow, encouraged by King Henry, had not only blown the remains of St Thomas à Becket from the mouths of his cannon, but stripped the Pembroke shrine of St David's bones.

'And jewels, mind you,' he added, 'which was probably more to the point of it. For his wee catamites to play with.'

'Priests and their catamites are what got us to this part,' Patten argued mildly, knowing the Laird of Hollows was debating purely for the sport in it and from no sense of pious anger. 'You mistake the reformers for what they are reforming, my lord.'

'A bishop is a bishop,' the Laird replied, pouring liberally. 'Which means women or young boys.'

'If that is so, then is his sin not redeemed at the last, my lord?'

'By God's own grace,' the Laird replied, sucking his fingers where wine had slopped.

'A gratis gift from the Lord,' Patten agreed, 'for faith in Christ and not earned by deeds or bought with indulgences.'

'Aha,' said the Laird, seeing the mire Patten was laying for him. 'Pure Luther that, and him a prelate of your reformers who is swiving some wee German whore.'

He thumped the table in triumph and made dishes clatter; folk looked round for a moment, paused to stillness, then went on with their work, preparing Hollows for the year's end feast, no more than three weeks away now. The Laird wanted his stone hall finished by then, even if the builders muttered about cold-cracked mortar and tried to up the price.

Katherina von Bora, Luther's properly legal wife and called 'die Lutherin' because of it, was hardly a wee German whore, though he, of course, was a priest. Reformed to the point of having a wife. Who was Saxon nobility, no less – Patten mentioned it and saw the cloud on the Laird's brow, as dark a menace as the ones which had only just cleared that morning and under which Patten had travelled, trembling and soaked, from Carlisle.

'Saxony,' the Laird muttered, and Patten knew why that name bothered him – Batty Coalhouse. Patten never spoke it aloud, all the same; no one did in Hollows, if they valued their skin.

'It is an awkward business,' he offered quietly, and the Laird did not need to ask what business he referred to; there were four men and a dog trembling in the undercroft and awaiting 'the Laird's pleasure' after bringing the news of the latest failure to bring The Man Who Could Not Be Named to a suitable end.

'Awkward for Clym bloody Hen Harrow, certes,' the Laird growled bitterly, then waved his cup so that Patten only just managed to get his crown hat out of the way of the spilling wine; he brushed the feather in it as if soothing a bird.

'He is some lad for the cutting of body parts,' the Laird went on sullenly. 'I shall mark that when it comes to his own.'

'Awkward for all, sir,' Patten answered smoothly. 'Sir Thomas, of course, has every faith in your ability to carry out suitable recompense on the man who committed such vile calumnies on the person of his son.'

And myself, he thought, and swallowed the gorge of fear at the memory of that day, the mad, snarling Graham men, the blood on the snow, and the way Otley's head had burst open...

He said nothing on it, all the same, for any calumnies visited on him were neither here nor there in the balance of Sir Thomas Wharton's scales; the Deputy Warden of the English West March wanted suitable vengeance for the discomfort to his son and the affront to his plans and honour. Above all, he wanted the still missing babe.

'Sir Thomas will have his recompense,' the Laird replied sourly, then offered Patten a lopsided grin.

'How is the younger Wharton?' he asked and there was more amusement than concern in his voice.

'Officially, he is hale and hearty,' Patten replied blandly.

'Privily?'

Patten's face remained slate blank, then he cleared his throat.

'He is festering with pox, his humours are unbalanced and, according to the old woman who tends him, he wakes night after night, screaming about a one-armed man and calling for Lord Otley to leave him be.'

'Christ betimes,' the Laird said in wonder. 'That's hagged, without a doubt. I would look to the auld beldame; check beneath her cot, Patten, and you will find a wee homunculus slathered with blood and young Tom's privy hair.'

His voice was light and laughing, and Patten sighed, seeing the way of it and what he would have to do.

'Young Tom's father does not think so,' he said, throwing some iron into his voice. 'Sir Thomas believes that the spell in it is simply the continued presence of this Batty Coalhouse in the world. So does Henry, his elder brother.'

He paused a moment to let the words seep through the sodden head that was the Laird, saw the eyes narrow and realised that at last he had the man's full attention, drink-fogged though it might be.

'Otherwise,' he added, stroking the hat feather as if it was the skin of an expensive woman, 'Sir Thomas may feel constrained to inform the king that the money he pays the Laird of Hollows is returning little reward. He may even feel constrained to ask permission of the king to re-examine the entire construct of Hollows Tower, lying as it does in an area which permits no permanent structures—'

The movement was swift, so swift that Patten barely had time for a yelp before the Laird's hand closed on his own, the pair crushing the hat feather.

'Constrained, is it?'

The voice was hoarse and low, and Patten felt the terrible crushing strength of the fist, felt his bones grate, and whined, high as a dog.

'I will give you constrained. You and all your bloody Whartons—'

'Husband.'

The voice slashed him like a slap and he blinked, then looked up into the sharp face, the needle stare; his hand relaxed and Patten drew his own out of the cave of it, nursing it and breathing heavy with the effort of not weeping. The feather drooped, broken and draggled as a drunken bawd.

'Wife,' the Laird offered her with a grudging nod.

'I have prepared hospitality for Master Patten,' the Lady said, as if nothing had transpired at all, as if they were all waxing philosophical or mathematical, like perjink proper folk of breeding in a fine hall. Discussing physiognomy, or King Henry's forthcoming nuptials with the Parr woman.

Patten managed a smile and massaged his hand; he did not look at the Laird at all when he spoke.

'I will, if I may, avail myself of it. I feel fatigued after my journey and have not quite recovered from a touch of ague I contracted at the Porte last year. During negotiations with the Ottomans.'

'Indeed,' the Lady said and ushered him, smiling, into the care of Grets, whose thick-woolled body, fat, chap-cheeked bannock of a face and waddling walk did nothing at all for Patten's mood.

But it ensured that, at least this time, there would be no unwilling upending and tupping of women in Hollows, the Lady thought. Though that horse had already bolted.

'Are you determined to ruin us?' she said, low and hissing hard, once Patten had gone. The Laird shifted, angry and uncomfortable.

'Threatened me,' he muttered. 'Bloody wee clerk – the Porte, indeed. As if he had had the ear of the sultan himself – and even if he had, what good did he do? The Ottomans signed a treaty with the French against the Emperor and Fat Henry. Bloody wee lowborn parish clerk from Billingsgate. His da is a clothworker, in the name of Christ...'

She did not point out that he was no noble-born himself, just Johnnie Armstrong, son of Johnnie Armstrong, and all the blackmeal rents paid to the hereditary head of the Armstrongs in the Debatable was what gave him his power. That and living where the only law was March law and that depended on strength; she did not like the thought that her husband's was failing, for all his breadth of shoulder.

'You need to be better tempered with Master Patten,' she said, keeping her voice low and without rancour, though the effort was trembling her. 'He is secretary to the Earl of Arundel, who has lent him to Wharton. Arundel is the closest King Henry Tudor has to a friend he can trust, so you need to consider that, my good lord. One wrong word will pass down that chain, and if Henry Tudor turns his face from you, then all the enemies you have made over the botched business of the wee Queen will come down on our heads here.'

He bridled and stared bitterly back at her.

'And who advised me to that?' he declared sourly. 'Who thought it was a perjink wee plan to kidnap a Queen?'

She waved one dismissive, irritated hand.

'The politics of it are sound – marry Scotland to England and end the war. No one is hurt and everyone gets to drink wine and eat sweetmeats at a wedding. Once done, the bairn is the next Queen of England and Scotland both when Fat Henry dies and his wee Prince Edward takes the crown. Fat Henry would have thanked us and wee Mary would have thanked us twice when she was grown.'

She shot him a stern look, like a mother at a child caught in a larder with jam round his mouth.

'Now no-one has thanks for us at all – and the babe remains a lost mystery. If you had not involved yourself with Batty Coalhouse...'

'Aye, well – the war you sought to avoid is coming, for certes,' he spat back. 'And it will be harder than ever.'

'Because of you and Batty Coalhouse,' she said, fighting to keep her rise out of her voice. 'Because of him and your mishandling—'

'Enough!'

The roar came with a slap of his hand on the table, so that the jug and cups bounced; folk stopped dead, paused for a moment, then slowly, careful, went back to what they were doing.

The Lady looked at him, at this golden lord she had once married, powerful and potent and moneyed. He looked back at her from pouched eyes, sullen as embers, set in thread-veined cheeks. His mouth was wet and slack and he did not look potent – though the fault could be with herself.

For a moment she felt a sharp blade of anger scar through the core of her at Mintie, at her ability to fall into a bairn from a single encounter, at her ruthless desire to rid herself of it. She dared sin on her soul for the thought – I would have stood the rape of it, for the child. Though it is too late. Too late for child, for all the gold of my days is spent...

Her husband, muttering and scowling, jerked her back to the bleak now.

'Here's you saying leave him be,' he was growling, standing now and pacing, swinging his arms. 'Here's a wee clerk frae Billingsgate threatening me with the wrath of Fat Henry if I leave him be. Here's you telling me to listen to the wee clerk from Billingsgate – and yet leave Batty Coalhouse be at the same time.'

He spat the name as if it was soiled fruit and saw the admittance of the insoluble problem of it in his wife's eyes, grabbed at it in triumph.

'You chap and chop, wife. It is a circle that will not be squared is Batty Coalhouse, and so—'

'I can get you Batty Coalhouse.'

The voice swung both their heads to where Mattie of the Whithaugh stood, stern and solid as a weathered fence post; beside him, Sorley twisted his hat back and forth in his hands.

'How so, Mattie Armstrong?'

'You have tried hunting him and failed,' Mattie said. 'Now let him come to you. Find something – or someone – he values and flush him from his hidey-hole.'

'If you dare lay a hand on the head of Mintie Henderson, Johnnie Armstrong of Hollows, you will rue the day you married me.'

Her voice was sharp and grating and the Laird winced. I already rue the day, he thought.

'Not her, begging your ladyship's pardon,' Mattie said, and indicated Sorley, who bobbed something halfway between a bow and curtsey. 'I set my boy here to watch Powrieburn for Batty, for I owe him blood, as you know. Instead, there is another flitting back and forth to that place. Wooing Mintie, I am thinking.'

'Will Elliot,' Sorley blurted, and the Lady was not surprised, even if her eyes widened. He will get poor commons from her now, she thought, unless the lass has softened in recent times.

'Elliot?' the Laird repeated, then laughed from the side of his face. 'There is fitting. Use one to repair the damage caused by one.'

'He is Land Sergeant at Hermitage,' the Lady added warningly. 'Have we not annoyed the powers on this side of the Border enough?'

'He will not be Land Sergeant for long,' Mattie said slyly. 'I hear Wicked Wat holds the writ for the Keeper's task. Unlikely he will keep Will Elliot on in his job.'

He paused and shrugged, seeing the effect Wicked Wat Scott's name had.

'Wat Scott will not have the Keeper's title for long,' he added, 'but long enough to do your good self harm, I am thinking. Best you rid yourself of Coalhouse now, before you have to bend all your thoughts on Wicked Wat.'

'Will Elliot is still the Land Sergeant,' the Lady argued, and Mattie cocked a sly head.

'No matter who sits in Hermitage, they will not want Will Elliot as Land Sergeant. A man who has betrayed his Keeper, no matter the cause? No man will trust him from now.'

Right enough, the Laird thought. Every man of power dipped his beak a little. Some did it a lot and there was money to be made in black rents and tithes, which was why even the likes of a Land Sergeant's position was sought after and could be bought.

The upkeep of Wardens was poorly provided in part because, that way, kings knew some of the black rents went on useful purpose – but everybody had to fall in with it, and if you could not trust your closest deputy...

'What makes you think Batty will come for Will?'

Mattie smiled like a weasel sensing rabbit.

'Will is sweet on Mintie and she has not sent him on his way. Batty will do anything Mintie asks, it appears.'

The Laird thought it over. He wanted to ask his wife if this seemed likely, if Mintie held such a power of the pair, but he did not want to speak to her at all, so in the end he nodded.

'Get me Will Elliot,' he said, and then, conscious of his wife's whetted iron stare, added: 'Gently.'

The Lady said nothing, merely watched as her husband, pointedly ignoring her, went off into a huddle with Leckie regarding what Patten had come for – apart from finding the missing Queen of Scots.

Wharton's plan to further Fat Henry's cause was to set the Names to their old feuds. The Armstrongs were being paid to put the Scotts and Kers to spoil; Croziers and Storeys from England would join in. The whole Border was about to flare into unholy fire and sword.

It would only be a lesser imp to the full Satan set for the spring, when the English would come in force. This was only Wharton being careful with his master's money and knowing the nature of the Borders men – he would not take fulsome assurances from the likes of Johnnie Armstrong, Laird of Hollows Tower, but set him to make some 'annoyance' among his neighbours, to prove his worth and mettle.

So Hollows would have to strike and at the English-hating Scotts.

She hated Hollows. The old tower had been torn down by the English almost two decades since, and this new one, moved to a better spot, had originally been spacious and wooden.

Now Johnnie wanted it built in stone, but that was hard to get, even plundered from his father's original, and so it had been built tighter, cramping everyone together. Most of the servants and retinue lived round it, clustered inside the barmkin wall like cooped chickens, for there was scarce room for Laird and Lady in the tower itself.

She looked round it and saw the reality of her dreams, writ in ashlar and flagstones – something supposedly fine and grand, made mean by circumstance. There was even a strange powrie stone being used as the lintel, which no one cared for; that and the reeking chimney and stale must of the cold-ruined mortar, already rotted and crumbling, was as good a metaphor for Hollows as any wee poet could devise.

And for her life, she thought, seeing men lever the new doorway slab over the pit there. By tradition, a bitter enemy was buried underneath it, so that walking across him every day was a constant revenge and a good omen.

The Lady thought she knew who her husband had planned for it.

He must have come in the night and asked the question of her, though how Batty had heard, out there on the cold-swept moor, that there might be doubt left in Mintie was a mystery in itself.

But Corbie was one of his names, Will remembered. The crow that no one notices, sitting in a twisted tree and watching, watching...

He stood with Bet's Annie, who was prim as a pursed lip in partlet, kertch and apron. Mintie, arms wrapped round herself under a riding cloak, peered from the hood of it and only the smoke of her breath betrayed her at all.

'It is clear enough,' Bet's Annie said, looking at the scrawl on the worn white of the feed store wall. 'Though how we are to answer it is another matter entire.'

The charcoal scrawl taunted them, a foot-high gibbet from which hung a stick man with a wide, toothed smile. Not hard to work out who it was meant to be, or what it asked – but answering it was not as hard as Bet's Annie made out.

'Strike through it,' Will advised sternly. 'That's message enough.'

'If he can see it, others will as well,' Bet's Annie responded, hitching up her bosom and wishing she had not had to point herself into the bones of the corslet, which seemed restraining more and more these days. I almost wish it was me bairned, she thought mournfully, for I know it is too much beef from too many licks at the honey spoon and that will not be shifted in nine months.

The thought made her guilty, made her look at Mintie and see a briefness of whey face; the voice, when it came, was firm.

'He will come and they will not see him.'

No one needed to know the 'they' she spoke of; once or twice Bet's Annie had seen a rider, Will had spotted a man heading on foot to his tethered horse, and even Mintie had seen someone, claiming it to be Sorley Armstrong from Whithaugh.

No matter the who, the why was clear – they would spy out Powrieburn in the hope that Batty would crawl back to it, cold and stiff and done up with hunger and thirst, him and his mount both. Then they would come for him – not to take him while he was inside, but to lie in wait and grab him when he left, sluggish with warmth and a full belly and a bag of fresh provisions.

Will had felt the eyes, making his skin goose up more than the snell wind off the moor. He had felt it again that day and now followed the women back to the house, muttering about staying a while, just to see.

None of the women were fooled, all the same, not even Mintie's ma, who struggled to rise or even make sense of the day now. Will moon-calfed after Mintie, and Bet's Annie, Jinet and Megs felt as much sorrow as laughter for him and his desire to please.

Mintie herself was aware of it, but the world still seemed like something seen from behind a veil, where wind and light and birdsong all seemed somehow muted, a land from which all colour had been leached.

She saw his wooing and wanted to tell him not to, that it was no use, that this fruit was rotted and spoiled and the seed fallen on stony ground.

Not only that, she was sure the missing part of her, the part ripped out with Hutchie's, had left that ground more than stony.

It had left it barren.

Riders came not long after and Bet's Annie saw them first. She was taking beasts out to the field for a taste of clean air and a lick of what sun there might be, for locking them up in the dark undercroft of Powrieburn did them no good.

She levered the feed off her shoulder and stood while the beasts clustered, shouldering one another to snatch at mouthfuls, for there was only mud and browned grass in their field. She unfastened the cord and shook it free, raised her head and saw the men, moving steady and slow, picking a way through the tarns and tussocks.

For a moment she was paralysed with fear – then she recognised one of them and the relief almost dropped her to the ground. By God, she thought, Powrieburn in winter was a time when no one came; now the place is like a high road in Edinburgh.

She bobbed a polite curtsey all the same, for the one she knew was a man she had been expecting to arrive.

Ower-The-Moss Hob Henderson was short and squat, with eyes that were familiar to anyone who lived in the Borders – wary and distrustful – and what skin could be seen beyond the beard of his face was flushed and peeling from some long-standing disease.

'Bet's Annie,' he acknowledged and jerked his head at the other two, without taking his eyes off her. 'This is my middle laddie, Hew. And Agnes's Eck of Saughtree.'

The middle laddie gave her a grin, and despite herself Bet's Annie was pleased with it, for he was a good looker and dressed in his Sunday best – a moss-green doublet slashed to show the corn yellow beneath and a wee blue cape and matching bonnet. The other might have been handsome, save that all his front teeth had gone, leaving monster yellowed wolf fangs on either side of his smile.

'Is the Mistress well?'

'Mintie or her ma?' Bet's Annie replied sharply, for she had an idea why the chief of the Hendersons in Upper Liddesdale had ridden out from Hobsgill. It had taken him long enough to stir his arse, she thought, and Mintie would not like it.

His shaggy eyebrows went up at her presumption.

'Mintie's mother. I hear she is taken to her bed. I hear also that Mintie is... with condition.'

With condition – there was a neat ride round the harsh fact, Bet's Annie thought, and her scowl showed something of it in her face. Hob did not care for it, nor for all the comings and goings he had seen around Powrieburn. He had come to put it right.

He said so and Bet's Annie glowered at him, her cheeks flushing.

'Is that the case?' she answered eventually, near panting with the effort of holding her temper, which was the best course. 'I am sure Mintie and her ma will be suitably tempered by your concern.'

Hob cared even less for her tone, less still for the way no one invited him or his men to unsaddle, or offered common hospitality let alone the due to the headman of the Hendersons of Liddesdale.

He was made fuming by the appearance of Will Elliot, for he had heard of the man and was confirmed in what he suspected – that the Land Sergeant of Hermitage was out to put his boots under the Powrieburn table. Which was mainly what he had come to prevent.

He saved his lowered brow and cat-spit of wrath for Mintie, all the same, when she finally drifted down into the yard and stood there, her face shrouded in the hood of a long riding cloak and her manner draped with rudeness. Her voice, he was forced to admit, had grit in it when she replied to Hob's demand to see the Mistress.

'I am the Mistress of Powreiburn now. My mother is taken to her bed and sleeps. What you have to say, you say to me, Master Hob.'

He had heard she was all whey and head-bowed, so this iron from her came as a surprise, enough to lift his brows. Still, he did not like to be reminded of how low the stock of the Henderson grayne had fallen, especially when it was delivered to him out the mouth of a young lass fallen from grace.

He did not say that, all the same. Instead, he introduced the two others and was disappointed to see no more than a turn of the hooded head as they bowed and grinned.

'I am leaving them here, for I have a mind to see Powrieburn with some men about it now that your da has gone, may God keep him.'

The boys piously added 'amen's' to that, but Mintie said nothing, and eventually Hob stirred in his saddle and looked from Mintie to Bet's Annie, then to Will Elliot, who kept to the back of all this, knowing what Hob was up to.

'Well?' snapped Hob at length. 'Have you no thanks for the kindness?'

'If kindness there was, then thanks there would be,' Mintie answered flat as a hand on a face. 'But there is not kindness. There is a search for advantage. Which one of these am I to regard as my future husband? The comely son? Or his gummed kin?'

'Ho, ho,' Eck declared, bridling, but was silenced by a wave of Hob's hand.

'The comely son,' he answered and managed a crooked smile. 'I would have thought that pleasing at least.'

The hood fell back and Hob felt the weapon of her face strike him; Christ and His Saints, he thought, she looks like Death warmed over. Mintie saw his look and then stared at Hew.

'Like your bride, then?' she demanded, and he flushed like the boy he was, grew angry with it and would have spat back something cruel save that his da held up a hand and stopped the words in his mouth.

'It makes sense to consider it,' he said in a wheedling tone, then glanced quickly at Will, scowling. 'Powrieburn needs a man's hand at it, not that of a too-young woman. Unless you have set your cap elsewhere, Mistress Araminta.'

'Will Elliot is a friend,' she answered, and Will, on the point of boiling up himself at all this, was struck dumb by that. A friend; he did not know whether to be joyous or weep, wanting that at least and having hoped for a lot more.

'My cap is firmly on my head,' Mintie went on, her voice level and firm as an old Roman road, 'and there it will remain. Powrieburn needs no man's hand over it – nor do I.'

'Aye, well,' Hob declared, 'Powrieburn is Henderson land.'

'It is my land,' Mintie answered.

'It is mine as your chief,' Hob retorted, closing one eye in a squinting scowl.

'It is Hepburn's, since you hold all your lands from him,' Mintie answered, almost wearily. 'So argue the bit with the noble who has fallen from courtly grace.'

'Christ,' Hob roared. 'You are an ungrateful wee squit, who needs to mind her manners and her place in life—'

'Steady, Hob.'

The voice was quiet but the steel in it rang, and Hob jerked to the sound of it, glowering now at Will, who had stopped leaning against the lintel and now stood, solid as a barmkin, with one hand on his hilt.

'So,' Hob sneered. 'Your bloody light o' love reveals himself—'

'I will not be married on to anyone,' Mintie said sharply. 'Mattie of Whithaugh tried this and his boys paid the price for it – you must have heard that, even in Hobsgill. Though you did nothing.'

Hob stroked his beard.

'I heard – and here I am. Are you threatening me with the same? Me? Head of your grayne? By God, Mintie, you sail close to being broken.'

'I tell you only what is true,' Mintie answered and turned from him as if he was not there at all. 'There will be no one married to me and Powrieburn will stay Henderson. The women manage well enough here, as another good friend told a peck of brigands who came here in the night. That was another time you did not come to the aid of your Powrieburn kin.'

She walked back into the undercroft, her voice trailing behind like a waft of blue peat smoke.

'Leave your lads if you must, but tell them they must do as I bid, or I will pack them back to you.'

'Pack them...' Hob began and then lost his words in the torrent of frustrated spray that came from his lips. By the time

263

he recovered himself, Mintie had vanished, so he rounded on Bet's Annie.

'Tell yon wee lass she will have a task to pack off these lads if I tell them otherwise.'

Bet's Annie shrugged and glanced at Will.

'So thought Will, Clem and Sorley Armstrong. Hen Graham and Dand Ker too. Batty Coalhouse changed their minds.'

'By God – is Batty her white knight then?'

Will laughed, so hard and hearty that Hob was left blinking and confused. Eventually he growled at the boys to dismount and take their gear into Powrieburn.

'Da...' said Hew, uncertain and not happy with the way matters had turned out, less happy still at the sight of his prospective bride. Bet's Annie smiled up at him, pretty and predatory with promise, so that he swallowed and lost his way with the argument against remaining.

'Batty Coalhouse,' Hob said, once his boys had been eaten by the dim of the undercroft. Will nodded, bitter with the words Mintie had spoken so vehemently.

Hob shifted his weight in the high-backed saddle and looked at Will with one eye closed and the other quizzical.

'Mintie will marry a Henderson,' he declared. 'As distant kin as will keep the kirk happy, but a Henderson for all that. No Elliots nor any else will be putting their boots under a Powrieburn table.'

'So you claim,' Will answered, as bland as could be managed by a fuming man. 'Mintie might have a thing to say on it.'

'Mintie has not a thing to say on it,' Hob answered sternly, 'being a young lass and me her feudal. Unless you or Batty Coalhouse wish to say it for her.'

Will, who did not want to add a quarrel with the Hobsgill Hendersons to his fearsomely growing tally of enemies, merely shrugged, and Hob took that for compliance. He shook his head in wonder and mock sorrow.

'Batty Coalhouse. He has a deal to answer for, that man,' Hob said finally, then touched his split-brim cap to Will with as polite a scowl as he could manage, reined round and left.

Batty will answer to the De'il, Will thought, but not to Ower-The-Moss Hob Henderson. Unlike myself...

He was still burning at his meekness hours later, when Batty arrived in the yard of Powrieburn, mouse quiet and leading Fiskie in. Will had gone to the undercroft to get out of the tension above, where no one spoke much and the dull pewter cloud that was Mintie hung over everyone. Her mother's plaintive mewlings, rapidly turning to a grating whine, did not help.

Batty by flitting moonlight looked done up and reeked of moss and moor, firesmoke, blood and unwashed staleness.

'You look like a sick dog's arse-end,' Will said, as Batty took Fiskie in the opened bastel house door, walking as if his legs did not bend. Batty had no answer, since it was no doubt the truth if he looked anything like he felt; his legs were stiff as wooden balks, his whole body under the clothes felt clammy, and all of him ached in various and painful ways.

It was no life was winter out on the moss, and he said so.

'Then come in from it,' Will fired back sharply.

'Just so,' Batty said, waving a weary hand and finding a smile for Bet's Annie and Jinet, tumbling down the ladder with delighted squeals, as if their favoured grandsire had arrived with nosegays and sweetmeats.

Fiskie was taken and unsaddled, Bet's Annie – with a sly look over one shoulder – produced a flask, which Batty cowped down his throat until his apple threatened to bob up and out his eyes. When he stopped, it was with a great sigh.

'By God, Annie, yon is as fine an *eau de vie* as ever graced a bishop's cellar,' he said, wiping his matted beard with the back of a grimed hand. He handed it on to Will, who took one look at where it had been and waved it away with a grimace that raised Batty's eyebrows.

He said nothing, merely moved to the Saul's stall, where the pair of them whickered to each other, meaningless sounds of affection.

'Were you seen?'

Batty looked at Will.

'I was, certes – but I will be away before they gather, so Powrieburn is safe.'

'So you say,' Will said bitterly, 'though it is not. Nowhere is, for you have set Liddesdale and the Debatable aflame.'

Batty said nothing, but stroked the Saul's whiskered muzzle.

'I have seen what that can do,' Will persisted hoarsely. 'Red murder is the least of it, for folk are left in the wake of a Ride and the misery and ruin goes on long after the event.'

He leaned forward, his face savage.

'Have you seen it, Batty? The ruin you cause? Bairns and pigs sharing the same filth because their roof is gone? Broken limbs and wounds that fester. Bairns starving because the mother is too wasted to feed milk. The pestilence that always follows, so that wee lassies the age of Mintie end up shivering and melting wi' agues, or so poxed with blisters that they can open neither mouth nor eyes.'

He broke off and paced three steps the length of the under-croft, then three steps back into the steady, stroking silence of Batty's hand on the Saul.

'That's what yours and Mintie's vengeance will unleash on the houses of my neighbours, Batty. Ordinary folk who are no part of any of this...'

He broke off and squinted, quizzical and venomous.

'I have seen that look on you,' he said, and saw Batty's head come up, thought triumphantly that he had scored a hit.

'That look,' he went on, 'that shows how killing comes easy to you.'

'It comes,' Batty said wearily. 'Nor is it easy. D'ye ken, Will, that sixty miles distant from either side of the Divide, life is all peace and lush? You should go there.'

'Or is it redemption?' Will persisted like a goad.

Batty turned and looked steadily at him, and Will took that as agreement, jumped on the idea and brandished it like a torch.

'Redemption,' he repeated, sly and soft, thinking as he spoke. 'Aye – Batty Coalhouse, the white knight, finding a way to rescue his soul for all the viciousness he did in the Saxonies. By coming to the aid of a damsel in distress – aye, and maybe getting his boots under her bed as a wee addition—'

The hand on his throat choked the sound from him and he found, to his horror, that Batty's face was close enough to his own for him to smell the sourness of his breath, the woodsmoke rank in his beard and hair. The eyes were cold and hard, with a spark in the middle like a fire inside ice.

'Don't carp to me about ordinary folk, Will Elliot. I have seen ordinary folk baying for blood and fire at pyres and breaking wheels for the entertainment in it. And don't wave poor, innocent neighbours and families at me, for I have never had much of either and so that means nothing to me.'

His voice was low, a *cilice* that rasped the silence. He let Will go and the release sagged the man to his knees, holding his throat and coughing to clear it, feeling the raw burn.

'I have never felt your God, Will,' Batty went on, half to himself. 'I have never met the man and would not know him if I did.'

He patted the Saul, turned to where Jinet was coming down the ladder, careful and steady with a bowl and spoon and a hunk of bread.

'God is fine enough in wee universities,' he added, moving to the siren smell of hot food, 'but he is a vicious bastard for misery in his everyday work.'

There was more he could have said, but had no way to convey it and so fell on the stew while his thoughts turned it to ashes in his mouth, and Will massaged his throat and stayed sullen-silent. Bet's Annie, who had crossed herself in shock at Batty's cursing of God, stood in the chill and waited, looking from one man to the other.

267

Redemption? Aye, well, mayhap, Batty thought. His soul was in the gust of guns, in the desperate reek of slaughtered men and horses, whole acres of both with their innards out and smoking with plagues of flies.

It was on the walls of shattered stone, in sieges seen from both sides, where men had been torn into travesties of God's creation by his expertise with powder and shot, in the frightening creep through mines and countermines. It was in the dazed little skeins of Will's ordinary folk, fleeing with their bundles while fire made a mockery of the blue sky.

Where was God in that? There was only cold dread and the black, inhuman face of war. Yet there was hope in Mintie, faint and fluttering as a bird's heart: He knew it and if he could keep it beating there was redemption in that, he thought.

Silly auld fool...

She came down the undercroft ladder into mid-spoon, saw the drip of it off the ragged moustache before he wiped it away. For a moment, a glorious little moment, he thought he saw the disapproving moue of her lips, half expected her to sniff, or even say: 'Men will wallow if left to themselves.'

There was nothing and he nodded to her.

'Mistress Mintie.'

'Master Coalhouse.'

Silence, save for the shift of beasts.

'You wish to ask me something?' Mintie demanded eventually, just as the moment stretched to an unheard whine along everyone's nerves.

'Just so,' Batty answered, handing the bowl to Bet's Annie. 'It is simple and it is this – are you still of the same mind? It seems there is a dissenting view.'

'I think you must do as you will,' Mintie declared flatly. 'Everyone has an opinion and all of them agree – Batty Coalhouse must be stopped.'

'Yours is the only opinion,' Batty countered, and saw her look him over, taking in the stained weariness.

Bet's Annie brought a bag of provisions and Jinet saddled up Dubs, for Fiskie would need some time of feed and warm. So too did Batty, and everyone saw it, even Mintie.

An old, one-armed, big-bellied man, she thought, skulking on the winter moss. Hardened in skill and resolve, she remembered from Tod Graham of Askerton's letter – such an age ago now, it seemed. Was he hard and resolved still?

'There is the justice,' Mintie said softly. 'He stole from me…'

Batty nodded.

'There is that. But none of the justice in it will bring back what he took – or what has since been lost.'

There was a long silence then, until Mintie turned away abruptly and went back up the steps. Batty let out his breath and took the reins of Dubs. Will tore off his hat and scrubbed his head with frustration.

'What was decided? Are you done with the affair?'

'Is she hurt still?' Batty asked Bet's Annie and had back a nod. Will fell silent, suddenly seeing the half-crouch of Mintie in a different light and alarmed.

'How bad is it?' he demanded and Bet's Annie shrugged.

'She will heal, given time,' she said. Then she squinted at Batty.

'Is there no word on the wee queen?'

It was a whisper, for few folk knew the Queen of Scots was missing and had been for over-long now. It was not something the Regent wanted bandied abroad, for he was now sure Fat Henry Tudor did not have her either, and it suited him that Fat Henry thought the bairn tucked up in her French mother's arms, safe at Falklands.

Sooner or later, though, it would all come out – unless the babe was found.

Outside, the two Henderson boys bobbed polite nods, admiring and awestruck at being close to the legend that was now Batty Coalhouse.

'We saw men,' blurted Eck.

'A mile away, but circling to the north,' Hew added.

'Good lads – well done.'

They beamed and preened under Batty's thanks, while Hew could not drag his eyes from the fearsome axe-handled dagg stuck in his belt.

Batty fastened his fodder bags and clambered into the saddle, grunting with the effort. Then he turned to Will.

'Watch out for Mintie,' he said, and his tuneless voice trailed off into the dark – *'syne that he has kissed her rosy lips, all underneath the Eildon Tree...'*

He will bring them down on him if he does not leave off with the Queen of Elfland, Will thought as he watched him vanish – then realised that was what Batty wanted, to drag the lurkers away across the moss, away from Powrieburn.

It left Will none the wiser as to what had been decided and he breathed hard for a while, the smoke of it curling back and making diamonds in his beard. Then, shaking his head and shivering with a tremble that had little to do with the snell wind curling round the yard of Powrieburn, he went into the undercroft.

Bet's Annie waited for him, patient as old stone and with his own horse saddled and ready, which was pointed. Will did not argue, simply took the reins from her.

'Will you be fine here?' he asked, and Bet's Annie, smiling like a boiled haddie at the bright-eyed beautiful Hew, spoke into his innocence with a throaty chuckle.

'As the sun on shiny water,' she declared, beaming, and Will did not know whether to smile for Bet's Annie or frown for worry about the boy.

He took the horse into the yard and climbed up, looking down as Bet's Annie came out briefly, wrapping herself with wool.

'She bleeds still, a bittie, though she will never complain of it,' she said and then frowned over it. 'It is better than it was, but moves slowly towards healing. Faster than her soul, Will Elliot, which may never be whole again.'

The words followed him like cawing rooks, trailing after him into the night so that he was hunched into his thoughts and letting the horse pick the way it knew well, all the way back to the stone slab of Hermitage. He was lost in wondering how in the name of all the pits of Hell he might start anew to track down the babe. Every surreptitious journey to some possible lead had ended in nothing at all.

The men came as a surprise to him, had taken him before he even knew he was grabbed.

'Aye, aye, Land Sergeant,' said one as they took his latchbow and sword, parry dagger and bollock knife, swift and easy as scooping sucklings from a bairn. Will blenched at the sound of that voice, for he knew it well.

Mattie of Whithaugh loomed out of the dim, leaning casually on his saddle-front and nodding with satisfaction; behind him, Will saw Sorley Armstrong grinning.

'You have a wee engagement,' Mattie said. 'With the Laird of Hollows.'

Chapter Seventeen

Hollows Tower

Friday, (2 March)...

Patten came into the hall almost unnoticed among the throng gathered round the high table where the Laird sat. In front of him stood a square man, blocky and pale, his hands bound in front of him, but his beard jutting with a defiance – though Patten thought it smacked of desperation. He remembered him, with a sudden spasm, as one of the men who had ambushed the column taking the royal bairn south.

Since then, he had made it his business to learn a deal about the men involved, and this one had been an official from Hermitage. Probably still was, Patten thought, and counted more than that these days. Bringing him here, bound and threatened, was a reckless move for the Laird of Hollows, and if he kept tweaking the beards of his betters they would eventually come at him together.

The Laird of Hollows wore an embroidered leather doublet over a clean linen shirt with a high, small-ruffed collar and a grey, fur-trimmed gown over that. Above his glower of brows was a black velvet hat with a panache of plume in it and Patten almost laughed aloud. Wee papingo, he thought, all dressed in his best feathers to make himself out noble, though the truth was that he was no more elevated than any shoemaker.

Yet he did have the money and rents from Hollows and elsewhere, not to mention the loyalty of every Armstrong on both sides of the Border for miles in every direction. Above all,

Patten added to himself, he was a robber baron in the Debatable Land, where his was the only real law.

It was this very fact Johnnie Armstrong was pointing out to the Land Sergeant of Hermitage, who had tried to bluster his hands free, at the very least, with the statement of who he was and what he represented.

'The law, is it?' the Laird replied, lolling back in his seat. He waved one expansive, ringed hand.

'D'you see any here who care for your law, Will Elliot?'

They all laughed, dutiful and savage. Like a wolf pack, Patten thought with a shiver, scenting blood; he did not like the tone of this matter, but the faint throb of his hand kept him from stepping forward to say so. Across the crowded flagstones, he caught the eye of the Lady, almost lost in the throng and consigned to the fringes as if of no account; her eye was glaucous as a fish.

'The Scott of Buccleuch will care,' Will replied, and there was a mocking burr of sound at that. The Laird flushed a little.

'Wicked Wat? Aye, I hear he is to take over as Keeper. If he had cared, Will, he would have come at me before, when Armstrongs burned him and took his gear and kine. Are you worth more?'

'His dignity is,' Will responded, hoping that it was so. 'He is Warden of the West as it is. Now he is Keeper of Liddesdale as well, and I am his Land Sergeant – an affront to me is a direct one to him. You step on that cloak at your peril, Johnnie Armstrong.'

Leckie started to growl about giving the Laird of Hollows his 'my lord' due, but a wave of the Laird's hand clicked his teeth shut on it. The Laird scowled at Will.

Will did not like that look. Holy Mother, he is eident to do me harm, he thought, and the sweat ran down his back in salt worms.

'I hear you will not be Land Sergeant at Hermitage for long – and though I dislike the thought of giving aid to Wat Scott, I do not think he would exert himself much on your behalf. Your death, in fact, would be to his advantage.'

It was too close to the truth for Will to argue against, so he contented himself with a glower and hoped his heart's thunder could only be heard in his own ears.

'If you are so much the law,' the Laird went on slowly, 'then you should be out on a hot trod for Batty Coalhouse. I have a pile of left arms and some of their owners waiting to be buried thanks to him.'

'Make a Bill,' Will answered shortly, knowing the Laird would never ride out to Hermitage, nor ask a Scott for as much as the time of day. Besides, any investigation or Truce Day trial of Batty would find too much at the Laird's own door.

'I have a better idea,' the Laird said, and the hall buzzed with a murmur of savagery; Will felt his bowels shift.

'He will come for you,' the Laird declared. 'You are fast friends, which is why you have not done your duty and gone after him in the first instance.'

'He is no friend to me,' Will declared, which was not exactly denying Christ three times, but was close enough for him to feel the taint of the lie.

'We will see,' the Laird said. 'I have a wee room prepared for you and will send a message to Powrieburn, one Master Coalhouse is sure to get.'

He turned to Leckie and smiled.

'What d'you think, Leckie – a left arm, like my poor lads?'

Will's mouth was so dry at the thought he could not speak at all, and it took him all his time to stand up – even then he sagged a little and had to step sideways to recover his balance. The Laird saw it and his head came up like a dog on the trail.

'Some toes, mayhap. Balance him up as it were.'

Now the hall was a buzz of vicious bees and Patten was more alarmed than ever, for it was one thing to hold such a man as the Land Sergeant of Hermitage, another thing entirely to mutilate or even kill him. He announced it, overloud because he was afraid.

His words hung in the air like a blast of chill air and everyone fell silent under the haar of it. The Laird looked round, his face flushed and threaded with veins.

'Master Patten,' he declared, rolling the name round his mouth like imminent spit. Then he smiled, which took everyone by surprise, not least Patten.

'Is correct,' the Laird added, and Will staggered with the lurching force of the relief.

'I am the Laird of Hollows and I do not attack unarmed men,' he went on. 'Not even the friend of such an infame as Batty Coalhouse.'

He made a gesture and Leckie stepped forward with a knife and cut the rope binding Will's hands; he fell to massaging life back into them, almost weeping with the prickle of returning blood.

Leckie took a linen-wrapped bundle from someone and then handed it to Will, whose sausage fingers fumbled to unwrap it; his basket-hilt sword and parry dagger fell to the flags with ringing clangs, and for a bewildering moment Will stood there, blinking.

When he looked up, the Laird was away from the table, one hand on hip, the other resting on the long hilt of the massive two-handed sword which had snicked the head off the Fyrebrande. The point made a sinister grate as he turned it slowly, smiling. He had shrugged out of the grey robe and stood in his shirt and hose.

'Now you have a better chance,' the Laird said, 'of keeping your wee bits on your person.'

Will became aware that folk had drawn back, all the way to the far walls and corners, and that only two people were left in the square they formed – himself and the Laird of Hollows.

The Laird hauled off his soft hat and flung it away. Then he spun the two-handed weapon lightly upright, bowed and fell into a stance.

'*Porta di ferro piana terrone,*' he said. '*Flos Duellatorum* of Maestro dei Liberi of Cremona.'

He saw Will's narrow-eyed incomprehension and, as much for the equally bewildered crowd, translated.

'Guard of the Iron Door.'

Of course it is, Will thought bitterly. Along with all the other fancy wee poses he no doubt has, culled from the manuals of arms. He shook life back into his fingers and hands, wrapped them round the hilts and set himself.

'Come ahead, then,' he said as firmly as he could manage.

Powrieburn

At the same time

The month had come in growling and swishing a tail of snow-wind, and if the old saw held true, would bleat its way out at the end, all lamb-soft and sunny. There was precious little sign of it that Bet's Annie could see, and the day, when she surfaced into it, was bitch-cold.

Normally she would never have slept in the feed store, which for all its fragrant contents, warm enough when you burrowed in, was a solid affair whose stones leached cold like a larder.

But it was private and she had crawled in with Hew, who was as eager as a leg-humping pup. Bet's Annie had forgotten how young boys were when presented with the mysteries of a woman and her head was muzzy with lack of sleep. Still, she looked at him fondly enough, for he had come back at her again and again, with seemingly boundless energy and enthusiasm, if no skill at all.

Now he woke and shifted to her, so that she felt the bar of iron on her leg and marvelled at it – Christ's bones, did he sleep with it up?

But she shoved him away, too weary to even think straight.

'Away, you muckhound,' she declared, scrambling up and blowing white breath onto her hands. 'If you have such fire in you, use it to clean out the stalls.'

'Ach, but Annie,' he wheedled. 'You are a braw as the sun on shiny water. Come here, for I love you.'

Preening despite herself, Bet's Annie was too wise to be cozened – and too dressed to be easily invaded. She buckled for a moment when he surfaced, naked and displayed – only the young and daft took every stitch off in weather like this, even for loving, so it was a fine sight for her, rarely seen. He shivered, slender and handsome, the bits which had been exposed to sun and weather brown against the rest of him like a cut loaf. Irresistible...

She was reaching for him when a voice cracked the moment.

'Hew, Hew – are you there?'

Hew cursed Eck to the ninth circle of Hell as Bet's Annie spun away with a laugh, leaving him to cover himself up.

Eck was shuffling and turning his hat in his hands, his breath smoking in the chill. He bobbed politely to Bet's Annie and blinked once or twice.

'He is in there,' she said, and began to sway away, knowing the effect she had. Eck cleared his throat.

'It was you I sought,' he said, and she turned, half expecting some stammering declaration of love – a lie that translated as 'I would like some of what Hew is enjoying'.

'Mistress Mintie is gone.'

The surprise of it made her mouth work like a fish. Gone? Gone where? With what? Or whom?

Eck looked anguished and told her. Gone early that morning. Saddled up Jaunty herself and left alone. No one heard, for everyone was asleep – the door and yett had been left wide open, he added, bright with the thrilling horror of that.

Bet's Annie fought the rise of panic. Gone. There was no good in it at all. She whirled as Hew sauntered out, swaggering for Eck's benefit and smirking knowingly at Bet's Annie.

'Can you track?' she demanded, which reeled him out of his bravado and he stammered a bit, then recovered.

'I can follow a leaping hare on a flagged floor blindfolded,' he answered and there was no boast in it – Bet's Annie marvelled at how a night's quim turned uncertain boy to confident youth. Like some alchemical, she thought. Or a witch brew. One more night's visit to my cunny and I will end up ducked or burned for having transmuted him into a man.

The thought almost made her laugh, while the boys scurried off, shouting, to saddle horses and fetch their arms. They were delighted to be on a quest, to be out and free of mucking out stables.

'Saddle one for me,' Bet's Annie called after them and was less shining on the moment, for she hated riding and that pleasant ache in her nethers from the night before would become a fiery shriek before the day was out.

But she could hardly trust two laddies to have sense – and she was sure Mintie was riding into trouble.

–

Miles away, Mintie rode in grey fog, veiled from the duck-egg sky and whirling cry of peewits, lost and looking for the Jerusalem of her soul. She wanted milk and honey, the sweetness of bairns still cauled from the womb, and knew only that it was not for her.

Not in this world.

She rode past black cattle, avoided the forge by the curling dog-tail of smoke. Thought of Agnes and felt sadder still.

The dew was sweet. The wind shifted to the west and felt warm; she realised spring was coming with a sunlight of bright cloth, and once it would have lifted her up like the sound of a treble choir.

She rode Jaunty down the long falls of elder and briar, yarrow, harebell and thorn bush, all the way down the black-mealed lands of the Armstrong, out past the huddled thumbnail defiances of the Grahams.

Out to the silvered Solway, sitting on Jaunty like a lop-lugged sack and lost as a shower of sparks from a log.

When rain and night came, she stopped and slithered off Jaunty's back, stumping on wooden legs to the shelter of a copse. No fire. No food. Jaunty whickered plaintively, and Mintie fondled the velvet muzzle for a moment, but offered nothing, not even the relief of unsaddling.

In the morning she climbed back up, and Jaunty, moody but loyal, carried her on. She made good time and only had to hunker down in the damp a second night. She remembered it had taken one more when she had come this way with Batty – but he would have been riding light, giving her time to think. It had made no difference then, nor would now, so she almost rushed to the end of it, down to the place she had chosen. Or which had chosen her, she could not be sure.

The boy knew her, peering from his huddled hidey-hole, his hands held in front of him as if in prayer, his herring eyes rolling. He remembered her, would have gone and welcomed her, save for the other one, the one he did not care for. The woman did not know she was followed by the one he did not care for.

Mintie did not know of the selkie boy, had left Jaunty as if she had never been anything to her, and Jaunty, not knowing the way of it, fell to cropping the windblown grass while her mistress gathered stones.

Fat, rounded and clean-washed, they snuggled in the apron, cradled close to her as any bairn would be – to anyone looking, she might have been a mother with a wean caught up to her breast in the safe snug of an apron loop, crabbing along the shingle.

As she wandered, picking her way down the long tumble of stones to the sighing sea, she sang softly of all the regrets and the things she was leaving, so that they began to fade, become like trees in a thick mist. No more than black bars, the memories of themselves.

The wind blowing the grass. The fish that jumped and left ripples. The cow licking her calf clean of newborn slime. The cautious sharp-shouldered stalk of a cat. The bee at the heather – first this year. The sun like a coin and the salt Solway breeze that spiced the air.

The boy ran for his ma, who came out too late, in time to see her up to her knees, the wet dress clinging so that she stumbled. Too late and too far away – yet someone was close and closing still, hurling off a stumbling horse.

She was numbed by the cold and breathless with it, but the world had faded, stalk by stalk, flower by scented flower, shrunk to a pale line between the sea and the duck-egg sky. She started to fall, tumbling into the heavy embrace of the stone bairn – and found herself snagged.

It bewildered her, half in and half out as she was. She could not fall, could not slide beneath the cold balm of the Solway coverlet and let the stone bairn carry her down and down with her hair like wrack.

There was splashing and a grunt, and suddenly the world cascaded back on her, so that the chill bit and she whooped in air. Then the realisation that she was held, by a single strong arm round her waist, firm-fastened and dragging her back to the land and the world and all the pain.

'Let me go…'

'No.'

She knew the voice. Batty. She tried to beat at him, to struggle, but he was a moving rock, a relentless progress towards the land, and she was carried out of the sea and up the shingle.

She became aware of the selkie boy and then his ma.

'Soft, soft,' the woman said and gathered her in, so that she was the bairn and the stone one tumbled out, back to all the other rocks of the beach.

'Let me go,' she managed before the grey swallowed her.

'Never,' she heard him say.

He cut and slashed, dashed in, scurried back, spun on his good foot, did every thing he could remember and some he had never tried, so that he started to pant and drool and sob with fear, frustration and fatigue.

To every attack, the Laird parried, smiling and easy and light as grace.

'*Porta di ferro mezzana,*' he would say. 'Guard of the Iron Door, in the middle.'

'*Porta di Denti di Cinghiale* – Guard of the Wild Boar's Teeth.'

And once, when Will thought he had at last forced an error and could strike at his exposed back:

'*Porta di Donna Sovrana,*' he had called, and the blade appeared across his back, the clang of Will's sword on it like a knell.

'Guard of the Queen,' he translated, turning light and easy so that Will saw the entire event had been deliberate.

It was all managed like a mummer's play, for the amusement and instruction of the gawpers. Patten saw this after a few minutes, when he realised that the Laird was parrying every-thing, creating no counterstrokes.

Patten knew the Italian sword manuals were considered far too vicious, concentrating on attack and almost always ending in one or both combatants dead or injured. That was for the single-handed blade. The two-handed sword manuals from the Italies were the opposite, too oriented to defence, unlike the Swiss and Germans – that was typical of the little robber baron of Hollows, Patten sneered to himself, to choose the worst of every fighting style.

Still, it did not matter much if you had mastered it, he conceded, seeing how the Laird danced with the huge, unwieldy weapon. Mattered less still if you fought an idiot and could afford the instruction in it; in the end, all Johnnie

Armstrong of Hollows was doing was setting his seal on the moment, showing the admiring crowd that he was still the Laird, Master and Champion of the Armstrongs.

Will did not see it until later, stamping and birling in the maelstrom of it and thinking he was fighting for his life. It was only after the man had exposed his back and shown that it had been deliberately designed to make a fool of him that Will realised what was happening and stepped back a little. His scowl stopped the Laird's smile.

He nodded, seeing Will understood. Then the next second Will saw the great sword whirl round, held by the ricasso, the blunted section of the blade, the hilt and quillons lashing into his face like a mace.

'*Mordstreich*,' the Laird called, and Will, his face shrieking and his eyes full of his own blood, did not need to know that it meant Death Stroke and was not Italian at all, but the altogether more vicious Swiss.

The next should have been the finish of it, a two-handed waist slash that might well have cut him through. Instead, as he staggered away and tried to dash the blood out of his eyes, he felt the heat and the sheer size of the Laird right up close, so that his wine breath fluttered Will's nostril hairs.

He had a brief bewildering moment when the sword whirled like a circle of light; then the Laird, his face impassive, drove the point through Will's instep.

Will shrieked, his face a red mist of his own blood, his mind a white light. When he came to his senses slightly, he realised he was slumped, clinging onto the ricasso, with both hands as if he kneeled at a crucifix; he was astounded that he had dropped his own weapons.

For a moment he let go of the two-hander, looked into the Laird's face and tried to pull away; the Laird smiled, soft and vicious, ground the sword in a small circle and drilled pain deeper into Will with every grate of small bones.

The removal of it, that sickening suck that lifted his foot like a marionette, brought Will off his knees, struggling as if in a net to keep the blackness from swallowing him. He could get to his weapons...

The second blow drove it through his other foot, a last vicious twist splintering the bones. The pain hit him, his eyes turned white as they rolled up into his head, and he gargled while the world roared like a great voice in his ears; as he fell to the flagstones, he realised it was the crowd of onlookers, cheering their Laird.

Solway Coast
Not long after

She awoke but did not move or want to be awake. She wanted to be dead and lay in the smoked dark hoping to be no more than a cloud on a star, feeling so small between them, trying to wish herself into oblivion.

There was a tendril of wind, draughting into the hut she knew she lay in, whispering night secrets to her with the scent of fox and earth and salt. She did not want that; it was life.

Life would not let her be. It clattered the lid on a kettle, sparked the fire with pops, muttered in the strange, incomprehensible way of the selkie boy, so that she knew where she was and no matter how she fought not to know, it was there, bright as day.

She tried, then, to be alone with the sound, as if there would be no sound except for her and that way she could banish it. But it would not be cellared and the scents betrayed her, with their harsh smoke, the fish, the savour from the kettle and the tang of something else – *eau de vie*.

Finally, there was the most traitorous of all, the tuneless grate of singing sound that dragged her back to the now and the pain and the anguish of failure.

'*For speak ye word in Elfin-land, ye'll ne'er win back to yer ain countrie.*'

She opened her eyes and saw him by the fireside, blood-dyed by the flames and squinting his face up into that strange grimace of displeasure that lied about his enjoyment of strong drink. He caught her looking and corked the flask with his teeth, grinning so that his curve of beard waggled.

'Back with us then.'

He wore a wrap of dirty blanket and his clothes were scattered and steaming all round the fireplace. So were her own, Mintie saw.

'If you hate it so much, why put it in your mouth?'

It was a voice like the whisper of moth-wings, but Batty heard it and grinned broader still at the memory in it of the old Mintie.

'By God, lass, if it tasted good we would never be done swallowing. It is only the fact that it tastes like the worst physick that keeps me this side of sober.'

There was a pause while Mintie blinked away the last shreds of the little sleep she wanted to be more, sucking in the echoes of strange music, the hiss of growing spring and the cold eyes of stars.

'You should have let me go.'

'The Solway is a cold embrace for a woman with a cuddle of stones mumming as a child,' he replied shortly. 'It is no life for a young lass, that.'

'It is an affront to life,' said a new voice, heavy and thick with grief and censure; Mintie turned to the face of Auld Nan, fierced by firelight into a vengeful angel.

'God hates me,' she replied wearily, and Auld Nan hissed her displeasure and rattled the kettle with a stirring spoon to show it.

The music, strange and thin, moved over her like the dancing rill of a burn giving birth in spate; despite herself, she turned her head – so heavy, like a huge gunball – to see the selkie boy with the pipe in his mouth, head waggling from side to side.

'Just so,' said Batty thoughtfully. 'There he is, poor wee twisted soul, witless and webbed, rolling-eyed and gabbling. Yet he is doing what neither the pair of us can do, Mintie – I can't play the wee pipes at all and you can't get up from where God has thrown you.'

He leaned forward a little.

'Look at him, Mintie. His fingers are fused, yet he plays and the music is in him.'

He stopped and they listened; at first it sounded like screeching cats to Mintie, but gradually she heard a melody of sorts, distinguished something like a merry jig. Sweet as snake venom.

'Mayhap that's the music they play in Elfland,' Batty mused and reached out to touch his doublet, sighing when he felt the damp.

Mintie was trembled by the music, wanted to get up and run, flee like a deer. Instead she cried, soft and silent, but Batty saw the betraying glint of her tears, heard the faintest whisper of her.

'He stole from me.'

Batty did not know whether Mintie meant just the horse and the money, or her father, or everything that had come after, but he knew Hutchie Elliot was in it even without the name. He sighed.

'I have said before – punishing Hutchie will not bring back the loss.'

'If God loved me, He would do it.'

The logic was unassailable.

'Am I to be an archangel, then?' he replied, trying to keep his voice light and feeling the crushing weight of it dragging his soul down, like Mintie's stone baby, into a darker sea than the Solway's firth.

'Michelangelo,' he said almost to himself, 'with fire and sword.'

Auld Nan heard it and crossed herself. Batty watched Mintie slide into the little death, breathing easy while the fire popped and the kettle lid clattered with savoury promise. There was the yeasty smell of good beer as Auld Nan fetched horn beakers of it.

There is yeast in me too, Batty thought, no more willed by me than beer has a choice – and it will out in the murder of a bride and groom with slow match entertainment, or vengeance for a young girl.

Batty had seen Auld Nan's fervent cross-signing for what it was – a warding against the bad sins of what must be done. Folk knew all about sin, or so they thought, but Batty knew everyone was born and situated in station differently from one another, and sin was particular to all of them. Dependent on self and circumstance.

For all that, a body felt guilt. Even if not master of self nor circumstance, the fool felt guilt and shame for it. It was senseless as the self-loathing of an idiot for being born that way – he looked at the selkie boy, listened to his music. No such loathing there, he thought. He is in himself, complete and needing no more. But priests would claim the sin in him made him monstrous, wrought it hard in texts and tracts and fierce mouthings about reward and punishment.

For all that he knew this, for all that he could deny God, Batty still felt accountable beyond the facts, wanted to atone, to flagellate and humble himself, to promise to be better.

So he would commit even more sins to expiate the ones already gone, for the new ones were in a Good Cause.

Who lay, breathing soft in the little death.

–

The riders came in the night, two wide-eyed boys and Bet's Annie, walking like a sailor and so weary she thought herself about to shatter to shards.

She was sagging with relief when she found Mintie alive and snugged up in a strange hut, with an eldritch boy the other lads eyed with cautious revulsion, Auld Nan the Solway Witch

– and Batty, big-bellied, solidly cheerful and grinning still, even if it never quite made it to his eyes.

Bet's Annie wiped even that mockery from him, saw the cold stone that replaced it when she told him what had happened just as they had started on their ride to find Mintie.

Two men had ridden up to the outer door of Powrieburn and Bet's Annie and the boys, just far enough away to see and yet not be seen, had heard Megs and Jinet shriek as the door was hammered. One of the men, Bet's Annie noted, was Leckie, the steward of Hollows.

But the men did not want in, only to leave a message.

'Boots,' Bet's Annie declared, slathered with the thrilling-sick horror of it. 'Bloody and rent at the feet and nailed to the door. He was awfy proud of those boots and would never have given them up willingly.'

She had not needed to say the name, for she could see Batty had worked it out, but she said it anyway.

'Will Elliot.'

Chapter Eighteen

Hollows Tower

Feast of St Gregory (12 March)...

The wind took the cage and turned it gently, but enough for the figure in it to wake with a start and a wail at the pain and horror of the world he found himself in. The two crows yarped alarm and flapped sullenly away, sodden with rain.

The Lady, feeling the harsh snick of wind up here on the half-done roof, watched the long, banded cylinder turn at the end of its rope, hoisted high on the arm of the raised gibbet whose struts strained with the weight. It will come crashing down on their heads, she thought moodily, as the workmen huddled miserably beneath it looked warily at the sound of creaking, then up at the groaning figure.

Serve them their just due if it did, she added to herself. And then, more bitter and savage than she had thought possible, she added the wish that her husband be one of them.

He was in the hall, of course, talking animatedly with Leckie about the upcoming feast for Lady Day, about rents and black-meal and how it was essential it all be gathered in. As if nothing untoward had happened. As if the world had not tilted and flung everything Hollows held dear to the edge of the precipice.

All he cares about now, she thought bitterly, is the rents and blackmeal, which will all be handed to the other man who stood by his table, with fistfuls of charts and plans and expense – Sandy Scrymgeour, master builder from Myres and the man creating Hollows in stone. Gold would be more proper, the

Lady thought, for every corbel and crow-stepped gable seemed to cost more than the last.

Her husband, flushed and animated with drink as much as enthusiasm, would not countenance another mason for the work, all the same – Scrymgeour was related to John, Master of Work for the dead King James; John and Sandy both had been ousted by the Regent in favour of a Hamilton kinsman and, as ever, any enemy of an enemy was a friend – even if he overcharged you on rubble and mortar.

Her husband was all energy and backslapping since he had humiliated Will Elliot and proved his continued prowess with the two-handed Armstrong sword. But it had not been his Lady who had rubbed ointment into the overtaxed muscles that night, even though she knew of it and what else had been rubbed and which of the remaining hoors had done it.

It was a mark of his disrespect that he had done it in a half-wood, half-stone tower no more than the width of a courtyard square and with three floors only; in a world of little privacy, he might just as well have swived the bitch fully naked on the high table at dinner.

That was now the measure of the man she had married, she thought, with a sick, sad loss, bitter as aloes. Energy wasted in pettiness.

All her life she had risen early, to dress herself and pray, sometimes in the pale quiet before the world sprang to life with demands on managing her husband's hall. Lately she had prayed with Father Ridley. He came every other day to provide balm for her soul and she looked forward to it more and more.

Ridley had just left her, on his way to Langholm and keeping as low a profile as he could in these awkward times, while still trying to make a living from God; the wee priest had a cruck house in the town and kept himself to himself, could not be persuaded to move out to the safety of Hollows.

'God's work is needed everywhere, Lady,' he had declared when asked. 'Even in Langholm.'

God, the Lady thought, is barely living Himself in these times – and I cannot rise early enough to thwart a husband determined to ruin us all.

She crossed herself and begged forgiveness, then came down the wind of steps – every fifth one a trap-step, slightly higher than the rest to catch the unwary or those creeping in the dark – into the smoking dim of the hall. On the way, she accepted the nods and bobbed curtseys of scurrying folk, though there were fewer in the cramped place now. That, at least, was a blessing.

Without preamble, she walked into the middle of her husband, Leckie and Sandy the builder, so that all conversation stopped. There was a pause, then Sandy tipped a knuckle to his forehead and, stung to it, Leckie offered a curt bow. Her husband fixed a smile on his face and nodded to her.

'Lady,' he said dismissively, and when she did not take the hint, broadened the affair on his face until it twitched his beard with effort.

'This is a conversation you are ill-equipped to join,' he pointed out, 'being among men as it is.'

'Oh, is it? Rents and levies and lamenting the price of stone-haulers is beyond the likes of me, is it?'

Her voice was dangerously pitched and the Laird reined himself in a little, as did Leckie. Even Sandy had been exposed enough in recent times to do no more than clear his throat at the woman's presumption.

'You would do better bending your mind to ending that abomination hanging from our roof,' she went on, glaring at them all. Leckie, who had arranged it, and Sandy, who had built the contraption, shuffled a bit and said nothing. The Laird glowered back at her.

'You are interfering in business which does not concern you.'

Leckie and Sandy winced at that and the master builder backed off a step or two, trying to be surreptitious about it and failing.

'So,' she said, her voice a gimlet that pinned them all there. 'Hanging the Land Sergeant of Hermitage in a cage from the roof is no concern of mine? Crippling him and nailing his bloody boots to a neighbour's door is nothing to me? Did you have some strange notion that I was clapped in an upstairs room with no windows or mind? Or that I had no say in matters? I may be the only female here bar your collection of draggletailed whores, Johnnie Armstrong, but I am neither one of them nor a dog to be kennelled at your whim.'

'God grant me the wish,' the Laird replied, and now Leckie and Sandy were stepping away from the table with no attempt to hide their alarm.

'Aye, you may think it. Every young lass's dream according to you, to be held awaiting your pleasure.'

'I brought the women for the English,' the Laird attempted and was ravaged by her shrill bark of bitter laughter. 'To save your honour...'

'Is that the case? To save my honour you huckled in every whore for miles? And yet some are here still, long after all the sprigs of English gentrice are gone.'

'By God,' exploded the Laird. 'If I had not, you would have been dragged in every nook and outhouse and gaffed like a salmon. Next time I will allow it and you need not look to me for succour.'

'Neither myself nor any decent woman has succour here, it appears,' she spat back. 'Mintie Henderson for one. The stinking-pyntled bastard-born who dishonoured her is still here and untouched, while you hang the law that demands him in a cage.'

'Christ's bones, woman – this is neither about Hutchie Elliott nor Mintie Henderson. The pair deserve each other, much good may it do them, for one is a vicious wee rat and the other a lass with a long neb and a loud voice. Besides – moderate your language. You are Lady of Hollows, not some fishwife in a scaling wynd.'

'Johnnie Armstrong,' shrieked his wife, the words ringing in echoes, stirring the stone dust and bringing all sound to a stop.

'After all you have dirled in my ears from cockcrow to compline from the day we were married on to each other, d'you think there is a wee naked filth of word left on the face of God's earth that is not acquent with Hollows Tower?'

'Well,' her husband roared back, his face bagged with blood. 'Here is another – get you to buggery, woman, and leave honour and men's work to men.'

'Honour, is it?' she said and her voice had gone low, still bell-clear in the silence that lingered on after the last outburst. She leaned forward into his fire of face.

'Here is honour, husband. Release Will Elliot. Make restitution to Mintie Henderson. Forget Batty Coalhouse. Before you lose all honour – and your wife besides.'

That rocked him and everyone saw it. But he righted himself and blinked a bit and his hand twitched. Wanting the comfort of the goblet, she saw and could not hide the sneer.

'Well – truly are the daughters of Eve related,' the Laird replied, breathing heavily. 'All you are missing, Lady, is an apple. The serpent you possess already... it is in your mouth and speaking to me – to *me* – of honour.'

He turned away from her then and made a deal of pretence at studying Scrymgeour's plans. Clearly ignored, the Lady drew herself up and stalked from the room. Like a tiger some of the onlookers thought admiringly.

–

Not far away, perched like a crow up among the trees dripping into the Esk, Batty crouched and watched the cage turn and tried not to see a wheel instead, braided with broken limbs and moving slowly – save when some passer-by spun it out of amusement and malice.

And the man on that wheel, Batty thought, barely in this world at all, had to watch the bewilder of it circling him – cloud, tall house, sky, steeple, endlessly repeated, slower and slower until someone spun it anew, until it faded into the fogged veil of a death too slow.

At least Will was upright, Batty thought. With his feet pierced like Christ's own he would be weak from shock and loss of blood, but they would have stopped the bleeding; they did not want him to die before he had served his purpose.

A gibbet on a roof made rescue hard to consider. No point in galloping down like some Roland, Batty thought, so he watched and soaked and tried to think of a way to get to Will, get him down and get him away.

Short of riding up with a band of Grahams, it did not seem possible.

The man on a bad nag caught his attention, moving away north. Langholm, perhaps. Or the inn at Mosspaul. Batty had seen the man before, coming and going at Hollows – a clerk then, off on the Laird's business.

Batty slid away into the drip of trees, noting the burgeoning green, the swell of buds. New life was coming through the wind and cold rain, and with the spring would come Fat Henry and a vengeance that would fire the land to ruin.

If I leave any of it, Batty thought savagely.

Langholm

That same night

Ganny was half drunk – again. Ridley did not care for how often that was happening, but had to admit that, so far, it had not spoiled his looks. If he was honest, the priest was forced to admit that it excited him, as if a marble statue, perfect and white, had flushed to lewd life.

Ganymede was no statue and less than lewd. He was querulous and irritable.

'I am going mad,' he complained, scowling so hard that Ridley despaired. 'I see no one save wee Jane here.'

'Well,' Ridley declared waspishly, 'you insisted we keep "wee Jane", so you only have yourself to blame if she latches you to her side. It's not some pup you can leave in the straw.'

'If it wasn't for her I would already be mad,' the boy spat back. 'You keep telling me it is too dangerous to go out.'

It was true and yet not so. Dangerous to Ridley, who was afraid 'wee Jane' might be recognised. The chance of the creature having been stolen from around here was slim, but Ridley had foul dreams about some shrieking mother declaring it, in public and at the top of her voice. Worse still, he was afraid of losing Ganny to some Hollows tough with a taste for such a boy and rich enough to turn his head. The thought of that ate at the priest nightly, made his possession of the boy all the more fervent, as if he was forming chains to bind him with.

Yet he knew he could not pen the boy up, but neither could he be constantly at his side to protect him. He tried a kiss, but Ganny backed away.

'Where have you been all day?' he demanded and Ridley sighed.

'Physicking the robber baron of Hollows,' he said wearily, then added with a touch of bite, 'the man who pays for this roof and the food you eat.'

'Is he ill then?' Ganny pouted.

'Don't,' Ridley pleaded. 'The wind will change and you will be stuck looking like that.'

Ganny squinted and Ridley sighed, gave in and waved a hand dismissively.

'The Lord of Hollows, as he calls himself, is choleric and his urine is sweet. Beyond that, I cannot tell, for I am physicking him at a distance, without his knowing, at the behest of his wife. He thinks I am no more than his wife's latest priestly plaything.'

'Euch,' Ganny declared, making an even worse face. 'You tried to kiss me after drinking piss all day?'

'Not piss, beautiful boy – urine. And I don't drink it all day – I don't drink it at all. I taste it, to discover, among other things, if the owner has *diabetus mellitus*. On the top of my tongue, d'you see? Like this.'

He waggled his tongue and Ganny waved with disgust.

'Christ, put that horror away. A pig's tongue is better looking.'

Stung, Ridley bridled.

'Pig's tongue, is it? This tongue has more learning in it than your entire head. More than your whoremongering head will ever gain.'

'Whoremonger? Where am I whoring then? I never leave this place long enough to waggle my bits at anyone else. Unlike you, pleasuring everything in this forsaken hole called Hollows. It is a wonder your foul instrument is still attached.'

'Foul instrument,' Ridley repeated, wondering where the boy had picked that phrase up from. 'Foul instrument?'

'Of pleasure,' Ganny added sullenly. 'I heard yon bishop say so, back in St Mary Merton. Foul instrument of pleasure he called you. He hadn't seen it, though – I had.'

Ridley shivered at the remembrance of the bishop. If the hordes had not launched themselves at St Mary Merton, he thought, my fate would have been much warmer. Then he caught Ganny's grin and found it infectious.

'Foul instrument of pleasure,' he repeated. 'That bishop would not know one if it hit him in the face.'

Ganny clapped his hands and laughed with delight at that.

'He would not know the difference between a sigh of love and a fart,' Ridley went on, and then, in the middle of Ganny's laughter, an entire thought struck him like a sounding bell.

'I have a mind to make you a bishop,' he declared, and Ganny looked at him, tilting his head to one side like a curious bird. Ridley felt the tumescence in him and his mouth went dry.

'A bishop?'

Nodding, moving closer, losing all his sense, Ridley laid it out. Soon the year changed at Hollows Tower, as well as everywhere else, and they were planning a Feast of Fools, for which they needed, of course, a boy-bishop. They would pay too.

Ganny clapped his hands with delight at the thought.

'I will buy some cloth of gold,' Ridley babbled, gathering Ganny to him. 'We can make cope and mitre from it – you will dazzle them...'

'And wee Jane can be the baby Jesus,' Ganny declared suddenly, bright with enthusiasm. He danced in a circle with delight, peeling off his clothes as he did so, and Ridley, who had forgotten the baby in the moment, had a wild moment of panic at the thought of it, at the idea of bringing it into public view. It was dispelled at once when Ganny fell on his knees in front of him.

'Oh God,' he said at the touch. The babe – a danger. But perfect, of course, for the Feast of Fools, where everything was turned on its head and servitors became noble and a boy-bishop scathed the holiest of sacraments. A girl-child as Jesus was perfect...

Perfect as marble, white marble like Ganny's cheeks...

Powrieburn
Five days later

Mintie lay in a labyrinth of memories and those who tended her thought she was numbed by grief and circumstance. Megs said so, scowling at the fact that now both the mistresses of Powrieburn were laid flat and of no use at all, but Bet's Annie scathed her and anyone else who voiced a poor opinion.

They were wrong. I am not blank, Mintie thought, nor frozen. Just the opposite; when you are frozen from the tragedy of your life, you can endure it. It's when you wake up that it drives you mad. When you wake to the knowledge that you are a palace of brothels, that all you were is now dead, all the hopes and dreams and the normal course of events for a life gone like smoke.

Everything that steps in the world must mark it, grind it, break silences and trails — save herself, who was no more than an interruption on the face of the moon. She found herself staring at her hands, folded in her lap and no more part of her than the whisper of another's breath.

To be dead in a world where you still walked and talked was to be in a bleakness that made the Bewcastle look like a garland of flowered gardens. Walking dead in such a place, with folk wrenching you back from running as fast as possible through the membrane of water that was no more than a door that led out and away.

There was no lodestone, no sign from God to bear her up with any ease, so she moved through the days like gossamer and silver beams. She tended to her mother, realising, with that faint part of her struggling like a trapped fly with reason, that here was a woman fighting to live and failing with every wheezing breath, even as young, healthy Mintie sought the opposite.

Realising too, with some sliver of shame, that she had brought this on her ma and everyone in Powrieburn, which only added to the bleak in her.

'She needs better help than us,' Bet's Annie declared finally. 'I hear there is a wee physicker priest at Hollows, catering to the Lady's soul — will I ask there for her aid, in the love of God?'

Mintie wanted nothing from the Lady of Hollows — but her ma wheezed and stirred, coughing, and the sliver of shame worked itself deeper, so she agreed, though she offered no help as Bet's Annie saddled Jaunty and Hew his own mount, the pair of them prepared to ride into the dark heart of the Debatable.

It was hard to bear, this world, but she would endure it still, Mintie thought, for a faint thread of hope called Batty Coalhouse and her justice.

Megs and Jinet waited for instruction and guidance, so she became what they wanted — prudent and smiling, modest, calm, candid and benign.

But she moved through the world with her head slightly tilted, as if listening to a sound no one else could hear. Jinet confided to Eck that she thought Mintie was hearing something in the distance and worried that it might be the last vestige of madness – a distant bairn's crying.

Mintie was listening right enough, but not straining to hear a child weep. She was listening to the soft sputter of a slow match burning down and down and down…

–

The whole truth of it was, according to Simoni, that a Medici was the Devil. And possibly God as well.

'The Magnificent Lorenzo was clearly the Devil, Alessandro the Moor possibly a lesser imp. Lorenzino, however, is an idiot…'

'Or God,' Batty said. 'Since you haven't mentioned a Medici in that role.'

Simoni waved his goblet, slopping wine everywhere. He belched and looked startled by it, then remembered his thread.

'Alessandro only thinks he is God,' he declaimed. 'Because he is grandson of the Magnificent. Or not, depending on who you listen to – some say he is really the bastard of Pope Clement VII, otherwise known as Guilo, nephew to the Magnificent.'

Batty was losing track; there seemed an awful lot of Medici in this small inn and he said so.

'Lorenzino is certainly the Devil,' Simoni went on, as if Batty had not spoken at all.

Batty was too fogged by wine to argue. Besides, Simoni was right about Lorenzino, the least of the Medici. Lorenzaccio, they called him – Bad Lorenzo – but only for going round decapitating statues at night in Rome.

'Perfectly Medici,' Simoni agreed, once they had laughed at the stupidly childish acts of Lorenzaccio.

'Yet there they are,' Batty declared, throwing his one arm in the general direction of anywhere. It would suffice, since they were in the Caravella inn, on the Via dei Pilastri, not far from the Gate of the Cross and Gallows. And anywhere you pointed in Florence led to a wall besieged by Medici.

Or their supporters, the French of Charles V. And Germans. And Swiss. And any other mercenary bastards who thought Florence could be plundered. But Alessandro and all the other little Medici, Simoni opined, were lolling in Bibbione, miles away from danger, eating cacciucco and insalata nizzarda, fagioli and good marzolino cheese, while we here in Florence exist on thin soup.

For certes they would be doing that, agreed Batty, pouring the last of the wine. And peacocks and pheasant. He knew Simoni missed the cheese above all, but was less convinced of the poor worth of their own fare; in his experience, even thin soup was better than some of the stuff he had eaten in his time and better than they would have if the siege dragged on.

'For sure,' Simoni agreed and raised his goblet. 'Of course, the siege will last as long as the wine does. And we have a lot of wine − even if you and your dogs suck it up like sponges.'

So they sat and drank while men clanked about in armour, ripping up homes along the Via Ghibellina for firewood, while others ran around putting out fires started by French guns. The streets were choked with noise and smoke. Whores grew rich, prisoners were pardoned if they could fight, and church bells rang for no reason.

Then Niccolò, the one they called Furbo − foxy − came running in, shouting. 'We can hear digging in the convent. Stab me up the arse with a rusty pike if I lie.'

Simoni threw down his goblet, so that wine sprayed everywhere.

'Fuck your mother, I told you so,' he yelled triumphantly.

This was when Batty knew it was a dream, for not only would Michelangelo Simoni never curse, he would never throw away good wine.

But still he could not wake from it.

Then they were outside the convent of St Theresa, shrouded in dust and shouting, in the middle of which was a strange droning that raised the flesh on Batty's body. They were the Angels of Michael, busy singing the Song of Moses − the Lord is a man of war. They were, in fact, men of Strozzi's company, abandoned here when that man took the army off to fight the Pope and the French; he lost and fled and now the Angels of Michael were stuck in Florence with everyone else.

They were clanking metal giants who wanted to rush off into St Theresa and start carving up the enemy who had come up through the old cloacae, then dug the last way into the convent.

But Michelangelo only wanted them stopped at the door, for he and Batty had discovered their digging ages before and the dust that coated everyone was proof that they had blown the floor of the convent open and were massing inside. They had to be kept inside.

'How long do you need?' he called out to the kneeling Batty, who lit his fuses and watched them like children.

'When you see me run,' Batty yelled back, 'try and overtake me.'

Then he plunged after Michelangelo, into the billowing mist of dust and shouts, where men struggled to press themselves out of the convent gateway into the street and the Angels of Michael swung into their faces like a door. They struggled and roared; flashes of fire split the gloom.

This at least had been real, but in this version of the mad dream-dash to perdition, Batty wore a salet and a back and breast, used a vicious basket-hilt cutter with 'Solinger hat mich' engraved on the blade. But that had been Michelangelo.

In reality, Batty had swung an old, notched sword – the same one he still had – and was counting.

One.

Two.

Three. He saw Michelangelo hurdle someone on the ground, failed to make the jump himself and half fell.

Four.

Five.

Six. Batty always half fell at this point in the dream, and no matter how hard he tried, he could not wake up from the next bit.

Seven.

Eight.

Nine. Batty blundered into the knots of struggling men, fighting and falling in the talus of rubble from older wall collapses. He took someone's flailing elbow in the ribs, a blow that made him grunt.

Twelve.

Thirteen.

Fourteen – he cut at a figure in torn blue, a jarring chop that carved a steak from the man's thigh and sent him reeling and screaming. *Fifteen, sixteen, seventeen,* in a mist of smoke and dust and wild swinging.

Eighteen. The sweat was running down him like mice in a burning wall.

Nineteen. The world slowed; he caught the black-bearded man under the chin, the sword stabbing upwards, coming out through his mouth and slicing his nose. It snapped. Dream-Solingen steel and it snapped. It always snapped.

Twenty. The man fell away and Batty was left with the hilt and a perfectly sheared nub end. Not even a jagged end, but clean, so that he did not have a weapon at all. It did not matter.

'Run,' he screamed, as he always did in the dream, as he had done when the moment was real. Then, though, it did not seem as if he ran through air thick as honey, his legs seeming unable to move. And, as she always did, the nun appeared, weaving like a sick crow, robes flapping, wimple torn, walking as if in a daze. And on fire.

In every other version of this, the man who appeared and caught him by the arm, dragging him away from moving to the nun, was Hans Kohlhase, his bearded face slick, his beard matted and blood all over him. The way he had looked on the breaking wheel, for he had never been in Florence; the reality of that day had been Michelangelo, hauling him away by the arm and deciding for him, in that hesitating moment, whether to save the nun and risk himself, or leave her to the fate of God.

Every time he dreamed this it had been the same – the convent and the street and the world vanished in a great blasting roar of flame, a sick flare of heat and a fist of unseen, casual savagery that flung them all to skitter and roll in the rubble. Stones and burning wood clattering round them. The nun on fire and screaming.

Always the same.

Not this time. This time the nun, her face Mintie's, was suddenly so close Batty could smell the cloves and nutmeg Mintie used in her hair while, incongruously, the flames that shrivelled her had no heat or substance to them at all.

'Die for me,' she said.

Newark Castle, near Selkirk
At the same time

'It is my considered opinion,' Wat Scott declared, 'that every man needs a woman, to share the burden of murder, the guilt of victory and the melancholic phlegm of defeat.'

He shifted his big beefy shoulders inside the casing of fine dark blue perse, slashed and brocaded in green; he stroked the grizzle of combed and trimmed beard that lay over his neat white-lace collar.

'To dry the tears of shame,' he went on in his growl of a voice. 'To scent with delicacy the smell of blood on your hands. To show you God's exquisite plan when all your slain rise up in dreams to challenge your very reason to exist.'

Batty sat and listened, stone-faced.

'I myself,' Wat went on, 'have recently gotten married on to a fine woman. My Janet is a helpmeet and all of the above what I have been saying, for I have fought in a wheen of affrays and seen my share of hempings, so my sleep can be troubled.'

Wat Scott leaned forward a little, his brows an arrowhead of irritation.

'But never has it been removed from me entire by the nocturnal shouts of another. Not even in any brothel.'

He looked round hastily and added loudly: 'Which I have never visited, only heard hearsay of.'

'I am sorry for it,' Batty replied wryly. 'Sorrier still to have dreamed it.'

'Aye, aye,' Wat declared sourly. 'But myself and Goodwife Janet are mightily puzzled by a burning nun and what Mintie Henderson of Powrieburn has to do with it. By God, the whole of Newark is. Nor does it make me consider your endeavour favourably. A man as hag-ridden as that, Master Coalhouse, is not filling me with confidence.'

'I am sorry for it,' Batty repeated, appalled at just how much had been revealed of his dreams and more shaken by the change of it than he cared to admit. He recovered himself and pretended to look round the hall of Newark to allow him time to chivvy his thoughts into a semblance of ranks.

Newark was fresh to Wicked Wat, handed to him a month or two before and still being furbished properly by his equally new wife. There were dust motes dancing in the shafts of sunlight through the small windows and a general bustle and beating of old hangings; Newark, Batty thought, was only a floor higher than Powrieburn and a mere rickle of flagstones wider than Hollows, yet it held the name 'castle', while Hollows did not dare be anything more than a tower.

Wicked Wat Scott of Branxholme and Buccleuch, however, was delighted with it, the more so since he had been in and out of wardings in Edinburgh, held at 'the king's pleasure' and only released the year before last. As he had always argued, how could he be in the purse of the English when Branxholme was a sooty lair of scorchings still, ten years on from when Henry Percy, Earl of Northumberland, had led the English to burn it?

Now Scott was the darling of the Regent, a bastion against the English he had once been accused of being too close to and, once again, lording it over the Kers of Cessford. So much so, as Batty told him, he had taken his eye off the Armstrongs of Hollows and paid the price for it.

'True enough,' Wat agreed and poured good ale from a pitcher, lifting his feet obligingly while a woman with a broom attempted to sweep and curtsey apology at the same time. 'You need eyes in your neck for this part of the world.'

'You should have stayed married to Jinty Ker,' Batty growled back daringly, and for a moment Wat scowled, then gave a mock shiver.

'God forbid. But no man can ever claim I did not exert my upmost to keep the peace between that widdershins race and myself. Jinty Ker was left-handed, like all of them, but she was as contrary in everything else she did and said as well. As bad as her da, and being married on to her was as good as sharing a bed with Himself of Cessford. Divorcing her was the best thing I did.'

He broke off, looked flustered for a moment, then added hastily: 'Besides marrying Janet Beaton, that is.'

The broom-woman swept away and Wat grinned at Batty.

'That told in a hall is repeated in a solar,' he said softly, tapping his nose. 'Janet will know it by nightfall.'

'The Kers of Cessford are no danger to you now,' Batty said, swallowing the ale and wishing it was stronger. He was flustered and ruffled by the dreaming, the third time in a week. 'The Laird o' Hollows is. He is planning more against you, to prove to Fat Henry that he is worth the hire.'

Wat knew it, and if truth was told aloud, would have been forced to admit he was more concerned than he let on.

'You need not tell me about the Laird of Hollows,' he declared, and riffled through the papers in front of him, lifting one.

'Item,' he read, 'on the eighteenth, men of Armstrong and Bourne took out of Cleuchbrae, within a few miles of Dumfries, four horses.'

He threw it down, picked up a fistful more.

'Item – on the nineteenth, of same took from Drumhill forty beasts. Item, on the twentieth, of same took at East Waperburne, hurting five men in peril of their lives in pursuit, twenty-four oxen and sixty sheep. Within half a mile of Branxholme.'

He flung the lists down.

'A hundred sheep and mares, more in oxen and kine, and twenty folk hurt,' he growled. 'All done by Armstrongs and Bournes from both sides of the Divide, and away, free as you please with their spoil – *my* beasts. And me not able to do a thing about it.'

'And all in a time when no Rides are usual,' Batty pointed out, impressed – as he always was – with the magic that allowed folk to put memory on paper. 'Still, we know the cause of it, the ruse that led to the wee Queen's kidnap.'

Wat shot him a look.

'Still no word on that, then?'

Batty shook his head and Wat closed one reflective eye.

'I hear you played a part in it.'

Batty knew what the Warden was at and smiled grimly.

'In the rescue. I do not know where the bairn is now. We were careless, I admit, but not treacherous, my lord.'

'Aye, well – still lost, all the same. The Regent is convinced Fat Henry has her and is biding his time before revealing it.'

'Better that than the wee lass is away with the Egyptianis, brought up as thieving wee besom,' Batty pointed out. 'Or found out and left in a panic on the moss for the foxes.'

Wicked Wat crossed himself.

'Heaven forfend – still, with the entire country scouring every brake and bush, that will reveal itself fairly soon.'

It had to, Wat thought, for a country with no wee queen was a nation in turmoil. You would not need a Regent, you would need a ruler – and, if it became known that wee baby Mary was dead or gone for good, then all the factions would draw apart and start snarling about their rights. With King Henry at the door, grinning out of his fat face and priming his big guns with Hollows-made powder, offering help and money to all of the factions while attaching their strings.

'The best man for the task of finding her is now caged at Hollows,' Batty said sternly. 'A Land Sergeant of Liddesdale. In your March, my lord. Bad enough the Laird spoils you blind without thumbing his neb at your station as well.'

'By God, we will see,' Wat scowled, the memory of his lifted beasts and ravaged households scouring the comfort from him.

Batty rubbed his pouched and prickled eyes. 'I can deliver the Laird of Hollows,' he went on. 'But I will need you and your men at his door. Perjink and proper Warden's men.'

'If there was a chance of knocking down Hollows I would be there,' Wat declared. 'With a thousand lances. None of it will do the least good if Hollows is barred, for two men and a three-legged pup could hold it against twice a thousand. But get me in and I will be there, with Bill and band.'

And a blaze of torches for burning that mill, if he could get close enough...

Batty sat for a while, brooding on the dream. Then he stirred himself.

'Hollows will be open to you and you will not need a thousand lances. Just the Warden's garrison. At dawn on Lady Day.'

'Lady Day? I had plans for Lady Day eve, involving jigging and wine and a deal of meat.'

'You and everybody else,' Batty replied. 'Including Hollows. They are holding a Feast of Fools on the eve of it.'

Wat laughed and slapped his knee.

'And you plan to make fools of them?'

He shook his shaggy head with amused admiration and his massive shoulders trembled with amusement.

'By God, Batty, you have iron in you and a neck of brass to match it. I will go light on the celebrating then and take a wee Lady Day ride out to Hollows, in company with a hunting party of a few score close friends. If what you say turns true, then I am in your debt.'

He raised his pewter mug, and Batty, after a pause, clanked his own against it, hearing it like a knell sealing the matter. The flame is at the fuse, he thought, and there is no going back from it now.

'How d'you plan on doing it?' Wat asked. Batty had no intention of telling him and simply shrugged, his one good shoulder lifting higher than the other.

'Loudly,' he said.

Chapter Nineteeen

Hollows Tower

Lady Day eve (24 March)

The day had been benisoned with sunshine, turning the land tawny, streaking it with green as new life struggled through the leached winter grasses. The last leprous patches of snow had gone and the Esk danced and sparkled.

Batty lay up in trees that were still skeletal and clawed but already budded to bursting. He lay there like a laired fox, watching while the day slid down from sun-warm to chill, watching the water in the river jig for the joy of not being ice, watching the slow progress of Bella driving more shod geese up to Hollows for the night's Feast of Fools.

He wondered how Agnes was faring after her encounter with Mintie. He wondered how Mintie was faring and if she would contrive another way to exit the world. If she was determined enough, he thought, a length of rope and an undercroft beam would do, but the long trip to the Solway and the business of the bairn of stones smacked of contrivance; if she had wanted the balm of oblivion, Batty thought, rope and beam were handier and quicker.

So he was sure it had been a desperate mummer's play for his benefit. She had invested her future in himself and had let him know it – at no small risk to herself, mind you; if he had been an inch shorter in the arm, a second later in the splashing dash to her, or a quim-hair less in strength, she would have slipped away whether she meant it or not.

There was, of course, just enough dark in her for that risk not to have mattered much. Batty was trying not to feel the weight of all that, and failing.

That will account for the dreams, he thought to himself. She has shaken me like a dog with a rat and all my sins are burst from the prison I fastened them in – Hans on the wheel, the burning nun I should have helped, the slaughter of Florence and the abandonment of it at the last. I should have taken up Michelangelo's offer, so that I would not be here, at this moment, about to do what I must.

Then he sighed. Hey-ho, you can only play the cards you are dealt, in life as in Primero.

So he watched the men moving to and fro, slow and deliberate in their movements, barrowing loads of saltpetre, hoisting loads of charcoal. In an outbuilding, far removed from the mill itself, yellowed alchemists forged sulphur out of fool's gold. The millwheel turned and the sound of grinding and shrieking told where the machinery whirled.

Wooden, of course, every toothed wheel and spoke and kept thickly greased but squealing like an ox-cart axle as they ground and sieved and spun.

There were equally noisy carts, lumbering up with loads of charcoal probably made from alder – nothing but the best for the Hollows powder mill, Batty thought. Others reeked with the produce of every privy for miles, carefully mixed with wood ash and mortar, then placed in piles ranked in order of age, the older having more of the vital saltpetre they needed. Everyone was encouraged to water them with their piss; they leached evil brown stains, spilling in sluggish runnels down to the Esk.

Then there were the kegs, no more than four or five a time, loaded onto wee ponies and led out south. To Carlisle, Batty thought, and on to Fat Henry's depots; he would pay well for good corned gunpowder, and it was small wonder the Laird of Hollows could afford to build his tower in stone.

He watched the shuffling, careful pairs who brought out the thick cakes, moving as if underwater. The charcoal and sulphur had been pulverised by the huge flat-edged millstones, the resulting mixture sieved to remove any impurities – anything that might cause a spark – and then saltpetre added and the whole mixed into 'wetten dough', a damp cake.

That went to the press for 'coming' – squeezing smaller – then was dusted and black-leaded to keep out the damp. Finally the cake, thirty or so Scots pounds of Hell waiting to happen, was taken out to the underground magazine and stored by these shuffling, cautious pairs.

Even the last dusting was reused, and working in the mill was a hard job, even when the turning wheel handled the heaviest parts of it. The only advantage to the work was that they only had to do it from light until it was too dark to see, for no lantern or, God forbid, torch was ever used.

Twice in the day a solemn party came out of the mill carrying the proving mortar, no bigger than a decent goblet, but black and heavy iron. They moved far enough away not to be a danger, then went through the motions of testing the batch – the bang scared up a protest of birds, the fist-sized smooth stone they shot sailed satisfyingly far, within acceptable range for the weight of powder.

Batty also watched the little knots of armed riders – Hollows men – out to collect the year-end black rents, extorting money from little steadings and holdings. He counted twenty or more out, knowing they would be gone all the next day and grumbling at missing the Feast of Fools. That left no more, Batty reckoned, than a dozen fighting men at Hollows, who would be working up a rare thirst at the promise of the coming revels.

Still, drunk or sober, there would be enough of them to defend the place if the doors were barred and the walls stood.

Batty watched the mill workers on into the dusk, until they stopped. The talk went up a level when they were free of labour and concentration. They fell to chaffering one another as much with relief at having got through another day as with the promise of a celebration, however small and mean, to bring the year round to *anno domini* 1543.

Better yet, tomorrow was a day free from work that not even the hardest taskmaster in the most lawless part of God's world would dare flout for the ill-feeling it would foment. They were happy and off to see wife and bairns, or women and drink.

The mill workers went off in twos and threes, pausing to wish the guards well as they lit their brazier on the bridge, only entrance to the mill itself and far enough away that no spark would carry. In the mill, Batty thought, would be the luckless man left to shiver in the cold dark, with only a cudgel for a weapon, there to keep out the casual thief or ragged-arsed stranger looking for shelter in a place seemingly abandoned.

Batty waited until the landscape silvered and the river turned to a plunge of moonshine. To his left, the bridge guards flitted shadows back and forth on the brazier; there were two only, with pikes and back and breasts, and helmets, all to show how important they were. To the right, Hollows loomed briefly against the dying light, a black spike glazed with the slight lambent light from its few high windows.

On the half-finished roof was another guard that Batty had seen in daylight, right next to the unlit beacon brazier and within taunt of the caged prisoner who hung there.

The cage hung out across the new crow-stepped gable, swinging to and fro and perilously close to the lattice of scaffolding erected for new work to begin. Too early and cold yet, Batty thought, for mortaring stone in place of that timber.

He squinted up at the dark tower. The banded cylinder had been empty for all the day and Batty wondered if Will had died. He thought not, in the end, because the cage was still there, waiting for an occupant. It was probable that the Laird had taken Will inside, if only to feed and warm him, treat the wounds he had; the Land Sergeant had to be kept alive, after all, for his purpose to be fulfilled.

He will be in the cage tonight, Batty thought, certes. Hung like a decorating bauble on the Hollows' Feast of Fools.

Eventually, as a dog fox yelped love to the dark, he moved slowly, stretching the stiff out of him. He was about to leave cover when he heard the muffled clap and clop of hooves and froze on the spot.

Three figures, dark and swaddled, ambled nags up to the bridge, spoke briefly with the guards. One of the riders was a woman and made the guards laugh; then the horsemen moved on into the dark, heading down to Andrascroft.

Batty thought for a fleeting instant that one of the riders was Bet's Annie, and wondered on that for a while; then he shook it from him and, lumbering like a soft-padded bear, went down to the river and the dark powder mill.

He went across the Esk, the cold of it biting like a dog's jaw. The water was not deep, but the thaw had spated it and he had to move slowly and carefully, feeling his way across the jumbled rocks of the bed.

Twice he slipped and managed – just – not to soak himself, which would have been a disaster to the slow match he had coiled round him. Still, he crawled out the far side cursing silently and beginning to shiver; he would suffer for this in days to come, with bone-deep aches and probably an ague and blocked nose.

If he had days to come.

The mill was dark, the wheel locked and still with the water gurring soft and creaming round it; he moved swiftly and silently to the walls, rolling like a sailor, keeping an eye on the men at the bridge. The night had enough winter memory in it to keep folk close to the flames, and Batty was happy with that – he did not want them wandering up to find out how the watchman fared.

He moved to the door, found it locked, slipped on. A powder mill was a sieve of entrances and exits, because a close-fastened structure acted like a barrel if the powder ever exploded. There was one entire wooden wall, a weak structure designed to funnel any explosions in the least destructive direction, but Batty thought the builders had never experienced what powder could do if it was all fired at once.

He found an opening and was in, pausing in the dark to take in the strange shapes. Those hanging things surrounded by toothed wheels would be the shakers for mixing the ingredients. The great bulk of the flat-edged millstones was easy to spot and the stink of nitre and sulphur and acrid alchemics caught his throat.

He heard a cough. Someone shuffled out.

'Who is there? Is any yin there?'

Querulous and rheumy that voice, fitting for a man who lived and breathed this fetid atmosphere for most of his long sleepless nights, Batty thought. Poor luckless old man, having to miss all the food and drink and bonhomie for a cold watch in this tomb. You stand poorly in the estimation of the Laird of Hollows, he thought. You stand as poorly in the estimation of God Himself.

Worse than all of that, you stand poorly in my path.

He moved to the sound, just as the man shuffled round the end of a block of millstone; they collided, both recoiling with the shock. With a sharp cry, the watchman lashed out and whacked Batty in the ribs with his cudgel, hard enough to make him gasp.

The next one will be at my head, Batty thought wildly, then drew from his boot and thrust in a swift, much-used motion. The watchman seemed to catch his breath with a sharp intake; the cudgel clattered to the floor and he paused, hung on the moment, then fell like a tree.

Batty straightened, wincing and panting. A punch, he thought, no more. Almost friendly... save that the fist had sharp steel in it.

Then he scowled – bloody old fool with a stick nearly ends me before I am started. If it had not been for ells of slow match...

He levered himself out of his jack of plates and uncoiled the slow match from round his body, while the man he had stabbed in the lungs gurgled and wheezed and bled. Batty paid him no more mind than if he had been part of the mill, a flagstone or a shaking vat.

He was annoyed for his ells of slow match, concerned more that it might get wet in the old man's spreading lake of blood than for the long, hard death the man was having. He had made that match himself, to a tried and true method so that he knew the burn-length – two spans an hour – and did not want any interference with it.

Good hempen cord, soaked in limewater and saltpetre for the nitre, washed in a lye of water and wood ash. Laid flat all of a piece, which was awkward since it was so long, but if you hung it up soaked the nitre collected at either end and vanished from the middle, so that all you got was a few seconds of dangerous flare and spit before it fizzled out.

Coiled like lengths of snake round the mill, it would burn steady, a series of winking red eyes leading down to several points. One would be to the magazine outside. Another was to the dust sieves, kegged and covered. Another was to an uncapped keg of the proving powder, left in the mill itself because folk anxious to be off and with a free day waiting could not be bothered taking it back to the magazine.

The slow match for the magazine was vinegar-soaked against the wet, though Batty was not exactly sure what this would do to the burn rate. Faster, certes, he thought, so he cut it longer. He could not afford to coil it round the dry of the magazine – too much powder in there and it would go off prematurely if he did. It would have to stretch out along the ground until the final moment and Batty was least sure of this one.

He hoped the ground was not too damp as he led the last, longest match to the magazine, half crouched to keep an eye on the guards at the bridge. Once down in the deep-ramped entrance, he cracked the wooden door easily enough, fed the match into the stacks of kegs and bundled cakes and scurried out like a fat rat from a ditch. He closed the door and barred it, making a muzzle out of the magazine.

Then he went back to the dark chill of the powder mill, to the acrid reek and the scurry of vermin attracted by the blood of the dead man. He sat in a corner and watched his breath smoke, glancing every now and then at the high-set window, looking for the smeared milk of a new dawn. He saw lights flicker where Hollows would be, thought he could hear the faint sound of laughter.

There had been other Lady Days, other celebrations of the change of year and most had been better than this, Batty thought. Even the one that heralded 1530, though that had also had a lick of death in it. He laid his head back against the rough wall, staring at the faint outline of another, seeing the ill-laid stones of the mill.

Done in a hurry, he thought. Flung up with more thought to getting it working than doing a good job. Michelangelo would be outraged, he thought, and chuckled softly to himself, wondering if the man still designed fortifications, or was bringing beauty from marble instead.

Not an elephant, though. On this same night a dozen years ago, Batty had sat with others round a flickering fire in a rubbled, pocked bastion of Florence, waiting for the raw new day of 1530 and the slaughter it would bring, listening to Michelangelo cursing the white elephant given to his former patron, Pope Leo X.

Batty put his head back against the rough stone and listened again...

'That catamite-lover,' Michelangelo growls, scrawling on the back of fields of fire and ranges as he did so, scoring the charcoal to fragments with his rage. 'Another Medici. Made us all immortalise that idiot beast, which died two years after he got it. They choked it with poor food, then fed it gold to make its bowels move – can you believe it?'

He shakes his head. Scrape, scrape, scrape. He is almost sixty and still full of manic energy, dark-haired, dark-bearded.

'Gold, in the name of God. But even in the short time it lived, the beast caused riots all the way to Rome. People wrecked a cardinal's

villa trying to see it – broke down walls and dug holes through houses.
Folk died.'

Scrape, scrape.

'Sereno wrote poetry to it – "such a spectacle has been observed
by Pompey, Hannibal, Domitian and few others". The Spaniard,
Naharro, wrote a play with a part for the beast. Folk loved this doggerel,
the Pope almost as much as he loved that elephant. He called it Hanno
and lavished attention on the big-arsed monstrosity, which someone
taught to bow to him. Would have been better teaching it not to void
everywhere – noxious animal. Until they choked it with bad feeding,
that is.'

Scrape, scrape, and the charcoal splinters fly while those spatulate
hands blur with manic intensity.

'If they had used the gold they fed it as a laxative to pay for marble,'
he says, 'San Lorenzo basilica would be finished instead of looking like
a dog kennel.'

Another pause, another head-shake, while his eyes flick from subject
to paper and his fingers fly.

'Noxious beast,' he mutters, then hawks and spits. 'Not as noxious
as Raffaello da Urbino, the little Pope balls-licker.'

He puts on a falsetto voice that makes folk chuckle.

'How would you like us all to immortalise the departed Hanno,
Your Immense Holiness? Fresco? Oils? Pen and ink? Stucco? Marble?
Intarsia? Leonardo might do something – though he is past his best
these days and never finishes commissions. Simoni has some slight skill
with majolica...'

The charcoal splinters to ruin finally, and he throws the remains of
it away.

'Little turd, Raffaello,' Michelangelo scowls, staining his clothes
as he searches for another piece. 'Died of swiving his mistress, La
Fornarina, and not before time. Thirty-seven years in the same world
as me was too long – the dauber was even about to be made a cardinal,
can you imagine it?'

He spits on his fingers, wipes them clean on his front so as not to
smudge new paper.

'Should have exhibited him in a cage, not the thrice-damned elephant, which we had to paint, sculpt and fuss over for years after it died.'

All the rough-arsed had loved Michelangelo's tales and the fact that he sat with them, the wonderful artist of beauty, the calculating genius of arc and range. Sitting sharing bad wine with the powder-stained, bloody-handed of Batty Coalhouse's company, who had to carry out Michelangelo Simoni's clever schemes for repairing the shattered defences, re-site the rabinets and culverins and demi-culverins.

'You are here fighting the Medici and the Pope,' Batty says to him. 'Yet the Pope is your patron. What will you do once this is done with?'

Michelangelo shrugs.

'Go back and sculpt for the Pope. Like you, I am a mercenary – you could be fighting for the French tomorrow. I will build and design and sculpt for the Medici if they ask and pay and give me something interesting to work on.'

He leans forward, his eyes intense, his spade beard quivering.

'I am a whore, no less than those on Rome's Ripetta wharf. A Florentine Republic, however, is the love of my life.'

That was then, this was now, Batty thought. I should have gone to stay with Michelangelo so that I would not be here now – I jalouse that his Lady Day in the Italies is a lot better than mine.

Yet he knew, now as then, that when morning came he would stagger himself upright on stiff legs, joints aching and the missing arm itching, take up his weapons and see how poorly he stood in God's estimation.

Powrieburn

That same night

Her urine smelled fetid, tasted sweet, and of the fifteen shades – five alone of green – the old Mistress of Powrieburn's expellant was verdigris. With her hooked nails, bloody teeth and fever,

Ridley did not need any astrology done; besides, he doubted if these people even knew the month of their birth, let alone the hour and day.

'Phthisis,' he announced to Bet's Annie and saw her incomprehension.

'White plague?' he suggested. He knew some folk named it that way because the victims became so pale. There was a flicker in the woman's eyes then, and Ridley sighed. Well, no matter – give her the help for it and never mind the Greek.

'Wolf's liver taken in a thin wine,' he went on. 'Lard of sow fed on grass. A broth of she-ass.'

It would not help, he knew, for the woman was too far gone, but it was always better to offer hope.

'Ground boar penis will ease her breathing,' he went on and then paused. 'You should know that ph... white plague... may spread.'

He paused then, for in some places Ridley knew that phthisis was considered vampirism since one victim invariably led to others suffering slow wasting, and there were ignorants who claimed this was the victim sucking their life in a desperate attempt to stay alive. The condition caused red and swollen eyes which became sensitive to the light, so sufferers preferred the dark – and that only added to the lore.

Ridley was fairly sure there were no such creatures as vampires and equally certain that those who believed it were quite capable of taking an old beldame like the Mistress of Powrieburn, knocking her on the head and then burying her with a stake through her heart.

'White plague,' Bet's Annie repeated slowly. 'Boar penis.'

'Ground,' Ridley added patiently, wondering if the entire household was wit-struck. The daughter sat with her hands in her lap, staring at nothing, and though Ridley suspected grief, he did not know of any version which placed a daughter within comfort reach of her dying ma and then let her sit and watch like a crow waiting for a lamb to die.

In fact, the only time the daughter – Mintie – had been animated at all was when she fixed Ridley in a corner and questioned him on childbirth, wanting to know about the soul of a newborn.

'Placed in the embryo by God,' Ridley had told her firmly, 'forty days after conception.' She had demanded he confirm it, grasping his wrist fiercely as she did so. Afterwards, she had sat like that, saying nothing, staring at nothing.

Ridley wanted away back to Hollows where he had left Ganny preparing to dress as a boy-bishop, crooning over baby Jane and chuckling as he wrapped her up to be little Jesus.

This evening Hollows would be a riot of drunks and folk made delirious with celebration and the topsy-turvy madness of a Feast of Fools. Ridley looked around him; this place is the exact opposite, he thought. Even for a household grieving over a slow dying it is bleak.

He wanted to leave but could not, for he had, at the very least, to offer the woman final Confession and Rites – nor would he get paid if he left before she died and did not think she would do it in a hurry.

Bet's Annie knew the scowling physicker she and Hew had brought from Hollows with the stiff blessing of the Lady was no true doctor, nor even a barber-surgeon – though he might be a priest. He knew a bit, but any cunning woman could do as much, for all he made a show of holding urine up to the light, swirling and sniffing and dabbing it on his tongue.

White plague. Bet's Annie knew the name well enough, though it was called differently here – Elfstruck. The Faerie had claimed the old Mistress of Powrieburn as sure as if the Queen of Elfland herself had arrived, all tinkling bells and white horse. Hag-ridden was another name for it.

She told the others that it was just the old woman's time, no more than age and circumstance, though she knew the Faerie rarely stopped at just the one. Perhaps in Powrieburn, though, which had a compact with the Silent Moving Folk…

She never spoke to Mintie, had had enough of the girl, in fact. Her ma lay dying there and not a word of comfort for her, just an endless brooding on her own condition, as if she was the only lass in Liddesdale who had ever been tupped against her will, or lost a child.

Mintie was only half aware of anything else, just the one thing.

Forty days.

Forty days. It circled and coiled round Mintie's head, in and out of her heart. Whether doctor or priest, he would be right – why would he not be? So what she had torn from herself had never had a soul. Unlike wee Agnes's mite, which went longer to term; for the first time, Mintie realised what she had done to Agnes with her desperate, wild talk.

Forty days. A priest-doctor said so, so it must be true. It was something, then, lifted from the stain on her own soul, something for the wee mite...

Her ma coughed and it was a ram on the wall of her. She almost heard the stones crack, felt the lurch as if she had been leaning against it. Then it collapsed, sudden and complete, and the world rushed in. She turned, blinking, felt the spate filling her so that she could hardly breathe.

'Ma...'

Bet's Annie, amazed, saw Mintie move to the bedside, take the withered, hook-nailed hands in her own, heard the cracked bell tone of her voice.

Christ be praised for this miracle at least, she thought.

Then a voice outside hailed them.

Jinet, closest to the small window, peered out and announced that a boy was sat on a horse in the yard.

'Dressed like a man,' she added with a half-laugh.

Bet's Annie clattered down to where Hew and Eck stood ready with drawn swords; she scattered them like chooks and unbarred doors into the pewter and milk dawn.

The boy sat on a fine horse, lance fewtered into the stirrup leather, iron hat on his head and a highly decorated musket slung on his back. Little shield, daggers, sword – he was every inch a warrior; it was just that the inches weren't many.

'Davey Graham,' Bet's Annie said formally. 'Unsaddle and welcome.'

Davey-boy grinned at her, then nodded to Hew and Eck, who were older and yet so much less that they did not care to know it.

'What brings you to Powrieburn?' Bet's Annie asked as Davey Graham slithered from the horse. On foot he was just a boy festooned with weapons as big as himself.

'My da sent me. To help in the rescue of the Land Sergeant of Hermitage.'

Bet's Annie laughed at the poor-tin lie of it.

'He did not, Davey Graham of Netherby. He would no more send his darling Davey-boy out on his own on such a task than he would mount a naked virgin on a milk white and send her into the Debatable with all his gold in two big bags.'

Hew and Eck laughed, which only deepened the red flush and scowl on Davey-boy.

'Besides that,' she added firmly, 'he would know that any such rescue would not be mounted from Powrieburn, since the man who would do it is long gone from this place. So do not lie to me, Davey-boy Graham.'

Davey frowned and opened then closed his mouth.

'I came to help,' he admitted and scuffed one boot toe. 'I like Land Sergeant Will.'

Bet's Annie recalled that it was Davey who had been with Will all the way down to Carlisle and back. It must have been a rare adventure for the lad, she thought, and he has clearly made Will a friend; her heart warmed to him at once. He would have to be got back to Netherby, all the same, before Dickon worried himself into a lather – and rashness.

'Get you inside – you look as if you could use broth at least. Bring your nag in and the lads will see to it. You can tell Mistress Mintie of your plans. What does your da say regarding Will being caged up at Hollows?'

'He says Will was daft to get lifted so easily. And he fought badly, he says, though it is hard to take on the Laird of Hollows and his two-hander. He says Will is cunny-struck.'

Davey-boy was happy now that he was not about to be sent off and happier still that the two lads were trying hard not to show their admiration for his wonderful gun. He was happy enough to repeat what he'd heard and not realise what he said.

Cunny-struck, Bet's Annie thought. Aye, well, Dickon and the Netherby Grahams had that right – bedazzled by the possibility of Mintie, Will had been weakened as badly as Samson. But what would the Grahams do about it? She asked as she followed Davey-boy up the steps.

'My da says it is a matter for Batty Coalhouse. He is angered at Batty for what he did with the Armstrongs we gave him.'

Well he might be, Bet's Annie thought, for it was a foul deed and now Batty is repaid for it – he will have no help from his new kin. Other than this daring boy, she thought, and was touched enough by it to announce Davey to the rest of the house as if he was being presented at court.

'He has come to help rescue Will Elliot,' she added to Mintie's back and saw the head come up.

Mintie turned then, so pale that Ridley whimpered, thinking her the next victim.

'Will,' she said, as if in wonder. 'Batty.'

Her face was misery, suddenly old and white as a blanched walnut.

'Christ in Heaven, Annie – what have I done?'

Chapter Twenty

They had demolished most of the last of the feast, when the Laird finally sent for his prisoners and Leckie half stumbled down into the undercroft with Davey's Pate, the pair of them red-faced with drink and cursing their luck.

The light made the prisoners blink, but Hutchie's eyes were rat bright and expectant as he looked the swaying pair over; even down here in the dark and cold he could hear the riot of the Feast of Fools.

Leckie had not known what to expect, but the friendly, confident nod of Hutchie Elliott had not been part of it and made him scowl. Hutchie merely grinned his still-white grin and nodded at the half-eaten pie clutched in Leckie's fist, a betrayal of custard cream fringing his moustache.

'Good vittles, then,' he declared brightly. 'Any left for us?'

Leckie recovered enough to growl, while Pate swayed and belched and blinked like a weary owl, his mind trying to grind out a sharp response and so far from it a week would never be long enough.

'The dogs have your portion,' Leckie managed, and after a long moment – while it pierced the fog of drink – Pate laughed, got caught in a great belch and looked surprised at it.

'You are called to the hall,' Leckie declared portentously and then waved to Pate, who fumbled for his keys, held them for a moment and blinked once more.

'Ah might boak,' he announced and shoved the keys at Leckie before turning away and vomiting copiously.

'Ach, you filthy whoreslip,' bellowed Leckie, leaping back from the splashing. Hutchie laughed and the dog barked.

'Don't try anything,' Leckie warned, suddenly aware of the crowd of men he had to release and that he was alone save for the retching Pate.

'Aye, aye,' Hutchie replied wryly, 'a quick blow to lay you out, shove the brace of you in your own cell and then fight our way through the hall and out into the yard, battle to the stables, saddle horses and away to freedom. Pausing only to thieve the silver and violate a woman or three on the way.'

'Less of your violatin',' muttered Sore Jo, picking his scabs. 'That's what landed us here.'

He dug Hutchie sharply in the ribs and for a moment they glared at each other; then the dog growled and Hutchie relaxed. He had not forgotten the strange contract the Lady had intimated with these others and did not trust them. For now, though, they were all mired in the same muddy dub.

Leckie opened the door and Pate moaned about 'bad pie' and 'nivver again'. They left him in the dark as they were shepherded upstairs by Leckie; their shadows bobbing and dancing in the torch he held high.

They came up into a blare of light and leprous heat, a beating bell of noise from bellowers and roarers, and a shrill shriek of drunk women; drum and flute fought and failed to be heard over it.

The fresh rushes had been scattered and littered with the debris of a rich table, spilled from torn-apart platters which still had the memory of the original, enough to water the mouth of Hutchie and the others.

Stuffed goose, Lombard-style with sliced almonds. Stewed pigeons with sausage and onions. Boiled calves' feet with cheese and egg. Sheep's pluck and bashed neeps. Fried veal sweetbreads and liver. Rob's Tam groaned and champed saliva onto his beard; the dog tore free from Black Penny and darted in to fight the wolfhounds for scraps.

'Well, well – the bold lads are here.'

The Laird sat at his high seat, bright in pale blue silk slashed to show the white linen beneath, though the fine suit was already stained with meat juice and wine. His face was a berry of seeming delight, in contrast to the stone of his Lady, who sat in prim dove grey, her hands in her lap and her eyes agate.

'It is right and proper,' the Laird bellowed, aiming to be heard above the din, 'that a Feast of Fools be graced by some of the greatest fools in Liddesdale.'

He slapped the table and rocked with laughter, which everyone dutifully joined in; the marzipan model of Hollows Tower teetered. The Laird waved magnanimously.

'Follow Leckie and he will tell you what to do. It is the Laird o' Hollows' pleasure to feast you and then send you on your way, with no bad cess atween us. Before that, you will entertain us as befits fools.'

He paused, drank, belched and then laughed.

'Save you, Hutchie. You will play your part in this mummery, but I will keep you close at my pleasure.'

Hutchie bowed, fighting the seethe in him. He followed the others out the door and down the steps into the barmkin yard to the accompaniment of laughter, only some of it good-natured, and a shower of small bones and bits of bread.

Down in the yard, lit by flickering torches, Leckie smirked and indicated a heap of filthy brown robes.

'Put them on and take up your censers, wee priests,' he declared, and Hutchie realised the robes were ragged, stained and stinking habits. The censers were buckets of ashes.

Then he saw the boy dressed like a bishop in cloth of gold, clutching a basket crib.

'The Boy Bishop and the baby Jesus,' Leckie declared. 'You are his clerics.'

Black Penny, more concerned about his dog than anything, merely struggled into the garments without a murmur; the rest followed, muttering.

Hutchie climbed into the slime of his own habit, took up the bucket, and then, with a sharp bark of laughter, Leckie waved them back up the stairs. They processed forward into the hall, waving the ash buckets back and forth until the contents spilled in a cloud, right and left.

Behind came the Boy Bishop, beaming and cradling his holy charge, reciting the Creed at the top of his shrill voice. As they came into the hall, a great roar went up and folk answered every 'amen' response with a bray like a donkey and great howls of laughter.

William Patten caught the Lady's eye, saw that it was jaundiced as his own; King Henry had banned the Boy Bishop abomination in England only recently, but it was such a well-established tradition that it would take more than an edict to end it. It might never end for the Scotch, he thought, looking at the greased delight on faces.

As entertainment, he thought scornfully, it is what you might expect from this unsophisticated outpost in a barbarian country. He warmed himself with the thought that soon he would have concluded his business here and be gone. He would give this Laird three days, though he did not think the missing royal babe would be found in that time; after that, he would inform King Henry of the truth of matters.

Hutchie, seething as he ducked food missiles from the laughing snarlers and growlers on their benches, processed round the small hall twice and found himself at the heels of the Boy Bishop, who had discovered just what it meant to be coped and mitred in cloth of gold and treated as a fool.

An outthrust foot made the boy stumble and Hutchie shot out a reflexive hand to catch the tumbling crib, realising that it was a real child a moment later. Then he looked at the wee face of it and the shock was like a dash of freezing water.

The Boy Bishop turned to thank him, then saw the frozen astonishment on the man's face; he snatched the crib from him and stumbled away.

Hutchie, bedazzled, ignored the flung bones and insults now. He had seen the babe, and even allowing for the sullen twist of her bawling face at being in this melee, he knew her well.

It was a marvel, though, how Mary, Queen of Scots had ended up in the charge of a Boy Bishop at a Feast of Fools.

And how no one else knew but him.

The powder mill near Hollows Tower
Dawn on Lady Day (25 March)

The sour milk sky smeared light in the high window and Batty stirred, stretching slowly to get the stiffness out; his movement set the rats scurrying from the body, now a vague outline in the dim, lying in a circle of sticky shadow.

Batty thought about it for a moment, shoved the regret away and shrugged; one more on the heap of bad cess on his soul. Let us see, he thought, levering himself up, if I have finally annoyed God.

He sang, soft and out of tune, for there was no one to hear but the rats and the long dead man: '*It was mirk, mirk night, there was no starlight and they waded in red blood to the knee.*'

Then he took a breath, pulled out his axe-shafted dagg and examined the wound wheel of it.

'*For all the blood that's shed on the earth, runs through the springs o' yon countrie.*'

He squeezed the trigger. It was not loaded, but the wheel spun and the sparks flew, catching the fine wool and charcoal. Sparks in this place; Batty almost heard the walls shriek, and with sweat running on him like lice, he puffed the faint glow into life, then lit a master match.

It was always the most danger, this part. He blew softly on the master match, then touched the smouldering end to all the others, one by one, the ends burning bright and red, each of them adding to the danger of a premature detonation. But the night was chill and damp, damp enough even in the mill.

He watched them. Like rat eyes in the dark, he thought. Then he scurried away, out of the mill, moving in a half crouched lumber, limbs stiff and sore.

He did not breathe normally until he was across the Esk, dripping this time because he had fallen twice in his haste and was soaked through.

Yet he lay back briefly and stared at the cloud-winked stars and got his breath back. Then he levered himself up and stared back at the mill, which would be silent and empty for only a little while longer, with no one bothering it, nor the dead man in it, nor the winking crimson eyes. Everyone would be too busy drinking and eating, jigging and laughing.

Feast of Fools, Batty thought, then took a deep, grim breath.

Yon sorry arse in the mill is only the first. By the time I am done here, Hell will seem a sunlit meadow.

Hollows Tower
At the same time

He swung and sometimes thought he was in his cradle, though why his ma had put his feet in the fire was a mystery; he called to her, hoping she would move his crib back a bit.

Then he surfaced into the horror, hanging in the banded cylinder out over the tower of Hollows, his feet shrieking with agony because he only had a narrow metal strip to stand on, and his arms were close to his sides so that he could not move them.

So he stood, all his weight taken on the balls of his bloody, stabbed feet, bound in banded metal and swinging.

'Will Elliot.'

The voice made him blink, but he was turned away from it. Then the vagrant breeze turned the cage in a sickening circle and he saw the Lady, wrapped against the chill up on the tower roof. Beside her were two men – Leckie, Will recognised. And the Englishman, the wee man who had pissed himself in the coach when the Grahams had attacked. It seemed another age since that, and he shivered. He had a name, the wee English, but he couldn't remember it...

He has fever, the Lady thought with alarm. My husband will kill this man with his carelessness.

She glanced at Patten and saw his grim look, the raised eyebrow. The Englishman saw the danger in this course, she knew – but Leckie, swaying and owlish with drink, was here because her husband had seen his wife leave the hall and set his drunken dog to watch her, so there was little that could be said or done.

My husband does not trust me, she thought bitterly, and that is what we have come down to, him and I. What does he think I will do? Drag the Land Sergeant of Hermitage onto the roof, knock the lock and free him – to do what? The man can hardly see, is almost certainly not able to stand, and all my husband's growling men between him and freedom.

She could only negotiate.

'He is fevered,' she said to Leckie. 'A blind man can see it and the air is chill. If he is left out all night, he will die.'

Leckie, aware that he had drunk too much, tried to marshall a suitable riposte but lost it on the march out of his mouth and degenerated into mumble and a wave of one hand that could mean anything.

'Bring him in,' she ordered sternly, and that sliced the fog in him.

'Naw,' he said, shaking his head and waggling a finger. 'Nawnawnaw – nay brininggin... bringin' gin. Hang, the Maister shays, and hang he will. Will will hang, so he will...'

He brayed with laughter, the sound shaking Will out of a slow sink into oblivion. He opened his eyes with difficulty, saw Leckie's red mouth wide with laughter, saw the pale marble of the Lady's face and the disapproving moue of the Englishman. Patten, that was his name...

Then, behind them all, a huge red flower blossomed in the dark, expanding like opening petals in all directions, a sick, swollen black and crimson bloom, leprous with menace.

A second later the heat and the massive noise blasted all sense away; Hell opened its throat and vomited all over Hollows Tower.

—

A concussive wave of light and sound knocked Batty to the ground, slamming the breath out of his lungs; for a single eyeblink the world was bright as day, etched in red with a huge flare of stretched shadows.

There was a time when he was neither in nor out of the world and, when he eventually decided he was still in it, he lifted his head and heard the singing emptiness of a strange silence.

Too close, he thought. Too much powder. Yet there was a flicker of pride at how all the slow matches had burned down almost together – no match with a slow match, that's Batty Coalhouse...

He rolled over and tried to get his breath back and heard pattering like running feet, raised his head a little and saw myriad small lights; nearby, shunked into the earth like a stake in a heart, a balk of timber smouldered.

The pattering was the last of the debris, fine as rain and some of it burning so that a mirr of fire fell all round him, hissing into the Esk; trees, stripped of their new buds, some uprooted, burned like torches.

He levered himself up slowly, checking limbs. There was the smell of burning hair and he patted and pinched out smoulders on the cloth of his jack. His sword was still slung, his single dagg stuck in his belt.

For a moment the vision of his father presented itself, the moment he waved from under the shelter of the Red Tower.

Or perhaps he was just stirring life into the match he was about to touch to the powder kegs that blew him and the gate to Hell.

Batty shook it away and got up, grunting. Somewhere ahead was Hollows, and at last hearing returned, so that the screaming seemed loud.

–

The tower shuddered as something massive struck it; a black wind whirred like a bird-wing between Patten and Leckie, with something darker still at the centre of it. The Lady was whirled away by it, struck and flung over the edge in an eyeblink by what Patten swore was a shattered segment of millstone.

The wind of it flung Patten backwards, skittering across the narrow walkway to slam into the slated peak of the roof. Leckie was flung the other way, colliding with the banded cylinder of the cage so that it swung wildly, right out in a half-circle, with Leckie clinging by instinct, like a barnacle to a wave-lashed rock.

Patten got up and staggered, panicked at not being able to breathe, turning in little jerky movements until he realised that the roaring he could hear was the slow, thunderous slither of the crow-stepped gable collapsing and taking half the roof with it, plunging down to the next floor. It left the curling wind of stair like the exposed nerve of a shattered tooth.

He lurched away from the tumble of falling stones, saw the incongruous sight of a half-circle of wood embedded in the wall. He had enough time to register it as part of a mill wheel before it tore free with an agonised shriek and fell into the huddle of buildings inside the barmkin, taking the wooden lattice of scaffolding with it in a great shower of timber skewers. He stumbled for the remains of the stair, looking for a way out and away.

Will's world tilted crazily and he lost his senses in the bewildering twists. The cage spun right round on its chain, out from the crenellated walls and all the way back to the other side; he

330

heard screaming and squinted down as far as his chin would allow.

Below, clinging on and staring up with his mouth a gaping sewer of shrieks, Leckie swung by one hand like a mad rope in a high wind, scrabbling furiously for grip with the other.

Will smiled as the cage lurched and banged Leckie into the stones, so that he tried to reach out and grab the wall. But there was no firmness left in Hollows Tower. It was melting like the marzipan model in the hall below, while the world seemed all fire and roaring.

Will moved his pain-burning foot onto the fingers and pressed hard, stamped until his own screams merged with those of Leckie, and when, fainting, he finally relaxed the pressure, Leckie fell away with a last despairing shriek.

Will had time to laugh one laugh. Then the cage gibbet snapped and sent him plunging sixty feet to the ground.

Chapter Twenty-One

Two miles east from Hollows
Lady Day (25 March)

The morning sun was barely up and staggering with weakness, yet it lit Ganny like a beacon. He glowed with golden perfection and dazzled himself; he whimpered and peeled off the cope – the mitre he had long since lost in the frantic desire to be gone from Hollows.

It had been after the smiling man had come to him, one of those wearing the stinking priests' robes who had acted as his processional escort. Ganny had known something was up the second this man, with his white teeth and slicked hair, had saved baby Jane from falling and seen who she was at the same time.

He knew her, that was clear, and that put Ganny in a blind panic – Christ, mayhap the baby was stolen from him, he thought. Yet the next thought was that a man like this, with winter in his eyes, did not have any child he cared for.

Yet he knew the babe and knew it was stolen.

'Fine looking wee lass,' he had said, smiling and easy when he had come to Ganny after all the hullabaloo had died down. Seated well below the salt, hoping for anonymity now that his role was done, Ganny had known he'd been sought out deliberately and his bowels, then as now, had turned to stone.

'Baby Jesus,' he had muttered back, trying to look winsome, though his top lip had stuck to his teeth when he smiled. 'Feast of Fools jest.'

'Aye, aye, good one,' the man had agreed, squeezing onto the bench close up to Ganny, so that the stink of the robes wrinkled his nose. The man apologised cheerfully, while another in the same robes stopped, looming over them both, and asked if they had seen his dog.

'No, Penny,' the man had replied, then took the other by the wrist. 'Get ready to move, Black Penny, dog or no dog. I have a money-making scheme that is surer yet than anything the Lady of Hollows has promised you.'

The man called Black Penny shook off the grip, scowling.

'Aye – what is it, then, Hutchie? Robbing wee bairns of their sweet sucklings?'

'In a manner,' the man called Hutchie had replied and winked at Ganny.

'This wee lad here has a bairn. It is not his bairn, is it, lad?'

'My father...' Ganny had lied, making Hutchie laugh; he had seen the sometime doctor come and go with the boy in tow. He knew the man was a priest fleeing from somewhere.

'Ridley? I fancy not, wee man. I fancy that priest is too old to be fathering the likes of you – or wee pretty red-headed babes like this.'

He was looking at Black Penny when he spoke, and Ganny saw something light in that man's eyes; his fear grew, so that it was all he could do not to flee there and then.

'No,' Black Penny had said, then peered closer. 'By God, it might be. You know it for sure?'

'As I know my hand's back,' Hutchie had agreed, and now Ganny was moving, so that Hutchie reached out and gripped his wrist.

'Not so fast—'

There was a fierce commotion, a great snarling and growling that scattered folk in a ring. The man called Black Penny had looked up and cursed.

'Beauchien—'

He leaped forward, collided with the man next to him and was flung away angrily with a drunken curse for his clumsiness.

He fell into another, who rounded on the thrower – in a second, fists and boots were flying, faces red and greased were exultant and snarling.

Hutchie lost his grip as someone tried to hit him; Ganny snatched up the crib and fled, haring in between bodies as if through a forest, straight out the door, down the steps and into the courtyard and away.

He had been running ever since, the first mad rush of it slowed to a trot, then a walk, and finally to a panting, heaving stagger which let him see the glowing gold of himself out on the bare moss. Like a torch in darkness, he thought.

He looked back over his shoulder; he knew they would be coming and he thought of just leaving the baby. But when he looked down at her, face squashed up in a wail because she was fretting, tired, needed changing, needed fed, he could not do it.

All his life Ganny had had nothing save his siblings. They had cowered in fear from their own parents and hugged their slim lives and each other. When Ridley had left, taking Ganny with him, he had nothing at all – baby Jane was all of his brothers and sisters in one, and he could not leave her on the wet moss for men like Hutchie and Black Penny.

He wondered who baby Jane really was. Valuable, or the likes of these men would not be bothered. He cursed Ridley for his stupidity in getting involved with it – but looked east, squinting into the blood of the sun and hoping to see the place called Powrieburn, where Ridley had gone.

Then he struggled on.

–

Not far behind, Hutchie and Black Penny and the dog followed after, grim as rolling rocks and on foot. Rob's Tam and Rob's Davey were still back in Hollows, for there had been no time to find them.

Black Penny fretted on that, for Clym's Bairns had been a family when all was said and done, and leaving them behind was abandonment, pure and simple. They would be punished for our escape, he had told Hutchie, who had sympathised with soothing words about going back for them when this business was done – while thinking that it was nothing to him if the two idiot brothers were hanged for it and good riddance.

'He is headed for Powrieburn,' Hutchie said at length and shook his head, laughing grimly at the joke of it. 'I am never done with that place, it seems.'

'We can't go there,' Penny declared. 'We have not even as much as an eating knife between us.'

'We have the dog,' Hutchie answered and they stared down at it, as it stared back, bleeding from a new rent on what was left of an ear and bright with tongue-lolling ecstasy at being out on the moss. Its teeth were a reef of all the daggers they would need.

'True enough,' Penny declared and patted the straked muzzle.

There was a sudden rumbling roar from behind them, making them turn and stare; a great pall of smoke rose up and a wind, feral hot as the breath of a great dragon, washed over them, rippling the stunted trees and moss grass.

'What in Hell was that?' demanded Penny fearfully, and Hutchie, who did not know and did not want to know, merely grunted and stepped out over the moss to where a golden cope lay like a trove on the wet earth.

He held it up; they forgot about what lay behind and struck out towards Powrieburn.

Hollows Tower

At the same time

Batty came up on the Hell of Hollows, shattered and surrounded by burning and shrieking. The horse did not care for it and balked, so he climbed off, wincing at the pain in his back where his own explosion had punched him.

Folk ran like chooks, making the same noises and with the same mindless panic; almost all of them ignored Batty as he stalked forward, leaning as if into a wind, the axe-handled dagg in his one hand.

A woman saw him, must have recognised the one arm and her shrieks went up so high only wolves could have heard her; she spun away, stumbling. A man saw her do it and peered, swaying; the eyes in his blackened, blood-streaked face grew wide with knowledge and he gave a grunt, fumbled for a weapon.

Batty, striding steadily towards him, did not want to be bothered, for he had seen the battered cylinder of cage and realised what had happened. When the man finally got a knife out, Batty's axe was splitting his neck from his shoulder and the man reeled away with a blood-clotted scream and fell to his knees.

Uncaring, Batty lumbered on to the cage, to the still figure inside it. He cursed; had he managed to kill Will Elliot with his rescue plan?

He struck the lock once, twice and burst it open, then levered the battered half of the cage up; Will groaned and Batty almost cried out with delight.

'You bastard-born one-armed son o' a hoor.'

The voice whirled him round into the twisted bloat of the Laird's stare. Blackened and bloody that face, and the first rays of the new day did nothing for it – but it threw golden shafts off the length of steel he held in his hand.

That bloody two-hander of his, Batty thought bitterly.

The Laird was humming with the horror of it, strummed with fire at what had been done to him and his. He had woken from a half-drunk snooze to the crashing roars of stones falling all round him, folk screaming and fleeing, falling crushed and bleeding.

It took him a long time – an age, it seemed – to suck in the fact that the roof was fallen in and the ceiling above him too, the whole lot crashing into the hall. When he realised it, he could only think he was under attack, that somehow great guns had been used on his precious tower; he lurched for the mantle and the sword, shoved and elbowed his way through the panicked throng, heading for the door to defend what was his.

Scotts, he had thought. Or Grahams. Even Fat Henry himself, his ears poisoned by that wee sleekit popinjay rat Patten...

Stumbling out, he had tripped over the body of Sorley Armstrong, crushed to bloody ruin by the crashing fall of the metal cage – and when he looked up, there was a one-armed man bashing open the lock of it.

The Laird of Hollows knew that Batty was somehow responsible for this. Then he saw, in a bemused blink, the flaming timbers and the remains of a millwheel, and knew what had been done.

The sheer destruction of it, the impudence of it – by God, the challenge of it – made him roar.

His first sweeping cut made Batty jerk backwards and almost stumble over the cage. Batty felt the last wicked point of the two-hander pink his jack of a few threads and he waved the axe-handled dagg threateningly enough to stop the Laird.

'By God,' Batty declared admiringly, trying to stretch time – somewhere, Wat Scott was coming, he hoped, fast now that he had seen and heard the explosion. 'I have lost a deal of belly pursuing this business and it is just as well, otherwise you'd had slice the pluck of me open, for sure.'

The Laird blinked. He had paused only because he'd seen a dagg, but he was now sure that it was unloaded and so was no better than a hand axe. Fixed with hate, he started in to swinging, calling out the cuts as he did.

'*Fendenti da sinistra*,' he shouted after the cut from the left.

'*Fendenti da destra*,' he roared as it came in from the other side.

337

Christ, thought Batty, he is decided on opening me like a side of beef – and he backed away, wishing he had loaded the dagg.

'*Sottani da destra*,' the Laird bawled, though Batty heard the whistling breathless of him. This, a cut from the bottom right upwards, Batty locked with the head of the axe, ran up the blade of it in a short step and was face to blood-bag face with the Laird for a brief moment.

'*Kopfstreich*,' he declared and rammed his helmet into the Laird's face. It isn't Talhoffer, or any other wee *Fechtbuch* of the art, he thought, but I can't read anyway.

The blow was not entirely full on, but it made the Laird curse and reel away, a new mark across his forehead, already seeping blood. Good, Batty thought, let it run in your eyes and blind you.

He was feeling more confident now – as much as you could against a man with several feet of ugly steel – for the Laird was half drunk, panting like a mated bull and bleeding badly. But hate kept the man fired and his skill, Batty knew, was considerable.

Then, in the middle of the whirling confusion of staggering, fleeing people, a man lurched out of the ruin of Hollows, weeping and roaring and heading towards Batty with a length of backsword raised high for a vicious cut.

It was not in any manual of arms, Batty thought in the fleeting second it took to recognise Mattie of Whithaugh, but it will cleave me all the same. Then he flung the dagg.

A dagg with an axe handle was no weapon balanced for throwing, so it showed how poorly Mattie stood with God and the Devil both – how poorly that whole family stood, Batty thought with astonishment – when the axe blade smacked Mattie in the forehead like it was slicing kindling.

The force of it stopped Mattie, though his legs kept going and ran out and up, so that he crashed like a thrown grain bag. The Laird stared in astonished horror – which gave Batty the chance to haul out his own sword.

Another Armstrong gone was what the Laird was thinking in that eyeblink when Mattie spreadeagled on the flame-lit earth and started making a lake beneath him, one that seeped to the fringes of the crushed Sorley nearby. By God – the entire of Whithaugh has been slaughtered by this man...

The slither of steel from scabbard snapped him back to Batty and he snarled and rushed in, frenzied with fresh hate.

Batty dodged and parried as best he could, while the Laird howled '*mezzani*' as he hacked swings from one side and then the other; Batty parried one and almost lost his sword with the sheer power of the blow.

After that he jigged about, making the odd riposte cut while the Laird swung and whirled and slashed, yelling all the while in Italian about 'Iron Door Guard' and 'Royal Guard of the True Window'.

When he started in to wheezing and the cuts slackened, Batty grinned a little.

'*Oberhow,*' he called out and banged down an overhead cut.

'*Sturtzhow.*'

And he slashed the plunging cut.

'*Das Lang Zorn ortt.*'

He thrust the Long Guard of Wrath at the Laird's face.

They were all parried, though the Laird was not quoting any manual now – the drink and the exertion were taking their toll – but Batty wanted the Laird worse still.

'The man that would the two-hand learn both close and clear,' he recited impudently, 'must have a good eye both far and near.'

He feinted, cut left and the blades rang.

'An in stop,' he said and thrust.

'An out stop,' he added, and parried the return – a weak blow that scarcely jarred him now.

'And a hawk quarter,' he said and ripped his edge through the stained blue doublet, a new slash that revealed more red than white.

The Laird backed off, his face paler and his eyes scrunched up with trepidation; Batty might have only one arm, but it was frightening in its strength.

'A cantle, a doublet and half for his fear,' Batty recited and gave all those half-arm strokes in a whirling display of strength and dexterity that the Laird was barely able to fend off.

'Two rounds and a half, with good cheer,' he finished, and suddenly the Laird found himself locked hilt to hilt, blinking through the drink-sweat into the curved quiver of Batty's beard. He thought another headbutt was imminent and started to reel back, but Batty grinned his undershot grin.

'*Gamba destra, calci nei coglione*,' he declared, and while the Laird was blinking the sense of that into him, Batty's right foot kicked him in the cods, as he had said.

The Laird fell back with a vomiting shout, the two-hander spilled from his grasp and everything forgotten save the white-hot screaming agony where his balls cowered.

Batty leaned on the sword like a cane for a moment, heaving in panted breaths, then straightened wearily.

'I cannot read,' he said, 'but I can listen and learn to those training with a manual of arms.'

He limped to where the Laird lay, took the point of his sword and laid it against the man's neck; the Laird was vaguely aware of it, lost in the agony of pain which seemed to flood sickeningly from his fork to the crown of his head and everywhere between.

'I would think on that,' said a voice, and Batty half turned to see Wat Scott, leaning casually on the high front of his saddle, his other hand outstretched as a perch for a hooded hawk. Behind him, mounted men spilled up to Hollows, lances and swords in their fists, with scarcely much to do except loot the place.

'I came hunting, as I said,' Wat went on, nodding admiringly to his fine hawk, which was nervous and fluttering with the noise and scent, turning its blind, hooded head this way and that.

'It would not do, Batty, to remove the Headman o' the Hollows Armstrongs entire,' Wat Scott declared, stroking the breast of the hawk to soothe it. 'His uncle will take the high seat if you do and he is a man of better judgement entirely. Better the Devil you know, as it were.'

Batty took the point away from the Laird's neck; he did not care one way or the other, and the cold of that when he said it made Wat's armflesh creep.

'Besides,' Wat added, trying to pierce Batty's armoured indifference, 'his wife lies a score of feet away – what's left of her, poor lady – and we will spoil his beasts, take all the monies we can, then burn the rest. His powder mill is gone entire and his tower is collapsed, so he is well paid.'

'Will Elliot?' Batty demanded and Wat nodded to where men were levering the Land Sergeant out of the cage.

'He is alive, but sore hurt, so he may yet die. We will care for him – and yourself, if you need it.'

Batty ached like a huge bruise, but if he did not go on it would not be finished, he knew.

'Hutchie Elliott.'

Wat nodded.

'I thought you would ask – no sign of him, but here is one who might tell us.'

He beckoned and two riders pushed a figure forward at lance-point – Rob's Davey, bloody and sullen, his sooted face streaked with tracks of weeping.

He was numb and raw, felt as if he had been split from crown to groin and one half of him stripped away; he had seen his brother running like a pillar of fire, like a torch, to hurl himself off the edge of the Hole, trying to plunge down into the Esk beyond and below, to put himself out. So he was dead, either broken by the fall, burned to charcoal or drowned. Probably all three.

Rob's Davey was done for and knew it – a Broken Man, a man with no Name, was the butt of everyone's hate and they would hang him simply for being here. Yet he did not care, for the world was a strange, shivered place without the other half of him in it.

He gave his last curse to Batty Coalhouse – pungent enough to strip enamel off Wat Scott's fancy neck collar – but provided the information they needed in return for the promise that they would fetch out his brother and bury them side by side, all perjink and Christian.

After he had been promised and huckled away to tree and rope, Batty took a breath and walked over to Mattie of the Whithaugh; the axe-handled dagg came out of the splintered mess of his head with scarcely a tug.

'East,' he said and squinted into the new day's sun. Powrieburn lay that way – could it be that Hutchie Elliott, desperate wee rat that he was, was heading for more mischief with Mintie?

The thought chilled him and he wiped the axe head clean on Mattie, then stuffed the dagg into his belt.

Wat saw it and stared, saw Batty take a last look round at the burning ruins as if seeing them for the first time. Admiring and appalled, Wat shook his head and there was no mock in it at all as his voice escorted Batty back to his horse.

'By God, Batty. Loudly you said and loudly you did it. The echoes of it will be a long time dying in the Debatable.'

Chapter Twenty-Two

Powrieburn
Not long after

Her ma fought hard all through that morning, and the man called Ridley showed that he was a better priest than a physicker when he murmured her through Penance, Anointing and Viaticum.

Then her ma asked for Mintie, and she went in a turmoil of feelings, of rememberings of this woman's strength being all there was between the world and wee Mintie, of her sureness and her teaching of things a woman needed to know. She was aware too of how she had been, asleep in a veil of smog it seemed, with the only light in it a firebrand...

'I am done,' her mother said and patted Mintie's fluttering, impotent hand. 'There is the truth of it and so I am called before God.'

Her voice was a wind through a web, no more, but the urgency in it was tangible.

'Make your peace, Araminta,' she whispered. 'With God and with yourself. Ask forgiveness of the one and forgive with the other. Else you are lost. This is the last good advice I can give.'

It was the use of 'Araminta' that broke her to silent, shoulder-shaking tears. Too fine a name for a wee sprout of lass in a corner of the Borders, her da had said, but ma had defended it fiercely.

'In this place, a Name is everything,' she had said. 'The Henderson one does not count for much, so I will give my daughter another name to be proud of.'

Eventually Mintie felt hands on her shoulders and was raised up into the soft concern of Bet's Annie, while the other women moved gently and quietly to the task of washing and swaddling the old Mistress of Powrieburn, who had passed out of the world with no more ripple than a gnat's wing on a pool.

Ridley, his eyes gritty from lack of sleep, was pleased that all had gone well – a gentle death and he had remembered the rites even though he had not had to use them for a long time. Now all he wanted was to accept his payment graciously and scamper back to Hollows and Ganny; when the daughter came to him, he was expectant and easily ambushed.

'Hear my confession,' she said, and Ridley, his heart sinking, could do nothing more than agree; they trooped down the steps to the undercroft, then out across the yard to the feed store. Bet's Annie stood with folded arms at the door to keep folk out, while the women washed and dressed and roped Mintie's swaddled ma by the legs for lowering through the trapdoor and out of Powrieburn.

First time the old woman has been out of the house in an age, Bet's Annie thought, trying not to listen at what was being said behind her back. I know most of it anyway, she said to herself; there is nothing there to shock me.

There was for Ridley, for he had been a cloistered cleric most of his life, taking confessions from other monks; Mintie's book of revelations was a stun on his sense.

'I am told only the Pope can forgive such a sin,' she said at the end of telling him about ridding herself of the child.

'Only God can forgive you,' Ridley blurted out before he had time to think. Then he took a breath or two. If this Batty Coalhouse was loose round Hollows, planning badness, then Ganny was perhaps in danger...

He dismissed it as preposterous. One man against the Armstrongs of Hollows?

Mintie sat on a hay bale, hands on lap, while Ridley sat next to her, shrouding his face with one arm and hand like the barrier of a confessional booth. She needs absolving and punishment, he thought – yet she is right. Only the Pope can lift this level of sin.

Then he sighed. What did it matter here, in this wild, northern place, with all of the south throwing out the Pope in favour of Fat Henry? The world was turning and God spun with it. Perhaps, then, it was the spirit of God Himself, so long absent from Father Ridley, that slid the justice and mercy into him.

'*Te absolvo*,' he declared. 'Your penance is to forgive. This Hutchie Elliott and yourself both, as your mother demanded – a deathbed request, which cannot be ignored. God is watching.'

Mintie took a deep breath then. She was not sure she could do it and said so, but Ridley sat like a stone saint, and finally she bowed her head in acquiescence and he signed the cross over her. Outside, they loaded her ma onto the pushcart, to take her for burial.

In the yard, the women stood by the cart, waiting patiently for Mintie and the priest, who now realised he was expected to preside over the actual burial too. Wearily wordless, he fell in with the procession, eventually noticing that they were all looking in the one direction, at a great black cloud on the horizon.

'Looks like rain,' Ridley said pointedly, in the hope of spurring them on to be done with the business.

'This is the Borders in springtime,' Jinet smarted back at him. 'Does a hirshel heft to a hill? Of course it will rain.'

Ridley had been around long enough to know that a hirshel was a herd of sheep and that Borderers believed such flocks clung to a particular hillside, never to be driven off save by force. It was, he understood, some kind of country proverb, but her attitude irritated him, for he was a priest deserving of better. He did not have long to feel aggrieved.

'No raincloud that,' Davey-boy declared, looking up from pointing out more splendid features on his gun to Hew. 'Smoke. Over Hollows.'

For a moment Ridley felt the chill in his bowels, then they dropped away entirely when two figures came round the side of the feed store. One was Eck, who had the second by one arm and was huckling it along.

A wee girl, folk thought at first, with a babe in a basket, a babe that wailed; Mintie's hand went to her throat.

The figure tore free from Eck and set the basket down with surprising gentleness, just as a sharp, piercing cry of recognition came from Ridley. The figure heard it and raised a tortured, frightened scowl of face.

'You bloody left me. They bloody chased me.'

The voice was no girl's and Ridley, even as he felt the shock at seeing Ganny and baby Jane here, felt a sharper pang at the sound of the boy's voice breaking.

Then Ganny was at him, nut fists beating at his chest until a big woman hauled him away, and Ridley, shocked, could only stare, knowing with the cracking bell of the boy's voice and the glare of the fierce, big-armed woman that the sweetness of Ganny was gone from him. Just like that, in an eyeblink, in a dung-covered yard in the middle of nowhere; he almost wept.

From the depths of the woman's apron where his face was buried, they heard Ganny weep and moan about being chased. Mintie, as if in a dream, moved wooden-legged to the crib and peered in it as if it was a nest of snakes.

The squashed face shrieked itself red with fury at being hungry and ignored, yet even through all that, Mintie knew the child well enough and fell on her knees in the mud, overwhelmed by what work God made to bring Mary, Queen of Scots to this place at this time.

–

The rooks were wheeling and rasping when the cavalcade came back from the Faerie stones, draped in sadness and their own thoughts.

Ridley could not believe that Ganny was gone from him, but each time he looked over at the boy, folded in one protecting arm of the big woman, he had such a glare that it melted his resolve to keep staring. And the voice had splintered the charms besides...

Bet's Annie knew what the boy had been, knew what the filthy wee sodomite priest had done and was determined that all of that was ended for the boy. Ganny, she discovered his name was, though it was Ridley's name for him – Ganymede.

'I had a name but I lost it,' he hiccuped, and Bet's Annie melted. Hew and Eck, having worked out the way of it, stared daggers at the priest and dared him to challenge Bet's Annie – while looking at the boy as if he was some Faerie apparition.

Mintie had worked all of it out, standing with her leaf-whirl of memories of her ma while the priest intoned the service and consigned her to the embrace of worms and Faerie. And all the time she wondered where the priest had come by the boy and where the boy had come by the babe, and if either of them knew what they had.

In the end she thought not, and was easier, then, when she handed coin to the priest and thanked him for his service.

'You may leave,' she said, 'whenever you care. The boy stays and the babe stays.'

Ridley did not argue, for he was sick of the babe and sicker still at the loss of Ganny. He made the coins vanish and trooped after the cavalcade, back to the bastel of Powrieburn where he would reclaim his horse and leave.

By the time they had reached the yard, the strange cloud had wisped away, the sun had come out and the rooks whirled and cried; Mintie was uneasy about that, but when the dog barked, everyone stopped.

'Davey Graham,' Mintie called, for they had left him behind to guard the door and the now sleeping baby.

There was silence, then a soft whistle came from nearby and a figure stepped from the feed store, with a slinking, ugly brute of a hound at his heels. Hew and Eck cursed and grabbed their hilts, but the figure chuckled and blew on a slow match.

'That's our caliver,' Megs declared indignantly and the man laughed.

'Put it from your mind, quine,' he said, 'for it is yours no more.'

Hew and Eck had their weapons half out when the fat barrel of the caliver turned on them like a Cyclops eye.

'Don't,' the man said softly.

'You have but a single shot,' Hew answered.

'Who will be the one to take it, then?'

Hew trembled on the brink of it, but Mintie was no fool and put a hand on his arm, stilling him as you would a skittish horse.

It scarcely even came as a shock to her when the second figure stepped from the undercroft, another caliver in his fists and the crib looped over the crook of one elbow. It was almost a satisfaction to see that it was Hutchie Elliott, for Mintie was sure the Queen of Elfland was hanging over Powrieburn. She had brought them all here for a purpose.

Bet's Annie saw the gun Hutchie held and gave a cry, both her hands rising to her mouth as if to keep the other shouts penned. Ganny, freed from her embrace, sank at her feet; and Ridley saw it, saw the men and knew them at once.

'Hutchie,' he said. 'Penny... don't hurt me.'

Hutchie sneered and now Mintie saw the reason for Bet's Annie's distress; the gun he held was inlaid and silvered and splendid – Davey-boy's own caliver, which the lad would not have given up lightly.

'Did you hurt the boy who owned that gun?' Mintie asked softly and Hutchie eyed her sourly. All that had happened to him had happened because of her – bloody wee lassie of no account; yet there were other feelings coursing in him, confusing and strong.

'He is not worried much about its loss,' Hutchie answered and Bet's Annie groaned. Mintie nodded, as if she had known all along, though it was only partly true and she felt a deep bone-ache of sorrow for the fierce boy who would never now grow up.

'He was called Davey Graham,' she said. 'Of Netherby. You will wish for a clean hanging when his father catches you.'

'Dickon Graham's lad?'

The question came from the one called Penny and the fear was in his face when he looked across at Hutchie.

'The same.'

'Dear God in Heaven,' said Penny, and the barrel of the caliver drooped.

'Keep your guard,' Hutchie snapped, though his own mouth was dry. Christ, of all the wee lads in the world, I had to cut the throat of the son of the fiercest Graham in the Borders. God's wounds — what was that wee lad doing here? All his life had been luck like this.

He glanced bitterly at Mintie. Her doing again. The babe stirred and murmured and he felt a savage surge of joy at the sound.

He had the prize and the getting away…

'I will take the priest's horse,' he said and moved to it, for it was saddled and ready. 'Black Penny — lead out the mare called Jaunty. Mintie will point her out.'

It was a calculated swipe of viciousness to steal her favourite horse and he saw she knew it. His grin was wolfen as Mintie moved past him, close enough to smell the staleness of his body. She indicated the horse and Penny led it out.

'It's not saddled,' he protested.

'Take the time if you choose,' Hutchie declared, mounting carefully and always keeping the caliver trained. 'But you will be here on your own in another minute. Hand me up the crib with the bairn.'

Muttering, Black Penny did as he was bid and then swung up on the back of Jaunty, who stirred and snorted at having such a weight and no saddle. Then Penny squinted into the distance and pointed.

'Someone is coming.'

Hutchie knew before it was more than a shadow who the someone was. He felt the bones of his face grow cold, as if he stared too long into a howling blizzard and then, blinking, realised that Mintie was watching him.

'Aye,' she said softly, almost sadly it seemed to Hutchie. 'You are right to be feared of him and I am sorry for lighting him all over the Border at you.'

'It's Batty Coalhouse.'

Black Penny spat that out and started working the lead rope, which was no proper bridle and reins, and needed, he thought, more viciousness to get the beast he rode to move.

'I forgive you, Hutchie Elliott.'

The words clattered out into the silvered air of Powrieburn's morning and everyone heard it, especially Hutchie, who felt that some spell had been laid on him and shivered; there was altogether a deal too much Faerie around this place.

But he managed the old, white, lopsided grin at her as he reined round to follow the urgent Black Penny out of the yard and away.

'Aye, wee Mintie – I will miss you, so I will.'

The words, viciously familiar, seemed only to be echoes of what they once had been and no more trouble to Mintie than a scattering of feathers. She smiled back at him and he felt a sudden rush of fear that sent him heeling the horse in a panic.

Mintie took a breath or two while folk cursed and ran here and there. Bet's Annie scurried to the undercroft, hoping not to find what she did, lying in a tarn of his own blood.

Then Mintie whistled once, twice. Jaunty stopped dead, spun on her hind fetlocks and came thundering back. Black Penny gave a shout, fell off and rolled, while the bewildered dog capered and yelped.

'By God,' said a familiar voice, the grating admiration of it bringing a rush of strange peace to Mintie, so that when she turned, her face was beatific.

'That's a fine trick you have with that beast,' Batty Coalhouse said as he passed her at a fast trot, heading out to the sprawled Black Penny and the dancing bark of dog.

For a moment Black Penny thought he might resist, but then he saw Batty's fist full of dagg – Clym's own axe-handled dagg, no less – and all the resolve blew out of him like old smoke.

In a moment the two Henderson boys had come lolloping up like pups, but their fists were full of steel and they eyed the monstrous dog warily.

'Leave off,' Black Penny said wearily to the dog and then stood up, swaying and favouring one leg. Batty looked down at him, leaning on the saddle front.

'Why did you come all this way?' he asked. 'And where is Hutchie headed?'

'To Hell,' Black Penny answered bitterly. 'Will you find someone to care for the dog after I am hemped?'

'You will see him, by and by,' Batty answered mildly, 'for the law will hang dog and man both for their crimes.'

Then he frowned down at the pistol.

'I wish I had stopped to load this now.'

Black Penny's look was sour, but Mintie was suddenly along-side Batty, mounted bareback on Jaunty and with her skirts caught up to let her ride astraddle. Batty looked at her with his eyebrows up.

'Hutchie has the wee Queen,' she said. Batty did not even begin to ask all the questions that crowded into his mouth, merely nodded and kicked his mount into her mud-spattering wake.

Tinnis Hill

Not long after

The bracken was changing, the green of it sharp enough to cut the eye after so long a time staring at a world of amber and gold, black and white. Now there was purple and a blush of Faerie gloves, not a flower Batty cared to see up on the moss and bracken hump of Tinnis, where the wind hissed.

'Faerie glove,' Mintie said, seeing him stare. 'They gave the flowers to the fox to put on his paws and make him silent while hunting. Pretty.'

She raised herself in the saddle a little and sniffed the air, for all the world like the fox she spoke of.

'Spring,' she said.

'Poison,' Batty grunted and jerked his beard at the pink Faerie gloves. 'Keeps evil at bay in a garden, but is bad cess if you bring it indoors.'

'True,' Mintie agreed, and her smile was the old smile, the sly, challenging smile, and he almost laughed aloud at that.

'It is a most insincere bloom,' she declared, and now Batty did laugh, but the sound was strange on Tinnis and he cut it off, remembering why they were there.

All about was the trickling lisp of water, motes dancing in the new sunlight, curlews churring and insects wheeping and whinging; the horses flicked and trembled at the bites. Yet somewhere death lurked.

Strange that a desperate Hutchie should have headed up Tinnis, Batty thought, and shivered, despite himself. As if the Queen of Elfland called him.

They moved on, shuffling up through the clinging bracken, across the scraped waste and past the crooked trees and the strange upright stones that lurched drunkenly, for all that they had been Faerie raised.

It was there that Mintie saw the horse, reins dragging on the ground and standing hipshot, one front leg raised. She knew at once that Hutchie had lamed it, flogging it hard up Tinnis, over bad ground.

'Careful, lass,' Batty said and levered himself off the horse. Mintie did likewise and they stood for a moment, looking at the huddle of man-sized stones. Then Mintie moved towards the horse, unable to stand and watch it suffer any longer.

She shouldered past a moss-grown stone and yelped with shock and surprise when Hutchie stepped out, caliver in his hand and the slow match smoking; his grin was feral sharp.

It was a reflex that she did not even think was in her, an act she had not thought of consciously — she shot out a hand and covered his like a lover. There was a moment when the surprise froze him, his eyes bewildered at the gentle touch.

Then she squeezed as hard as she could and smothered the match in his grip, so that it ground its burn into his palm. He roared and backhanded her, a blow that flung her away to crash and roll in the bracken, right to the feet of Batty.

He hefted her up with a steel grip, steadied her, then let her go, drew his sword and stepped between her and Hutchie, who had dropped the caliver and was flapping his scorched hand. Then he realised Batty was there with his hand full of steel and he backed rapidly away, hauling out Davey-boy's stolen backsword. They crouched, eyeing each other.

Hutchie took in the solid confidence of the man he faced, the undershot jut that made the untrimmed beard spring up, the narrowed fox eyes in a face like a bad map. His jack had been coloured and neatly stitched once, but was dangling with torn threads, a uniform dung colour stained with rust where rents had leaked water into the metal plates. It could also have been old blood, Hutchie thought, remembering Batty's reputation.

Then he sneered. One arm. Old. And by the looks of those pouched eyes, almost done up.

Batty saw the sneer and knew what was coming, watched the cunning eyes in that handsome, florid face with its white smile. He wore no more than doublet and shirt and fat breeks and hose, but Hutchie Elliott was as dangerous as a cornered rat for all his lack of armour.

'I am better than you,' Hutchie said suddenly.

'Aye, aye, so you say,' Batty replied mildly, watching the eyes.

'You are a broken dog, Batty Coalhouse,' Hutchie said and suddenly lunged with a roar.

'Here is your death.'

The blades clashed and Mintie, dazed and jaw-bruised, heard the grunts of them as they fought, circling and stamping.

Hutchie cut and slashed, but Batty was nowhere near and the air healed quickly. His next was a thrust that whicked past Batty's ear and would have taken him in the mouth if he had not jerked; he stepped in close, to where Hutchie's furious eyes had gone boar-slitted, and spat in his face.

Reeling away, Hutchie cursed and Batty thought he had him – he whirled his wrist and slammed his blade down, just as Hutchie parried. The sheer strength of the blow made Hutchie cry out and the backsword went flying from him – but Batty heard the sharp, high ting and saw most of his own blade whirl like a scythe through the air.

Then he stared at the nub end he had left, perfectly sheared, a clean-cut edge. Like the dream, he thought dully.

Hutchie, shaking life back into his numbed hand, gave a cry and lashed out with a foot, catching Batty on the shins and staggering him. He followed it up with a roundhouse left hook which drove into Batty's belly like a ram on a wall.

Mintie heard the whoosh, saw Batty stumble away, saw the kick that sent him sprawling. Hutchie, staggering wildly, looked round for his sword but spotted the caliver, spotted the last wink of the slow match and laughed.

He darted for it, swept it up and blew the match back into life, swung the red eye of it and fastened it to the lock, while Batty sucked in air and pain and looked up at the caliver muzzle, big as a cave.

My match, he thought, which I made and gave to Davey-boy Graham for his splendid new gun. Any other match would have been crushed of life with what Mintie did, but not mine. No match with a slow match, he thought bitterly. And now it kills me.

'Don't,' said Mintie, holding out one hand to Hutchie, who grinned his white grin at her.

'You don't need to do this,' she went on. 'I forgive you. You can go free. But you need to hand ower the babe, Hutchie. Is she safe and well?'

Hutchie blinked slowly, then nodded and glanced quickly round, found what he wanted, took a step or two back and rattled the crib with a kick; the bairn woke and wailed.

'A fortune in that wee cry,' he said.

'You will never spend it,' Batty wheezed and wondered if he could get the axe-handled dagg out and throw it twice as magically in one morning. Hutchie knew of the dagg as well and was not about to leave it with Batty.

'Fork out that pistol – slow, now – and toss it here. It is fine, and Clym Hen Harrow would rather I have it, for sure.'

Batty threw the pistol at his feet. So be it then, he thought, and levered himself off his knees. You can only play the hand you are dealt, in life as in Primero.

'You cannot keep the babe,' Mintie insisted. 'They will hunt you over bog and moss forever, Hutchie, even if you were to make them hand money for it.'

Hutchie knew it, but wanted something from all this. He stood in what he had and what little he had contrived to steal, and was, he suddenly realised, no better fortuned than when he had killed Mintie's father – a horse and a brace of guns. But now, he thought, every hand in the Borders is against me – aye, and further, if I keep this bairn.

'If I hand you the babe,' he said, 'you will give me a head start, at least, on the fine horse there which is not whistle-struck?'

Mintie nodded.

'And put out the slow match of Batty Coalhouse?'

He was looking at Batty when he said it and her small 'yes' tore his eyes to her. He grinned his white grin.

'And will you come with me, wee Queen of the Powries?' he said. 'Ride away with me and be my love?'

There was only the sound of curlews and Batty wheezing. Then Mintie seemed to surface from somewhere else.

'I forgive you,' she said.

He blew on the match and started to shake his head.

'No, no, wee Mintie,' he said, puffing the glowing end until it sparked a little. 'You will never come away with the likes of me.'

His voice was bitter as old aloes as he raised the caliver and sighted.

'Nor will Batty be put out save by death.'

Mintie put out a hand, just as Batty started to move. Slow, he knew even as he did it. Slow and old and still too fat...

She went between the caliver and him just as the priming pan flared and smoked. The explosion was loud and vicious – and wrong.

There was a shrieking scream from inside the great egret plume of smoke. Batty lumbered to a halt like some wounded bear, blinking bewildered as Mintie, arms flung wide, stood like Saint Joan to take the ball.

Which had not come.

Instead, Hutchie lay where he had been flung, writhing like a cut adder, his hands a mass of blood, and his face – Gods, his face. Mintie, her mind shifting back into the wonder of being alive and whole, saw it an instant before Batty swept her away, but it was enough.

More than enough, Batty thought, for the ravaging of a burst barrel in a flawed piece of cheap did awful damage. He left Mintie then and moved to the baby in the crib, picked her up and brought her back, pausing only to look once at the writhing, moaning ruin of what had once been Hutchie Elliott.

There was little left of the swaggering ranter to hang, nor would they have to fasten his hands to keep them from supporting himself on the rope's end, for he had little of them either.

Mintie had seen it and was weeping. That was because of all the forgiveness she had been storing up, Batty thought, as he handed her the crib, then went back to fetch the horse and the axe-handled dagg. He took the caliver too, seeing now that the ivory on it was only bone and the silver gilt tawdry. Bloody Egyptianis had cozened Davey-boy after all, Batty thought, with a badly made gun that might have blown up at any of its firings. Still, his da might like to see what killed his murderer.

Then he bent to where Hutchie moaned in a mask of blood, the raw, wet blubber of lips puffing out pink froth and no meaning, the splendid white teeth of him blown to pulp and splinter. Mintie would think he offered some comfort, a little mercy of soothing noises, but Batty had none of that left.

'Not smiling now, you sow's arse,' he whispered and went on, leaving him there. Then he helped Mintie and crib and himself up onto their horses and turned for Powrieburn with the lame one hobbling along at the hind end.

Mintie, lost in a crimson world of agony from Hutchie's blow, was only dimly aware, with the fading sound of his choking wheezes, that they were leaving him to die with the Tinnis Faerie.

Powrieburn, Liddesdale

Lady Day, 36th Regnal Year of James VI of Scotland (25 March 1603)

Time snows over all our deeds, Mintie thought, smothering memories, leaving blanks. But not mine, she added fiercely. Three years aulder than the new-dead queen and still to the fore, looking into a future that no longer had the wild Rides that Trottie and the rest of the household feared.

Perhaps the Faerie took Hutchie, Mintie thought, lying back in the canopied bed, and smelled the bracken and the new earth. She fancied she could even scent out the perfume of the foxgloves, the Faerie flowers whose kiss was death, but that may just have been conjured by the memories of that day, brought back by the distant carillon of bells tolling for the dead Elizabeth I, by the grace of God no longer Queen of England.

She had worried about leaving Hutchie wounded and dying. But when Wat Scott sent riders to fetch the body, there was none to be found, only old blood. So either he had been carried off by friends or Faerie – but whatever had happened, neither Mintie nor anyone else had seen or heard of him since.

Wicked Wat Scott had to be content hanging Black Penny, which he did – though Mintie managed to get a reprieve for the dog and it lived a long time as a faithful guard at Powrieburn; if it missed its old master, it never gave sign of it.

Neither did Ganny. Mintie swept him into Powrieburn and Ridley vanished. Ganny became Arthur Henderson, went on to better learning in Edinburgh and became a lawyer there. Now he had sons and grandweans of his own, and Mintie thought that the best thing she had ever done – and the nearest she would get to children of her own.

The wee Queen was delivered quiet and secret to a sternly delighted Regent and a grateful, weeping Dowager Queen, and the rewards for it helped Powrieburn, for Mintie was smart enough to ask for contracts to supply the court with horseflesh rather than a bag of easily squandered gold. What others had as reward – Batty for one – remained a mystery.

Fat Henry did not come in the spring, though everyone scrambled about in expectation of it. The King of England had too much on his mind and the official chroniclers wrote that it was the threat of invasion by the French that kept his army in the south.

The truth, of course, was Catherine Parr, the lecherous old goat's last fling. And him with a festered leg as well, Mintie thought. Men are swine if left to their own.

Fat Henry came the next year all the same, sending his earls to land at Leith and despoil the place in an orgy of viciousness that stayed in the memory of those in a Scots army who could only watch and fume. There were rebel Scots with the English too – but Johnnie Armstrong of Hollows was not among them.

He was nowhere, Mintie thought. Left glowering like a spider in the ruins of his home, nursing his cods and his wrath and unable to do much about either. The loss of Hollows, his wife and his dignity crushed him like a nut in a steel fist; he died a few years back, she recalled, an old muttering sink of hatred and self-sorrow, and the Armstrong tower passed to a new Laird, some kin or other. Now that would end too with the union of the borders.

The years rolled away from Mintie like the Esk, and she closed her eyes and followed them for a while. Bet's Annie had married Hew, for he bairned her soon after and Ower-The-Moss Henderson had little choice. When he died – 1553, she thought, or 54 – Hew took over as head of the Hendersons and Mintie never had a lick of trouble about marriage or inheritance from that day.

Will Elliot never recovered from what had been done to him, though he lived on a while longer, hirpling about in some position in Fife, she heard. He died in 1548, which was young. She was told that it was 'strange circumstances' but not more, so Mintie thought the folk who told her were being kind and not saying that he had done away with himself, because he had been broken to what he considered nothing – unable to ride or walk like a man. Or court the girl he wanted.

Mintie felt guilt for that, but only a little. It was the way of things, ordained by God, and she could find no more feelings for Will deeper than she had – which were not enough for marriage. As Batty would put it – you can only play the hand you are dealt, in life as in Primero.

Batty. She heard from him in 1545, when he came back to lay flowers on the grave mound of the Saul, who had died quite gloriously in the spring – in the middle of an ecstatic roll in a new meadow, kicking his hooves in the air as if he was young.

Batty had been unchanged and working for anyone who would pay, wore a new shirt, breeks and a hat with a feather – but the filthy old jack of plates was the same, the axe-handled dagg was still snugged up in his belt, and Fiskie was loaded with the same old saddlery and scuffed holsters.

He stayed the night and they played Primero, and he said that when he was done siting rabinets and culverins all over Berwick for the English, he would go back to the Scots. Or take Fat Henry's coin and start the process of knocking down what he had helped build at Leith or Haddington. Either that or go and see Michelangelo in Rome. If that man still lived.

Mintie, never sure if he jested or not, simply laughed at the thought of Batty sharing confidences with the Pope's artist. But next morning Batty was gone before she was up and she never saw him again.

She heard various rumours of him after that – he had gone to Ireland with the English, or Germany to fight in the wars there, or was pursuing someone called Maramaldo up and down the east coast and elsewhere. None of what she heard mentioned Michelangelo and she was a little sorry about that.

It had been a wheen of years ago and he was dead and gone, for she recalled him saying that he had been born with the century.

They were all dead and gone, she thought with a sudden chill that had nothing to do with the cold March breeze. All the ones in Powrieburn now are strangers to those times; I am the only one left who remembers.

Time has snowed over it all, save me. She drew the coverlet up and was about to call out, waspishly, for Trottie to come and close the window and stop wailing about the threat of riders. There would be an end to them now, but they would go out in fire and sword, she knew.

Then she heard – or fancied she heard – the gentle singing. It leaped her heart into her throat and she knew it could not be him, not after all these years, that it had to be someone else. If it was anyone at all.

But it hung on the breeze, gentle as a baby breathing.

'And he has gotten a coat of the elven cloth, a pair of shoes of the velvet green. And until seven years were gone and past, True Thomas on earth was never seen.'

Author's Note

There are three Walls in Scotland, all built for the same reasons. The best known is Hadrian's, but the Antonine is still a visible scar and more than a footnote in history books. The one no one mentions nowadays is the Scotch Dyke.

Built in 1552, a decade after the events of this tale, the dyke marked a final agreement by England and Scotland concerning the Debatable Land. Two parallel ditches flank an earthwork bank a dozen feet wide and the height of a man, which runs for about four miles west from the Esk and once cut the Debatable in half, to keep the Scots away from Carlisle. At either end was placed a boundary stone marked with a cross pattée.

Little remains these days. There is no monument to it and even maps omit it – but it was, literally, the defining moment when the Debatable Land was officially incorporated into the territory of both countries.

The Borderers ignored it, of course. They thought it no more than a nuisance to moving stolen cattle back and forth, and continued to raid and counter-raid much as they had done before, right up to the Union of the Crowns in 1603 and even beyond. They simply went round one end and back the other. Which tells you all you need about the nature of the Borderers, on both sides of the Divide. When they decided to abrogate responsibility for a stretch of Border land, both countries agreed that there would be 'no firm raisings' – in other words, no-one could build houses or fortresses.

Since the point of the Debatable was that no-one was prepared to police it, the imhabitants ignored that – the result, among others was Canobie, nowadays the village of Canonbie, the 16th century equivalent then of a Wild West frontier town. Even today there are scarcely more than four hundred inhabitants – though it is much more peaceful.

Similarly, Hollows Tower was built with no reference to 'firm raisings' and still exists, built in stone and perched above the Esk – it is now called Gilnockie and is the Armstrong Museum; you can even get married in it these days. There is a mill near there too, but it belongs to the much later wool industry; there never was a powder mill.

The Armstrongs of Hollows – now Gilnockie – have no doubt been maligned here and were no better nor worse than other Names in the area. The Laird I have here is fiction, but the father I give him was not. Johnnie Armstrong of Gilnockie was the Lord of the Borders and his fate at the hands of the king is as described. He had five sons, not just the one I shamelessly use here – but the sheer power, defiance and outlaw nature of the Armstrongs was too good to pass up for this story.

Powrieburn is complete invention, as is everyone in it – though Tinnis Hill is not, and remains as defiantly Faerie as when I saw it on my travels.

Batty and Will are also imagined, though Batty's past as one of the Kohlhase family of Saxony is real enough. The story of the Kohlhase horses is well-known in Germany and has been made into several films. I also placed Batty at the Siege of Florence, all part of the embryonic wars of religion on the continent. Michelangelo was there, as described and arranging the defences.

Hepburn, the Keeper of Liddesdale, Arran the Regent, Thomas Wharton and Wat Scott are all real, as is the the plot to kidnap the new-born Mary Queen of Scots, fomented by Henry VIII following the death of King James and the refusal of the Scots to fall in with his plan to marry the baby to his son, Prince Edward. Such a hare-brained scheme was never implemented, but the delicious what-if of it was too good a plot to ignore. After all, another wild plot of Henry's was put into operation and succeeded – the assassination of Henry's implacable Catholic foe, Cardinal Beaton.

The Borders was – and is – a beautiful, wild, bleak place. And though their hospitality to strangers is improved, there remains a hardy, suspicious, brave breed still living in the Debatable Land.

I hope I have done them all justice.

Glossary

APOSTLES – A collection of wooden, stoppered flasks filled with an exact amount of powder and ball for a single pistol or caliver shot, which made for quicker and more reliable loading. They were suspended by a cord from a leather bandolier worn by arquebusiers, seven flasks in front and five in back, for a total of twelve, hence the name.

BASTEL (OR BASTLE) HOUSE – Probably derived from the French *bastille*, a family dwelling along the Scottish-English border designed for defence against raiding. It had one-metre-thick stone walls, a slate rather than thatched roof and was two storeys high. The lower floor was used to secure beasts – cattle and horses – and had a double door, the outer in stout wood-timbers, the inner a metal grille called a 'yett'. There was an internal ladder to the upper levels, which might also include a garret space underneath the roof, which was usually drawn up at night and the trapdoor closed. The windows were small or even just arrow slits.

BARMKIN – A defensive wall built round a castle or keep, usually with a walkway for sentries.

BIRL – To spin round.

BILL – An official warrant, issued by a March Warden or the like, demanding that a suspected miscreant present himself for judgement. If ignored – fouled – then someone appointed by the authorities would go and fetch him. This was Batty's job until open war ended all Warden activity.

BLACKMEAL – A payment made 'off the books' to answer extortion or threat from a neighbour. Paid, usually, in goods particularly grain (meal) or livestock, it was the basis of ensuring some measure of peace along a Border area essentially ruled by the equivalent of Mafia mob bosses. The origin, of course, of the word 'blackmail'.

CALIVER – An improved version of the arquebus, in that it had standard bore, making loading faster and firing more accurate.

CRUCK HOUSE – A building made of frame of curved timbers set in pairs. Used to build small huts up to large barns, it was the simplest cheapest building method of the medieval age.

CRUSIE – A simple container with a wick that provided light.

CUSTRIN – A rogue, base fellow or varlet.

DAGG – A pistol as opposed to a long-barrel musket.

DEBATABLE LAND – An area ten miles long and four wide whose ownership was disputed between Scotland and England, resulting in edicts against either country settling it. The area's people promptly ignored this and powerful clans moved in, notably the Armstrongs. For three hundred years they and others effectively controlled the land, resisting all attempts by Scotland or England to interfere. It became a haven for outlaws of all sides.

FOUTIE – Despicably underhand.

GRAYNE – Borders word for 'clan'. 'Name' is another version of it.

HEMPIE – A rogue likely to be hanged ('hemped').

HIRPLE – Limp.

HOT TROD – The formalities of pursuing reivers, usually by the forces of the Wardens. Up to six days after the siezure of any cattle by thieves taking them across the other side of the Border, the forces attempting to recover them and apprehend the guilty were permitted to also cross the Border freely in pursuit. They had to do it with 'hue and cry, with horn and hound' and were also obliged to carry a smouldering peat on the point of a lance to signify the task they were on.

HUNKER-SLIDING – Someone creeping while crouched; obviously up to no good.

JACK – The ubiquitous garment of the Border warrior – the jack of plates. Most ordinary Border fighters had a jack, a sleeveless jerkin with either iron or the cheaper horn plates sewn between two layers of felt or canvas.

JALOUSE – To surmise or suspect.

JEDDART STAFF – A Scottish polearm, said to have originated in Jedburgh and consisting of a spear point, a thin glaive on one side and a hook or spike on the other. Able – by Border riders – to be used horsed or on foot.

KERTCH – A kerchief, usually used by married women to cover their hair.

KISTING – Funeral. A kist is a chest or a box.

KITHAN – A sneak-thief.

LATCHBOW – A cheap crossbow, light enough to be used from horseback, with a firing mechanism as simple as a door latch. The power was light but at close range it would wound or kill an unprotected man and knock the wind out of one wearing a jack.

PERJINK – Proper, neat.

PHTHISIS – Sixteenth-century term for pulmonary tuberculosis or similar wasting disease.

PRIMERO – 16th century poker where you attempt to bluff your competitors out of betting against you. Players *vie* or *vye* by stating how high a hand they are claiming to have and can flat-out lie to overstate it. It was played using a 40-card deck, but there are no surviving written rules, only descriptions.

RAMSTAMPIT – Blustering loud boaster.

RIDE/RIDING – The raids mounted by one reiver family, or Name, against another, either for robbery or revenge. Depending on how many family members and affiliated Names you could get to join you, these were brief affairs of one night or ones involving several thousand men who could lay waste to entire villages and towns on either side of the Border. The usual Riding times lasted from Lammas (Aug 1) to Candlemas (Feb 2).

SCUMFISH – How raiders got people out of their bastel houses – the modern definition is 'to disgust or stifle' which is what raiders did, by getting on the roof and throwing damp burning bracken down the chimney, essentially smoking out the inhabitants. The defenders kept covered wooden buckets handy, forked the burning bracken into them and closed the lid until the contents could be thrown back outside.

SKLIMMING – Moving fast. Can also mean throwing stones across a pond.

SLORACH – Any bog or morass or filthy mess you might step in.

SLOW MATCH – Early firearms were called 'matchlocks' because they were ignited by a smouldering fuse, called a slow-match, brought down into the pan. Keeping a slow-match smouldering required constant vigilance, a good manufacturer – and no rain. By the middle of the 16th century, wheel locks, were being made. More reliable, they had a spinning striker that created a flint spark as igniter.

SNELL – Cold, icy.

STRAVAIGIN – Wandering or scattered.

TESTOON – Coin minted during the last days of Henry VIII, with more copper than silver in it, so that the portrait of Henry on one side wore down to the copper on his embossed nose; they became known as 'coppernoses' as a result. Eventually became the English shilling of pre-decimal currency.

YALDSON – Yet one more insult: son of a prostitute.

Border Reivers

A Dish of Spurs
Burning the Water